FALL
OF
EMPIRES

LEGACY OF THE LOST TRILOGY

BOOK 3

FALL OF EMPIRES

MADDIE JENSEN

For information contact: maddie.jensen94@gmail.com

Cover design by CelinGraphics
Map design by Cass Maren
ISBN: 978-0-646-89054-8

First edition: May 2024

10 9 8 7 6 5 4 3 2 1

To Mum,

For showing me what being a strong woman looks like.

CONTENT WARNING

This book contains mature themes including brief descriptions of violence/physical abuse, war, death, sexual content, PTSD, miscarriage, and implications of sexual assault.

Reader discretion is advised.

Razmara

PROLOGUE
DEACON MORROW

"You can't do this."

Boots clicked a loud and frantic staccato down the corridor, ringing out against the granite grey stone. Lord Thom Dyre of Gethsemane followed the freshly minted King of Genera down the corridor with dogged determination. Godspeaker Myron trailed a few paces behind him, his own steps making no sound, though his lined brow was furrowed into a deep frown.

Nicodemus had begun to change and transform, like a butterfly emerging from its cocoon. At first, a mournful silence had settled over the capital, along with a wild storm that had raged through the city for days. Cobryn Morrow had ruled Genera for over twenty years. The Warmonger, his youngest wife Gretchen, his son Jacen...all dead within a matter of hours. Lilith and her daughter Ayesha were nowhere to be found, but it was assumed they'd fled the country.

After the storm passed, the winds of change passed through Genera, luring all the rats and spiders from their hiding holes and into Nicodemus. Nobles who had quarrelled with Cobryn graced the court, vultures circling like they were hovering over a carcass, desperate to ingratiate themselves with the new King.

Lord Isak Delmar, one of those risen to grace by Cobryn's hand following the Island Wars, had come to simper at Deacon's feet to prove he would serve the new King as faithfully as the old. Lady Ariadne Pavlos, a sharp-eyed woman who'd lost her husband during the Island Wars, had curtsied deeply, but in her wicked smile lingered a gnawing hunger for power.

Deacon Morrow refrained from rolling his eyes as he spun to face them both, Lord Dyre's expression defiant and Myron's more difficult to read.

It had been two days since the bodies of the dead royals had burned on the pyres, though Jacen's funeral had only been at Lord Dyre's insistence. Despite Deacon proclaiming far and wide that Jacen was a traitor who had killed his father and stepmother, Lord Dyre felt Jacen still deserved the same funeral rites as his family.

Lord Dyre had been an unexpected addition to court at Nicodemus, and not particularly a welcome one. Deacon had not seen the man since he'd been a teenager, after Annaliese—Lord Dyre's sister, Cobryn's beloved first wife and Jacen and Vida's mother—had died. Unfortunately, he had not been among those who had come to court to earn Deacon's favour.

No, Lord Dyre had vehemently opposed Deacon from the moment the crown touched his head. Not that it was surprising—the man had lost both his niece and nephew within the space of a scant few months. Lord Dyre had expected to see Jacen on the throne, and the fact that it was Deacon instead clearly did not sit well with him.

Godspeaker Myron was yet another thorn in Deacon's side, proving that even so early in his reign, there would be challenges. He was a particularly odious member of the Godsvoice, the holy church of Genera. The man was all quiet disapproval and judgemental stares, the voice of tradition wrapped in the deep blue robes of hypocrisy. Deacon was aware of Cobryn's dealing with the Godsvoice and knew the corruption that ran deep within the church.

"This goes against tradition." Myron's soft contempt dug beneath Deacon's skin, making him prickle with irritation. "The mourning rites are quite clear, Your Majesty. It must be observed for the full period of a year."

"I am the King, Myron." Deacon folded his arms over his chest, staring him down. "My brother, gods rest his soul, had three wives in his lifetime—two of them at the same time. You are now telling me I'm not even permitted one?"

2

"It's not about the number of wives." Lord Dyre spoke more impatiently than the Godspeaker, ire flaring in his eyes. "It's about who you intend to marry. The girl is freshly widowed. You cannot wed her. The rules are clear."

How little Lord Dyre knew of Nicodemus, Deacon mused. The man had last been in the capital for Annaliese's funeral nearly two decades past. The loss had broken the tenuous tie between the Dyre family and the King. Though Deacon had not been privy to their final conversation, Cobryn and Lord Dyre had parted on bad terms.

"We are in a time of turbulence." Deacon inhaled deeply to prevent himself losing his cool with the two insufferable men. The fresh scent of rain lingered on the air, mingled with the withering of the flowers and crushed sunset leaves strewn across the stone across autumn demanded. "Cobryn is dead, as is one of his wives. The other has fled with their youngest child, and Jacen became a kinslayer. I hardly think my choice of wife merits this much fuss."

Deacon had sent men he trusted after Lilith and Ayesha. He liked to think the woman was not a threat, but one of Cobryn's children surviving could pose problems in the future, and it was an issue he wanted eliminated. These were not matters he wished to share with Myron and Lord Dyre, already firmly entrenched in opposition to his rule.

"Beyond tradition, it is cruel." Lord Dyre's jaw clenched. He must have been forty by then, with a receding hairline and grey flecking his beard. Like Cobryn had been, a man inching past his prime. "She has lost the man she cares about, and you would force her to wed you?"

Deacon waved a dismissive hand. He was not about to be lectured on morality by the nobleman of the city-state with the highest crime population in Genera. It was said that Gethsemane was crawling with thieves in the streets, and that pirates proudly donned their colours even as they docked in the harbour.

"It is not force, Lord Dyre. It is a choice."

"Hardly a choice at all, when she knows the alternative would involve you harming her family."

Deacon turned his back on the men and continued down the corridor, sliding a brass key from his pocket. As he turned down a narrower corridor, the torches lit his path down the hall. Deacon slid the key into the lock and twisted until it clicked.

His hand hesitated over the knob for a moment. He did not know what to expect on the other side of the door, though his triumph was undeniable. Deacon might have lost the war for Basium, but he had gained everything else he wanted—including its Queen.

He turned the handle and stepped inside.

The room was dark, thick with the sickly-sweet scent of Obscurate. Carissa Darnell was perched on the edge of her bed, back straight as a rod. She glared up at him, red-rimmed eyes burning with hatred. Even pale as death and lifeless as a ghost, even with her lips twisted in derision, she was beautiful.

"Are you satisfied now?" Her voice was hoarse but venomous.

The smoking of Obscurate was difficult for the user the first time, or so Deacon had heard. It had been a shame to suppress all that wonderful dark power of hers, but he couldn't have her attacking him. It had not been without cost—one of the Merciless Ones, Fernandez, had been killed in the effort of capturing and subduing Carissa. Even without her power at her disposal, the young woman had fought tooth and nail against coming to Nicodemus.

Deacon cocked his head to the side. "You think this is about my satisfaction?"

Her smile was bitter. "You'll spin some web of lies about how it's not, but we both know the truth. *You* killed Cobryn and Gretchen. You framed Jacen, you killed…"

Carissa choked on the words, fresh tears welling in her eyes. She and Jacen had clearly loved each other. His loss had hurt her deeply, but it had created an opportunity for Deacon. Despite the conflict between Carissa and her brother, she still stood to inherit Basium. That aside, she was a powerful Primordial, the only woman Deacon considered near his equal.

"I know what happens now." Carissa hissed the words, pushing herself to her feet. She did not cut an intimidating figure, at least half a head shorter than Deacon. "I know what you *want*."

Deacon should have wed Carissa years before when Cobryn had first conquered Basium. He was a patient man, but he was not waiting any longer, not when she was within his grasp. All rules could be broken, especially when he was the most powerful man in the country.

"You will marry me and become Queen of Genera." Deacon smiled as she shuddered in revulsion. "You still have family in Basium. Your brother, your son…"

"Don't you touch them," Carissa snarled, causing Deacon's smirk to widen. Carissa's son with Jacen, Zephyr, would always be her weakness. She would never risk any harm befalling her child. She was similar to Lilith that way, protecting her child even when it put her in a dire predicament.

"It's simple, Carissa. You know the solution."

"You won't just leave Basium." Carissa's hands balled into fists, but he noticed how she swayed on her feet. The Obscurate could have some unpleasant side effects. "It's not in your nature."

"If your brother sees sense…"

"He won't surrender to you. Not after everything that happened during the Conquest."

Deacon shrugged nonchalantly. "Then if he will not capitulate, he will die."

Tears spilled down Carissa's cheeks. She rubbed her arms and shivered as though overcome by a sudden chill. Her teeth chattered, and he wondered whether fluctuating temperature was another side effect of the Obscurate. She stared up at him like there was some mercy to be found and choked back a sob when she saw none.

"You destroy everything you touch," she spat. "Just like Cobryn."

"What is your answer?" Deacon knew the truth. They both did. He had proved time and again the cost of resistance, and Carissa would never risk her son. With Jacen dead, she had realised just how far Deacon would go to achieve his ambitions. One way or another, he would achieve his goal, just as he had ascended to the throne of Genera.

Carissa grabbed his wrist with surprising strength. Her skin was clammy against his, but her grip was firm. Her violet-blue eyes glittered with anger, but it was not the sort of hot rage that burned down cities. It was a deeper rage, something cold as winter snow.

"You can't keep me caged forever. The darkness will always come out." Her smile was brittle, the promise of something terrible lingering in her eyes. "When it does, I will make sure it swallows you whole."

Deacon ignored the icy shiver that raced up his spine, sudden and unwelcome. He would be damned if he feared the girl. Her magic was suppressed. She had no supporters in Nicodemus. She was in his territory, alone, without any chance of rescue or escape. Nothing about her should be frightening.

So then, what had been the cold dread he'd just felt?

"Bold words, but not what I was looking for."

"Yes." The word was a guilty whisper. She released his wrist and looked away as though unable to stand the sight of him. "What other choice do I have?"

"None." He caught her by the chin and pressed a kiss to her cheek. He could taste the salt of her tears on his lips. "Until our wedding, darling Carissa."

Deacon strode over to the door and pulled it closed behind him, turning the key in the lock until it clicked once more. He was not astonished in the slightest that Lord Dyre and Myron had remained outside the entire time, mere feet from the door. He wouldn't have been surprised if they'd listened in on the conversation. Lord Dyre's expression was one of undisguised disgust, Myron's utmost disappointment.

"You will regret this." Lord Dyre offered a mocking bow, seemingly oblivious to the gravity of threatening a king. "Your Majesty."

The nobleman stormed off, leaving only Deacon and the condemning silence of the Godspeaker. The man's dismay was palpable. It was only after a few moments that Myron spoke.

"This decision will cost you popularity, my King. It will cost you men such as Lord Dyre, men you want on your side."

"My side?" Deacon arched an eyebrow in confusion. "Godspeaker Myron, you act as though we are at war. For the first time in many years, there is peace, both here and among the countries under our governance."

"We do not have Basium," Myron reminded him coolly, clasping his hands. "Do you think they will forgive and forget what happened to them?"

"I think they are a fractured nation, especially without a queen." Deacon's tone was curt. He did not appreciate being questioned in the matters of politics, especially by a Godspeaker. "They will struggle with only their boy king, Sebastian. I intend to watch and wait, not strike immediately. I am not a fool."

Myron's smile was tight. "Forgive me for saying so, Majesty, but yes you are."

At Carissa's first wedding, Deacon's arm had been entwined with hers as he had led her down the aisle in the absence of a living father figure. At her second, he stood at the end of the aisle, his blue silk shirt reminiscent of the Godspeaker robes, drenched in the sunlight filtering in through the windowpanes and spilling across the silver velvet of the carpet that ran the length of the palace cathedral.

"It is not too late to give this up." Godspeaker Myron's voice was soft in Deacon's ear as he stood with his hands clasped. "I have warned you; this goes against tradition. If you proceed, you will anger the gods."

"The gods or you, Myron?" Deacon responded, eyes flicking to the insufferable Godspeaker. As the most senior of the Godsvoice within the palace walls, it had fallen to Myron to officiate the ceremony, and his disdain was palpable. "My ancestors were the ones who created these traditions, not the gods. My ancestors, like Cobryn, would understand that some rules can be bent."

"Bent, not broken," Myron muttered.

Deacon refrained from sighing in exasperation. Myron was so rigidly devout that he could not understand that circumstances varied. Allowing Carissa the entire year's mourning period would give her plenty of chance to wriggle free of his grasp, and he did not intend for that to happen. Deacon had already lost Basium; he had no intention of losing its Queen too.

Deacon inhaled the scent of sage and mint that permeated the cathedral, punctured with the floral notes of the roses lining the pews. The opulence that had gone into decorating the cathedral spoke to the importance of the wedding, a king's wedding. After Cobryn's death, it felt right that the nobility had something to celebrate beyond just a coronation.

A sharp gasp ripped through the quiet chattering, followed by a sea of whispers, rustling about the cathedral like leaves in the wind. Deacon turned to face the yawning mouth of the cathedral's entrance to see his bride making the slow walk down the silver velvet carpet. It was not the fact that there was no father figure on her arm that made Deacon tense, but rather her choice of garb.

That little bitch.

Instead of white or even her house colours, Carissa was dressed all in black. The lace veil over her face was not white for marriage, but black for mourning. It was such a stark contrast to the typical white, so different to the neutral hues among the attendees, that it struck a bold chord.

Deacon's hands clenched into fists by his sides. Making a fuss would only serve to fuel the flames of Carissa's scandal. He was forced to bear the indignity in silence, eyes flicking to Myron and noting the shock and pity in the Godspeaker's expression. As Carissa approached the dais, she reached out to draw back her veil, her eyelids coated in glittering gold and the smug twist of her lips painted a rosy pink.

She stood by Deacon's side in silence as they recited their vows. He expected her to falter, the words trembling in her mouth, perhaps even the sheen of tears in her eyes. Yet Carissa remained unmoved, speaking her vows in perfect clarity, eyes dry and hard as marble. He silently fumed at the fact that she had taken the moment from him, for all talk would be about how the Queen had worn mourning black to her own wedding.

It was Deacon's victory, not Carissa's, and yet…that was not how it felt. The honey sweetness of triumph had soured on his tongue, like the bitter aftertaste of biting into an overripe fruit. Once they had recited their vows, Deacon caught Carissa's chin and kissed her hard. The crowd cheered, perhaps mistaking the movement for passion instead of what it was: a desperate grasp for control.

"You wore black," he hissed, keeping a firm grip on her chin as he drew back.

"I am still in my mourning period." There was an undercurrent of soft violence in Carissa's voice. "Just because you don't respect the traditions of your country does not mean I am the same."

Deacon's icy smile masked his rage as he released her, turning to the crowd.

"Please, feel free to make your way to the banquet hall for the feast. My wife and I will join you shortly to celebrate this momentous occasion."

There were several suggestive whistles and hoots from the assembly as they filed out from the pews, and Carissa visibly flinched, the first chink in the armour she had donned for the wedding. Deacon threw Myron a terse look, and the Godspeaker silently made his way from the cathedral as well.

Deacon crossed over to the pews, plucking one of the roses from where it had been wound around the wood and turning it over in his fingers. One of the thorns nicked at his thumb, but the pinprick was far less an irritation than Carissa's stony silence. When he glanced at her, his freshly minted wife, she remained on the dais, as cold and beautiful as any of his ancestor's statues.

"You will regret your choices, Carissa."

"As will you." Carissa's eyes glimmered with dark amusement, flashing her teeth in a savage smile that promised danger. Her mocking laugh rang through the cathedral, its echo cold and haunting. "Till death do us part, husband."

Since he had first revealed his power as a teenager, everyone had looked at Deacon with fear in their eyes. They dreaded what he was capable of, and out of that terror had come respect. Even Cobryn, who had been closer with Deacon than anyone else, was wary of his younger brother's might. He would never have admitted as much, but the sharp gleam of trepidation was difficult to disguise.

Yet…there was none of it in Carissa's eyes. It puzzled him and roused an impatient fury within him. He wanted her to recognise that he was in charge there, not her. He wanted her to be afraid of him.

Deacon caught her by the throat, fingers tightening enough to make her grimace. He was losing his cool, but he would not be thwarted by Carissa. He would not be questioned. He would not be undermined. He finally had it all, and while her subtle microaggressions were thoroughly annoying, he doubted her defiance would withstand him. Stone eroded over time. He would bring her crumbling down.

"We should be enjoying the feast." Deacon traced his bloodied thumb over her bottom lip, his anger pulsing into delight as she shuddered. "I believe you remember what comes after that."

Dread flared in Carissa's violet-blue eyes, her smile brittle as glass. Despite her obvious disgust, she stood firm and refused to tremble, reaching up to wipe the blood from her lip with nonchalance.

"Of course I remember. Don't worry, I will do my duty."

He had anticipated a protest, an excuse, something to bring back the sugary sweetness of her denial that it was happening. Instead, he received resigned acceptance, and the taste of ash in his mouth remained. Carissa was a practical woman who had already been shackled in matrimony once. He supposed he should not have expected any flight of fancy.

Carissa pried his hand off her neck, stepping back and once again donning her veil of mourning. He wished to rip that stupid piece of lace from her hands, to violently erase any remnants of Jacen that lingered on her. But such actions would appear erratic and born of fury, and Carissa's mocking laughter still rang in his ears.

Deacon had always seen there was a darkness in her, but he wondered how deep it dwelled, how far down he had to dig to reach the bottom of a patience honed with ancient power and years of trauma. She had never been a woman he had underestimated, but he had been foolish to expect the tearful pleas of a desperate girl from her.

He could feel her insincere smile burning with the promise of destruction.

"They will be waiting for us in the banquet hall. Shall we, *husband?*"

ONE
THE TRAITOROUS LADY
BELLONA LENORE

Bellona trailed her fingers through the cold blue-green water as the gondola made its way down the streets of Theron. Several other gondolas passed by, their occupants nodding their heads to the Lady of Theron. The trill of birdsong rang over the waterways, and Bellona smiled and closed her eyes as a fresh breeze brushed over her freckled skin like a caress.

Once she would have considered it a drowned city. But over the past year, as it became clear it would be difficult to drain Theron of the water Deacon had flooded it with, she had come up with an alternative solution. The waterlogged streets were accessible by gondola, and as Bellona watched the sunlight shimmering off the water's surface in sparkling flecks of gold, she relished Theron's beauty.

"You haven't said a word since we got back." Cristofer Santana, Bellona's husband and Lord of the Ciroccan city of Ornella, watched her with apprehension from where he sprawled across the other side of the gondola. "What's wrong?"

"Coming back just reminds me what we've come back to," Bellona said, the cool water dripping from her fingertips as she leaned back into the gondola.

Cristofer and Bellona had spent the past month and a half in Cirocco, staying with the royal family. She had enjoyed getting to spend more time in her husband's homeland, but returning to Basium meant the burden of her responsibilities landing firmly back on her shoulders. Each new day brought the prospect of war closer to her doorstep, despite the fact that there had been uneasy peace in Basium for a year.

"Bell! Bell!" The high-pitched cry came from the street's edge. Little Zephyr Morrow, all of eighteen months old, toddled fearlessly down a set of steps toward the water with a wide smile, Eirian Faustus chasing after him. The gondola rocked violently as the child threw himself from the ledge to embrace Bellona, and the reprimand died from her lips as she held the boy close to her chest.

"As you can tell, he's missed you very much." Eirian, Bellona's lover, had an amused smile adorning her lips as she reached a hand to help her out of the gondola. Cristofer scooped up Zephyr as he too stepped onto the path, looking happier for it with colour returning to his cheeks. He was not one for water travel.

Bellona looked down at the child in her husband's arms. Zephyr resembled his mother more every day, and Bellona's stomach twisted at the thought of her best friend. The news that Carissa was in Genera—that she'd married Deacon Morrow, the man she hated most—had taken some time to process. Bellona was under no illusion that Carissa entered the union willingly.

Unfortunately, where Bellona saw tragedy, Sebastian's supporters saw opportunity. Only days after the letter of Carissa's fate had been received, Sebastian's coronation was held in Marinel. Bellona had declined to attend, bitter that instead of working to save Carissa from a horrific marriage, her brother had chosen to take her crown.

Sebastian had not taken Bellona's rejection well, and things had taken a worse turn when a letter had arrived requesting custody of Zephyr. Despite Sebastian being the boy's uncle, Bellona did not trust those surrounding the impressionable young King. Sebastian might have Zephyr's best interests at heart, but his advisors saw another potential contender for the throne.

After the apparent murder of Quintin Faustus by Jacen Morrow, a story Bellona found suspicious at best, General Orien Luce and Priestess Juniper Diem had become the military and religious advisors to the young King. She did not know either of them well, and therefore they had not earned her trust. Bellona proclaimed herself Zephyr's guardian, refused to hand the child over, and refused to swear fealty to the King.

Bellona did not know if she would ever see her best friend again, or what sort of woman she would become. She vividly remembered her mother's fate at the hands of a Generan soldier, the atrocity he had committed before he had killed her. The idea that Carissa was suffering through that, over and over again…

For nights following the news of Carissa's marriage to Deacon, Bellona had recurring nightmares of what had happened to her mother. But instead of her mother's face, it had been Carissa's. The unspeakable atrocities that Carissa was likely suffering in Genera were worse than death. She was a prisoner yet again, in a cage she had no hope of escaping from.

She swallowed back bile. Bellona took her loyalty to Carissa seriously, and though she had failed to protect her friend, she would not fail to protect Carissa's son. At first, she had resented the child's presence—Bellona had never been overly fond of children—but as the weeks stretched into months, Zephyr's constant presence had become more of a soothing balm than an irritation.

Everywhere in the boy's features, she saw reminders of his parents. Carissa's piercing eyes, Jacen's easy smile. Bellona never considered herself close with her best friend's husband, but Jacen had not deserved what happened to him. Jacen had been in the way, so Deacon had callously murdered him.

"Has he behaved?" Bellona asked, linking her arm through Eirian's as they headed up to the castle. Behind them, Cristofer was laughing and wrestling an excitable Zephyr. Her husband had taken to Zephyr immediately, besotted with the child that had been unintentionally left in their care.

"He has." Eirian's body was tense, her shoulders rigid. "Sebastian wrote again, Bellona. He's not asking this time. He's demanding Zephyr be released into his custody."

Bellona scoffed. Over the past year since Carissa had been brought to Genera, all she'd heard from Sebastian were insistences that she had over his nephew. She doubted the words on the parchment were his. Why would an eighteen-year-old King have any interest in his toddler nephew unless it was political?

"Did it read like the writing of the young King, or that of his advisors?"

Eirian's silence was answer enough, and she glanced over her shoulder at Cristofer.

"You're going to drop him if you aren't careful."

"Charming as ever, Eirian." Cristofer offered her a broad grin capable of thawing even the coldest of hearts. "How has Theron been in our absence?"

She gave him a pointed look. "Best discussed when young Zephyr here has been put down for his nap."

"Nap?" the child repeated indignantly, his violet-blue eyes narrowing in a manner reminiscent of his mother.

"Yes," Bellona said sternly, before her tone grew lighter. "If you ever want to grow up big and strong, then you should have your nap."

Bellona cast one look back at the shimmering water, the gondolas gliding gently across the surface. If she had managed to turn the shit situation of Theron's flooding into something spectacular, she hoped the same could be said regarding Sebastian's intense interest in obtaining custody of his nephew.

Bellona read over the letter from Sebastian, her lips silently mouthing the words on the parchment. Cristofer sat across from her with a stern expression on his face, while Eirian paced and forth in front of the window. Bellona swept her ginger hair—cut short just above her shoulders for practicality since her early days as Zephyr's guardian—out of her face.

"You've been staring at that thing for a while now." Cristofer's voice was gentle but firm. "It's just words, Bell."

"A traitor to the crown." The words were spoken with barely concealed anger, her voice quavering at the effort of holding back her rage. "He has labelled me a traitor to the crown for refusing to hand over Zephyr."

"It's more than that, Bellona." Eirian ceased her steps, leaning over the back of the chair beside Cristofer. "You also didn't swear fealty to him. You know how that looked when it was Lord Ambrose refusing to swear to Carissa. It creates unease."

"Oh, then by all means, let's go to Marinel and swear fealty." Bellona slapped her hand down on the table, the letter pinned under her palm. "Let's go and bow to a pretender king."

Cristofer and Eirian exchanged worried looks. Goddess above, how she hated when they did that. The three of them were close enough to know each other inside out, and that look was how Cristofer and Eirian silently communicated that they thought Bellona was overreacting to something.

"Bellona…" Cristofer reached across the table and rested his hand over hers. "We don't know if Carissa is coming back."

Bellona snatched her hand from his, pushing herself to her feet. The chair scraped noisily from under her as she stood, tears pricking at the corners of her eyes. He was right, and she hated it. For a year now, Bellona had acted as though Sebastian was warming Carissa's throne, as though she would come back to Basium to claim it.

Bellona wanted nothing more than to march on Genera and rescue her friend. Cristofer and Eirian had talked her out of it. Deacon had three countries at his disposal, despite losing Basium. Bellona would go to war for Carissa, but who would follow? Many in Basium had condemned the young woman to her fate. To them, she was as good as dead. For all her magic, all her dark power, Carissa had been trapped by the only man who could outmatch her.

Would peace with Sebastian allow them to save Carissa? Somehow, Bellona doubted it. To Orien and Juniper, having Carissa gone suited their purposes. They would present whatever argument they could to turn Sebastian against trying to save his sister.

"It's Carissa." Bellona's voice was sharp as flint. "You don't know her like I do. If anyone can escape that monster, it's her. She's one of the most powerful

Maleficium this country has ever known."

"Don't you see that something's wrong?" Eirian leaned further forward over the chair. "If it were that easy, she would already have done it. They've been talking about how much Obscurate has been imported into Genera. What if…"

Bellona's stomach turned and bile rose in the back of her throat at what Eirian was insinuating. Carissa was a match for Deacon when her magic was at full strength. If she had no magic at all…

A shrill scream drew Bellona from her thoughts, making her whirl back around to face her husband and her lover. Their expressions reflected her own confusion, and the three of them rushed for the door. When Bellona stepped into the corridor, the first thing she noticed was the door to Zephyr's room—situated just down the end of the hall from the conference room—was flung wide open.

Panic flared through her and she sprinted down the corridor, heart hammering in her chest as she ignored Cristofer and Eirian's shouts of warning. When she burst into the room, a man in black stood over Zephyr's bed, but he spun to face Bellona at the intrusion. She noticed one of the guards who was typically stationed outside the little boy's quarters on the ground, his throat slashed open.

"Ah, the Lenore bitch." A grin spread across his heavily scarred face. "Good."

Bellona reached down to her belt, tugging the knife she kept there free. These days, it was foolish to be unarmed despite the truce with Sebastian. The man lunged for her, and she took a few stumbling steps backwards as he swung his sword, as though he meant to cleave her in two.

He was not a big man, but most people were bigger than Bellona. She used her smaller size and greater speed to her advantage, ducking and twirling so that she was behind him. He turned on her with surprising speed, but she was ready for him. Feinting for his stomach, Bellona dropped her knife and caught it with her other hand, stabbing him in the thigh. As the man screamed in pain, she wrenched the blade free and shoved the knife into his throat.

As the man gurgled and died, collapsing on the ground with a scarlet stain spreading under him, Bellona turned her attention to young Zephyr. The child sat curled in the corner of his bed, wide-eyed, hugging the sheets close. When Bellona inspected him, she saw no visible sign of injury. As she scooped him into her lap and held him close, kissing the top of his head, Cristofer and Eirian ran into the room.

Cristofer immediately made a beeline for Bellona and Zephyr, whilst Eirian knelt beside the man's corpse, checking him over.

"Are you all right?" Cristofer asked, taking her face in his hands. When she nodded, he pressed a quick kiss to her cheek. "Don't ever go running in unprepared, Bellona. He could have killed you."

"I found this." Eirian rose from her position over the dead assassin, a bloodstained page in her hands. Bellona only needed to see the stamp of the black swan to know what it was, her heart thundering in her chest as her fury intensified.

Sebastian Darnell had tried to have her killed. He had tried to have Zephyr abducted or murdered. Perhaps he hadn't been the one to issue the command, but if he had stamped the letter, he must have known what it was for. Bellona had given him the benefit of the doubt, believing him to be an innocent bystander, but the letter was proof of his crimes.

"What does it say?" she asked with barely controlled ire, bracing herself for the answer.

Eirian's eyes scanned the parchment. "Lady Lenore is henceforth to be detained and brought to the capital, along with Prince Zephyr Morrow. If she should resist, any injuries or death resulting are not to blame on the Crown."

"Bell…" Cristofer rested a hand on his shoulder, his dark eyes pleading with her. "You don't know that's from Sebastian himself. General Luce could just have easily taken the stamp and used it himself."

Sebastian had been one of the people who'd protested strongly against Carissa utilising the Blood Rite in the war. Though he might not be directly responsible for what had happened to her, unease settled over Bellona like a cloak. Within the space of a few weeks, Jacen was dead, and Carissa was gone.

"Regardless, the crown has made a move against me." Bellona held Zephyr tighter to her, silently promising that she would die before anyone touched the child. Her eyes flicked up to Eirian, furious and full of retribution. "If the King considers me a traitor to the crown, he's seen nothing yet."

Two
The Bitter Queen
Carissa Darnell

If there was one place Carissa was most at peace, it was the gardens.

Nicodemus's palace gardens were not as abundant with plants as Marinel's, to Carissa's bitter disappointment, though still she took refuge amongst the thick trees and the few flowers that bloomed in Genera's harsh climate.

Jacen's fiddle rested in her lap, one of the only remnants Carissa had left of her first husband. Despite the fact he'd been dead a year, the thought of his sweet smile still made tears prick at her eyes. The fiddle was one of the things she could cling to that reminded her of him, the only thing Deacon hadn't yet wrested from her grasp.

She had slowly trained herself to play the instrument, knowing Deacon would not waste money on lessons. She would never be as good as Jacen, but she hoped to replicate the beautiful music that had once brought cheer to the dining halls around Basium. Thus far, her attempts were pitiful, and despite the impatience that swelled within her, she planned to master the instrument no matter how long it took or how much it made her fingers ache.

Of all the things Deacon had subjected her to, taking away her power was the most heinous. The Obscurate dulled the senses and was used more widely in Harith for Imperium and Maleficium who wanted to suppress their abilities. Carissa needed it in daily doses, and she had already experienced the consequences of refusing to take it. She rubbed her wrist, a chill ghosting up her spine.

"Your Majesty." It was Godspeaker Myron, with his dry, quiet voice and watchful eyes. At first Carissa had not taken well to the man, but over time, it became apparent Myron was not one of Deacon's most avid supporters.

"Godspeaker." Carissa indicated the patch of grass beside her. "Come, won't you sit with me?"

It was Myron who brought her news of home. Carissa's heart ached when she thought of Basium, of the people she'd left behind. Her best friend, her brother, her *son*. What would they think of her? She shuddered, wondering if perhaps it was best she didn't know the answer to that.

Carissa had spent the early days of her marriage in a haze of Obscurate-muddled, wine-drunk confusion. She had thought it best she felt nothing. These days, Carissa saw there was no use in waking to a throbbing head and bile rising in the back of her throat. She needed to be sharp as a blade to survive Deacon, especially if she hoped to have any chance of being free.

It was hard to think of the honeyed taste of freedom when all she had was ashen imprisonment on her tongue. It had been a year, and she had not managed to break her shackles. Carissa was patient, building the foundations from the ground up, but there was no telling all of her work would not come toppling down.

"Have you any word from Basium?" Carissa asked, taking care not to let desperation colour her tone as he sat stiffly beside her.

"I have, none of it good." Myron sighed heavily. "Things have not improved between Lady Lenore and King Sebastian."

Carissa could not say she was surprised, though disappointment welled within her. Since she had been taken, since news of her marriage to Deacon had reached Basium, her best friend and her brother were on the brink of civil war. Word had it that Bellona had custody of Zephyr, and refused to hand him over despite Sebastian's insistence that he should be the one to raise his nephew.

"I spoke to a medic this morning." Myron rested a hand over hers, his skin papery and dry. "The King is displeased."

Carissa clenched her jaw as nausea roiled in the pit of her stomach. Deacon had made it quite apparent he wanted a child from her, an heir. She would do anything in her power to deny him that. Thus far, her prayers to the goddess Elethea had been answered.

If she was Bellona, she would have resisted every part of the marriage with all the stubborn fibres of her being. If she was Bellona, she would have tried to murder Deacon in his sleep rather than subject herself to him.

Unfortunately, she was not Bellona. Carissa was not a warrior, but a survivor. When Jacen had returned from the Island Wars, a man that Carissa had not known and loved yet, she had treated the issue of their marital bed with a cold, business-like detachment. She had done the same with Deacon, casting aside pride and the shreds of her dignity and giving him exactly what he wanted. It gave her no pleasure, but she would rather be an active participant and have some small degree of control over her situation.

"I don't want to have this conversation." Her words were icy, a cold warning issued with nothing to give it weight.

Fortunately, Deacon was currently preoccupied with Nocturnum. The event occurred annually in Genera and was perhaps the biggest celebration in the country. It was said to be a night where the gods walked amongst men, a night of festivities and mulled wine. Carissa would don her most difficult mask—that of the smiling, benevolent monarch. It had always been a part she played well, but playing it as Deacon's wife was the hardest.

"A word of advice, my dear." Myron's gaze was pitying. "Give him what he wants."

Carissa's lips twisted into a bitter smile. "Isn't that just the problem, Godspeaker? No one says no to Deacon. No one defies Deacon. It's through giving him what he wants that he's gotten this far."

She supposed her agreeing to marry him hadn't helped matters, but she had not truly had a choice. If she hadn't wed him, he hardly would have let her go. Carissa might never be free again, but she would prefer to endure the hell that was life as Deacon's wife rather than see her family and friends endangered.

She was not a fool—one day, perhaps sooner rather than later, Deacon's greedy gaze would return to Basium. He would want the country that had defied him, just as he'd gained the woman who'd refused him. For the moment, he had his hands tied. Deacon did not speak of such matters with Carissa, but Myron did.

Harith was growing unruly, despite the best efforts of Deacon's older sister Relda to maintain order. Wendell had gone silent since learning the awful fate of Gretchen, and that quiet was troubling. Even within Genera, Deacon had enemies. He was not a popular monarch, and his decision to defy the traditional mourning period and marry Carissa regardless had only solidified that.

"Do you pray, Your Majesty?"

"To whom?" Carissa threw him a quizzical look, the light breeze kicking her coal-black hair back from her face. "To the goddess Elethea, yes."

"Perhaps you should consider praying to the Generan gods," Myron suggested gently. It was not the first time he had said as much to her, and she was reminded of the fact that while he might be her ally, he was also a member of the Godsvoice. Events like Nocturnum were intensely spiritual for him.

"You don't think they favour Deacon?" Carissa's tone was sour, the acidic taste of defeat all too familiar on her tongue. "They've granted him everything he's wanted so far, if you believe in them."

"Not everything." Myron's eyes flicked up to the whispering leaves of the trees overhead. "Not a child."

Carissa remembered when she had discovered her pregnancy with Zephyr. It had been through Miriam's visions, and she had been a mix of hopeful and terrified at the idea of being a mother. The thought that she might give Deacon a child—it was a thought she could not entertain. Every time she lingered on the possibility, it made bile rise in her throat and her stomach coil into knots. No matter the cost, she could never give him an heir.

She was aware, to her delight, that he had taken a mistress in the form of Ariadne Pavlos, a widowed noblewoman in her late twenties, which seemed to occupy some of Deacon's time and give Carissa respite.

At first, Ariadne had seen Carissa as an obstacle, but she was sharp as shattered glass, quickly realising that the Queen cared nothing for her ambitions. These days, Ariadne was quick to shoot her a fleeting smile or a wink, as though they shared some sort of conspiratorial secret. She was one of the few people at court that Carissa actually liked, though many would have found it strange that a queen should favour her husband's mistress.

"It may help," Myron continued, his quiet words grating on her nerves like steel across stone. "Obscurate would be dangerous for an unborn child. He would not risk subjecting you to the drug if it might cost him something he wants."

No Obscurate. The thought lit a spark within Carissa, a dark and dangerous idea that clawed its way out of some deep pit within her. There was nothing she wouldn't do to be free, nothing she wouldn't do if it meant returning to Basium. She had long since forsaken her pride, stripped herself down piece by piece until she was a hollow shell. *That* was how she had survived Nicodemus.

The cost of her whirlwind idea would be high, though she would be the only one paying it. Deacon was a clever man, and if he detected the whiff of a lie or a farce, there would be no mercy. Carissa needed to be convincing. She would once again be donning a mask, the only mask that could push forward her plan: the mask of the subservient wife.

Carissa received a summons to dinner—it was a command, not a request. Deacon always acted as though he gave her a choice, but when resistance resulted in someone around her being punished for it, was there really a decision?

Carissa approached the dinner table as one might a battleground, though armed with only her words. The Obscurate made her magic inaccessible. She felt it the clearest when she had her bleeding, but even then it was an incomprehensible tugging at the back of her mind. When she reached for it, the Obscurate muddled her grasp too much for her to take a hold. It was frustrating, but she had given up on trying. The drug was too strong for her to fight.

Carissa had dressed in a very deliberate manner for tonight's dinner. Often insistent upon her house colours of cream and gold, or else a varying shade of purple to bring out her eyes, she had decided upon a black silk dress with silver detailing. Morrow colours. She did not wear fur to stave off the chill, leaving her arms bare, goosebumps dancing along her skin. The dress cinched in at the waist and dipped low enough to draw attention to the swell of her breasts.

Goddess above, she hated herself for what she had to do. She hated herself each time she did it, though that night was most important of all. Typically, it was to claw back some control of her own, but she hoped in that instance, it would lend well to the long game she was playing. A game to obtain her freedom.

"Dear wife." Deacon seated himself across from her, smiling even as she gripped her knife and fork tightly and glowered at him over her salted pork. "Preparations for Nocturnum are underway. I forget you've never experienced it—it's quite the celebration here in Nicodemus."

How laughable that she had once been at the pinnacle of power, the Queen of Basium who had sent Deacon and his army fleeing back to Genera. She was little more than a glorified prisoner, a shining trophy for Deacon to put on display, as Cobryn had done with Lilith and Gretchen.

Once, Carissa had believed that Deacon wanted her for her magic. She wasn't so certain anymore. After all, if that was the case, why wouldn't he let her access her power? Was he afraid of her blood magic? She dared not mention her magic or the Obscurate, for fear that breathing a word of either would undo the knots she was carefully tying to fashion his noose.

"I look forward to Nocturnum." The words were not quite a lie. Though not

25

typically one for parties, Carissa didn't mind the odd celebration on occasion. Her heart tugged her thoughts in the direction of Jacen, wondering how he would have celebrated if he was in Genera.

If he was alive.

"You and Myron have become quite close friends." Deacon tilted his head to the side, the warm candlelight throwing his bright hazel eyes and high cheekbones into sharp relief. A physically handsome man, with such an ugly heart. Carissa inhaled the rosemary and warm Ciroccan spices on her food, reminding herself that she had to think with her head. She could not let her emotions rule her, not even her hatred of Deacon.

"Am I not permitted friends?" Carissa tilted her head to the side, dark hair spilling like oil over her shoulders. "Godspeaker Myron is insistent on converting me to your faith, especially before Nocturnum. He wants me to offer my prayers to your gods."

"I see." Deacon did not sound convinced, but there was no suspicion sparkling in his eyes. Perhaps he thought Myron and Carissa traded gossip behind his back. If he thought anything more sinister, surely he would have done something about it.

"It does get lonely, you know." Carissa allowed a defensive note to creep into her voice, words drifting in the murky realm somewhere between truth and lie. "I don't have Bellona. I don't have anyone here. I have to make new friends all over again."

"Carissa." Deacon made the single word a sound of exasperation, setting his knife and fork down with a clatter against the porcelain plate. "I never once denied you the ability to make friends. I am, however, questioning your interest in befriending a middle-aged man who is more dedicated to the gods than any living being."

"My first father, you and Cobryn murdered during the Conquest." Carissa's voice was hard and cold as marble. She pushed herself to her feet, chair scraping back against the tiles at the speed with which she rose. "My second, you drowned in Theron. Is it any wonder I seek a paternal figure you won't kill?"

Carissa recalled the plays she and her brothers had put on as children for their parents, a charade of too-heavy costumes and quarrelling between the siblings. Peregrine insisted on playing the dashing hero, assigning Carissa and Sebastian roles as villains or fools. Theodore participated on occasion depending on his level of interest, and Peregrine bent to whatever role Theodore deigned to accept.

Initially, the plays had been extreme theatrics, Sebastian tossing himself across the makeshift wooden stage when his character perished. Over time, the performances had become polished. The tears were a shimmer in the eyes instead of hysterical crying. Natural actors, their grandfather Patrick had called them after one of their last performances.

A performance, Carissa thought, often had as much raw honesty as there was deception. There had to be something real in it, or else it wouldn't work. She gripped the edge of the pine wood table so hard that her knuckles gleamed white, swallowing the lump that itched in her throat whenever she thought about Kato's fate.

"So, you feel alone. Isolated." Deacon arched an eyebrow, leaning back in his chair to observe her. Carissa noted the way his eyes swept down from her face to rake over her body. Triumph and revulsion surged through her in chaotic unison.

"Isn't that what you wanted?" Carissa's every step was a slow, deliberate movement that pulled her closer to him, her arms folding over her chest and her chin tilting upwards. Her mouth twisted in contempt.

They both knew the answer to the question. Cobryn's strength had been in his violence, the sheer physical power that he possessed. Deacon's magic was a force in itself, but his true strength lay in his manipulation. He wanted Carissa to feel isolated so that hope for escape became impossible. He was wary of potential friends like Myron who could become another person Carissa relied upon.

He feared his loss of control. It was why he had taken her magic; it was why he wanted her to feel that he was the only constant in her life now. Carissa thought perhaps she might be one of the few people alive who knew Deacon inside and out, his awful ambition and the things he would do to attain his goals.

Deacon eased himself to his feet, a curiosity softening his features as he examined her. She remained still and silent, letting him see whatever he wanted to in her expression.

"If that's what you think I intended, you don't have any idea what I want."

"Don't I?" There was a menacing softness to Carissa's words, her stomach and her heart plunging into freefall as she took a last step to close the distance between them. A smile as sharp and brittle as broken glass twisted her lips. Then, like a siren's song luring in a drowning sailor, she dragged him down to kiss her.

Deacon kissed back with fervour, as she knew he would, his arms twisting tight as ropes around her waist. Carissa gripped his shoulders and tugged him close against her, her kiss as hard and unforgiving as the raging ocean in a storm. She pushed down the horror and disgust at her own actions. It was a business transaction. Nothing more, nothing less.

As Deacon picked her up and set her on the table, cold lips descending down her neck, Carissa tilted her head back and let her black hair spill down her back so he couldn't see her victorious smile.

Deacon wanted an heir, and so she would pretend she was giving him one. Why would he question another of his apparent victories? What reason did he have to doubt the pregnancy that Carissa would soon announce, hesitantly and with defeat in her voice?

That time, she was the cat and he was the mouse—and without knowing it, he had fallen right into her trap.

THREE
THE LYING PRINCESS
LILITH MARWAN

Lilith didn't ever think she could be a ruler. It wasn't as though she didn't have the temperament for it—it was the fact that she found meetings to be tedious. That was especially the case for the latest meeting, consisting of her aunt Queen Samara, her cousin Prince Cairo, spymaster Ishtar Haroun, and his lover and secret ally, Relda Morrow. They were an unlikely group of associates, Lilith thought as she cast around the room.

For many years, Lilith believed Relda was the same as her older brothers—interested only in domination, enjoying the power she held in Harith. It turned out that Relda was the Fox, second-in-command to an underground resistance determined to cast off the weight of the Morrow Empire. With Cobryn gone, it was becoming easier, but they knew better than to flaunt Relda's true colours. Deacon had to think he had Harith and Wendell under control...for the moment.

The meeting room had a much more casual atmosphere than the rectangular oak table and straight-backed chairs of Cobryn's conference room in Genera. Harith's meeting room had comfortable, plush chairs adorned with colourful cushions, and a round table so they could sit anywhere they liked and still observe one another.

Ishtar lounged in his chair with a languid grace. Lilith owed him a debt, a debt she was yet to repay. If not for Ishtar, Lilith wasn't certain she and Ayesha would have made it out of Genera alive.

He had also helped them keep a dangerous secret...a secret that, a year on, was almost ready to come to light. For all his quiet indifference, Ishtar certainly cared about people more than he let on—especially Elyes, his bastard son with Relda.

"Has there been any word from Bao?" Lilith asked, though she doubted the answer would be much different to the last time they'd met.

"Nothing new." Cairo raked his fingers through his dark hair. Lilith could smell the Obscurate on him, and wondered if the others could too. She had quickly discovered since returning to Dalal that her cousin partook in the drug, which he claimed eased his high levels of anxiety. Though suspicious, Lilith couldn't think why Cairo would lie to her.

"Meaning?" Relda persisted.

"Meaning they're impartial." Samara scoffed, her many bangles jingling against one another. "They won't be for long, not when Deacon decides they're next."

"Do you think it will be them, not Cirocco?" Lilith questioned, her gaze flicking to her aunt. Samara wasn't getting any younger, the stiffness in her joints beginning to show in the slowness of her gait. Her aunt said she wanted to retire peacefully, and planned to abdicate her throne to Cairo once his daughter was a few years older.

"Cirocco is too close with Basium." Samara shook her head slowly, her earrings and beads in her hair jingling at the movement. "It would be a far greater risk than to attack them. No, Deacon will want Bao."

"What about Wendell?" Ishtar leaned forward, dark eyes inquisitive. "We haven't heard from Stefan in months."

Lilith couldn't say she was surprised, though a stab of familiar guilt pierced her at the mention of the King of Wendell. She would never shake her memories with Gretchen, the woman who had been Cobryn's youngest wife and the only person who truly understood the torment Lilith experienced.

Gretchen had been pregnant with the Warmonger's child when she'd been ruthlessly killed by Deacon. Drowned in the river—Lilith thought it was a horrific way to die, and she still wished there was more she could have done to save Gretchen.

"I don't think we will be for a while," Lilith admitted, pushing aside her thoughts. "What happened to Gretchen...it hit Stefan hard. He hates Deacon, but he fears him more."

Fear was a powerful weapon, one that Cobryn had always wielded with great efficiency. Deacon was even more terrifying, considering the strong magic that flowed through his veins. The only thing that gave Lilith comfort was the knowledge that Deacon was an unpopular King. Despite his brutal nature, Cobryn had at least maintained some degree of approval from the Generan people. Either Deacon didn't care, or he had given up on trying.

They had also learned that Deacon had abducted Carissa Darnell and forced her to become his wife. Lilith understood better than anyone what the younger woman was going through. It was a brutal fate, far worse than Carissa deserved. As if the girl hadn't been through enough in her life, she was married to the monster who'd ripped her family to shreds in the first place.

"We need to convince him that standing against Deacon is his best option." Samara's brow furrowed. Lilith silently agreed with her aunt, but how were they meant to accomplish such a task? Stefan was far more weak-willed than Gretchen had been. If he was to stand against Deacon, he would certainly need assurances.

"What would you say is our best course of action?" Cairo turned his attention to Relda. If anyone knew Deacon, it was her. The woman had viewed her younger brother's choice of wife and recent choices with disdain.

"It's been a year." Relda steepled her fingers, contemplative. "Things have been quiet...too quiet. From what I've heard, my brother is not faring well. He faces political opposition within his own court. The time to gather our allies is now, while Deacon is at his weakest."

"Would war not unite them?" Apprehension laced Lilith's words. She did not want them to make a fatal mistake. "They are at odds with each other. Shouldn't we let them battle for dominance, rather than lash out against Genera and cause them to unite?"

"I said gather allies, not wage war." Relda arched an eyebrow. "I agree we cannot risk them banding together, but Deacon is the true enemy here, not Genera as a whole. The time to reach out is now. We must know who our friends are."

"We do have another weapon at our disposal." Ishtar spoke quietly, and panic rose within Lilith as his eyes flicked to hers. "Ayesha."

Lilith missed her daughter, heart aching at the thought of Ayesha. Upon her flight from Genera, one thing had been obvious to her: Deacon could never be allowed to find a child of Cobryn Morrow. Although the youngest of Cobryn's children, and a girl at that, Ayesha had a strong claim to the throne which could challenge Deacon's.

"My daughter is not a weapon." Lilith's eyes narrowed. "She is not a piece to be used in whatever game you want to play."

"Revealing that she's alive could turn the tides in our favour," Relda insisted, leaning forward and resting her elbows on the smooth surface of the table. "At the moment, the only reason Deacon hasn't been torn down is because there are no viable alternatives."

Lilith's eyes locked onto Ishtar's, and he gave a small nod. She took a deep breath and steeled herself. Ayesha was only twelve, and she would do anything in her power to prevent her child becoming a monarch. If it meant sacrificing something she'd kept close to her chest, then it was time. The secret she and Ishtar had worked so hard to keep found its way out of darkness and into the light.

She sent a silent prayer to Eislanon, the Harithian goddess of treachery and sin, for she doubted any of the other gods would stand by the lies she had told, even if they were for the greater good.

"There's something I need to tell you all. Something I should have told you a year ago."

The familiar saccharine scent of Obscurate clogged Lilith's nostrils as she packed her things. It had been several weeks since she had gone to visit Ayesha, and although the girl was growing more independent, Lilith needed to see her— especially after the abrupt turn the meeting had taken.

Heaving a sigh, she swung open the door and padded down the corridor to Cairo's room. Sure enough, the blue smoke was wafting out from under his door. Lilith rapped once and then turned the handle. Surprisingly, the door was unlocked, and she blinked through the haze of smoke.

"You have to stop smoking the Obscurate." Lilith folded her arms over her chest, inspecting her cousin with barely muted disapproval. "Inara can't grow up with a father who…"

"With a father who does what?" Cairo glared over at Lilith with red-rimmed eyes. "Do you think this is what I wanted to be, Lilith? You have your little secrets, and I have mine. I take the Obscurate because I have to."

"What does that mean, Cairo?" Lilith's words were gentle as she seated herself beside her cousin, watching as he put out his pipe. Whatever was happening with Cairo, it had gotten worse over the past year. When she had visited Harith before, when Cobryn had been alive, she'd not even noticed him taking Obscurate. It was harder to tell when he *wasn't* using the substance.

"It doesn't matter." He shook his head, eyes flicking up to meet hers. "What matters now is what we plan to do about Deacon. That man can't stay in power."

"It's not as easy as that."

"You just made it easy." Cairo's brow creased in confusion. "What you told us at the meeting...that's our answer."

"Maybe I shouldn't have said anything." Irritation coloured Lilith's tone. "I'm not forcing someone onto the Generan throne. That wasn't what I meant."

"How is she?" Cairo's expression morphed into something more sympathetic.

33

"Ayesha, I mean. It can't be easy for her, being out in the jungle with only one companion."

"She's adjusted to it better than I thought," Lilith admitted, raking her fingers through her dark hair. Ayesha had always been a quiet girl, but in the past year, she had thrived out in the jungle. If she was frustrated at being kept from her family, it didn't show. Instead, she had learned many skills—perhaps not ones that benefitted her station, but important for her survival nonetheless.

"Give her my love, won't you?" Cairo smiled.

There were about a dozen questions that Lilith wanted to ask Cairo, about the Obscurate, about what his intentions for Genera were. Instead, she settled on comfortable silence, not wishing to cause an argument with her cousin before her departure. There would be time for such conversation upon her return.

"I will." Lilith eased herself off the bed. "Take care of yourself while I'm gone."

Cairo's smile waned only slightly. "Don't I always?"

FOUR
THE LOST LORD
THOM DYRE

By the Trinity, he despised the capital.

Thom Dyre cast a disdainful gaze over the four towers at each of the compass points of the city of Nicodemus. The mountains looming near were beautiful, but the city itself was better off avoided. Thom preferred his home city of Gethsemane, with its weaving streets and dark alleys and the bridges that linked it all together. Nicodemus was too orderly, too many straight lines and squares. It was far too neat for his liking.

For a typically dull city, Nicodemus was ripe with cheer. The approach of Nocturnum had a habit of breathing life into even the most wretched of places. No wonder Thom had avoided the capital after the death of his older sister, Annaliese—there were too many memories there. It had only been when Cobryn had met his untimely demise and Deacon had ascended the throne that Thom spent more time in the capital.

The first people Thom met with, as always, were Godspeaker Myron and Ariadne Pavlos. There was a temple down near the city gates—next to a brothel, amusingly—where Myron would meet with Thom and Ariadne. These audiences had commenced soon after Deacon's coronation, an unlikely alliance formed when the nobleman and the Godspeaker had realised they had a mutual contempt for their new King.

Ariadne had joined them later, only a few months previously when Myron had managed to befriend her and draw her into their schemes. At first, Thom had not trusted the woman, particularly knowing that she was Deacon's mistress. It became clear that despite being ruthlessly ambitious and wanting the best for her two children at her late husband's estate, Ariadne had a strange kindness to her that was displayed in the most unusual of circumstances.

"Lord Dyre, welcome back to Nicodemus." Myron's voice was full of dry mirth as he approached, lowering his hood. "Just in time for the Nocturnum celebrations too. Excellent timing."

Ariadne sprawled gracefully in one of the velvet couches, twirling one of her errant brown curls around her finger as she examined Thom. The three of them had few things in common, but one was that they were all better listeners than they were talkers, picking up on court gossip with sharp ears.

"I can hardly wait." Thom shook his head slowly, sarcasm colouring his tone. He was a man who preferred the solitude of his library and the company of books over wild festivities. "How are things here? Has our beloved King been hard at work?"

"Indeed." Myron sighed heavily, glancing at Ariadne. "Deacon has launched ships, headed to Bao. He also risks conflict with Harith in his search for Ayesha."

Ayesha, the sole surviving child of Cobryn Morrow. It wasn't good enough for Deacon that she was gone—he wanted her found, and most likely he wanted her killed. It did not matter to him that the girl wasn't even thirteen. She posed a problem if she ever came out of hiding, and he wanted that problem eliminated. Though the girl was not Thom's niece, he felt a surge of sympathy for her.

"The Queen?" Thom pressed. The encounters he'd had with her had left a distinct impression.

Thom could see why his late nephew, gods rest his soul, had loved Carissa. Beneath the surface, the raven-haired prettiness, there was a steel like Thom had never seen. Cobryn's younger wives, the women who had come after Annaliese, had not married him by choice. Likewise forced into a marriage she had not wanted, Carissa could have hidden herself away, as Lilith had done. Instead, she showed her face at social occasions, she behaved with grace, and there was always a benevolent smile on her lips.

How strong did she have to be, he wondered, to endure it? She was a woman who refused to be broken, who donned the mask of dignity and civility again and again. Unspeakable things must happen beyond the public eye, but Carissa endured with poise. Thom had rarely met a woman of her youth who was *that* strong. She was the picture-perfect Queen, and it must have been killing her inside.

Deacon had been a fool to marry her. A beautiful woman, but not one worth losing popularity in an already-uneasy country for. Cobryn's younger brother, forever in his shadow, having lost his patience with it all at last. The story went that Jacen had turned on his family, killing Cobryn and Gretchen in a bid for power before Deacon had taken him down—but that did not fit with what Thom knew of his nephew's character. Far more likely Deacon had committed the murders and blamed a dead man.

"Bearing the burden of being Deacon's wife as best she can." It was Ariadne who spoke in her melodic voice that time, leaning forward with glimmering grey eyes. "She still adamantly refuses to have any child with him, though lately…"

"Lately?" Myron repeated the word sharply.

"Typically, she shares his bed on the odd occasion. Recently, it has become more frequent, though I couldn't say why."

Thom's brow furrowed. Carissa hated her husband and wished for as little contact with him as possible. What reason would she have to share his bed more regularly? Perhaps, after a year as Deacon's wife, Carissa had been broken down into the submissive role that he wanted for her. He turned his mind to the matter of Carissa's home country.

"Basium?"

"Still on the brink of civil war." Myron raked a hand through his thinning salt-and-pepper hair. "Lady Lenore refuses to hand over Prince Zephyr, and word has it that King Sebastian is furious about it."

Thom ruminated over his knowledge of the two most powerful players in Basium. Lady Lenore had recently come to power, her father Kato having sacrificed himself during the flooding of Theron to allow his people the chance to escape. Then there was Sebastian himself. He was a boy of eighteen, nowhere near as self-assured as his sister had been at that age, and heavily reliant upon senior authority figures such as General Orien Luce and Priestess Juniper Diem.

"What does she think will happen?" Thom asked, Lady Lenore's stubbornness perplexing him.

"It appears she is still holding out hope that Carissa will return to Basium to claim her crown." Myron's expression was sorrowful.

"I should speak to the Queen." Thom heaved a sigh, bracing himself for an audience with Carissa. It wasn't as though the woman herself was emotionally taxing—it was facing someone who had been through so much trauma and remained so resilient. It was a physical reminder that even Deacon's wife, *especially* Deacon's wife, suffered as a result of his triumph.

"Come, we can return to the palace together." Ariadne smiled and offered her arm. Perhaps she might have once attempted to seduce Thom into marrying her so she could become Lady of Gethsemane. Since then, she knew him better, and seemed content in her role as Deacon's mistress.

As they left the temple and headed up the street to the palace, Thom took in the decorations beginning to adorn the city. Skulls with candles placed in them, bones gleaming ominously in the sunlight, webbing that might have been real. Ariadne observed him with a strange smile.

"I'm happy you are in Nicodemus for Nocturnum, Lord Dyre. I know you aren't fond of celebrations, but this is something special."

"May I ask you something?" Thom blurted out. It was a question that had been on his mind for some time. Ariadne nodded. "When you first came to the capital, I know you were only interested in power, in what your ambition could bring you. With your husband dead in the Island Wars, you thought it was time you established yourself. You could have just become Deacon's mistress and ignored Carissa's predicament entirely. Why didn't you?"

There were a few beats of silence between them, broken by a man on a swaying ladder hammering a bone against the side of the building.

"Ambition is not evil, Thom." There was a reprimand in Ariadne's tone, a defensiveness he had not expected from such an unflappable woman. "I reach out with both hands, and the gods grant me both ambition and compassion. The two can coexist. Carissa is no threat to me, and so of course I pity her for what she endures."

Ariadne's oldest child, her daughter, was five years old. Perhaps she looked at Carissa and thought that could be her daughter's fate in ten or fifteen years. Perhaps it had been her own fate, for Ariadne remained enigmatic about her relationship with her late husband. Thom felt shame wash over him. He had been wrong to judge so quickly and harshly.

"I meant no disrespect, Lady Pavlos."

"I know." Ariadne grinned. "Such a shame you are not interested in marriage or children. We would make a formidable couple."

Thom had never been interested in such matters, but unfortunately his mother Odessa pressed the importance of them. Thom was forty, and at the age where he needed to consider what would happen to Gethsemane if he passed. A marriage of convenience might have worked, but what woman would be happy with such an arrangement?

Turning his mind from the daunting prospect he'd faced for the past twenty years, he focused on the ominous decorations flooding the capital city. For a celebration, Nocturnum certainly did bring with it a curious feeling of dread.

The Queen of Genera so often wore a mask of polite greeting, her smiles forced and stiff. When she greeted Thom with joy glittering in her violet-blue eyes and a grin spread across her features, flinging her arms around his neck in an excited embrace, his heart warmed. Was it his presence that had caused Carissa happiness? If so, he was grateful for it. The poor girl needed some light in her life.

"It's so good to see you, Uncle Thom." She insisted upon addressing him as such, despite the fact that Deacon disapproved. If Jacen was alive, it would have been an appropriate greeting—but his nephew was dead. They'd all seen his body burn on the pyre. Carissa should not be treating him with such casual familiarity.

She smelled of lavender and sandalwood. It was a calming scent. The last time Thom had seen Carissa had been some months prior for her twentieth birthday, and he recalled how the same scent had washed over him. He wondered if it was soothing for her as well, or if it was to wash away the sickly-sweet odour of the Obscurate she was forced to take.

"Carissa." Thom linked his arm through hers and allowed her to lead through the corridors into the gardens, the scent of fresh pine wafting on the cool air. It was certainly her favourite location within the palace—apparently, the Queen had always had an affinity for gardening.

"You're quiet," Carissa noted, tilting her head to the side. "You've been to the capital more times in the past year than you have in the last two decades. What is it about Nicodemus that changed?"

It was a regret Thom had. His sister's death had driven him away from court, and he had missed forging relationships with his niece and nephew as a result. With Jacen and Vida both dead, and all Thom was left with was a hollow space in his heart where his family should have been.

"Its king," Thom admitted. "After Annaliese died, I was content in Gethsemane with my mother, Odessa. Cobryn's reign was not always pleasant, but things only became turbulent once Deacon ascended the throne."

The truth was also more complicated. The less he involved Carissa, the better. If Deacon discovered she was plotting against him, Thom shuddered to think what he might do to her. The girl had already been through enough. She knew he and Myron were not in favour of Deacon, and that was all she needed to be aware of.

"I take it he still plies you with Obscurate."

Carissa's smile soured. "He will continue to, unless I fall pregnant. He wouldn't want to risk the drug on his child."

The thought that Carissa was made to take Obscurate at all turned Thom's stomach. For a man who had once been intrigued by her dark magic, all Deacon had proved was that he was afraid of it. Why else would he have suppressed her power entirely?

Thom's eyes raked over the decorations that had been put up in preparation for Nocturnum, similar to the ones out in the streets. There were false nets with hand-crafted spiders strewn over the bushes. Small bats hung from the ceiling, and skulls had been fitted into place over the candles. Thom could remember how excited the Nocturnum festivities had made him as a child. These days, the prospect merely exhausted him.

"Will you be participating in Nocturnum?"

"Of course." Something devious glimmered in Carissa's eyes. "I've heard it's quite the spectacle."

What are you planning, Carissa? The way her eyes lit up and the emphasis on the word 'spectacle' gave Thom cause for concern. The Queen would doubtlessly deny that she was plotting anything, but her coming alive with an almost savage glee said otherwise. Thom could only hope it was something harmless, else he feared for her safety. No one was untouchable in Deacon's court.

FIVE
THE FUGITIVE KING
JACEN MORROW

The attack came from above.

Jacen whirled around, sword drawn and gripped tightly in both hands. His ambusher was far smaller than him, and wiry . She was a maelstrom of dark braids, a knife in each of her hands as she lunged at him. He quickly grabbed her wrist and twisted, making her cry out and drop one of her knives. Jacen swept her feet out from under her. She fell to the ground, and he breathed heavily as he stared down at her.

"Again."

Ayesha Morrow glowered up at her brother with impatient hazel eyes. She would be thirteen in a few short months, and already she was taller than her mother, with a slim frame reminiscent of her sister Vida. As Jacen's lungs burned, a twitch in his stomach made him grimace, pressing a hand to the place where Deacon had stabbed him.

"Does it hurt?" Ayesha's frustration morphed into concern, eyes widening as she inspected him. "We can stop."

"No," Jacen said, but the way he rasped the word made Ayesha roll her eyes.

"We're stopping." The words were a command. It was Jacen's turn to prickle with annoyance now—not at Ayesha, but at the fact that even a full year after Deacon's attempt to murder him, the wound hadn't completely gone away.

It was a miracle Jacen was alive at all, something he had Ayesha's mother Lilith and Harithian spymaster Ishtar Haroun to thank for. A Primordial with the ability to heal, Ishtar had brought Jacen back from the brink of death—but not without cost. The wound might have knitted together with only a silvery scar as proof it had even been there, but the phantom pangs continued to plague Jacen a year later. When he overexerted himself, it felt like being stabbed all over again.

Jacen's first thought after his recovery was to return to Genera and defeat Deacon once and for all—but he'd known it was folly. Lilith had convinced them that everyone was better off believing he was dead. There would come a time to reveal he'd survived the attempt, but it needed to be a card they played to thwart Deacon. So, he had remained in hiding in the Harithian jungle, miles from the capital of Dalal, with only Ayesha for company.

Jacen watched his younger sister as she hauled herself up into the treehouse they shared, legs dangling from the ladder. It had been imperative to hide Ayesha as well—she was another key player in the fight for the Generan throne, and Lilith believed that Deacon would send assassins after the girl.

At first, Ayesha had struggled with her mother's absence. She'd spent hours staring through the trees as if waiting for Lilith to return. As she spent more time with Jacen, that had changed. A year ago, Ayesha hadn't even managed to catch a knife when he'd tossed it to her. Since then, months of training had forged the girl into a formidable fighter. Smaller and faster on her feet than Jacen, she was clever and used her agility to her advantage. She had always been a quiet girl, watchful of those around her. In her sullen silence, Jacen had seen strength.

"Drink some water." That was the only warning Jacen had before a water skin bounced off his head, causing a yelp of surprise. He scowled and picked up the skin, taking a swig while pointedly ignoring Ayesha's snickers.

Sometimes, he was reminded that his youngest sister was still a child. Whilst mature and perceptive, every now and then a small action would make Jacen recall just how young she really was. It had been at Ayesha's insistence that Jacen had trained her in combat, and their conversation about it was imprinted vividly in his mind.

"I know what happened between my parents." Ayesha jutted her chin up, staring at him with those piercing eyes. "I know Father raped Mother. I want to make sure that never happens to her, or me, or anyone I care about."

Jacen hadn't the heart to tell her that being a trained fighter didn't stop such things. Being a warrior did not make you impervious to harm, and he had learned that the hard way. He had been impressed by Ayesha's resolve. Every time he thought she would give up, she proved her resilience. Ayesha had not been a quick learner, but she had been a determined one.

The sound of a horse neighing made Jacen tense. When he looked up, he saw that Ayesha had paused, hand on the hilt of one of her knives. After a moment she relaxed, smiling down at Jacen.

"It's just Mother."

Of the few visitors Jacen and Ayesha received, Lilith was by far the most frequent. Sometimes she was accompanied by Ishtar, who would silently check over Jacen to make sure he had healed. Even he couldn't explain the way Jacen burned with agony at times. All he had said was that healing wounds was never a precise art, and that there was the chance Jacen might continue to experience some discomfort.

A small price to pay, considering that he was alive when all the odds had pointed to him dying.

Death drew Jacen's thoughts to Gretchen. His father's youngest wife had scarcely been older than Jacen, and what had happened to her had been cruel and unjust. Jacen still remembered her blank eyes staring up at him without seeing, remembered the swell of her stomach, a baby that would never be born. What Deacon had done to her was sickening, making Jacen's stomach twist even a year later.

Lilith was alone today, slipping out of her saddle with inimitable grace. Ayesha climbed down from the treehouse, eyes bright and smile wide as she raced over to embrace her mother. She might have grown more independent in the past months, but she was still pleased to see Lilith whenever her mother visited. Likewise, Lilith's expression warmed at the sight of her daughter, and she held Ayesha close.

"It is wonderful to see you both."

It might have been Ishtar's healing magic that saved Jacen, but it was thanks to Lilith he was alive. She had retrieved him from the riverbank, alongside the jackal helm of House Morrow—a relic currently sitting untouched in the treehouse.

Jacen feared that helm; what it might make him become, should he put it on. Ayesha was old enough to understand what it represented, but in that, she was fearless. To her, the helm was something that could be changed, a symbol that could be twisted into meaning whatever they chose.

"It's good to see you too, Lilith." Jacen strode over, sheathing his sword. His stepmother could have left him to die in Nicodemus, but instead she had chosen to bring him back from the brink of death. Jacen owed her a lot, and it was at her insistence that he didn't ask too many questions. He wanted to hear about his wife, his son. He wanted to hear what Deacon had turned Genera into.

Lilith had promised answers would come in time, and so Jacen had tried to content himself with life in the jungle. At least he wasn't alone. He enjoyed Ayesha's company, but he missed his family. Lilith deflected any mention of them. It had been a year now, and all she would say was that both Carissa and Zephyr were alive.

"How is your training, Ayesha?" Lilith inspected her daughter. Over the past few months, Ayesha's slim frame had been forged into lean muscle. With little else to do in the jungle, the girl enjoyed her sparring sessions with Jacen. She also had a habit of climbing up and down the trees, much like the monkeys she tried to entreat out of the dense canopy.

"Good. I'm strong, Mother. I'm ready."

Jacen grimaced at the onset of the ongoing debate between Lilith and Ayesha.

With the fact that he was believed dead, there had been discussion amongst Ishtar and Relda about putting Ayesha on the throne when the time came. Lilith adamantly refused to let her only child sit on Genera's throne.

"No. We've talked about this." Lilith's tone was curt before she turned her attention to Jacen, her next words silencing Ayesha's protests. "I told them you were alive."

"What?" Jacen's stomach coiled with dread. "Who did you tell?"

"Only Samara, Relda, and Cairo." Lilith sighed deeply. "I felt I owed them as much. It's been a year. There was only so long I could hide you."

"This is because you want *me* on the Generan throne." There was no accusation in Jacen's tone. Lilith wouldn't let him walk away from who he was—Cobryn's son and heir. Deacon might have stolen the crown from him, but Lilith would be damned if she would let the title of monarch fall to her daughter.

"The throne was always your destiny." Lilith's eyes flicked up to the treehouse. Ishtar had said the treehouse had been built by Cairo when he had been a teenager, not even known to his mother Samara. It was a few storeys high, winding over several levels of branches, and Jacen often thought Cairo must have a solid carpentry skillset.

"You still won't tell me about Carissa and Zephyr?" Jacen pressed. He asked every time she came, and every time her lips pressed into a thin line. She'd explained that she wanted him focused on recovering his strength, but he had long since recovered. There was more that Lilith wasn't telling him. Jacen believed that both his wife and son were alive, but Lilith held back because she didn't want him rushing into something. Only, what was it she thought he would rush into?

"Soon, I promise."

"How can you promise that?" Jacen demanded, folding his arms over his chest, impatience coursing through him. "It's been a year, and you still won't tell me anything about them. You would be beside yourself if it was Ayesha."

Lilith's jaw clenched. "Things are not well in Basium. I will explain when I know more, but for now, that is all you need to be aware of."

"Not well?" Jacen repeated the words incredulously. Was that due to Sebastian vying for the throne?

Lilith glanced back at her daughter, who had remained in stubborn silence after her mother's rejection. Unimpressed, Ayesha gestured to Jacen, who sensed he was about to be drawn into an argument between mother and daughter.

"He doesn't want the throne, Mother. Why can't you see that?"

It would be a lie to claim she was wrong, so instead Jacen stayed quiet. He would take the Generan throne if there was no other option, but his year in the jungle had given him much time to think. He wanted to stay in Basium with his wife and son. As much as he loved his country, Nicodemus had not been home for some time. He was not the sole Morrow heir, and he saw no reason why Ayesha was unfit to rule the country, aside from her youth.

"Enough." Lilith's eyes flared with irritation, rare in a woman known for her utmost composure. "You are right, Jacen—you have been living in the shadows long enough. Pack your things and ready yourselves. We're going to Dalal."

SIX
THE SHADOW PRINCE
SEBASTIAN DARNELL

Sebastian had never believed that ruling Basium would be easy, but he'd also never thought it was going to be so hard. In the year since Carissa had vanished and he'd been crowned undisputed King of Basium, he'd dealt with his fair share of problems. The most persistent was, of course, Lady Bellona Lenore.

After word circulated of Carissa's presence in Genera, her marriage to King Deacon Morrow, Bellona was adamant that she would never bend the knee to Sebastian. She had insisted that they join forces and save Carissa, but Sebastian was wary about lashing out at Deacon. They had driven him back to his home country.

Bellona had been nothing but a thorn in his side since the moment he had been crowned. That did not mean he wished harm to come to her, so when whispers of an attempted assassination on the woman reached Sebastian's ears, he immediately went to see General Orien Luce.

"I need allies." Sebastian threw open the doors to the General's room. The man had been drinking, judging by the pitcher on the table. Sebastian slammed a fist down beside the pitcher as Orien, big and burly with a full beard, rose from his seat. "Do you know how hard it is to have allies when someone tries to fucking kill a key noblewoman?"

Orien had been in Marinel during the Conquest, almost seven years ago. He had been a captain then, and almost all his men had died trying to prevent the Morrows from breaching the city. He had fled to Isadore, disillusioned and ashamed. It had only been since Sebastian's coronation that he'd arrived in Marinel once again, with a new title granted by the King and a drive to see the Darnells back in power.

"You are being dramatic, Your Majesty." Orien frowned at the irate expression on Sebastian's face. "Our goal was to obtain the boy, your nephew Zephyr. Bellona's intervention was...an unfortunate complication."

"The man had a letter with my seal!" Sebastian exploded, unable to contain his anger. Due to Orien's actions, and potentially Juniper's too, he had been implicated in what had happened in Theron. "Lady Lenore marches for Emlen."

"With an army?"

"I have no idea," Sebastian admitted through clenched teeth, "but if she wanted, she could amass one. She has Cirocco, or did you forget that?"

Sebastian doubted Orien had. Cirocco was involved in a series of border skirmishes in Olin, a major city in southeast Wendell. Olin was the first step to gaining control of Wendell's heavily guarded southern harbours, which they would need to ensure Wendell didn't launch an attack on Bao. Word had it that Deacon had already sent several ships to the island nation.

"I have not forgotten." Orien's voice was cool. "I merely thought..."

"That's just the problem." Sebastian scowled. "You are making decisions without consulting me."

The tension between the two men was palpable, a sour film on Sebastian's tongue. Orien's nostrils flared as he inspected the young King. Deep down, Sebastian wondered what Quintin would have been like if he'd survived to see him crowned. Guilt twisted in Sebastian's gut, and he pushed aside the thoughts of his former mentor...and the terrible crime he'd committed to save his sister and nephew.

"You do need me." Orien's voice was quiet, but certain.

"Why?" Sebastian folded his arms over his chest. "Give me a good reason, Orien. I don't want to push you away, but your decisions..."

"We need strength," Orien snapped. "Strength and decisive action, neither of which you apparently possess."

The words cut beneath Sebastian's skin like a knife. The truth then, out in the open. Orien believed that he was weak. Orien thought that Sebastian was nothing without a firm guiding hand, just as Quintin had. Sebastian would prove him wrong, and hurt dictated the young King's next action.

"This is your final warning, General Luce. You've been an invaluable asset, but I will not have a civil war as Genera did. Next time you or Juniper come up with a plan, you're to discuss it with me first."

Sebastian turned and marched from the room before he could question the harsh choice. If Orien saw him as malleable, he would prove that he didn't need his old mentor to make decisions, and he held the threat over the General's head that he could send him away. Sebastian was no longer a child, lost and confused. He was a man, and his youth didn't make him a fool. The sun was setting over Orien and Juniper's influence, but it was only rising over Sebastian, burning bright.

Sebastian's wife Meliora had a preoccupation with a fat black cat that the servants in Marinel said had once belonged to Carissa. The creature's name was Soot, and she doted upon the cat. Sebastian quietly preferred dogs, especially when Soot kept bringing them dead mice. When he entered the room to change into some plain clothes, Meliora was sitting on the floor rubbing the cat's stomach as Soot purred loudly .

"I did it." Sebastian unclasped his cloak and tossed it onto the bed, the words making Meliora look up and Soot scamper away. "I warned General Luce what would happen if he made a decision without my consent."

It had been something they had discussed for some time. Meliora, level-headed and calmly intelligent, had always viewed Orien and Juniper with apprehension. However, she was prone to let Sebastian make his own mind up about the pair. A relieved smile spread across her features as she eased herself to her feet.

"Because of what happened in Theron?"

A dull ache throbbed at Sebastian's temples. "It's only gone on to cause more issues. Bellona is marching on Emlen."

Meliora bit her lip at the mention of her home city. Sebastian knew that Bellona was not a fool—she wouldn't go and attack. Nonetheless, she was a hot-headed woman, one Orien claimed was ruled by passion more than logic. Why she was headed to Emlen was unclear, but if she had an army at her back, Sebastian would know about it already.

"Zephyr wasn't harmed, was he?" Meliora asked, wringing her hands.

"No." Sebastian shook his head, raking his fingers through his black hair. "That doesn't make it any better. With my seal on the letter, it doesn't look good. Denying knowledge or involvement looks like I'm trying to wash my hands of something because it didn't work in my favour."

Meliora nodded slowly. "So, what do you want to do?"

She was always willing to give advice but left the final decisions up to Sebastian. He could think critically for himself, and unlike her father and his new advisors, Meliora always gave him the time and space to do so.

"For now, we need to wait and see." Sebastian fished some of his old clothes out of a trunk. "There is no point in taking action when it could just be seen as further hostility. It's Bellona's move, and we need to let her make it."

"Where are you going?" Meliora asked, watching as he changed out of his formal attire and into the old clothes.

"To the forge." It had become a habit. In her time in Marinel, Carissa's stress relief had apparently been tending to the gardens. Sebastian found peace in the heat of the blacksmith's forge, wiry limbs working metal into swords. The blacksmiths he visited were always happy to see the King, and it felt good to have the familiar tools in his hands once again.

"Are you sure you don't need to rest?" Meliora asked gently. She walked over and wrapped her arms around Sebastian. He was fortunate enough to have married for love—something his sister had never done.

Sebastian's stomach turned at the thought of Carissa. Married to a monster like Deacon Morrow—he supposed she hadn't really had much of a choice. She had truly loved Jacen, and he was dead. Meliora said that Carissa's fate was worse than death. With all that power, how was she still a prisoner in Nicodemus? Rescuing her was folly, particularly when Deacon still had three countries at his command.

There hadn't been any word of progress in the skirmishes between Wendell and Cirocco. If Cirocco managed to take back the southern harbours, they might turn the tide in their favour. Moving against Deacon, even to rescue his older sister, was a move that Sebastian simply could not afford to make—not alone, his realm still fractured as the divide between him and Bellona grew every day.

"We need Bellona." Sebastian's voice was hoarse as realisation dawned upon him. "We need her, and Orien has turned her against us."

"She was against us before that, my love," Meliora reminded him softly. "But there is still hope. She is not an unreasonable woman. It's not too late to make peace with her."

Sebastian prayed to the goddess Elethea that his wife was right, because if he could not make amends with the Lady of Theron, Basium could soon fall at the mercy of Deacon once again. The only way to move forward was united, and he hoped that it wasn't beyond reach.

"You keep dreaming about the cave." Meliora swept a strand of black hair from his face, examining him with a worried look.

Sebastian didn't deny it, though he disliked that his nightmares continued to wake her. Over the past few months, his dreams had only become more relentless. The same cave, the same bones, the same implacable voice hissing to him through the darkness. It meant something, but he couldn't have said what.

"That hardly matters."

"It does matter." Meliora's words were firm as she rested her hands on Sebastian's shoulders. "Perhaps you should speak with Juniper. She's your religious advisor, after all. Maybe she can help you interpret what the dream means."

Sebastian suppressed a shudder. Orien was, at least, forthright about his opinions. Juniper was harder to read, an unsettling serenity like an impenetrable shield. Her expressions were neutral, even her dark eyes betraying nothing of her feelings. He could not deny that Meliora was right, though. If anyone could tell him what his dreams meant, it was the Priestess.

"All right." Sebastian pressed a kiss to his wife's forehead. "I'll visit her after I go to the forge."

Sebastian sought out Juniper in the library with ash-marked fingers and a sense of elation swelling within him. Being at the forge always cleared his head, the tension fleeing from his shoulders as he hammered molten metal. The Priestess had her own methods of clearing her head. Juniper liked to read in the early hours of the evening, and he found her rail-thin form at a table with a battered old volume in her hands. She placed the book down and eased herself to her feet.

"Your Majesty. I didn't expect…"

"I came to seek your guidance." Sebastian gestured for Juniper to sit, and he pulled up a chair across from her. She remained quiet, face bathed in shadow and flickering candlelight. "I've been having dreams. Or rather, the same dream over and over again."

"You think it might be an omen?" Juniper asked, her words curiously framed somewhere between question and statement.

Legend had it that the goddess Elethea fell in love with a mortal and had two sons with him: Deimon and Phobian. Whispers in the chapel and scrawled ink on yellowed pages suggested that the twins had both fallen in love with the same woman, a seamstress that Elethea gifted the power to weave fabric from the stars—the first Imperium.

The twins fought over the seamstress with such terrible ferocity that the woman fled the city after Deimon and Phobian battled for her affection, a duel that ended with both of them perishing. Elethea's tears of grief created Lake Carpus, and nine months later, the seamstress gave birth to a baby boy. The first King of Basium, whose female descendants always held great power.

No one knew which of the twins had fathered the boy, and it was a secret that the seamstress kept until her dying day.

Before the Conquest, the Darnell family were considered goddess-blessed. Perhaps they had always been goddess-cursed, since the seamstress had delivered a child of gods' blood.

Sebastian shook his head. "I...I don't know what it is. But it's always the same. I'm in a dark cave. There are bones and skulls beneath my feet. A cloaked figure enters, but I can't see their face. A voice tells me I'm there to find salvation."

"I see." Juniper's words were soft, barely audible above the wind howling outside, rattling the windowpanes. "How long have you been having this dream?"

Sebastian hesitated, staring down at his soot-smeared fingers, the scent of metal and smoke from the forge still lingering in his nostrils.

"About a year."

"A *year*?" Juniper repeated, leaning forward so that her whole face was illuminated by the candlelight. "Then I certainly think this might be an omen. Recurring dreams like that have meaning, especially over such a long period of time."

"But how do I know what it means?" Sebastian asked, frustration rising in his tone despite his best attempts to quell it.

"A cave." Juniper was silent for a long moment, her expression as impassive as ever. "Do you recall the legend of Jameson Burnett?"

Sebastian's heart thudded against his ribcage, and he nodded, swallowing hard.

"Then you recall that he met his demise in a cave." Juniper shifted back, darkness consuming her features once more. "His cave, a place where his victims were buried. It was in this cave that your grandfather Patrick defeated him."

Unease rippled up Sebastian's spine. "You think it's that cave?"

"I can't say for certain." Juniper shrugged her shoulders. "I am not the one having the dreams, after all. There is only one person who could confirm it, and he has not been in the public eye since long before you were born."

"General Tycho Salus." Sebastian knew the name from his history lessons. No one had seen Tycho in decades, since Sebastian's father Frederick had been born. He had wanted to live a quiet, private life. The man had been one of the few survivors of Jameson Burnett's demise, and Sebastian wondered if it had worn heavy on his soul. Whatever had happened that day, none had spoken of it.

Defeat weighed heavy on his shoulders as he realised the chances of him learning the truth of his dreams were slim if it depended on finding Tycho.

"A word of caution, Your Majesty." Juniper rose gracefully, picking up her book and tucking it under her arm. "I would take care who you disclose these dreams to. Omens are not always from the goddess, and this sounds very close to a vision, either of the future or the past."

"I don't have magic in my blood," Sebastian protested hotly. Magic tended to pass down to women in his family, skipping a generation between Miriam and Carissa. He liked to think if there was magic in him, he would know about it. Yet the cold itch of truth scratched at him as Juniper's words sank in.

Could he have magic flowing through his veins? Miriam had visions of the future. Could Sebastian have inherited that power, or was it something different entirely? Lurching to his feet, knees trembling, Sebastian swiftly departed the library with a far more troubled heart than he'd arrived with.

SEVEN
THE NIGHT QUEEN
CARISSA DARNELL

Nocturnum descended over Genera like a shadow under the light of a full moon. The streets of Nicodemus were filled with music and laughter as Carissa descended the steps to join the fray. The festival was yet to officially commence, as the partygoers moved into the city square for the sacrifice. From what Carissa had gathered, the celebrations began after the ritual sacrifice of an animal—typically a boar or wild dog.

She watched with a sting of envy as the citizens laughed and twirled through the streets, the pulse of the drumbeat reverberating through the ground. Carved pumpkins leered down from their perches, candles within, most bearing sinister expressions. Skulls gleamed in the warm glow of the dozens of blazing torchlights. A small smile tugged at the corners of Carissa's lips, and she wondered if she might just enjoy herself tonight.

"Your Majesty." It was a rich female voice, and Carissa swivelled on her heel to see Ariadne Pavlos sauntered down the palace steps with fluid grace. Her mahogany ringlets cascaded down her back, threaded through with plum and burgundy ribbons, her dress a stark ivory in contrast. She tilted her chin up and smiled dazzlingly.

"You look beautiful." Carissa's dress was black as night, as dark as her hair, with modest gold detailing across the bodice. The only ornament she wore was a heavy gold necklace looped around her neck.

"I know." Ariadne's characteristic smugness was a welcome warmth as she linked her arm through Carissa's. "Are you ready?"

"I'm not sure," Carissa admitted, gnawing at her lip as a tightness in the pit of her stomach wormed its way through the heady scent of sandalwood and campfire smoke. "I've never celebrated Nocturnum before. I don't know what to expect."

"Then allow me to show you." As the drums beat deep throughout the city, Ariadne led Carissa into the crowded streets. There were a few whispers among the revellers as she did so, but Carissa ignored them, tilting her chin and holding herself tall and imperious, the way she imagined her grandmother Miriam had in the streets of Basium when their people first called them 'goddess-cursed'.

Ariadne weaved through the congregation with practised ease, offering out benevolent smiles like they were candy. Many of them watched her pass, spellbound eyes catching on her hair and her dress. Carissa could not say she blamed them. Ariadne was beautiful like a knife, sharp and cutting, glimmering at times in the right light. Reaching out of the velvet-draped tables edging the street, she picked up two glasses and thrust one into Carissa's unexpecting hands.

"What is this?" Carissa asked, a pleasant heat blossoming beneath her fingers as she stared down the deep red liquid. Her stomach coiled at the resemblance to fresh blood, but rich cloves and sharp citrus wafted up rather than the harsh metallic scent of blood.

"Mulled wine." Ariadne arched an eyebrow as she took a deep gulp of her own drink. "It's just warm spiced wine. Give it a try."

Tentatively, Carissa raised the glass to her lips and let the mulled wine wash over her tongue. The richness of the spices caressed her mouth and slithered down her throat. It seemed stronger than regular wine too, though Carissa would take no more than a few sips. She needed to have her wits about her, even tonight. Especially tonight.

"This is…very nice," Carissa admitted, taking another sip for good measure.

"Shall we dance?" Ariadne asked.

Setting her half-finished wine on the table, Carissa offered Ariadne her hand.

The older woman took it with a grin that hinted at delight and decadence. Stepping forward, Ariadne pushed off her foot into an effortless spin, hair whirling about her like a fan. Carissa was not too familiar with Generan dances, far more technical than anything she'd danced in Basium. Nonetheless, she caught their twined fingers and raised them above her head as she twirled past Ariadne. Her wedding ring sparkled in the firelight.

How she wished she could cast it into one of the bonfires lining the roads.

Carissa's gaze flicked to the large dais at the far end of the street, a marvel of marble that they'd spent the better part of the afternoon assembling. That would be where the sacrifice would take place, in full view of the revellers.

What an odd sight they must make. The King's wife and his mistress, with joined hands and shared smiles. Or perhaps it was normal—Cobryn had several wives. The citrus aftertaste of the wine coated her tongue, a bitterness that coincided with that of Deacon's refusal to take Ariadne as another wife. Releasing Ariadne's hands, she traipsed toward the dais on unsteady feet.

Deacon already stood on the marble, along with Myron and several other nobles and Godspeakers. The King's eyes were rimmed with kohl, and he was dressed all in silver, shimmering beneath the light of a hundred candles. He noticed Carissa at the front of the crowd and a malevolent smile curved the corners of his lips.

She gripped Ariadne's arm as the older woman slipped forward to stand by her side. A sultry smile crossed the noblewoman's lips as she tilted her head to the side and inspected Deacon, who offered her an answering smile. Carissa's shoulders loosened at the knowledge that her husband would have another bed to share tonight, and all it had taken was a smouldering look from Ariadne.

"Bring forth the sacrifice!" Deacon called, spreading his arms wide for a dramatic flair.

As the servants scurried forth, Carissa's breath caught in her throat. It could be no coincidence. In front of thousands of Generans, she struggled not to panic as she watched the servants bring the animal to the stone table in the middle of the dais.

A black swan. The animal on the sigil of her brother, Sebastian Darnell.

Deacon stepped forward with a curved knife in his hands, closing his eyes and muttering something under his breath, before swiping the blade across the swan's throat. The audience erupted into cheers as Deacon, the nobles and the Godspeakers moved forward to collect the animal's blood. It was tradition to drink the blood of the animal to acknowledge its sacrifice.

Blood. The Obscurate still ran deep through Carissa's system, but if she got enough blood into her...

Gathering her skirts, Carissa made her ways up the steps, fighting back the trembling in her limbs as she examined the dead swan. Deacon wanted to get under her skin, and he'd done so. It was a warning—of what he could do to her brother, of what could happen should she attempt to rise against him. Carissa struggled to breathe, as if she wasn't getting enough air into her lungs.

"You did that on purpose," she choked out, seeing his kohl-rimmed eyes fixated upon her.

"Whatever do you mean?" Deacon cocked his head to the side, but his hazel eyes gleamed with malice. "It's a ritual sacrifice, Carissa."

"You know what I mean." Carissa began to doubt her sanity. Was she reading too deeply into it, or was she right in believing Deacon was messing with her head? "It's usually a wild boar, or a dog, or a horse. Thom told me so. It's never a swan."

"It's an animal, Carissa." Deacon arched an eyebrow, sighing dramatically.

Ariadne called for him with a broad grin, having followed the Queen up the steps, and he turned away, immediately engaged in a far different conversation. Carissa fumed silently, gripping her skirts in clammy hands. He was toying with her. He had to be.

"You look stunning tonight, Your Majesty." Myron was dressed in the traditional formal blue robes of the Godsvoice, and Carissa noticed with rising hope that he had two drinking horns, one in each hand. With Deacon occupied, Myron silently handed over one of the drinking horns. Her anxiety over Deacon's antics forgotten, Carissa braced herself for the metallic tang of blood, far different from the sweet spice of the mulled wine.

Deacon swivelled to face her, eyes widening in alarm as he took in what Carissa was holding. Daring emboldening her, she raised her drinking horn as if in toast before taking a deep sip. Beside the King, Ariadne's mouth parted in shock, and she gripped Deacon's arm. She too realised precisely what Carissa was doing.

The metallic tang of blood on her tongue made her grimace, but she pushed through the unpleasantness. Ritual sacrifice hadn't been practised in Basium for many years, and Carissa herself considered it an outdated tradition. In that instance, it worked in her favour. For the first time in a year, she had blood directly in her system, and a warm tingle raced through her as her magic battled the Obscurate for control.

A pleasant giddiness came over Carissa as she handed Myron back the empty drinking horn, descending the steps to join in the beautiful chaos unravelling. The beat of the drums resonated through the streets, the Generan people laughing and dancing and dodging through the crowd. Carissa was a creature of darkness, and tonight she embraced it, the flickering of the lanterns casting shadows across her smile.

Would the blood be enough to push past the Obscurate? Her monthly bleedings weren't, but her magic had always been strongest when she absorbed blood directly into her system. It beckoned to her, more vividly than it had in months. It was there beneath the surface, an itch she couldn't quite scratch.

It was said that the gods walked the earth during Nocturnum, and even though Carissa did not believe in the Trinity, she could feel the energy thrumming through the crowd. Tilting her head back to look up at the full moon, Carissa closed her eyes and allowed all the sensations to wash over her. The heady scent of frankincense on the soft night breeze. The music pulsating, the beat of the drums echoing her own heartbeat. The delightful tingle of her magic, fighting to be freed from its cage.

"Carissa." Someone caught her arm and she started, eyes flying open. It was Thom, a puzzled expression on his face as he examined her. "Are you all right?"

"Why wouldn't I be?" Carissa tugged her arm from his grasp, instead catching his arm and twirling. She didn't know the steps of the dance that many of the Generans were performing currently, but she had watched long enough to improvise. When she spun back to face him, his eyes were serious and his mouth twisted in a grim line.

"Deacon's pissed, Carissa. What did you do?"

Carissa laughed, the first mirth she'd truly felt in months. "I drank some of the swan blood. If our wickedly clever King didn't want me partaking, perhaps he shouldn't have sacrificed a *black swan*."

Thom stepped back to the beat of the music, ducking under her outstretched arm and then turning to face her. His movements were stiff and awkward. He was not much of a dancer—he often preferred the company of books to people, making her wonder why he indulged in Nocturnum at all.

"I know you're upset…"

"He baited me. Of course I'm upset."

"Don't take unnecessary risks." Thom released her hand, gripping her by the shoulders, his eyes urgent. "I promise you'll be free of him one day, but…"

"You've said that for a year now." Carissa's eyes narrowed, a sharp edge cutting into her words. "I don't need you to liberate me, Lord Dyre. I can free myself."

Thom's brow furrowed, and she realised she must sound ungrateful. It was a mercy in itself that anyone in Deacon's court wanted to help her, and she was throwing that help back in Thom's face.

"Lord Dyre, Carissa." Deacon's voice was cool, but his eyes burned with fury, a smile forcing its way upon his lips. Alarm coursed through her as she looked for Ariadne, finding her speaking in murmurs with Myron. "My apologies for the intrusion. I'm pleased to see you both enjoying Nocturnum, but I must borrow my wife."

Before giving either of them a chance to speak, he grabbed Carissa by the arm and steered her out of the throng of people, the warmth of the bonfires and the flickering of the lanterns swallowed whole by a cool darkness that prickled at her skin. With a snarl, he slammed her against a pillar, sending a wave of pain up her spine.

"What the fuck are you playing at?"

"Whatever are you talking about?" Carissa's mask remained firmly in place even as Deacon's slipped. She tilted her head to the side, examining him with a smug smile plastered across her lips. "I would have thought you preferred I participate in Nocturnum rather than sulking in my room all night."

"I'm talking about the swan blood."

"Let's talk about the swan itself." Carissa jutted her chin upwards. For a tense moment, silence fell between them. *Stalemate.*

Seeing Deacon's anger at her consuming the blood made her realise the truth: he really was afraid of her. He was afraid of what she might do if she had her magic back. There was only one reason he would allow her off the Obscurate, and Carissa remembered Myron's sympathetic words: *A word of advice, my dear. Give him what he wants.*

Carissa knew what she needed to do, the first step in her path to freedom. She had been pushing things in that direction for weeks, patience pushed to its absolute limit as she concocted a lie, a situation so horrific to her that Deacon must believe it true. Tears welled in her eyes and spilled down her cheeks, lips twisting into a bitter smile. Deacon's eyes raked over her, confusion pinching his brow at her sudden melancholy turn.

"I'm with child."

Astonishment came over Deacon's face first, his lips parting in shock. A surprised laugh clawed its way out of his mouth, his teeth gleaming in a flash of candlelight as a broad grin spread across his features. The nausea that Carissa felt was all too real, bile rising in her throat at the glee in Deacon's eyes. She turned away and vomited into a bush, eyes burning with tears.

"This is excellent news." Deacon watched her with growing confidence as she wiped her mouth on the back of her hand. She didn't want it, wished there was another way to gain her magic back, but she needed to play the game even dirtier than Deacon. The only way that Deacon would surrender power was if he thought he was getting something in return. Victory was Deacon's weakness.

When Myron glanced at her, hands clasped tightly and eyes full of concern, she hoped he could see the victory in her tight smile.

EIGHT
THE ASSERTIVE LADY
BELLONA LENORE

The turrets of Emlen rose out of the morning mist, looming over Bellona's entourage. She inhaled sharply through her nostrils, the scent of fresh rain and dawn's dew heavy on the air. A flock of birds soared overhead, disappearing into the trees. With the peace and quiet, it was easy to believe they were there on pleasant business.

Bellona had not come with an army, because it wasn't war she wanted. It was answers. She had not risked leaving Zephyr behind in Theron, so the child had accompanied them on the road. Cristofer, however, had remained behind—in that instance, Eirian's company would be more beneficial. Her lover was, after all, originally from Emlen.

Like Theron, Emlen was a city devastated by battle. They had recovered better since they had not been flooded by a lake during Deacon's attack. The drawbridge creaked and groaned as it ground to a halt, allowing Bellona and her company passage into the city. She had always found it cold and unwelcoming, but perhaps that was retrospective, knowing the city was Sebastian's stronghold.

As they entered the familiar courtyard—the statue of Farran never having been repaired following Carissa's destruction of it when she had saved Jacen's life, its remnants cracked and chipped—Bellona dismounted her horse and crossed over to take Zephyr from one of the men. Ever since the Merciless Ones had betrayed them and abducted Carissa, Bellona had kept her circle close and tight-knit. No one was there who had not earned her trust.

"Lady Lenore." Lord Cyprian Ambrose approached, his smile benevolent but tight. Crow's feet stretched out from the corners of his lips, lines across his brow. His age was beginning to show. The nobleman was not alone—his son and heir, Jarl, stood in stony silence beside him.

"Lord Ambrose." Bellona rested Zephyr on her hip. Having the toddler in Lord Ambrose's presence was a deliberate move. The games of court had always been Carissa's arena. Bellona was more adept at trading barbed words, honest truths, and clashing blades.

"I see you have brought the King's nephew."

Bellona pursed her lips. "You say that as if one of his parents isn't still alive. Zephyr is, first and foremost, Jacen and Carissa's son."

"Forgive me." Lord Ambrose wrung his hands, while Jarl folded his arms over his chest as Eirian appeared at Bellona's side. "I know why you have come, Bellona, and I assure you that I had nothing to do with the attempt on your life."

"I don't think you did." Bellona didn't bother with false pleasantries since Lord Ambrose had pushed them aside with such ease. "I'd prefer to discuss this inside, if you don't mind. It's been a long journey, and my ward could use his rest."

"Of course." Lord Ambrose gestured for them to accompany him inside. Jarl hadn't said a word yet, but his silence spoke volumes. He was a hot-headed young man with a sharp tongue, not too unlike herself. What had Sebastian been saying about her, she wondered. Rumour of her stubbornness and unwillingness to pledge fealty had spread fast across Basium—ironic, considering Sebastian's supporters had been doing the exact same thing when Carissa had been in power.

Once Zephyr was safely in Eirian's care, Bellona accompanied Lord Ambrose and his son to the conference room. She wondered where Lady Ambrose was, though she didn't question the woman's absence. Perhaps she was at court in Marinel, with her daughter Meliora. Once the doors had closed behind them, Bellona whirled to face Lord Ambrose.

"Bellona, you must understand." Lord Ambrose held his hands up defensively. "I no longer have dealings with Sebastian's advisors. Quintin Faustus was greatly beneficial in Sebastian Darnell's rise to power, but he is dead now. These new advisors, General Luce and Priestess Juniper, expressed...problematic ideas."

She smiled humourlessly. "Such as trying to kill me?"

"I knew nothing about that." Lord Ambrose pulled out a chair, gesturing for her to take a seat. When he realised that she wasn't budging, he sat instead. "I have not spoken with them in months."

"Why?" Bellona demanded.

Jarl sneered. "That's hardly any of your business."

"Show respect, boy," Lord Ambrose barked, scowling at his son. "This is the Lady of Theron, and you will behave with the courtesy you were raised to show."

Where had that courtesy been for Jacen? Bellona tried not to think of dear, dead Jacen. She regretted the callousness with which she had treated him when he had been alive. Despite his complicated past and conflicted nature, Jacen had only wanted to be reunited with Carissa. It was too late for Bellona to recant her judgement.

Jacen should have been with his wife and son. Instead, he had died alone, murdered by his own uncle. It made Bellona want to scream at men like Lord Ambrose, shake them hard. These men had been the ones who had condemned Jacen to whatever fate lay in exile. If they had allowed him to stay in Basium, he would still be alive.

"General Luce and I had...a disagreement." Lord Ambrose stared into the crackling fire of the hearth. "The King wished to assist his sister in escaping her...unsavoury fate."

"You mean the part where she was abducted and forced to marry the monster who murdered her first husband." Bellona's tone was scathing. "It doesn't need to sound pretty, Lord Ambrose. That's what happened to Carissa. The *Queen*."

Lord Ambrose flinched, and even Jarl had the grace to avert his eyes. Bellona was done tiptoeing delicately around the subject of Carissa's fate, as though it only merited whispers behind closed doors. Everyone knew what had happened to Carissa.

"Yes, that fate. General Luce argued that Genera was Deacon's territory, this would be seen as declaring war, and it was beyond our jurisdiction. It was not a short debate, but it resulted in my departure from Marinel."

"What did he say?" Bellona asked, her contempt for the man growing every moment.

"That it was out of our hands." Lord Ambrose sighed heavily. "Unfortunately, he managed to convince the King of this as well."

"You're all cowards," Bellona snapped, unable to bottle up the anger that flared through her, letting her simmering surface crack. "I would march into Genera for Carissa. I would go to war for her. She is my Queen, and she has earned my loyalty and my respect."

"You make it sound so easy." Lord Ambrose pinched the bridge of his nose. "My dear girl, don't you think all of us wish we could do that? Deacon Morrow still holds Harith and Wendell."

"He'll lose both," Bellona responded. The battles in Wendell's southeast had been going for months, and there had been nothing more than rumours of unrest in Harith.

"He hasn't yet." Lord Ambrose shook his head slowly. "You want Basium, a country that has only just driven the Morrow Empire out, to face the might of three countries?"

She prickled with indignation at how much sense he made. "We have Cirocco. Maybe Bao."

"Bao will remain solitary. They have for many years."

"You don't know that."

"You are making a plan for war based on assumptions." Lord Ambrose stared up at her with desperate eyes. "Don't you realise how dangerous that is,

Lady Lenore?"

Her chin jutted upward. "You don't want war with Deacon Morrow."

Lord Ambrose looked weary as he gazed back into the flames. She realised how hot-headed and impulsive she must seem to him. The man had seen Basium fall and rise again. He wanted to avoid the same thing happening. Bellona understood that, but the cost could not, and would not, be Carissa.

Bellona looked to Jarl, who had been uncharacteristically quiet throughout the exchange. There was a troubled expression on his face, brow furrowed as his eyes flicked between Bellona and his father. She made a mental note to speak to him later, as she felt he knew more than he was letting on. Was it to do with General Luce and Priestess Juniper? Was it regarding Sebastian?

"Your father was a good man. A strategic man, and a skilled battle commander. But even your father knew his limits, and he knew not to wage war against those more powerful than him. You are so much like him, but you are young. Learn your limits, Lady Lenore. Some battles aren't worth fighting."

"Thank you for your words of wisdom, Lord Ambrose." Sarcasm laced Bellona's tone as she recognised the conversation was over. Without a goodbye, she flounced from the room—only to spin on her heel when someone gripped her arm. Jarl's eyes were wide as he released her.

"I need to talk to you. Later, alone." At her exasperated expression, he lowered his voice and continued. "It's about Sebastian."

The wind whistled low through the castle as Bellona moved in swift silence through the corridors to meet Jarl out by the decimated statue of Farran. The young man stood with his head craned back, face tilted up to examine the moon and stars, obscured by dark clouds. He turned to face Bellona with his hands in his pockets.

"I didn't know if you would come."

"Why wouldn't I?" Bellona arched an eyebrow. "You told me that you had information, so here I am."

"I remember when the statue fell." Jarl's lips twisted in the ghost of a smile. "Sebastian had tried to kill Jacen, and Carissa used her magic to protect him. I can't believe we didn't see she was a Maleficium then."

Bellona heaved an impatient sigh. "Spit it out, Jarl."

"I remained in Marinel, after Father left to come back here." Jarl's voice was soft. Bellona had expected passion and fire, but perhaps he had learned to curb his temper in the past year. "I saw more than he did. General Luce is a bad influence on Sebastian, and Priestess Juniper is worse. Her ideas are more than troubling. Their combined hunger for power would see Basium fall into civil war."

Bellona barked out a laugh. "I take it you mean they're the ones who tried to have Zephyr kidnapped and me killed."

Jarl shrugged. "I couldn't say for sure, but it wouldn't surprise me."

"So, what are you saying?"

"Any resistance to Sebastian's reign is a threat." Jarl's eyes were wide with urgency. "First it was Carissa, and now she's gone. Haven't you realised how hard General Luce has fought to prevent Sebastian going after her? It's not to ensure we don't lapse into another war. It's to ensure Sebastian has no competition for the throne."

Bellona shook her head. "That isn't true, though. Zephyr…"

She paused as she considered what she had been about to say, realisation dawning upon her as Jarl's lips tightened into a grim line. She had suspected that General Luce believed even little Zephyr to be a threat, but she had been aware it could be her paranoia and quickness to condemn him and the priestess. Hearing the idea out in the open, floated by someone else, made her absolutely certain.

"You as well. They would stop at nothing to rid Basium of any opposition to Sebastian's reign. It's not something my dear brother-in-law wants, but… between them, they have more influence than Sebastian would care to admit."

They were dealing with two dangerous people. They might not have magic, but it was a different sort of power entirely. General Luce was respected by the military. Priestess Juniper was held in high regard by the church. Bellona had been wary of Carissa's younger brother, the boy who had consistently pranked them when they had been children. Now, she was afraid for him.

NINE
THE HONEST PRINCESS
LILITH MARWAN

Every step that drew Lilith and Jacen to the castle's meeting room intensified the queasiness rolling in the pit of her stomach. In that room, Jacen would be confronted with the truth—and she worried how he was going to handle it. Jacen and Carissa had loved each other deeply, and once he heard about everything that had transpired in Genera since their escape...

Jacen initially wanted to disguise himself upon entering the capital, but Lilith advised against it. It was time that whispers started to spread. Word would soon reach Deacon that his nephew had survived and was in Dalal—which was precisely what Lilith wanted. Deacon thought himself victorious, but his reckoning was coming.

The meeting room was well-occupied. Cairo stood by the fire, dark eyes reflecting the flames. Ishtar and Relda lounged at the table. Samara had given her apologies—she had other business to attend to. Lilith wouldn't blame her aunt if she was apprehensive about the idea of Cobryn's eldest son returning to Dalal. But Jacen was not his father, something Lilith had known for years.

Jacen's eyes scanned the room, taking in the grim expressions of everyone present. The simmering anger in Relda's expression. The hurt in Cairo's. Rather than asking questions, he took a seat and looked expectantly at Lilith. He looked older than a man of twenty-three, grimness etched around his eyes and mouth. She took a deep breath, steadying her trembling hands, knowing she would have to be the one to finally give him answers.

"You wanted the truth. So here it is."

"All cards on the table?" he asked.

Lilith nodded, her hands twisted in the hem of her silk shirt. "Carissa is in Nicodemus. After we fled, everyone thought that you were dead. Deacon ascended to the throne and paid some Ciroccan mercenaries to abduct Carissa."

Horror gleamed in Jacen's eyes at her soft-spoken words, mouth opening in shock as he listened to what had become of the woman he loved. Lilith didn't blame him. Carissa's fate was like a personal blow. Had she not been a similar age when she had been brought to Nicodemus against her will? Did she not know the horror of a man's shadow looming over her in the darkest hours of the night?

"No," Jacen croaked. Relda turned her face toward the fire burning in the hearth, and Ishtar's jaw tightened.

"He married her. She is Queen of Genera now."

There was no way to soften the blow. It was not only Carissa's worst nightmare come true, but Jacen's as well.

"So, you left her there," Jacen snapped, glowering around at all of them. Relda's face betrayed her shame, unable to meet her nephew's eyes, while Cairo and Ishtar's expressions were more guarded. "You left her to *him*."

"We had no choice," Relda insisted, her attention turning back to her nephew. "Jacen, we don't have the power to move against Deacon, not yet."

Jacen slammed his fist down on the top, making Lilith jump. He pushed himself to his feet, eyes burning with anger. Lilith had never seen Cobryn in his features before, but the fury flaring in him was a frightening likeness.

"You don't understand what she's been through—"

"Excuse me?" Lilith's voice pitched dangerously soft. Everyone in the room fell silent, tension covering them like a thick cloak. She was not a woman prone to anger, but Jacen's words had roused an ice-cold rage in her. He immediately realised his mistake, hazel eyes flaring with alarm.

"I didn't mean…"

"I am the *only* person who understands what she's been through." Lilith's voice trembled as she struggled to hold back a decade's worth of pain. "Unless you want to count Gretchen. You remember what happened to Gretchen? How violently she was killed, for no other crime than she bore Cobryn's child?"

"Lilith…" Cairo spoke that time. She ignored him.

"Your father abused me in every way imaginable for ten years. You are frustrated? My every move was made at the risk of violence, every word I spoke was able to rouse Cobryn's ire if said on the wrong day. No one came to rescue me, Jacen."

The words might as well have been a slap for the way they made Jacen flinch. He sat back down in stony silence. Lilith let him think, let him dwell on what he had learned about Carissa. It couldn't have been easy to hear what had happened to her, but that did not justify his outburst.

"My son?" Jacen asked.

"Safe in Theron, with Lady Lenore." Lilith was relieved to give him some good news, at least. "She refuses to hand him over to Sebastian, who has claimed the throne in Carissa's absence."

Jacen did not appear surprised by the news. His nostrils flared, lips pressed into a thin line of displeasure. To Lilith, it looked like he was trying to prevent himself reacting further. Perhaps it had not been a smart move to keep the truth from him, but the last thing Lilith had needed was her half-healed stepson attempting to wage war to get the woman he loved back.

"We're done here." Jacen's chair scraped backward, and he marched from the room without a look at any of them.

Relda sighed heavily, rubbing her temples. "He's angry with us."

"I noticed," Ishtar replied dryly.

"He needs to be left alone." Lilith leaned back in her seat, folding her arms. "He's had some shocking information relayed to him, and he needs time to process it."

73

By the others' expressions, they were not startled that Jacen had reacted the way he had. Relda had known Jacen since he'd been a small boy, though she had not seen him in many years. As Lilith stared at the door that Jacen had slammed shut behind him, she wondered exactly what sort of revenge his furious mind was concocting for Deacon.

Ayesha had made a lot of her time exiled in Harith's jungles—her slim limbs were toned, her form more wiry than thin. Lilith watched her twirl a knife around the table, the ease with which she flipped the blade between her fingers. She was no longer a helpless child. As she approached her thirteenth birthday, Ayesha proved she was a young warrior in the making.

Lilith sat beside her daughter, wondering how best to impart the distressing information. She didn't wish to coddle Ayesha, and the girl knew more than many her age how cruel a place the world could be. That didn't mean she wanted to subject Ayesha to more than she could handle.

"There is something I told Jacen that I should also tell you." Lilith kept her voice soft and gentle.

"About Carissa?" Ayesha's eyes flicked up from the knife. "Cairo already told me."

Damn him. Lilith fought back a wave of annoyance that her cousin had spoken to Ayesha first. Something must have shifted in her expression because Ayesha scowled, jamming her knife blade-first into the table.

"I'm not a child. I don't need you to try and make it sound all nice. I know what's happening to Carissa. It's the same thing that happened to you."

Though startled by her daughter's words, Lilith kept her composure. "What do you think about that?"

Ayesha was silent for a few moments, her gaze on the jewelled handle of the knife. It had been a gift for her twelfth birthday, and already the weapon showed signs of use, the handle worn from being in Ayesha's hands so often.

"I can understand why Jacen is angry and upset. It's a horrible thing to happen. But...doesn't that mean Deacon's marriage to Carissa would be illegitimate? It's based on him thinking Jacen is dead."

"That's right," Lilith confirmed. Whilst Generan tradition dictated that a man could have up to five wives, it was not the same for women—they were only able to have one husband at a time. Since Jacen had survived the attempt on his life, Deacon's marriage to Carissa was invalid.

"Why didn't you tell him sooner?" Ayesha asked, her brow furrowing as she met her mother's eyes for the first time in the conversation.

Lilith ran her fingers through her hair. "I thought Jacen would do something foolish."

"Like what?" Ayesha cocked her head to the side.

Lilith swelled with love for her daughter. Despite the hard conversation they were having, Ayesha was taking everything in her stride. She wasn't angry that she hadn't been told; she was just looking for logical reasons. Lilith was forever reminded at how mature and level-headed she was for her young age.

"Riding to Nicodemus to rescue Carissa, trying to attack Deacon."

Ayesha chewed at her lip. "Yes, that does sound silly. Uncle Deacon is very powerful, and Jacen has no magic."

Lilith ached with pity for Carissa. No one should have to endure that, and she had meant what she'd said to Jacen—she understood the young woman's predicament better than anyone.

"I wanted to help Carissa. More than anything."

Ayesha slipped her hand through Lilith's and squeezed gently. When she looked at her daughter, she saw something fierce and bright burning in her eyes.

"We'll help her. We'll bring him down."

TEN
THE PLOTTING LORD
THOM DYRE

Thom had come to the conclusion that nothing Deacon Morrow did was harmless or without gain. When he learned of a specific magical advancement occurring within the streets of Nicodemus, he knew that there was no chance the King was unaware of its existence.

Carissa, desperate to escape the confines of the castle, had begged Thom to bring her for his investigation. He hadn't the heart to tell her no, especially since Carissa made it her business to know the people of Nicodemus—both nobles and commoners.

"I heard the news," Thom said as they took a turn down another narrow pathway along the back streets of Nicodemus. "Are congratulations in order?"

Deacon was always a man who celebrated his triumphs, and word had circulated the court that Carissa was expecting. Due to the development, she had also been taken off the Obscurate—Deacon would not want anything to harm his unborn child, after all.

Carissa's lips twisted into a bitter smile, but her eyes gleamed with triumph. Thom was a person used to watching from the shadows, reading their social cues. That look didn't speak of a defeated woman carrying a child she didn't want. His arm tightened in hers, and he pulled her to a halt.

"Carissa. What game are you playing?"

"Deacon gets everything he wants." Carissa gave a light shrug of her shoulders. "But there are sacrifices. I knew once he learned of my condition, he would have to take me off the Obscurate. It was a risk he was willing to take."

"Your condition?" Thom arched an eyebrow pointedly.

"I'd never give him what he wants." Carissa spat the words with relish, eyes glittering with euphoria. "I just let him *think* I had."

By the Trinity, this woman is going to get herself killed. Thom sucked in his breath and refrained from berating her. If Carissa had made such a claim, the cogs were working in her mind. She was planning something, and he had the distinct impression she wasn't ready to tell him what.

"You're playing with fire, Carissa."

"No, I'm just playing Deacon at his own game, and this time I intend to win." She tilted her head to the side. "Now, are you showing me these magical advancements or not?"

Though troubled by Carissa's scheming, Thom nonetheless dutifully led the way down the streets to the medical centre where he'd heard the advancements were taking place. Both he and Carissa had dressed in commoner clothing to avoid looking like nobles sticking their noses where they didn't belong.

Thom cast around the centre with a growing sense of fascinated horror. A few feet away, a woman had her teeth clenched as a healer loomed over her leg. Though Thom couldn't see the precise process, he could see enough. Beneath the healer's fingers was both the woman's flesh and bright red rubies. Thom's heart hammered in his chest as he realised the healer was welding the flesh with the gemstone to create what appeared to be an artificial foot.

Genera was known for its abundant jewel mines, but never had he imagined the gems that had been discovered were being used for that. When the woman flexed her ruby foot, Thom's stomach churned as her toes wriggled like actual flesh.

Who was funding the operation? He truly hoped that Deacon wasn't using the royal treasury to fund magical experiments. Another healer in forest green robes approached Carissa and Thom, gaze darting suspiciously between them.

Carissa hoisted an unconvincing smile across her features.

"I came on behalf of my employer. The one who runs all of this." Thom hoped that he was being vague enough that they wouldn't ask for a name, but implied he knew enough that they understood who he was talking about.

"Does His Majesty approve of our progress?"

The healer's words made Carissa press a hand over her mouth and confirmed Thom's fears. So, Deacon *was* behind it. It didn't make sense to Thom. How did it benefit him? Why would he be approving the use of expensive gemstones to create new limbs for those who had lost them?

"I feel brand new." The woman with the ruby foot approached with a wide grin. "Ready to serve."

"To serve?" Carissa repeated with a quizzical look, drawing the woman's attention to her. Recognition widened her eyes, and Thom realised they weren't as inconspicuous as he'd hoped.

"Your Majesty." The woman bowed stiffly. "Your husband has been most generous. I know these are only trials, but I thought it was worth the risk. A position in the army is hard enough to come by, let alone to keep once you become injured."

The army. Of course, how like Deacon to develop a way to make his soldiers harder to kill. Thom was apprehensive about the King's endgame. Nothing good could come of what Deacon was doing here. Likewise, Carissa had gone pale, her eyes wide as they flicked between the woman's face and her ruby foot.

"I know." The woman laughed. "Emerald would have suited me better, no?"

"Thank you for your time." Thom caught Carissa's arm and steered her from the medical centre. Once they were outside, she took a few steadying breaths, her eyes closed. What they'd seen had Carissa spooked. Did she know something he didn't? Or did she merely think, as he did, that Deacon would do something terrible with the advancement?

"We need to talk to Myron and Ariadne." Carissa's eyes were troubled.

Thom nodded in agreement. If anyone would share their concerns and be able to shed some light on what the King might be planning, it was their allies.

The Godspeaker was at prayer when Carissa, Ariadne, and Thom entered the chapel, and they waited in tense silence for several minutes before Myron entered. Ariadne had stifled her horror well once she had learned what the King was up to, but Thom had seen the shock flare in her eyes nonetheless as she sat down. Myron would undoubtedly be no different. His eyes darted between them, a wry smile tugging at the corners of his lips.

"You three look as though you've seen a ghost. I have heard that after Nocturnum, the spirits of the dead…"

"It's nothing to do with the dead," Carissa interrupted. "Quite the opposite."

Thom let the Queen explain what they had seen in the medical centre, Myron's brow furrowing deeply by the end of the tale.

"This is concerning. More so now that Deacon will know you two have been poking around in his business."

"I am hardly the only one interfering in matters." Thom straightened, inspecting Myron critically. "You handed Carissa the drinking horn with swan's blood on Nocturnum, when you knew how that might go."

"Here we go," Ariadne muttered under her breath, rolling her eyes and flopping back dramatically in the seat she'd taken.

"The Queen indulging in celebration is hardly cause for alarm." Myron waved a dismissive hand. Thom begged to differ, especially since they all knew that she had come dangerously close to using her magic again during Nocturnum. What would have happened if she had? What would a woman caged and abused for a year, her magic suppressed, do if she suddenly had control?

"You need to be more careful." Thom folded his arms over his chest. "You are expendable to Deacon. If you're openly working against him…"

"Then what?" Myron arched an eyebrow, undeterred. "He would kill me?

79

It would only serve to make me a martyr, and cause dissent in Genera. Enough people despise the King already. Murdering a member of the Godsvoice would upset what delicate balance there still is."

Of course a Godspeaker would welcome death, an opportunity to be accepted into the halls of the gods. It was a concept that Thom couldn't fathom, the idea that he was comfortable enough with death that he didn't fear Deacon's wrath. Thom knew there were worse things than death, as did Carissa.

"What are you two planning?" Thom's eyes flicked between the silent Godspeaker and the Queen, whose eyes burned with vicious satisfaction. Ariadne remained quiet, watchful. He didn't think she had known Carissa would drink the blood at Nocturnum. Ariadne's role was different, designed to keep the King's eyes on her.

"Liberty," Carissa said simply, before she took a deep breath and continued, "I'm going to be free, Thom."

"Then what? Return to a country that your younger brother rules and hope he's willing to get off the throne?" Thom couldn't help but sound doubtful.

"Would you prefer I stay here?" Carissa bared her teeth, the fractures in her indifferent mask beginning to show. "Under Deacon's control? I want to see my son again, Lord Dyre. Throne or no throne, there are still things for me in Basium."

A small, approving smile curved Ariadne's lips, and Thom was reminded of her own children back home at her estate. She rarely mentioned them, did not complain about their absence, but Ariadne had crafted her role well. The only danger was if she was caught consorting with Thom and Myron, Deacon's suspicion of her would rise.

"Might I make a suggestion?" Ariadne remarked, causing the other three to look to her and her smile to broaden. "Deacon thinks he has power here. He thinks he is in control here. Why don't we prove him wrong?"

Thom hid his bafflement. "You want the King to realise how dire a situation he is in?"

"Not directly." Ariadne drummed her fingers against the arm of her chair. "The King won't publicly announce Carissa's alleged pregnancy yet, it's considered bad luck. But if we were to make another kind of announcement, say about the situation in Wendell, and utilise Carissa…"

"Me?" Carissa's brow furrowed. "How?"

"You and Deacon can both speak to the people." Ariadne tossed her hair over her shoulder. "We can see then if the people's love for you eclipses their fear of him."

Thom nodded slowly, starting to see the merit in the idea. Carissa was no longer hiding in the castle pretending she didn't exist. The people knew who she was, knew her position. Seeing the reaction of a crowd to her compared to the King might give them a good indication of where they stood.

"This might be a clever idea." Myron held up a hand when Ariadne flashed a grin. "But it could also be dangerous. We must go about this carefully. If Deacon suspects he is being deliberately upstaged, he will not take it well."

Ariadne's eyes flared with wickedness. "Leave the King to me."

True to her word, Ariadne did handle Deacon. The following day it was announced that the King would be giving a speech on the situation in Wendell, and that Carissa would be present at the occasion. She stood beside Deacon with her hands clasped demurely, staring down at the crowd that had gathered at the foot of the steps. Thom remembered that Carissa hated public speaking, and her tense posture betrayed that fact.

"By now all of you have heard of matters unfolding in the Wendellian city of Olin." Deacon's voice lacked the distinctive booming volume that Cobryn's had carried, but he was audible nonetheless. "We will have to send reinforcements south to secure the city, as it appears that Cirocco is determined to obtain it for themselves."

The crowd remained in restless silence. Ariadne, resplendent in a dress of sky blue, flicked Thom a knowing look.

"Once I know the numbers needed, I will arrange for the march south to Wendell, and will make sure that Olin is ours. We will make sure the Ciroccans know that."

These words were followed by some scattered applause and a cheer or two, but otherwise the crowd remained relatively quiet. Deacon's gaze flicked to Ariadne, who moved forward to rest a comforting hand on his shoulder. Carissa took the opportunity while he was distracted to step forward, taking a deep breath.

"We want a strong Genera. We know that the army and reserves have faced many battles over the past decade, and we commend you on your strength and resilience. My husband does not ask this for Wendell's sake. He asks for it for the sake of Genera."

Whispers started amongst the crowd as the Queen's words piqued their interest. Many of them would never have heard her give a speech before, and certainly not to Generans. Deacon's expression was one of astonishment. Thom could see wariness in the tense set of his jaw.

"We have known a year of peace. A year since withdrawing from my home country of Basium, and has it not been a glorious and prosperous year?"

Fuck. Thom's hands clenched into fists by his sides. That wasn't the angle that they'd wanted Carissa to take. By the way Ariadne worked quickly to mask her shock, she felt the same way. Yet the people were murmuring in agreement, and that caused a smile to curve Carissa's lips.

"If we secure Olin, we will know a longer peace. We will turn the tide in our favour and welcome a new era in Genera, an era in which we can grow and focus on internal matters rather than expansion. Genera will be strong and you, its people, will reap the benefits."

Cheers rose through the crowd, and Thom realised that even if Carissa had gone off-script, she was saying precisely what the people wanted to hear. They were tired of war, of winning battles simply for the sake of expanding the Morrow Empire, when there were matters in Genera that needed solving and funding. Carissa was promising them the one thing she knew Deacon would not give them, so they would turn on him like a pack of rabid wolves when he went back on his word.

Deacon was livid, though he controlled his expression enough that the only hint of his anger rested in the gleam of his hazel eyes. Carissa's promise was not one he would keep, but the crowd's response proved it was a popular idea.

Even without magic, even in a gilded cage, they loved her. When Carissa looked triumphantly at Deacon, and Thom noted the shock on his face, he realised the King feared that more than anything. Carissa raised her arms and utilised her greatest weapon: a dazzling smile. As the cheers grew to a deafening roar, Thom was certain that Deacon Morrow was on borrowed time.

ELEVEN
THE FAMILIAL KING
JACEN MORROW

Jacen was not particularly in a mood for visitors, but when had he ever gotten what he wanted?

At the sharp rapping on his door, he sighed heavily, leaning over the sink where he'd been splashing his face with water. Pushing himself away from the basin and donning a shirt, he threw open the door to see his Aunt Relda. She raised her eyebrows expectantly, and rather than argue, Jacen groaned and swung the door wider to allow her inside.

"Make yourself at home, Aunt Relda."

She had certainly done so in Dalal. Relda had been Jacen's age when she had been stationed in Harith, tasked with protecting Cobryn's interests. Perhaps that had been what she'd done in the beginning, but after becoming Ishtar's lover and having their son, Elyes, things had clearly changed. Jacen hardly knew his aunt anymore.

Relda sprawled in a chair in the far corner of the room, pinching the bridge of her nose and sighing in response to Jacen's glower.

"By the Trinity, Jacen, lighten up."

"Lighten up?" Jacen repeated, his brow furrowing more deeply. "I don't think what I've heard about Carissa calls for 'lightening up'. You still have influence with Deacon, surely you could have…"

Relda barked a laugh. "Influence with Deacon? That time has long passed. Deacon hasn't communicated with me at all since he took the throne. Perhaps my dear little brother realised that the person who knows him best would have recognised precisely what he'd done."

"You could have done something. The Generan people would have supported you."

Jacen registered the ridiculousness of his words even as they fled his mouth, but he refused to believe that there was *nothing* that could have been done to help Carissa.

"Unlikely," Relda scoffed. "I have been in Harith for a decade. Many of the Generan nobles no longer trust me—which they aren't exactly wrong about."

"What do you mean?" Jacen frowned.

"You have probably heard word about this resistance in Harith."

Jacen folded his arms over his chest. "Yes, and that you've done nothing to discourage it."

"Well, of course not." Relda's smile was wide, eyes gleaming bright. "I am the Fox."

A chill slithered up Jacen's spine. He'd heard about the Fox, second-in-command of the underground resistance. Perhaps not underground anymore—they grew bolder every day. The idea that his aunt was part of it, that she'd been part of it all along...it was shocking, but in some ways, it also made sense.

Jacen was not the only Morrow who was disillusioned with what their family had become. Relda had simply taken action.

"Why?"

"I saw what my brothers did." Relda's face contorted with the shadow of anguish. "When Lilith married Cobryn, I knew that I'd seen enough. I wanted no more part in enabling them. If I'd openly stood against them, they'd have killed me. So, I did the only thing I could, and I wore the mask of the satisfied sister while becoming instrumental in planning their downfall."

Where Jacen had been hesitant, Relda had been proactive. Where Vida had succumbed to the pressures of their family's expectations, Relda had defied them completely. She had done what Cobryn's children could not. Jacen remembered Deacon's story, the tale of their father's murder. Had Relda stood idly by as Deacon drowned the man and realised just how much horror her younger brother was capable of committing?

"You're smarter than Vida and I were."

"Ah. Vida." Relda's mouth turned down in displeasure. "Your sister was many things, but deserving of such a death was not one of them."

Vida had betrayed her friends. Vida had chosen to side with their family...but could he really blame her? She had only seen one future for herself, and that was what she had chosen. Vida had sealed her own fate. If not for her own actions, she might still be alive.

"I know what you wanted to do." Relda leaned back in her chair. "Tell me, how do you think things would have gone, if you had known what happened to Carissa? If you had marched on Nicodemus, in all your foolish bravery, and tried to go to war with Deacon?"

Jacen knew how it would have gone. It would have ended in his death, for real that time. Nothing would have been accomplished. Lilith had been logical in her choice to keep the information from him, though it didn't stop his frustration. What horrors had Carissa endured? How much abuse had Deacon subjected her to, in the year she had been his wife? The thought made his stomach churn.

Carissa's worst fear had been what Deacon would do if he had been the one to marry her. Now she was living in that hell. Neither of them knew yet that the marriage was invalid, but that didn't erase Deacon's actions. Legitimate or not, Deacon had still vested the sort of violence upon Carissa that Jacen had fought to prevent.

"I would be dead," he ground out. His response to Carissa's fate had been emotional, not logical, and he could acknowledge that. After he'd had time to cool off, he realised what folly it would have been to take Deacon on without any form of a plan. If Lilith had told him right away, he'd have rushed into it, half-healed and burning with fury.

Relda's eyes burned with triumph. "Precisely, and then where would we be?"

"I don't want the Generan throne." Jacen shook his head fervently, the thought of it making his shoulders stiffen. "You have other options, but it won't be me."

"Ah." Relda heaved a sigh. "We worried you might say that. You realise that our next option is your twelve-year-old sister?"

"Is that such an awful option?" Jacen raised his eyebrows. "She will have strong women like you and her mother to guide her on the right path. Ayesha might be young, but I've spent the past year in her company. She would make a fine queen."

"Perhaps you should talk to her about it yourself," Relda suggested, pushing herself to her feet. "See what she thinks about you handing over the burden of a crown."

A sudden thought struck Jacen as his aunt crossed over to the door. His father had utilised his children as pawns in his game, but what about his siblings?

"Relda. Why did Cobryn never make you marry someone?"

"He tried." A tight smile crossed Relda's lips, something dark glimmering in her eyes. "I was betrothed to a minor lord from Genera's south when I was eighteen. A man who had a predilection for abusing servants. Apparently, he had a few bastards by a handful of poor maids in the capital. So, on the night of our wedding, I emptied shards of glass into his wine and watched him drink it."

Fuck. Jacen winced at the thought of it, his mind drifting to how Cobryn would have punished her for such insubordination.

"Surely Cobryn knew it was you."

Relda scoffed. "Of course he did. He realised I was sending him a message. Only a few years later, he conquered Harith, and saw merit in placing me here to enforce his will. He may not have respected me, but he quickly saw I wasn't as malleable as he had believed."

The sound of metal grating made Jacen grimace as he pushed open the door to Ayesha's room. Peering in, he saw that his sister was sharpening her knives with determined focus. She looked up at his approach, setting the knives down so their blades glittered ominously in the candlelight.

Even in the capital of Dalal, Ayesha kept her wits about her. He had seen her in the training yard with their cousin, Elyes. More than combat, she knew about which plants were poisonous, how to keep herself alive in the wild. The quiet little princess had become a fierce huntress.

"Keeping them sharp." Jacen nodded approvingly. "That's good."

"You taught me well." A smile crossed Ayesha's lips as she lifted her chin up to stare at her big brother. "You've been upset about Carissa. How are you feeling now?"

"Better," Jacen admitted, sitting on the edge of her bed and patting the spot beside him. "I wanted to talk to you about something. I want you to be honest with me."

Ayesha's brow furrowed as she sank down beside him. "I'm always honest with you."

"How would you feel about becoming Queen of Genera?" It was a big question, and Ayesha mulled over her answer. If she adamantly refused, Jacen would rethink his stance. He didn't want the throne, but he wasn't about to give it to a girl who had no desire for it and was far too young to sit on it in any case. He could see Relda's point and understood Lilith's reluctance. But the person whose opinion mattered the most was Ayesha herself.

"I know Mother hates the idea, but I don't." Her eyes flicked up to meet his, fierce and resolute. When Cobryn had been alive, Ayesha had been a ghost of a girl, drifting silently around Nicodemus and taking care to vanish when things got tense between her parents. Since the Warmonger had died, Jacen saw in

Ayesha everything Cobryn had not—tenacity and resolve.

"So, you'd be all right with it?"

"If you didn't want it, I would accept it." It wasn't outright happiness at the idea of being Queen of Genera, but the hesitant acceptance of a girl who recognised the burden that was being offered to her. She would take it from her older brother if it was what he wanted. Jacen felt a swell of love for his little sister, and he pulled her into a tight embrace. She tensed, but then wrapped her arms around him.

"I love you, Ayesha. I would never make you do something you weren't all right with. If that means wearing a crown I don't want, I would do it for you a thousand times over."

"How about we decide when the fighting is done?" Ayesha suggested, a sly smile spreading across her lips. "We can have a duel and the loser has to take the Generan throne."

Jacen couldn't help but laugh. "Perhaps not a duel, but yes, we can decide at a later date."

He prayed to the Trinity that they both survived what was to come. Neither of them were giddy over the idea of ruling Genera, but if one of them was killed, the other would have little choice in the matter.

TWELVE
THE PARANOID PRINCE
SEBASTIAN DARNELL

Juniper's summons made dread gnaw away inside of Sebastian, though he could not have guessed why she wanted him. He entered the chapel to find her, head bowed before the golden likeness of the goddess Elethea. Had Juniper told someone about his dreams? Could she want to discuss them further? He wiped his sweat-slick palms on his pants and approached her.

"You wished to see me."

Perhaps he should not have interrupted her at prayer, but if it was that urgent, certainly the goddess could wait.

"Your Majesty." Juniper unclasped her fingers and rose. She wore a smile in the same way the people adorned their homes with decoration, pleasant to look at but with no promise of what was inside. "I have been thinking about the matter of Quintin Faustus."

Sebastian frowned. Quintin had been dead for over a year. "What of him?"

"More on the manner of his death." Juniper observed him with an eerie calm. "It seems odd to me that Jacen Morrow would have killed him."

"Why is that?" Frustration seared up Sebastian's spine. No one had ever questioned his story, and since Jacen had died not long after, it wasn't as though anyone could have asked him. It had been the perfect cover story. "Jacen was exiled from Basium for murdering a man loyal to the crown."

"To escape," Juniper pointed out, her head tilting to the side and a crease pinching her brow. "But he was already leaving Basium. Killing Quintin in cold blood hardly makes sense, especially since he barely knew the man."

"Maybe he found out that Quintin was the leader of the Jackals and therefore behind attempts on his life," Sebastian suggested, his heart thundering in his chest.

"Perhaps." Juniper didn't appear convinced, and that lack of conviction made queasiness roil in the pit of Sebastian's stomach. Did she know something? Surely she would not have brought the matter to his attention if she suspected him.

"Are you requesting to launch an investigation?" he asked.

"I'm not entirely certain yet." Juniper's cool gaze raked over the King. "I think it might be prudent, but I wish to gather more information first."

"Of course." Sebastian nodded, hoping he looked more composed than he felt, his street instincts screaming at him to run, battling with his years as a prince dictating he show decorum and discretion. "Thank you for bringing this to my attention, Priestess Juniper."

Swivelling around, he turned and walked out of the chapel, his heart beating in time to his short, sharp footsteps. What did it mean? What had prompted Juniper to think about Quintin's death to begin with? He'd told no one what happened that night, but he would have to be careful.

"Sebastian!" His wife's voice made him spin on his heel. She ran over to him with a gleeful expression on her face, and he pushed aside his trepidation for her sake. Anything that pleased Meliora should certainly please him as well. "I have news to share."

"What is it, my love?" Sebastian caught her by the waist as she flung herself at him, a flurry of joy wrapped in a silk dress.

"I'm with child."

Sebastian was overcome by a whirlwind of emotion. Carissa had become pregnant quickly in her marriage to Jacen, but he hadn't anticipated that the same would be true for Meliora. It was a joyous moment—and yet tainted with dread, for Sebastian feared what it might mean for little Zephyr. How would Orien and Juniper react when they learned that the King was expecting a child of his own?

"That's fantastic news." Sebastian grinned and kissed the top of her head. "How far along?"

"The healers think around three months." Meliora's smile broadened, so brightly that she practically glowed. He couldn't bring himself to think of the negatives, considering how thrilled she was.

It hadn't been something he had processed as a child. The youngest of four siblings, Sebastian had few obligations. Even growing up in Emlen, knowing he would one day become King, his mind had not been on marriage and children. Meliora had changed all of that without meaning to, and he couldn't imagine his world without her.

"There's something I have to tell you too." Sebastian hated having to break her bubble of excitement, but he felt the time for secrets between them was over. Meliora was his wife, and she had proved her love and loyalty time and again. "You must swear to me that you won't tell anyone."

"Of course." Meliora sounded indignant that he might think for a moment she could betray him. "Sebastian, what's wrong?"

"Jacen never killed Quintin Faustus." Sebastian's breath hitched as he inhaled. "I did."

"What?" Meliora's expression morphed into one of horror. "But why?"

"He was planning to kill Carissa and Zephyr." Sebastian kept his voice low so as not to attract attention, his voice cracking over the words as he remembered what he had done that night. "I was upset, and he tried to comfort me that he would do the dirty work but I...I couldn't let that happen."

A solemn silence sat between Sebastian and Meliora for a few moments. She still looked shocked, but realisation dawned across her features at Sebastian's words. She too had known how fervent Quintin was in his beliefs.

"You did the right thing. He was dangerous."

"I *did the right thing*?" Sebastian hissed in disbelief, having been prepared for a chastising or even cold silence. "Meliora, I murdered the man who saved me from the Conquest. He helped me, and I repaid that with treachery and blood."

Meliora's expression grew firm, lips pressing together in the way they did when she was resolute about something.

"Quintin saved you because he saw the potential in doing so. It was never simply a kind act for a frightened child, Sebastian, and we both know that."

Meliora was so often kind and compassionate that he forgot there was steel in her too, and it made him love her even more when she showed it.

"I think Juniper knows," Sebastian said, and suddenly he wasn't a king, but an eighteen-year-old with all his fears and troubles being dragged kicking and screaming into the light. "She doesn't believe that Jacen killed Quintin. She told me as much."

"Sebastian." Meliora took his face in her hands, fingers cool against his cheeks. "Breathe. She doesn't know anything, or she would have said something."

He nodded slowly, taking a deep breath as she'd instructed. A small smile graced her lips, and he realised he'd been so caught up in the idea that his dark secret could be revealed that he hadn't focused on her news. He pressed a kiss to the top of her head and rested a hand on her stomach.

"We'll soon have other things to worry about in any case."

Meliora tilted her head back, her hair catching the sunlight. "If it's a girl…"

"You want to name her Sidonia?"

"No." Her smile was warm enough to melt his heart. "Imogen. After your mother."

A wave of nostalgia, the old pangs of the Conquest mixed with more recent anguish, washed over Sebastian. He gathered Meliora tight in his arms and held her close, inhaling her honey-sweet scent. He was grateful for her, the girl who always brought him back to reality when he lost himself in his nightmares. If only little Sebastian, who had first met a quiet girl who liked to embroider and blushed in his presence, could have known how far they'd come.

Thirteen
The Brutal Queen
Carissa Darnell

The knowledge that the Generan people loved her more than they feared Deacon was intoxicating to Carissa. Thom had not been pleased that she had gone off-script, essentially promising something that Deacon would never deliver, but it had been a deliberate move on Carissa's part. He might control her, but she possessed a power that Obscurate could not take away: the faith of Generan people disillusioned by war.

"You took a bold risk, you know." Ariadne swirled her red wine in its glass as she sat sprawled across a chair in the Queen's chambers. There was a feline grace about her, effortless and fluid.

"Deacon wouldn't touch me." Carissa shook her head fervently. "Not when he thinks it would risk a child that doesn't exist."

"About that." Ariadne leaned forward, eyes gleaming with urgency. "You may have bought yourself time, but that move also expedited the speed with which you must leave the capital."

Alarm pounded against Carissa's temples. "What do you mean?"

Ariadne was quiet a moment, taking a sip of her wine. "Deacon will be enraged. He will only tighten his hold over you. The time to flee Nicodemus must be now, Carissa. Otherwise, I fear for your safety and wellbeing."

"What about the rest of you?" Carissa asked, realising she was loath to give up any of the few friends she had in Genera.

"We'll be fine." Ariadne gave an elegant shrug of her shoulders. "Thom will probably return home. With you gone, my position with Deacon will become more imperative."

Carissa cracked a smile. "Ah, the real reason you want me gone."

"How well you know me." Ariadne acknowledged Carissa's smile with a wicked one of her own. "The King has seen many people here love you now. He has too many suspects to pinpoint anyone."

"He will hunt me." Carissa rubbed her arms as though to ward off a non-existent chill. "I don't know if I can make it back to Basium."

"Then don't go back to Basium." Ariadne made it sound so simple, but there was something lingering beneath the cool facade, making Carissa narrow her eyes.

"Where would I go?"

"Have you considered that Deacon has many enemies here in Genera?" Ariadne arched an eyebrow. "Oh, the capital might be full of sycophants, but think about where else you could go."

Carissa considered her options. Thom and Myron had often spoken of the fact that there were many who opposed Deacon's reign. There were two families that hated the Morrows more than anyone, two families who had been displaced during the Island Wars.

The noble families of Severino and Philemon had been scattered and lost in the years since the civil war. The houses of Delmar and Pyralis had been installed, but members of those old families still existed. It was desperate, to think they might trust her, support her. What was she but a broken Basiumite Queen?

It was a move Deacon wouldn't anticipate. He knew how badly she wanted to return home, and so he would scour the border for any sign of her—little knowing that she was headed west instead of south.

"The Generan Islands," Carissa murmured, and triumph flickered in Ariadne's eyes, making her certain that was what the older woman had meant.

"That's a big risk. I don't know if they wouldn't just hand me straight back."

"Isn't it worth that gamble?" Ariadne asked, finishing her wine and setting her glass down. "You could hide there until Deacon gives up on finding you, and then you could return home."

Hide. It seemed a coward's move, and yet, what choice did Carissa have? She would rather risk death than the idea of being recaptured and dragged back to Nicodemus to face Deacon's wrath. Bile rose in her throat at the thought, and she nodded fervently in agreement with Ariadne.

"You're right."

"The Generan Islands." Ariadne sprang to her feet and poured them each a glass of wine, raising hers in toast.

Carissa clinked her glass against Ariadne's. "The Generan Islands."

The time had come for Carissa to flee Marinel. She could feel her magic burning within her, begging to be used. If everything went according to plan, she would be able to kill Deacon whilst she did so. She hadn't told Thom and Myron, or even Ariadne, about that part of the plan—because they would believe it a great risk. Carissa no longer cared about the risk. She wanted Deacon dead, and she wanted to return to Basium. Unfortunately, both of those goals seemed far beyond reach...until recently.

Dinner with Deacon was always a tense affair. Carissa never knew what the man was going to say or do, how he planned to torment her next. She ate in silence and didn't speak first, choosing not to incite conflict no matter how much she wanted it. The sumptuous vegetables and marinated meat were tasteless on her tongue.

"I spoke to the healers today." Deacon's voice was light, but when Carissa looked up, his eyes were as wild as the sea in a storm. Her stomach twisted with horror as she realised what had happened. Her lie had been exposed. *Goddess, no. I thought I had more time.*

"How interesting. What about?" Carissa's hands shook as she raised her goblet to her mouth, but she did her best to remain calm. Deacon had a habit of getting under her skin, and it could be his way of worming the truth of her condition out of her—at least, she could hope so.

"It's strange. None of them recall diagnosing your condition. In fact, one of them was adamant that you had just started bleeding."

Fuck. Carissa set her goblet down hard. "What are you trying to say, Deacon?"

"You aren't pregnant." Deacon's chair scraped back as he sprang to his feet, and Carissa tensed. She reminded herself that she wasn't helpless. That time, she had her magic on her side —but he would know that. He would be ready for that. She'd wanted the element of surprise, but she no longer had it.

Deacon crossed over and grabbed Carissa by the arm, hauling her to her feet. She was ready for him, slamming her fist into his face with enough force that he staggered back. When he pressed his fingers to his nose, they came away scarlet. The seductive allure of his blood sang to Carissa. She could use her own magic, or she could use his.

Deacon backhanded her across the face, sending Carissa to the ground. She landed hard, grimacing as everything spun. She could taste the metallic tang of blood on her tongue, but she relished it. Her magic roared to life within her. She just needed to pick a target—and she found one. Deacon's sword was in its scabbard, hanging on the back of his chair.

Carissa rolled onto her stomach and reached with outstretched fingers. The sword slid from the scabbard and shot across the room, just as Deacon grabbed her to flip her over onto her back. It all happened so fast that for a moment, Carissa didn't understand what had happened—until she heard the sound of metal cleave through flesh and felt blood spray across her face. Something hit the ground with a wet *thump*.

Deacon screamed. As Carissa eased herself to her feet, she saw that he clutched the stump of his right hand, oozing crimson. She fought back bile as she took in the metallic stench of her victory. Holding up his sword and pointing the blade at him, she saw it clear as day in his eyes: fear. He was afraid of her. In the deepest, darkest part of her, she was viciously thrilled.

"You'll never fucking touch me again," she hissed at him, gaze flicking to the door.

Deacon lunged for her with incandescent rage burning in his eyes. She tried to slash at him with the sword, but she didn't know how to use it. Cutting off his hand had been sheer, dumb luck. The right move at the right moment. Deacon gripped the blade with his free hand. She imagined that there was so much pain coursing through him that the edge nicking his fingers wouldn't have perturbed him.

"You'll beg me for death," he snarled, yanking the sword from her hands.

She couldn't kill Deacon in that moment—even with him at his weakest, even when she had the upper hand. If she stayed and tried, she would wish she hadn't. Too many guards were loyal to him; too many nobles would be desperate for a noose around her neck.

Cursing angrily under her breath, Carissa chose freedom. She whirled on her heel and sprinted through the open door, the fresh air kissing her skin as she fled the palace.

With her bloodied dress, people's initial reaction was to step back and allow her to pass. Considering how badly she had injured Deacon, he would want her hunted down and dragged back just so he could bring her to justice himself. That thought spurred her on, driving her down through the streets of Nicodemus even as she gasped for air; her lungs burned.

The hint of a smile dawned on Carissa's face at the thought of freedom, of a shimmering sea and islands she had never been to. With her plan for her flight in mind, she headed down to the main gate, and the drawbridge that controlled passage into and out of the city.

Shouts rose up from the castle, a bell tolling that Carissa didn't understand the meaning of. It wasn't the deep bell that tolled for death, and though she wished he would, she doubted Deacon would die from losing his hand. Gathering her skirts, she sprinted for the drawbridge—and her stomach twisted when a group of soldiers stepped into her path. They were clad in the black and silver of House Morrow, the jackal embedded on their tunics. These were Deacon's men.

"Your Majesty, we must escort you back to the castle." One of them moved toward her, hand lingering on the hilt of his sword. *Brave man. Foolish man.*

"You will do no such thing." Carissa's words rang hollow, her eyes darting between the men. They moved cautiously around her, as though she was a rabid animal that could strike at any time. There were five of them.

"By order of the King."

How had Deacon gotten word out so fast? Carissa was rarely astonished when it came to Deacon anymore. She held her chin high, feeling the magic blazing through her veins. There was a wildness to it, a feeling Carissa recognised. She was not in control of it. No longer hindered by the Obscurate, it threatened to burst forth like water from a dam. She did not want to hurt these men, yet she feared that was what would happen should she delve into her magic.

"I am the Queen. You will let me pass."

"We can't do that." The man's voice was apologetic.

These men are going to die. A tear slipped down Carissa's cheek. She did not want to harm anyone else, but she'd been given no choice. Taking a deep breath, she straightened up, reaching out to her magic and letting it course through her. Was it Deacon's blood, splattered across her face, that made it roar to the surface? Or was it her own blood, her split lip puffy and sore?

Goddess above, she had missed the tingle of the magic at her fingertips. She had always known that it was powerful and seductive. But she realised it was also uncontrollable. Having been on the Obscurate for a year, her magic suppressed...she had no idea what she was capable of. She reached forward, hands outstretched towards the drawbridge. The soldiers shifted nervously, uncertain.

Carissa took a moment to feel the heaviness of the drawbridge, the metal chains that pulled it up and lowered it down, the weights attached to those chains. She remembered the last words her grandmother Miriam had spoken to her. *Take all that pain, all that rage, and use it to build something better.* Sometimes to bring about the new world, it meant tearing down the old one.

Under the weight of Carissa's magic, the chains snapped, metal flailing about as it disconnected from the post it had been connected to. One of the men shouted a warning as the drawbridge slammed open, a loud *boom* resonating as the edge of the wood hit the stone with force. As the dust flew up in the air, the soldiers closed in on Carissa. She needed no weapon to fight them with. She was a destructive force herself. No one would get in the way of her freedom.

The first man, the one who had spoken to Carissa previously, charged at her. Terrible power rushed through her, and all it took was a moment, her fingers flaring in his direction. His neck snapped, the *crack* making her teeth clench as his body toppled to the ground. The soldiers watched their comrade go down with wide eyes, before another of the men sneered defiantly in Carissa's direction.

"Fuck the King's orders, kill her!"

That was what Deacon had feared, she realised. He knew better than any that she was a weapon all on her own. Carissa only needed blood to make her magic work. She didn't need moisture in the air or the roiling sea.

As the next man rushed at her, sword raised, Carissa concentrated harder. Trying to control her power was like caging a raging storm. She never knew where it would strike next, with what ferocity. It was almost too much for her, and still she persisted. She would rather her wild magic than be powerless. She would never be powerless again.

When she lifted her hand, the bones in his legs snapped like twigs.

He screamed as he collapsed, the shock on the soldiers' faces enough distraction to allow Carissa to sprint across the drawbridge. Her heart thudded against her ribcage. The thought of the violence she'd committed repulsed her, nausea rolling in the pit of her stomach. Yet what choice had she had? What was an act of cruelty against Deacon compared to the many horrors he'd committed against her?

As Carissa fled Nicodemus, her sins weighing down on her shoulders, she promised she would never be helpless again. That, one way or another, she was going home.

FOURTEEN
THE CONCERNED PRINCESS
LILITH MARWAN

The saccharine scent of Obscurate stopped wafting through the halls of the palace, and Lilith was surprised to realise that Cairo was weaning himself off the substance. She didn't ask questions, since in the past he had always been evasive as to why he imbibed it in the first place. She focused on being proud of his efforts coming off the drug, his dark eyes shining with a lucidity she hadn't seen in months.

Cairo had even begun attending meetings with Ishtar and Relda. That day, they were joined by the leader of the resistance himself, Khaled Elam. Meeting with him always made Lilith's stomach flutter with butterflies. The former general and current leader of the resistance in Harith was commonly known by the moniker of the Wolf, a code name passed through rebels to maintain secrecy.

He was joined by Jameela Khalil, a woman with the power of prophecy. She had been the one to predict that Gretchen would never bear Cobryn a child. Had she known that Gretchen would die so horribly? Had she seen and not wanted to say anything?

"So, Jacen Morrow has been alive for a year, and no one knew about it other than yourself, your daughter, Relda, and Ishtar?" Khaled's good eye inspected Lilith critically as she shifted in her seat. "We have trusted you. Do you not trust us?"

"It isn't a matter of trust." Lilith shook her head fervently. "I did what I had to in order to protect my daughter and stepson. All it would have taken was one slip of the tongue, and Deacon would have sent someone to slip a knife through his ribs."

"She's right," Relda said. "She's not the only one who hid the truth, either. I never spoke of it because it wasn't my secret to share. The word's out now. All we have to do is decide our next move."

"I am more concerned that Deacon is aware of the situation." Jameela's eyes flicked to Ishtar. "As concerned as I am about the third city-killer."

"Not this again," Ishtar muttered, though Jameela's words roused curiosity in Lilith.

"City-killer?"

"You must not have heard the prophecy of the three city-killers." Ishtar's tone was one of wry amusement. "Don't worry, I'm sure Jameela will tell you all about it."

"It's not a joke, Ishtar," Jameela reprimanded, before she took a deep breath and continued. "I had a vision of three cities destroyed in the time of the Morrow Empire. Three mages who did the damage. Two men, one woman."

An icy chill ran up Lilith's spine. The sort of sheer power those mages would have to have in order to destroy *cities*. She couldn't even begin to fathom it. Her mind was drawn to the destruction of Elyes, how magical involvement had always been suspected in the city's fall. Was it possible that had been one such instance?

"How many of those cities have fallen?"

"Two." Jameela's sly eyes flicked to Lilith. "Deacon Morrow became the second city-killer when he destroyed Isadore."

"The first city-killer?" Lilith asked, partially afraid to know the answer. "The third?"

The hint of a smile graced Jameela's lips, but her eyes were like steel. The idea that another city was yet to be destroyed made Lilith's stomach turn. How were they supposed to prevent it? What mages in Razmara could be as powerful as the feared Deacon Morrow?

"One day, the truth about all three will come to light. For now, Deacon's identity is the only one I care to expose."

Lilith could tell she would get nothing more out of Jameela, just as the woman had refused to elaborate when she had told her and Gretchen's futures. How sorely Lilith missed Gretchen. How she wished the younger woman was still alive. They could have made a beautiful world together, but instead Lilith was expected to do that on her own.

The trill of laughter and the clash of steel were an odd mix to Lilith's ears as she left the meeting room, stopping to peer over the balcony and into the training yard. The evening sky darkened into hues of orange and purple, but even in the twilight, she could make out the glimmer of Ayesha's jewellery and the familiar mop of dark hair of her opponent, Elyes.

The cousins had often practised sparring since Ayesha's return from the jungle. They were perfectly balanced: Elyes with his sudden growth spurt and all the uncertain strength of a fourteen-year-old boy, and Ayesha with her determined ferocity and the speed of a striking snake. Lilith rested her elbows on the balcony, leaning forward to watch them.

Ayesha wielded dual scimitars, twirling them by her sides and sinking into a low stance as she watched Elyes pace back and forth like an agitated animal.

"Come on, then," she called.

Elyes grinned and lunged, but there was nothing but cold focus on Ayesha's face as she blocked him with her scimitars, using them to push him back. Surprise flashed across Elyes's face, his grin vanishing like water sifting through sand. They became a flurry of steel and spinning dark hair, trading blows hard and fast even though their weapons had been blunted to prevent them from seriously hurting each other.

She's good, Lilith realised. *They're both good*. The thought should have comforted her, but instead it awakened a cold dread within her. Ayesha and Elyes were children, and yet they had been forged into warriors because necessity demanded they be able to protect themselves. When they fought in the heat of a real battle, there would be no laughter, no smiles.

"Ayesha." Lilith traipsed down the steps, examining her daughter with the wary gaze of a mother whose child was growing far too fast. Elyes drew back, the sharp ring of steel resonating as he dragged his blades back from Ayesha's. The girl glanced at Lilith, lowering her scimitars and striding over.

Lilith remembered a child who had hidden under tables or behind furniture at the first sign of her father's violence. Ayesha had tiptoed around Nicodemus like a ghost, a girl who didn't want to be seen or heard. She might as well have been blessed, Anointed with invisibility. But Ayesha did not have magic as the Anointed did. She was simply good at disappearing, and it had broken Lilith's heart to realise she preferred it that way.

The year she had spent in the jungle with Jacen had changed Ayesha. Lilith had seen her daughter's progress during her visits, but it was since Ayesha had returned to Dalal that she truly saw just how much the girl had grown up. She strode with her head held high, confidence in her steps and resolve burning in her eyes. She had always been rake-thin, though her form had shifted to lean muscle. She would not be a child much longer, Lilith knew.

"Can we talk?" Lilith asked. Ayesha jerked her head in a nod, and Lilith led her daughter into one of the many gardens that the palace of Dalal boasted, the one with a fountain bubbling in the middle of it. The vegetation there grew thick, wild and untamed. Ivy weaved its way around stone pillars and the fountain's circular base. The few flowers that had appeared were big and bright, yellow and orange sunset hues bringing life to the garden.

"Is something wrong?" Ayesha tilted her head to the side.

"I know you spoke with Jacen about the Generan throne…"

Ayesha made a noise of impatience. "Not this again! I know it's not what *you* want, but it's not about you."

"Ayesha." Lilith's voice was stern, and she held up a hand to silence the girl's protests. "I am not going to argue with you about it. I have seen how strong and capable you've become. You have the makings of a true monarch."

Ayesha blinked rapidly, too young and inexperienced at masking her emotions to conceal her surprise.

"You...you agree with me?"

Lilith sighed deeply. It was more complicated than simply agreeing or disagreeing. The Generan throne had belonged to bloodthirsty jackals for two generations, men who wanted nothing more than to set the world on fire and watch it burn. Genera needed stability. Genera needed peace.

"I will not make Jacen take the throne if he doesn't want it, nor will I stop you from sitting upon it if that's what you want."

Ayesha jutted her chin up. "Is it because you don't think Jacen will make a good king?"

"Of course I don't think that," Lilith responded indignantly. "Jacen is not Cobryn. Neither are you. When the time is right, we will make a choice about Genera's future, but I want you to know I will not ignore Jacen's thoughts, or yours."

Ayesha observed her mother critically. "You aren't treating me like a child."

Lilith put her arms around her daughter and pressed a kiss to her forehead. She understood the danger facing both Ayesha and Jacen. Deacon's ire would be focused on his nephew, but there was no chance he would spare his niece, not when she was a contender for the Generan throne too.

Lilith was overcome by a surge of maternal protectiveness, not only toward Ayesha, but Jacen as well. It was true there were less than ten years between them, but his mother had died when he was only small, and he'd not had a positive female figure in his life since Relda had been sent to Harith after it had fallen.

Whatever it took, Lilith would defend the children of Cobryn Morrow until her dying breath. She would support them in their choices, but she would also guide them with a firm hand. It seemed strange, to have hated her husband so much, and yet possess so much love and admiration for his children.

A child of Cobryn Morrow would sit on the throne of Genera. The only question was, which one?

FIFTEEN
THE HOMEBOUND LORD
THOM DYRE

News of Carissa's flight from Nicodemus spread across Genera like wildfire. In the pandemonium that followed her escape—and Deacon losing his sword hand in the process—Thom planned his move out of the capital, determined to return home to Gethsemane.

Of course, such plans did not go without notice, which was how Thom found Ariadne Pavlos striding into his rooms without invitation as he slammed shut one of his trunks. The woman's eyes flicked from Thom to his packed belongings, a hint of a smile curving her lips.

"Abandoning ship?"

"Don't be ridiculous." Thom raked his hair out of his eyes. "This past year I may have visited Nicodemus more than in the past two decades, but Gethsemane is still my home. I don't have any need to be subject to the King's wrath."

"Yes, well." Ariadne's smile was tight and didn't reach her eyes, a far cry from the woman so comfortable with wicked grins and devious glances. "Not all of us have that sort of luxury."

Thom masked his astonishment. "You could return to your estate at any time."

"No, I can't." Ariadne planted her hands on her hips, eyebrows raised. "Don't you see how suspicious that would look if we both suddenly departed the capital? I must stay and comfort our dear King over the escape of his wife, even if it means listening to the despicable things he promises to do once he gets her back."

Thom was silent for a few moments. Carissa's escape had been reckless, hampered by her desire for vengeance, for blood. He could hardly blame her for lashing out at the man who'd abused and manipulated her, but it had only made Deacon all the more furious. Ariadne, however, was yet to register astonishment at the Queen's flight.

"You knew." Realisation slid over Thom, cold and unwelcome. "You knew that Carissa was going to flee Nicodemus."

"I thought it was best that only one of us carry that secret." Ariadne mimed sealing her lips and tossing away an invisible key. "For how can someone admit to something they don't know? He's not going to find her, Thom. That I promise you."

Thom regarded her with begrudging admiration. A year ago, he would barely have spoken a handful of words with Ariadne and Myron. Yet there they were, the two of them the closest friends he had in the snake's pit that was Nicodemus.

It would have been easy for an ambitious woman like Ariadne to be jealous of Carissa's status, or desire to take her place. But for as cunning as Ariadne was, she was also perceptive. She knew exactly what sort of man Deacon was, and while she might have been content as his lover, Thom didn't think she'd ever want to be his wife. Ariadne had not wanted Carissa gone for her own gain. She truly valued the younger woman's wellbeing.

"You know, I'm going to miss you." Ariadne reached out and rested a hand on Thom's arm. "Even if you and Myron bicker like an old married couple. You're one of the only people I can be honest with in this gods-forsaken place."

"Well, now that I'm gone, I trust you to be less honest." Thom couldn't help but smile, the warmth of her fingers searing through the fabric of his shirt. "In fact, I think you should lie at every given opportunity."

"To the King? Certainly." Ariadne laughed. He was reminded of the fact that her position wasn't just about her. She had two young children back at her estate, and one false move could mean a grisly fate for them as well as her. Like Carissa, like many of the Generan court, she walked a very fine line.

"Be careful." Thom brought her into a hug, making Ariadne yelp in surprise at the unexpected demonstration of affection. When he drew back, there was a tenderness in her eyes. "Stay close to Myron."

"You act like a father making sure his children behave in his absence." Ariadne's words were bold, but her smile wavered slightly. "We'll see you soon. That's a promise."

A smile tugged at Thom's lips as he took in the myriad bridges and labyrinthine layout of his home city of Gethsemane. How many times had he and Annaliese got lost in the streets as children? Too many to count, by his reckoning.

By the Trinity, it was good to be home. Thom had found the court of Nicodemus utterly stifling, and had only been there to speak with Myron, Ariadne, and Carissa. Since the Queen had fled, things in Genera were bound to get tense. Deacon knew his wife would want to return to Basium, and as such he had contacted agents at the border to keep an eye out for her.

Heaving a sigh, Thom removed his cloak as he strode into the hall, none too surprised to see his mother sitting imperiously in the grand oak chair.

Odessa Dyre was known as the Mistress of Webs, and for good reason. Despite her old age and frail stature, she was the head of a spy network that had originated in Gethsemane, but now extended across the entirety of Genera. Odessa even had people stationed in the court of Nicodemus. All of them reported directly back to her.

"Thom." Odessa rose with creaking bones, a warm smile crossing her lips at the sight of her sole surviving child. After she had lost Annaliese, Odessa had been inconsolable, and her grief was part of the reason that Thom had rarely left Gethsemane following his sister's death. Then Odessa had found a purpose, and Thom marvelled at how strong and driven his elderly mother had been since.

"Mother." Thom embraced her. She smelled of rosewater, the thick silks of her dress soft against his skin. In the last few years, Odessa felt the cold more than ever before due to her advancing age.

"I would ask how the capital was, but I already know." Odessa's eyes sparked with amusement, lips curved into a smile. "The King is not handling things well."

Odessa was one of the few people who dared to laugh fearlessly in the face of a man like Deacon. She had already lost her daughter and both of her grandchildren. What else did she have to lose ? Thom both admired her courage and resented her lack of caution.

"When has he ever?"

"There is more news."

Praxidike Stefanos walked into the hall, eyes darting between Odessa and Thom. The young man had been one of Jacen's few friends, and upon learning what had happened to Jacen, he had thrown himself wholeheartedly into supporting Odessa's spy network. He was one of her most valued agents, and when he wasn't in Gethsemane, he travelled all around Genera.

That day, there was something like hope sparkling in those dark eyes. Thom had seen how Jacen's death had destroyed Prax, watched him drink away his sorrows and gamble in the shadowy dens in the back streets of Gethsemane. He had even talked about sailing away in one of the city's many merchant vessels before Odessa had convinced him to join the cause.

"Jacen Morrow is alive." Prax's words vibrated with barely contained excitement.

Thom threw a sharp look at Odessa. The last thing Prax needed was encouragement that his friend might be alive. His mother arched an eyebrow, and Thom sighed, turning to face Prax. He did not lack empathy, but he was not a man of soft words and half-truths.

"That's not possible. He was burned on the pyre. Deacon delivered a killing blow."

"The body on the pyre was a decoy," Prax insisted. "Even Deacon doesn't know the truth. Jacen is alive, and he's hiding in Harith along with Lilith and Ayesha."

Prax's conviction was admirable, but Thom still didn't see how it was possible. Jacen could never have recovered from that kind of massive blood loss, unless there had been a Primordial on hand. Prax must have sensed Thom's doubt, his eyes narrowing.

"Look, I wouldn't say anything unless I was certain. The last thing I want is to believe he's alive if he isn't. There was a man who healed him—Ishtar Haroun."

The name rang a bell. Thom didn't think he'd met the man, but from recollection, he had been Harith's ambassador who had frequented the court of Nicodemus before he too had vanished following the Morrow massacre. He didn't know if the man had magic, but he supposed he couldn't count it out entirely.

Thom remembered Jacen as a child—the boy's soft smile, the gentle way he'd explained to Vida, squirming impatiently, how they could care for a bird with a broken wing. Despite the fact that he had grown up to become a soldier, as a little boy there had not been a drop of malice in him.

"Jacen is not our current concern. From the sound of it, he has allies in Harith. Right now, we need to worry about Carissa."

It wounded him to dismiss the joyous tidings of his nephew's survival. Thom wanted to celebrate it, but he was a man focused on the facts. Jacen was among friends and allies. Carissa had no one. A chill raced down Thom's spine at the thought. A terrified woman, one who had just gained her magic back... What kind of destruction could she wreak? What would she do if an enemy caught her first?

Prax's brow furrowed. "I bring you this, and you want to do...nothing?"

"No." Thom raked his fingers through his thinning hair. "Jacen's survival changes the game as we know it. But Carissa is alone in a country she doesn't know. If Deacon manages to get his hands on her again, I dread to think what could happen."

Thom had come to regard the young woman as a daughter figure. His stomach coiled at the idea of what Deacon was capable of. Cutting off his hand had probably seemed a wonderful idea to her at the time, a taste of bloody revenge, but the King had never been angrier in his life. No one crossed Deacon, especially not the girl he thought he had broken.

"She isn't even safe in her own country," Prax argued. "Not now that her brother has taken the throne. Sebastian won't be pleased to see her."

"Lady Lenore will." Odessa spoke quietly before her voice rose. "Yet another underestimated woman. If we reach out a hand to her, I believe she would take it. We need to bring Deacon down, and we cannot do it alone. Neither can she."

All Thom knew of Bellona, he had learned from Carissa. Lady Lenore was new to leadership, her father Kato heroically sacrificing himself to prevent many of Theron's citizens from drowning when Deacon had flooded the city. Only a handful of years older than the Queen, Bellona was a force to be reckoned with—a powerful ally or a formidable foe. Thom preferred the idea of the former.

"She has Cirocco at her back," he agreed. Cirocco was currently involved in skirmishes in Wendell to take control of the southern harbours, as they fought to send a Wendellian ship to Bao. If Bao thought that the other countries all stood against Deacon, surely they would join in. If they thought Wendell was lost, they would hesitate.

"Bellona wants Carissa back as Queen of Basium," Prax pointed out. "That's bound to cause tension with Sebastian."

"Sebastian has little power in Basium." Odessa waved a dismissive hand. "The boy has been too busy in his power struggle with Lady Lenore to make any real progress."

Thom pitied him. Sebastian was barely eighteen years old. He deserved better than Odessa's contempt, but his mother was right—Sebastian's decisions had not been popular.

"We shouldn't shun Sebastian so easily." Prax folded his arms over his chest. "He has married well, making allies within Basium. Even if Carissa does ascend the throne with Bellona's support, she will need more than just that to stay there. She will need the backing of other nobles."

"What would you suggest we do?" Odessa asked, a hint of steel entering her tone as the young soldier went quiet.

"Mother." Thom's muttered word was a warning. Prax didn't need the weight of Odessa's disdain bearing upon him.

Prax straightened up. "We should…"

"We write to Lady Lenore." Odessa gathered her skirts and seated herself with regal stiffness in the oak chair. "Once we have her response, we will plan our next move. For now, we keep an eye out for Carissa. If my grandson makes a move from Harith, we will consider that also. But the King is angry, and we must show patience and restraint for just a little longer."

There was a ledge on which Thom had liked to sit as a child. It overlooked the shimmering canals that ran through Gethsemane. From it, he had listened to the crews of ships singing sea shanties. He had watched the lights moving in the streets below as the citizens laughed. Thom was an observer, and there was no place better to people-watch than the ledge on the west tower.

Often Thom had done so with Annaliese, the two sharing a cup of mead she'd snuck from the kitchen and some bread and cheese. His older sister had managed to charm everyone she met, sweet and kind-hearted with a laugh that could make even the sternest of men smile. She had managed to win Cobryn's heart, the only woman who had done so. When she died, Thom often thought Annaliese had taken Cobryn's heart with her.

That night, when Thom went out to the ledge, he was surprised to find that it was already occupied. Of late he was a man who enjoyed his solitude, but Prax typically made for pleasant company. Thom was silent as he sat beside the younger man. In the canals below, two merchant ships had docked side by side. Sailors jumped from one deck to the next. On the upper deck, a shaggy-haired man played a lively tune on the fiddle.

"I remember when Jacen used to play like that," Prax murmured, finally breaking the quiet.

"I heard he was excellent with a fiddle." Thom smiled. Jacen had inherited his love of music from Annaliese. She had loved the fiddle as a girl, though she hadn't particularly been skilled at it. What made Annaliese shine was her genuine desire to see people laughing or dancing.

She had always shone as bright as the sun, and he had been content in her shadow. He still kept to the shadows, but there was nothing that burned as fierce and true as Annaliese.

"What do you think he will do now?" Prax twisted his head to examine Thom. "Jacen, I mean. Once he learns that the woman he loves has been abused by his monster of an uncle, do you think he will stand idly by?"

"I don't expect so," Thom admitted. "However, it would be a rash and unwise move to try and fight Deacon—even in his current state. Jacen would certainly know better than that."

If they all survived, Thom would atone for neglecting his nephew. He would become the sort of uncle that Jacen deserved. He would spend time in Nicodemus, regardless of his distaste for the capital. He prayed to the Trinity that his chance at giving Jacen a supportive family had not come too late.

SIXTEEN
THE MALICIOUS LADY
BELLONA LENORE

Upon her return to Theron, Bellona learned from Eirian that they had captured one of the Merciless Ones—Sienna Rodrigo. Bellona remembered when she'd first met the woman, how warm Sienna's laugh had been, how she had instantly liked her. It had been a poor judgement on her part. Sienna and the rest of the Merciless Ones had betrayed them. They had chosen a fortune from Deacon Morrow over loyalty to Cristofer Santana.

The copper-haired woman was held prisoner deep in the bowels of Theron's dungeons. Bellona left it a few days when she returned—she did not want to appear overly eager. Nonetheless, a desire for vengeance burned deep within her. Not for her, but for Carissa. Every horror that Carissa had endured in Genera was because of Sienna and the rest of her group. Apparently, the woman had been caught trying to sneak across the border into Cirocco—where the Merciless Ones had become wanted fugitives following their treason.

"You don't have to be here for this." Cristofer's voice resonated through the dungeons as he followed Bellona down the stone steps. Getting answers out of Sienna was not going to be easy, but Bellona was determined to do anything in her power to make the woman talk. When it came to getting Carissa back, there were no longer any lines she wasn't willing to cross.

"Of course I do." Bellona turned to frown over her shoulder. Her husband understood the importance of what was happening there, why it was important to *her*. She did not relish violence but understood in some instances it was necessary.

She doubted that Sienna would give her any answers without provocation.

"Have you ever tortured anyone before?" Cristofer asked, and Bellona's silence was response enough for him. "It's ugly work."

"I'm not here because I think it'll be pretty." Bellona's voice was curt. She didn't shy away from the horrors of the world—she never had. She didn't care what it took to get closure. She didn't care what it cost, even if it was her soul. Her fingers lingered on the knife she'd strapped to her hip.

Sienna was strapped down to a table in her cell, but she still managed to cast a contemptuous look at Bellona upon her entry. Her lip curled in derision, and she stared stubbornly up at the ceiling. Cristofer waited by the door, arms folded over his chest, as the wrought-iron gate screeched close behind Bellona.

Bellona's eyes raked over the table. Not a table—a stretching rack. Sienna was tied down spread-eagled, arms and legs held in place by several ropes. Bellona had always known the sort of torture instruments her father kept in the darkest pit of Theron, but she had never seen them firsthand. Her stomach coiled, but she ignored the apprehension.

"You don't scare me, Lady Lenore." Sienna's tone was scornful as Bellona approached, looming over her. Bellona wasn't surprised; she didn't scare many people. She was a small, slight woman, and it meant she was often underestimated. She didn't need Sienna's fear. She needed the truth.

"You betrayed Cristofer. More than that, you betrayed the Queen."

Sienna sneered. "She wasn't my queen."

"You abducted her," Bellona seethed, leaning her weight on the wheel of the stretching rack above Sienna's head. "You took her to Genera, to a man you knew would rape and abuse her. What had Carissa ever done to earn something so horrific from you?"

"It wasn't personal!" Sienna spat.

Entire body shaking with anger, Bellona turned the wheel. She hadn't been prepared for how Sienna's bones cracked and popped, making the woman cry out in pain. She gritted her teeth against the sound, against knowing she was the source of it. Bellona knelt to murmur in her ear.

"I will take you apart, piece by piece, until I find out why you sold out my best friend."

"Money," Sienna said the word as though it was simple. "I did it for money. We all did. I once said to you we value it over loyalty, and you were the one who seemed to think we were somehow more noble than that."

Bellona recoiled as though she had been slapped. She wished there had been a better reason, one she could understand. But for a woman whose word was her oath, she could not see how money could make Sienna commit such an atrocious crime. Carissa had endured hell because they wanted *money*?

"What about your fucking morality?" Bellona asked, grabbing a fistful of Sienna's copper hair and yanking back hard. Over by the door, Cristofer's brow creased, but she studiously ignored him. "Where was that when you abducted her?"

"I didn't care what Deacon did to the bitch."

Bellona saw white hot rage. She slid the knife free from her belt. She heard Cristofer shout her name, but all she was focused on was Sienna's cruel words. If they spared her, she would go on to create more chaos in her wake. She would hurt more people, people like Carissa who deserved better.

"Bellona." Cristofer grabbed her arm, his voice low in her ear. "If you do this, there's no coming back from it."

"That doesn't matter to me," Bellona snapped, her voice cracking with the weight of her rage.

"Yes, it does," he said gently, sliding his hand down so his fingers closed over hers where they gripped the knife. "You're a woman of justice, not vengeance. Every decision you've made in the past has been to protect the people you care about. There's nothing in this but malice. You know that."

He was right, and she hated it. As much as Bellona wanted to succumb to her

119

fury and plunge her knife into Sienna's heart, it wouldn't make her any different from Cobryn and Deacon and the people she despised. With a roar of anguish, she tossed the knife aside and pressed her face into her hands. Sobs shook her frame, and Cristofer enveloped her in his arms and held her close.

"You aren't a monster, Bell," he whispered into her hair. "You're human. You're right to be angry, you're right to want Sienna dead. Resisting that urge makes you the better person here."

Were there better people and worse people? Bellona wasn't so certain anymore. She wrenched free of Cristofer's arms, not even sparing Sienna a backward glance as she marched from the dungeon. Her heart cried out for revenge for the best friend the woman had betrayed, but her mind spoke more clearly: if she had surrendered to violence, she would be taking one step closer to being like the men she loathed.

Bellona couldn't sleep. She slipped out of her room with her bow and a quiver of arrows and dragged out a target in the courtyard. By the light of the moon and the stars, she fired one arrow after another, imagining that the target was Deacon Morrow's smirking face. Fury made her hands shake, her shots sloppy. In a fit of anger, she hurled her bow to the ground. Her breath fogged out in an irate mist as she tilted her head back, staring up at the blanket of stars overhead.

Why would the goddess Elethea wish such a cruel fate upon Carissa? Was it atonement for the sins of her ancestor, Jameson Burnett? For a year now, Bellona had struggled to find a reason for everything that had happened, and she could find none. Her prayers went unheard and unanswered.

"I was looking all over for you." A man's voice made her whirl around. Cristofer walked across the courtyard with something gleaming in the moonlight. Bellona licked her dry lips and picked up her bow, fingers tightening around it. "I have something for you."

It was a weapon in his hands, small and silvery and shiny. Bellona accepted the weapon, marvelling at how light it was in her grasp. Her heart hammered in her chest as she thought of Cristofer comforting her in the dungeons. Had he believed, at that moment, she might have killed Sienna?

"In my culture, it's tradition to give your husband or wife a gift after a year of being together." Cristofer smiled sheepishly. "It's called the Gifting, a way to prove how well you've come to know one another. This is a javelin, a small one. It's often used for sport in Cirocco, but it's also a deadly weapon."

"It's stunning." Bellona let a small smile creep across her lips. "I don't know how to thank you, or what to get you in return."

Cristofer shook his head. "It's a Ciroccan custom; I don't expect anything in return. I thought it was just a good time for you to have this."

"About the dungeons…" Bellona drew in a deep breath. "I almost lost control."

"But you didn't, Bell." His voice was gentle as he watched the way her knuckles went white as she clutched the javelin. "Wanting to hurt someone and acting on those urges are two entirely different things."

"Is it bad that I still wish her dead?" The words were scarcely above a whisper, trembling with the fear she felt in saying them.

"No." Cristofer kissed the top of Bellona's head. "We will do everything in our power to save Carissa, I promise you. But we both know killing Sienna wouldn't have accomplished anything. It would have made you feel worse; it would have stained your hands in blood hard to scrub off."

Bellona had killed before. She had killed to save Jacen's life; she had killed during the heat of battle. Cristofer was right, though. Murdering an unarmed prisoner to sate her appetite for revenge was not the answer. Bellona was stronger than that, stronger than the desire to bring the ultimate cruelty upon others whether they deserved it or not.

More than anything, Bellona missed her best friend. She remembered the months she'd been separated from Carissa when she fled to Theron following

Miriam's arrest. At least then, the threat of violence had not been so close to the Queen.

Hefting up the javelin that Cristofer had gifted her, Bellona bared her teeth and hurled it at the target with all her might. It missed without even scraping the target, skittering off into the darkness like all her lost prayers to Elethea.

Bellona read over the letter with a deep frown etched across her features. She had heard of Jacen's maternal uncle, Lord Thom Dyre of Gethsemane, by name only. He was more of a scholar than a fighter, a man who preferred solitude and books to the games of court. He had not been seen in Nicodemus since the death of Annaliese, his older sister and Jacen's mother—until Deacon had been crowned as Genera's King.

Eirian sat by the fire, tugging a brush through her pale blonde hair. Her eyes never left Bellona, observing as her lover set down the letter and sighed. Lord Dyre had asked for an audience in Theron. He had given a list of reasons why they would make excellent allies.

It was hardly the only news that had trickled into the city over the past few days. Jacen Morrow was alive, a shocking revelation that saw him in Dalal with his younger half-sister Ayesha and stepmother Lilith. Carissa had fled Nicodemus after taking off Deacon's hand. Privately, Bellona wished she'd taken off both. The Queen hadn't been seen since.

"Do you think this is a trick?" Bellona asked, waving the offending letter in the air.

"I don't believe so." Eirian shook her head, setting her brush down. "Lord Dyre risks a lot sending a letter like that. Deacon would be too concerned about licking his wounds. What does he have to gain by sending Lord Dyre to meet with you?"

Bellona privately agreed, but that did not dispel her suspicion. It was a natural state for her—after the Merciless Ones had abducted Carissa, she wondered if she would ever trust again.

"So, you think I should agree to the meeting?"

"I think he's right in saying we both need allies," Eirian pointed out. "Goddess only knows what's happening with Sebastian in Marinel. Carissa hasn't been seen since her escape. Jacen is in Harith. The Ciroccans are already fighting border skirmishes down in Wendell. We need more than that. We need a sound victory."

Bellona sank into a chair. Deacon was at his most vulnerable. The time to make a decisive strike was now. But without Carissa in the game at all, with Jacen's next move unknown —what were they supposed to do? Everything had seemed easier with Carissa by her side.

Come home, Carissa.

"Then we accept Lord Dyre's invitation. He can come to Theron, and we debate our next move from there."

Bellona stared into the flickering flames, a heaviness settling upon her shoulders. Was that how her father had felt during times of tension? How had he handled the burden? She missed her father too. Kato had left a gaping hole inside of her when he'd died, and it was like a scab she kept picking, never fully healed.

It had been difficult to let herself mourn him. Unexpectedly gaining custody of Zephyr had occupied all of her attention for the past year as she begrudgingly learned to care for the boy, first a baby and then as a toddler. Devoting that energy to something positive was a good outlet, yet it didn't stop the pain of Kato's death searing beneath her veins, an angry brew she had been forced to cork up.

She had infrequent nightmares of the tunnels, of an empty darkness and the ache that came with her heart breaking over and over. She mulled on what she could have done differently, on how they could have saved him. It was to no avail, for there was no solution to a problem one year buried.

The warmth of the hearth dried the tears that slipped down her cheeks almost as soon as they had spilled from her eyes. She reached up to wipe her face nonetheless. The grief was no longer sharp as a blade against her skin, its edge dulled to a bruise she was reminded of when it knocked against something.

Whether a great pain or a slight pain, Kato's death still hurt.

SEVENTEEN
THE NOSTALGIC KING
JACEN MORROW

With the secret of his survival out in the open, Jacen was living on borrowed time. The fact of the matter was that he could not remain in Dalal. The only question was what direction he should take. Word had reached the city of what had unfolded in Nicodemus—Carissa had cut off Deacon's sword hand and fled. As of yet, there was still no sign of her, but everyone knew she would be returning to Basium. The news brought Jacen vicious satisfaction.

Despite Deacon being at his weakest and most vulnerable, he was also at his angriest, a wild and wounded animal. To attack would be folly, and Jacen acknowledged it as such. To venture to Basium himself, with Sebastian and Bellona at each other's throats and turmoil surrounding them both, would also be a bad idea.

"Where would you have me go?" Jacen asked, hazel eyes darting between Relda and Lilith as they sat quietly across from him, the two most powerful women in Harith other than Queen Samara. "What would you have me do?"

He relied on their wisdom. Ultimately, he was the one who would have to make the choice, but he was open to taking suggestions.

"You need to think about this yourself, Jacen." Relda's voice was sharp and laced with impatience. "You are a grown man. It is not for us to instruct you. Whoever sits on the Generan throne, you must be the one to win it. What do you need?"

In her steely eyes, Jacen could see Cobryn, the lessons his father had drilled into him throughout his childhood.

"Allies." Jacen was reminded of his quest to gain them for Carissa when she had fled Marinel. His goal had been for his wife to take on Deacon with an army at her back. He thought Harith would be enough, but he realised what Relda was saying—he needed Generans on his side to gain the throne. His uncle was not a popular king, and there were many who would pick an alternative. Jacen was presenting them with one.

"Years ago, your father went to war with Philemon and Severino." Lilith's voice was soft, but her eyes glittered with fervent fire. "He had the noble families who ruled there killed. The survivors fled as he installed new families, like House Pyralis."

It hadn't just been Cobryn, Jacen recalled with sick guilt churning in his stomach. That was a war that Jacen had been an active participant in. Upon realising what Lilith was insinuating, laughter bubbled up in Jacen's chest before emerging from his mouth.

"You want me to convince the same houses that I helped destroy to assist me?" He couldn't disguise his disbelief, shaking his head slowly. "I may as well go and beg Deacon for the throne back."

"Don't be dramatic." Relda rolled her eyes, kicking her boots up on the table and leaning back in her seat. "It has been many years since the Island Wars. You were only seventeen, and many would remember that. You were young and impressionable."

"Old enough to make my own choices." Jacen slumped forward in his chair, sighing deeply. He was coming to the swift realisation that he had very few friends. "I was a major part of the Island Wars. I killed members of those noble houses."

"You think I am without sin?" Relda arched an eyebrow. "Do you think coming this far in Harith was easy? It wasn't. Instead of complaining about the fact that I wasn't trusted, I worked on earning that trust."

"There is also your mother's side of the family," Lilith reminded him.

Jacen only had vague memories of them. Lord Thom Dyre, younger brother of Jacen's mother Annaliese, had not been to Nicodemus since Jacen had been a child. Their mother Odessa even less so—Jacen thought perhaps the last time his grandmother had been in the capital had been just after Vida's birth and Annaliese's subsequent death. Blood didn't make a family—Deacon was proof of that. How did he know he could trust the Dyres?

"You don't know unless you try," Relda said, and Jacen reasoned that his doubt must have shown clear as day on his face. "I would start with the former Island lords and then try your mother's side of the family."

The last person Jacen went to see before his departure was Ayesha. With his bags packed and horse saddled, he found Ayesha reading in her bedroom, humming a Harithian song she had learned under her breath as she curled against the cushions.

His younger sister was the most important thing in the world to him, and he intended to make that known. He had noticed Ayesha spending more time with Elyes. The two cousins were close in age, and Jacen thought it was nice she finally had a friend her own age to spend time with.

"You're leaving." Ayesha looked up from the book in her lap, snapping it closed. "Are you sure I can't come with you?"

"Unfortunately not." Jacen smiled ruefully. It would be nice to have a companion on his journey, but it was far too dangerous for Ayesha to accompany him. Instead, she would remain in Dalal, where it was safe. What would become of Ayesha now? Would she return to their jungle hiding place, alone?

"I'm not afraid." Ayesha's chin jutted upwards. "I can protect myself too."

"It's not just about that." Jacen rested a hand lightly on her shoulder. "There's a lot of tension with the families I helped displace in the Island Wars. The last thing I want is for them to use you against me."

Ayesha wrinkled her nose. "Well, I wouldn't let them."

Jacen chuckled, kissing the top of her head. "It's not always as easy as that."

Ayesha sighed heavily. "So, you're going out alone then?"

"I'll be fine," Jacen said. He watched as Ayesha sprang off her bed and crossed the room. His stomach twisted when she picked up the jackal helm that had been a symbol of dread for both of them. Ayesha crossed back over and pressed the helm into Jacen's hands, even as he recoiled from it.

"Take it."

Jacen shook his head vigorously. "You know what that helm symbolises, Ayesha. Everyone who sees it lives in fear of war."

"So, make it mean something different." Ayesha's eyes sparkled as she pushed the helm at him more insistently. "Father isn't here anymore. The helm isn't his. It's yours. You decide what it represents."

Ayesha's wisdom shone out like a beacon, and he was overwhelmed with love for his little sister. It could not have been easy, being the youngest child of the Warmonger. Ayesha had grown up witnessing the violence her father had committed against her mother, and she was old enough to realise what happened behind closed doors. There was some of Cobryn's tenacity in her, but also Lilith's unyielding kindness. She would make a great queen, if that was what she chose.

"I'll miss you," he said. "I miss how simple the jungle was."

"Well, we couldn't have stayed there forever." Amusement coloured Ayesha's tone, her eyes sparkling as a rare smile crossed her lips. "We have important things to do. Duties."

"That we do." Jacen ruffled Ayesha's hair. Though he hesitated, he picked up the jackal helm and tucked it under his arm. Ayesha was right—it was up to Jacen to decide its legacy now. "Behave while I'm gone, won't you?"

Her grin turned wicked. "Never."

Examining the jackal helm and its wicked gleam in the candlelight, Jacen had an idea, and he pressed it back into Ayesha's hands. She turned it over in her fingers, a mixture of shock and delight on her face as she looked up at him.

"What are you doing?" she asked.

"You said I decided what it meant." Jacen smiled fondly. "I've decided that it belongs to you. The littlest jackal of House Morrow."

"I put it on," Ayesha whispered as she tucked the helm under her arm, "when you were healing in the jungle, before I was sent there. Something about it called to me. I think maybe I had my own idea about what it meant to me then."

"You see? It's meant to be yours." Jacen pressed a kiss to Ayesha's forehead, marvelling at how tall she was growing. "Maybe you can change what that helm means, just as I might stand a chance with the lost noble families."

EIGHTEEN
THE AVENGING PRINCE
SEBASTIAN DARNELL

Priestess Juniper's investigation hung over Sebastian like a dark cloud that refused to lift, the constant promise of rain lingering above him as he tried to clear the sky again. She had not spoken with Sebastian about the incident since their meeting in the chapel, and yet the silence on the matter brought dread rather than respite. No one could possibly know the truth...or could they?

Everywhere, enemies closed in around him. Far in the north, a wounded Deacon Morrow undoubtedly plotted revenge. Bellona Lenore might have returned to Theron, but would she forgive the attempt on her life? Carissa had vanished following a brutal attack on Deacon, and no one had seen her since.

The crown is heavy; don't put it on unless you wish to bear its weight. Sebastian had never wanted to wear the crown. It had been a choice made for him. Carissa wore it far better than he ever had, and a childish part of him yearned for his older sister to come and take it away from him. But what had that sister become? What was Carissa now, a Maleficium who had been caged and abused for a year? Her savagery could be seen in her attack on Deacon, justified though it might have been.

Amidst the chaos, Jarl arrived in Marinel. He and Sebastian took a turn through the gardens upon his arrival, late in the evening when the sky's hue had darkened to a deep blue and the stars twinkled overhead.

As always, Sebastian marvelled at the care his sister had taken of the place where their family had been slaughtered. The plants had grown wild when she had disappeared, and Sebastian hadn't the heart to employ a gardener to cut them back. He wanted them to be overgrown.

"Meliora is with child." Sebastian wanted to start with the good news, the knowledge that there was some happiness to be had in a world that seemed to be constantly getting darker. He had won the throne, but it wasn't enough. He saw the grim expressions of the people whenever he took to the streets. Marinel wasn't Emlen, where they knew him. In Marinel, he was the King, no matter what forge he visited or how sweat and ash stained his skin as he beat molten metal into shape.

"That's excellent news." Jarl's face split into a grin. When he noticed that no smile was coaxed from Sebastian, his brow furrowed. "Are you not pleased?"

"Of course I am." Sebastian didn't want to give his brother-in-law the wrong impression. "I'm nervous and excited. But there's so much happening that I fear for Meliora and the baby."

"Ah." Jarl craned his neck back to peer up at the stars. "Bellona returned to Theron."

Sebastian's stomach twisted at the mention of Lady Lenore. Bellona was as headstrong and fearless as her father, according to the rumours he'd heard. He didn't know the woman well enough to pass judgement, but he was aware that she would rather die than hand Zephyr over into Sebastian's custody.

"What did she want?"

"Answers." Jarl cast a meaningful look at his brother-in-law. "You can't blame her, considering the attempt on her life."

"It was not my doing," Sebastian snapped, irritated at the mess that Orien had created. Or was it precisely what the General wanted, to sow the seeds of discord between Carissa's best friend and her younger brother?

Winter's chill had settled over Marinel, the dusk winds carrying an icy bite that made Sebastian wrap his arms around himself. He inhaled sharply through his nostrils, wishing more than anything that he could be in the glorious heat of the forge. He wasn't meant to be a monarch. Like he worked molten metal into shape, so the people around him melted him down and moulded him into a creature of their own liking.

"I wasn't meant to be King," he muttered.

Sympathy, surprising in its rarity, flashed across Jarl's face. "But you *are*. The Morrows are gone, and here you stand in spite of all they've done."

"Is it worth it?" Sebastian's voice cracked over the words. "Carissa is... Thinking about her, thinking about the rest of my family, it aches. They have all suffered, only for me to be here. This shouldn't have cost *them*."

"We are your family now," Jarl reminded him, resting a supportive hand on Sebastian's shoulder. "Meliora and I. Our parents."

The words coaxed a soft smile to Sebastian's lips. Family didn't end in blood. Perhaps instead of being the one forged, he needed to take ownership of his own life and create himself into the man he wanted to be. No more blaming people like Quintin, or Orien, or Juniper. Sebastian would transcend their expectations in pursuit of his own.

Sebastian woke from nightmares of the cave, a cold sweat across his brow despite the chill of the night. He pried the tangled blankets from his body, evening out his breathing even as his heart raced. Was it really the cave where Jameson Burnett had committed his heinous crimes? He thought it was a fool's errand to seek out Tycho, and so had not bothered to do so. Why bring an old man out of a comfortable retirement for Sebastian's superstitions?

He considered Juniper's words. Could it be true that he might have magical blood in his veins, like his grandmother and his sister? Miriam had been a prophet, whose visions of the future had shown her the fire that would consume Marinel in the Conquest. Yet how could that be the same when it was the same thing, over and over again? It was more likely a dark omen, though Sebastian could not have said what.

Sebastian walked over to the sink and splashed his face with cool water. He could not shake the feeling that darkness was coming. War was going to show up at his door sooner or later, and whilst he might have the support of Emlen and his father-in-law Lord Ambrose, who else did he have?

Pushing himself away from the sink, Sebastian crossed over to the balcony, shoved the narrow doors open, and stepped out into the fresh night air. He walked forward and gripped the ledge with both hands, staring down at the lights in the city below.

These were his people now. He needed to protect them from whatever came next. He could no longer wait for Lady Lenore to make the first move—he had to reach out the hand of friendship to Bellona. Like it or not, they needed each other. If Basium was fractured, it would never survive.

"You've been tossing and turning all night." Meliora's sweet, soft voice made him turn to see that she had sat up, peering at him from her position on the bed. Sighing, he moved away from the ledge and closed the doors as he stepped back inside. He had not wished to wake her with his nightmares, but perhaps the pregnancy was part of it.

"I'm all right." Sebastian raked his fingers through his dark hair. "Just the cave again."

"You still don't want to find Tycho?"

Sebastian resisted the urge to scoff. "He would laugh in my face and see me off, whether I'm the King or not."

Meliora's hand flew to her stomach, brow pinching in pain. Sebastian crossed over and lit one of the candles, bringing it over and bathing her in its warm glow. When Meliora threw back the blankets, the bed sheets and her nightgown were soaked with blood from the hips down. Sebastian's stomach lurched, horror consuming him in its cold grasp as he realised what he was seeing.

Meliora pressed her hands to her face and screamed.

Sebastian considered himself a religious man, one who offered his prayers to the goddess Elethea. However, when the goddess offered nothing but cold silence and a bleak future in return, Sebastian was prone to taking matters into his own hands. Even Quintin, a former member of the Priesthood, had always said that while the goddess deliberated, mortals took action.

It wasn't action that Sebastian prayed for, kneeling in the chapel before the goddess's golden likeness. It was an answer.

The medics had expressed bewilderment over Meliora's miscarriage. Such things did, of course, happen naturally. However, there had been high amounts of cildana—a mildly poisonous plant—in her system. In small doses, it was not enough to be lethal, at least not to Meliora. But to their unborn baby, it had been deadly enough.

Sebastian choked back a sob, tears burning in his eyes as he thought of how Meliora had locked herself away in their room, refusing to speak even to Jarl. She was devastated by what had happened, even more so because it meant that someone had deliberately caused her to lose the child. Who could have wanted such an outcome? Who stood to gain by the terrible ordeal Meliora had endured?

"I don't ask for mercy." Sebastian's tear-streaked face jerked up to glower at the golden statue. "You have never granted it. Not to me, not to my dead family, not to my sister through the horrors she must have endured in Nicodemus, and certainly not to my sweet wife. I ask for justice."

Silence permeated the chapel, as Sebastian had commanded that no one be allowed to enter. He wanted the time and space to grieve his child's loss alone. His grandmother Miriam had lost all of her babies, all except Sebastian's father Frederick. Some women found it more difficult than others. Yet, Meliora's miscarriage was not of natural causes, and it amplified Sebastian's grief and woke a deep rage within him.

They were young, and there was plenty of time to have children, as the medics had said in an attempt to soothe Meliora's despair. Sebastian recalled how Quintin had once said it would be a mercy to kill baby Zephyr. Could there be an agent operating under the same assumption when it came to Sebastian and Meliora's child?

"You'll give me nothing but silence," Sebastian spat, easing himself to his feet with impatience flaring within him at a goddess who had nothing to offer him. "Fine. Then I will not beg your forgiveness when I bloody my hands once I discover who has done this to my wife."

There was someone in Sebastian's court who did not want him to have an heir, and that meant that there was danger lurking within the castle. Perhaps not outright, but a subtle menace that was all the more horrifying for its secrecy. He would root it out, rip it up, crush it beneath his feet.

Sebastian had thought about what sort of man he wanted to be, and he had come to the truth of it. Dire situations often revealed a person's true colours. Sebastian's were red, the colour of Quintin's blood as the light had left his eyes, the colour of the sword he hammered when it was hot.

He would have blood. He would have vengeance. He had always known that Carissa had her darkness, and now he recognised it in himself.

NINETEEN
THE HOPEFUL QUEEN
CARISSA DARNELL

The Generan countryside was hell. Most of the mountains had been close to Nicodemus, and Carissa had braved them on foot as much as she was able. At one of the first towns she came across, she had spent almost all of the coin she had on a horse. It was a gentle creature, a dappled mare named Liberty, which she had thought quite fitting upon purchasing her.

Liberty was the only company Carissa had, and made the journey across Genera that much quicker. Carissa stopped into several small towns to get more food and water, taking care to conceal herself lest someone discover her identity. Her only solace was that Deacon's spies would expect her to head south instead of west.

Once she reached Gethsemane, she would be safe. The city was relatively close to the coast, and Lord Dyre was her ally. All she had to do was make it there. The idea that she would have to subject more soldiers to a brutal, gruesome fate like she had in Nicodemus...she couldn't bear to think about it, guilt churning in the pit of her stomach.

Her magic surged through her veins after months of disuse and repression, and Carissa was finding it harder to push it back. Would it consume her, as it had Jameson Burnett? Every now and then she would use it to her advantage, killing and poorly skinning rabbits and other small animals to eat. It was a far cry from the lavish lifestyle she was used to, and she struggled to adjust to the long days in the saddle with blisters on her thighs, and the bitterly cold nights during which she rarely found warmth.

She was more than just a queen. She was a Maleficium. Instead of being used as someone else's weapon, she would become her own. Carissa's display in Nicodemus had proved her power. She had never doubted how strong her magic was but feared it might wane after months of Obscurate.

Carissa still experienced withdrawals from the drug, often feeling cold and nauseous, her body riddled with shakes. The sensation was familiar, as she had experienced similar symptoms during her pregnancy with Zephyr. However, she had bled, which eased her already-frayed nerves. It was just withdrawal, nothing more.

Tonight's town was called Apollonia, and Carissa longed for the warm heat of a soaking bath. She didn't have much money left, so it would probably be the last town where she could afford an inn before she reached Gethsemane. It was full of rickety buildings and haphazard streets with loose cobblestones, so the stay would be cheap. The last person anyone would expect to find in such a dilapidated town was the Queen.

"Hear what happened in the capital?" It was a gruff man's voice, and Carissa paused to listen intently.

"You mean to the King?" A woman that time, derision entering her tone. "It's no more than he deserves."

"You can't say something like that," the man responded, lowering his voice until Carissa could only just make out his next words. "It was the Queen that did it to him. Finally had enough of him."

"Don't blame her." The woman scoffed. "The man brings nothing but war and violence. She promised peace, and it was a pretty promise. Maybe she believed it. The King wants war, though. All the Morrows do."

Carissa bit down on her lip. She had thought the people admired her, but perhaps they believed her nothing more than a pawn in Deacon's game, someone for them to pity. Maybe they had cheered because at least her naive promise had seemed easier to swallow than the bitter pill of the truth. After tying Liberty to a post outside, she slipped into the inn, ensuring her hood was pulled up so people couldn't see her face.

"A room for one, please." She placed several coins down on the counter, deepening her voice. The scent of freshly-cooked meat and rosemary made her stomach grumble, but she couldn't think about a hot meal when a loaf of bread from the baker would be so much cheaper.

"Sorry, love." The innkeeper threw her an apologetic look and pointed a finger across the room. "The young gentleman over there just took the last one."

Carissa was overcome by a surge of frustration. She had been looking forward to a bath to ease the ache in her bones, and she felt the soreness of her stiff frame all the more acutely since she realised she wouldn't be getting it. She didn't look where the innkeeper was pointing, lest her irritation with a stranger show. It wasn't the man's fault that he'd obtained the room before her.

"Excuse me." It was a familiar voice, one that made Carissa tense. *It wasn't. It couldn't be.* "If the lady wants to have the room instead, I'll gladly give it up and get a refund."

Carissa's fingers trembled as she reached up to tug her hood down, turning to face the man who had spoken.

Jacen. It had to be some kind of cruel trick. Her first husband had been murdered by his uncle. The entire continent of Razmara had heard about it. His body had burned on the pyre. His hair was longer and there was stubble across his normally clean-shaven face, but it was him. She stared up at him with a mixture of confusion, horror, and wonder. When Jacen finally looked down at her, recognition dawned in his eyes.

"*Carissa?*"

"This can't be real," she whispered. The knot that had tied itself tight in her stomach since she had fled Nicodemus began to loosen, her knees trembling with relief. A sense of sudden ease washed over her, fresh and soothing as the rose-imbibed water she drew her baths with.

"I can explain everything." Jacen reached out and grabbed her arm, but Carissa lurched backward, colliding with the counter. Pain radiated up her spine as her breath came in ragged, her chest constricting. Hurt flashed in Jacen's eyes, and she wished she could take that away. The feeling of someone seizing hold of her like that brought her back to Nicodemus, to Deacon, to a dark room with a thick silver duvet on the bed...

"I'm sorry," she choked out.

The innkeeper was looking suspiciously between the pair of them. Drawing a shuddering breath, Carissa gathered the shreds of her composure.

"We know each other. It's fine. We'll both share the room."

"Very well." The innkeeper's eyes still darted between them, but he handed over a brass key, which Carissa took with a forced smile. Beckoning for Jacen to follow, she headed up the stairs, looking for the room number embedded into the metal of the key. A thousand thoughts spun through her mind as the floorboards creaked beneath her feet.

How was he alive? Why was he in Apollonia?

Carissa turned the key in the lock until it clicked, and only once they'd both entered the room did she shut the door. When Jacen moved across to seat himself on the bed, Carissa didn't stray from her position by the door.

"How?" Her voice broke on the single syllable. "How are you alive?"

Jacen's survival brought feelings of delight and horror. She wanted to embrace him, hold him close and never let go, yet she couldn't. Her body was rigid with tension as she awaited an explanation. Her marriage to Deacon was illegitimate. Deacon's own claim to the throne was invalid.

"Ishtar Haroun healed me." Jacen clasped his hands, refusing to meet her eyes. Did he feel guilty? "I was close to death, but...he brought me back from the brink. It still took weeks before I could move like I used to."

Carissa nodded slowly. She didn't want to push blame onto Jacen's shoulders, but she had to wonder why the man who loved her hadn't managed to communicate, in an entire year, that he was still alive. Jacen finally looked up at her, grief and guilt mixed in his expression as he took in the tense set of her shoulders.

"I didn't know." Jacen's eyes brimmed with tears. "About you, about what Deacon… Lilith kept it from me until recently. If I'd known…"

The fact that he was on the verge of breaking apart over it made Carissa's own eyes well with tears. She moved over to sit beside him on the bed, and she let him take her in his arms and hold her close.

Carissa had thought she would flinch away, but with Jacen she was warm and safe. With Jacen, she had nothing to fear. Even after a year apart, the world melted away when it was just the two of them. Tears coursed down Carissa's cheeks, but she was smiling. She had Jacen back, and the tension that had riddled her shoulders lightened at seeing him once again. She thought of warm nights in Emlen, the scent of cedar and pine.

"I'll kill him," Jacen promised, hatred in every word, "I'll kill him for what he did to you."

"I love you," Carissa sobbed, burying her face in the front of his shirt. "I love you so much."

Things would not go back to normal, at least not for a time. She trusted Jacen with her whole heart, but the damage Deacon had done would be difficult to undo. Deacon had not broken her, though. Nothing could destroy what she and Jacen had. Not his uncle, not the year that they'd been separated with no knowledge of each other's fates.

Carissa breathed in his scent, different from before, laden with sharp spice and musk. For the first time in over a year, a sense of security washed over her, loosening her tense limbs. It was like nothing could ever harm her. Her fingers linked through Jacen's, his hands callused and strong in hers.

"Why are you in Apollonia?" Jacen asked, the words vibrating through his chest. "I thought you would be heading back to Basium."

"That's what Deacon and his spies believe." Carissa drew away from him. "I need allies. I already have Lord Dyre in Gethsemane…"

"My uncle." Something sparkled in Jacen's eyes. "I'm looking for allies as well. I spoke to Lilith and Relda, and they think I should attempt to convince the Island nobles who were displaced during the war."

"I was going to seek them out too." Carissa nodded fervently. "Maybe together, we can earn their allegiance."

Together. It had been a long time since they'd promised to do things together. With Jacen by her side, Carissa was no longer a mess of anxiety and fear of her power. She was always stronger and more stable with him. The year apart had changed much, but not the love they shared.

"Then we will go home." Jacen took her face in his hands and pressed a kiss to her forehead, his lips gentle on her skin. "To our son."

"This war comes first," Carissa reminded him softly. "As long as Deacon lives, we will never be safe. Zephyr will never be safe. We need the Generan throne, and for that, we need more than just Lord Dyre. We need to reinstate the Island nobles."

Sharing a bed with her husband was strange. Though Jacen kept to his side and gave her space, Carissa found sleep difficult to come, her pulse racing as she stared up at the ceiling and how darkness and light from behind the curtains mingled. Jacen had offered to sleep on the floor, but Carissa hardly thought that was fair.

It had been a long time since she'd shared a bed with him…with anyone, really. In Nicodemus, she had at least been granted the small mercy of being able to sleep alone, though even then she had nightmares of dark shadows and wicked smiles.

Slowly easing herself up out of bed, taking care not to kick off the blankets and wake Jacen, Carissa tiptoed over to the window and drew the curtain back just enough to peer through. The cobbled streets below were empty, and she could hear a dog barking in the distance as the winter winds whistled by, rattling the windowpane.

Jacen had agreed easily with the plan to reinstate the Island nobles. Apparently, it had been something he had discussed with Lilith and Relda in Harith. Carissa was pleasantly surprised that Relda was on their side, having feared she was another of Deacon's loyalists ready to seize control. Nonetheless, Carissa knew Jacen well enough to know how much it must weigh on his conscience. He had, after all, participated in the Island Wars.

"Carissa?" Jacen's voice, thick with sleep, made her release the curtain and glance back over her shoulder at him. He sat up, rubbing his eyes and examining her blearily. "Are you all right? Why aren't you sleeping?"

"Not tired," she lied, shrugging her shoulders in a nonchalant manner. The last thing he needed was her anxiety on top of everything else. In the moonlight, she could see the silvery scar on his torso, the sole reminder of Deacon's attempted murder.

How could he still remain so soft and gentle despite everything he had been through? Carissa was like broken glass, all sharp edges, cutting away at anything that came close to her. She'd donned the mask of the benevolent Queen easily enough, but it had only ever been that: a farce. She had endured hardship for years, but at what point did you buckle under the weight of it?

"You can't sleep, can you?" Jacen patted the spot beside her on the bed, and Carissa sat down stiffly, crossing her legs and sweeping her tangled black hair out of her face. "Do you want to talk about it?"

"Not really," Carissa admitted, her eyes dropping to her intertwined fingers so she didn't have to see the hurt flash across Jacen's face. It wasn't that she didn't trust him. It was that it had been a year since she had seen him, and though he had his own demons to battle in that time, she didn't think she was quite ready to talk about hers.

"I heard you cut off Deacon's hand." Jacen's words were followed by a tense silence, as though he didn't know how she would react to them. When Carissa looked up, finally meeting his eyes, she wondered if he saw all the rage and anguish there.

"I wish I'd stabbed him in the heart instead."

Carissa did not regret fleeing, but she did regret that she hadn't killed Deacon. She was smart enough to know that a fight would not have gone well for her, and instead of risking losing such a battle, she'd escaped. The thought of Deacon's fury made knots tie in the pit of her stomach, despite the fact that she was far away from him.

"He killed Cobryn, didn't he?"

"Gretchen too. I went down to the river, and she was…" Jacen broke off, the pain in his hazel eyes glimmering in the darkness. He didn't have to elaborate because Carissa remembered hearing about it. Gretchen had been found dead by the riverbank where they had been camped, drowned in the water.

Carissa placed her hand over Jacen's, linking her fingers through his. They had both seen horrors, experienced more pain and devastation than they deserved. There was a beast in Carissa that hungered for more blood, more violence, against the man who'd hurt them so badly. She pushed it down, knowing no good could come of such reckless action.

"We can get through this. Together."

The hint of a smile danced at the corners of his lips as he squeezed her hand. "Together."

TWENTY
THE VIGILANT PRINCESS
LILITH MARWAN

Ayesha was restless since her brother had departed Dalal. Lilith could not blame her—Jacen had been a constant in Ayesha's life for the past year. As her thirteenth birthday passed, Ayesha's mind was focused on learning and training. Cairo had gifted her a pair of small scimitars, having seen the ones she practised with, and the sound of steel clashing rang through the yard as Lilith walked through the castle corridors.

"You're fast." Cairo sounded impressed. "Good. You can use that and your small size to your advantage."

When Lilith rounded the corner and saw them in the yard, Ayesha was grinning, and Cairo wiped sweat from his brow. When the girl saw her mother, her smile faded, especially when Lilith beckoned. She lowered her scimitars, breath fogging out in the cool evening air.

"You should get cleaned up for dinner, Ayesha."

The girl sighed dramatically. "Yes, Mother."

Sheathing her scimitars, she strode back inside, leaving Lilith with her cousin as he lifted his shirt to wipe his sweat-slick face with it. She folded her arms across her chest. Whilst she appreciated Jacen's training, the last thing she wanted was for Ayesha to be forged into a child soldier, especially with the burden of a monarchy hanging over her head.

"She's young, Cairo. You forget how young."

"She's thirteen." Cairo's brow furrowed. "She's barely a child anymore.

She's seen things others her age have not. If you coddle her, you'll only frustrate her. She wants to be useful. She wants to be a warrior, like Jacen."

"But she's not Jacen!" Lilith exclaimed, her frustration boiling over. "I won't have her become some weapon to be utilised…"

"What are you talking about?" Cairo sheathed his own scimitar, cocking his head to the side. "Cobryn is dead, Lilith. I know he tried to shape his children into an image of what he wanted them to be, but this is what *Ayesha* wants."

Lilith took a deep breath, trying to expel her baseless worries. Cairo was right; she was being far too protective of Ayesha. The girl had pleaded for Jacen to teach her how to fight, and it was with Lilith's approval that he had. She was no reluctant child soldier, but a strong-willed girl who knew what she wanted, everyone else be damned.

"Relda wants us to meet. We're discussing the recent developments in Genera and what we're planning next."

"Ah, politics." Cairo smiled wryly. "How exciting."

Lilith gave him a sharp look. "It's important, Cairo."

"I'm aware." Cairo held up his hands defensively. He had been more involved of late, perhaps realising that as his mother was getting older, his time on the throne had appeared on the horizon. Samara was no weak old woman, but age crept up on all of them like a weed sooner or later.

Cairo followed Lilith through the corridors to the meeting room, where Ishtar, Relda, Khaled, and Samara were already waiting. He didn't bother excusing himself to change, realising the urgency in Lilith's tone and that his sweat-riddled attire would have to be acceptable for the meeting. By contrast, Lilith was dressed as impeccably as ever, sweeping into the meeting room and holding the door open for her cousin to follow.

"Good of you to join us, Cairo." Relda's voice was dry, and her eyes flickered with amusement as she took in the prince's dishevelled state. "You've been spending a lot of time in the training yard."

"I'm rusty." Cairo practically threw himself into a seat, leaning back and blowing out a relieved groan as he stretched out his limbs.

"We need to talk about the Generan throne." Khaled's voice was low and without a hint of humour or lightness. "Jacen has gone to the Generan Islands in search of allies, but we cannot base our plan on his success. Neither can we be certain he will survive the voyage."

Lilith's stomach twisted with dread, and she was glad that Ayesha did not hear such words uttered. The girl was full of steely surety in her brother. The idea that he might not return at all would have devastated her, putting a chink in the hard armour that Ayesha was developing. Lilith folded her hands in her lap, glancing around the table at the others.

"Jacen doesn't want the throne of Genera." Cairo shook his head slowly. "It should be Ayesha."

Lilith's blood ran cold at the thought of her daughter on that throne. She said she would support Ayesha's decision to placate the girl, but her daughter was still a child and ignorant to the burdens of ruling. In a lot of ways, Ayesha was wise for her age, but she didn't need the burden that came with leadership. She didn't need Cobryn's legacy. A child was no monarch, and she shook her head fervently.

"I would die before I let my daughter sit on the Generan throne."

Ishtar arched an eyebrow. "Don't you think that's slightly dramatic?"

"You don't know." Lilith stared reproachfully at them all. "None of you know what it would mean to be a Morrow monarch after an empire falls. Ayesha shouldn't bear the weight of that on her shoulders. She's just turned thirteen."

"What other option do we have?" Cairo threw his arms up, despair and impatience colouring his tone as he glowered at Lilith.

"There is one other option." Relda spoke quietly, but everyone fell silent at her words. "My son, Elyes. He may be a bastard, but he is of royal blood. He could technically sit on the Generan throne."

Elyes was barely a year older than Ayesha, a quiet boy with clever eyes who was quick on his feet. As Relda's son by Ishtar, she was correct in saying that despite his bastard status, he could inherit the Generan throne if Jacen and Ayesha both turned it down. However, as he was not of age, it also meant that Relda would become regent.

"Relda." Cairo clasped his hands in front of him, leaning forward. "Is this about Elyes, or about you?"

She arched an eyebrow. "In what regard?"

"Are you sparing Jacen and Ayesha the Generan throne, or are you making a play for it yourself?"

Chaos erupted at the table. Relda's expression darkened and she bared her teeth, eyes flashing danger as she leaned forward. Cairo's jaw clenched and his eyes narrowed as he stared her down. Ishtar slammed his hand down, making Lilith jump.

"This isn't a power grab, Cairo." His voice was curt. "It's the only logical option. If Jacen won't sit on the throne, and Lilith doesn't want Ayesha on it, Elyes is our last choice."

"Have you asked Elyes if that's what he wants?" Lilith looked between Ishtar and Relda. They were the boy's parents—if anyone knew Elyes's ambitions, it would be them.

"No, but we will consult him." Relda leaned back in her chair, stretching her arms behind her head and interlocking her fingers. "I am a concerned mother too, Lilith. I only want what's best for both Elyes and Genera."

"There is more." Samara looked up from the letter she had been consulting for the duration of the meeting. "We no longer have the luxury of deciding our next move. Deacon Morrow and his army have left Nicodemus. They march for Dalal."

Panic bubbled in Lilith's chest, and for a moment she forgot how to breathe. It had been a year of peace, but the sun had set on that blissful era, and rose over a blood-red dawn. Would it really come to war again? Lilith chastised herself for hoping that with Deacon alive, there could be peace.

"My dearest brother will know by now that we are the reason behind Jacen's survival," Relda admitted, though the wideness of her eyes betrayed the calmness of her tone. "He will take his wrath out on Harith, so we need to be prepared."

Cairo's dark skin paled as though he had seen a ghost, and he lurched out of his chair and marched from the room abruptly. Was it the thought of war that perturbed him? Cairo had been present during the Fall of Elyes, the city after which Relda and Ishtar's son was named. It would not surprise Lilith if the thought of something similar happening perturbed him.

The thought to follow Cairo occurred to Lilith, though no one did. Most likely he would not want to be disturbed, and so any important conversation that happened could be relayed to him when he was not so shaken by the prospect of battle.

"Elyes and Ayesha need to be prepared." Ishtar raked his fingers through his hair. "Deacon will target them above all else. He will want to ensure, with Jacen's survival, that any other potential rivals will be crushed."

The idea of Deacon coming for her daughter made Lilith's skin crawl. She had suffered enough at the hands of the Morrow family. Deacon would not touch Ayesha, not while Lilith still drew breath, no matter the cost. Jacen was the true threat to Deacon now, but he would never discount Ayesha. Deacon's spies had been searching for the girl ever since they had fled Genera.

"Deacon will be sorry he came," Relda promised, getting to her feet and sauntering from the room, leaving Lilith wondering what the woman had planned. Her thoughts were drawn back to her cousin and his visceral reaction.

"Ishtar." Lilith's voice was soft but managed to capture the spymaster's attention. She gnawed at her lip, wondering how best to ask the question on her mind. "Cairo seems disturbed when we talk about war. I remember him being at the Fall of Elyes. Is that why he's so afraid?"

"Fear doesn't even begin to explain it." Ishtar shook his head slowly, and the grimness in his eyes made her certain there was something more to Cairo's reaction, something that even Ishtar could not describe. "The Fall of Elyes was a devastation to our people. It practically handed Harith to Cobryn on a silver platter. There is some part of Cairo that blames himself for how things went that day."

Lilith's brow furrowed. "Why?"

"I suppose because he was one of the leaders, young though he was." Ishtar shrugged his shoulders, brushing off the question as though it was a cobweb on his shoulders. "It's something you need to discuss with him, Lilith. I'm not in Cairo's head."

Lilith had offered prayers to both Jessefer and Sierity, the Harithian gods, during their respective seasons of summer and winter. She was beginning to wonder if she might have to go further for answers. When things went wrong, the treacherous Eislanon, who had attempted to overthrow the other gods, was blamed as the goddess of eternal sin. If Eislanon had been present that night, observing in the aether as Elyes fell, perhaps only she had the answers Lilith sought.

Sleep evaded Lilith, slipping through her fingers like water. Harith was not as cold as Genera in winter, a fact for which she was grateful as she padded barefoot through the corridors, the torching burning low in their metal brackets. The buzz of an arrow whizzing free from a bow as she stepped out into the cool night air made Lilith peer down over the balcony into the training yard.

Apparently, she was not the only one who found difficulty in sleeping. Cairo stood with a bow in his hands as he faced down the row of targets, his dark skin bathed in the warm glow of torchlight. Ferocity and shadow danced across his expression as he picked up another arrow and stretched the bow taut. Deciding to join her cousin, Lilith traipsed down the stairs to the buzz of the arrow flying and finding purchase near the centre of the target.

"It's late."

Cairo spun on his heel, the tension leaving his shoulders when he realised it was just her. He strode over to remove the arrows from the target. When he returned to his prior position, Lilith reached out a hand, palm up. Cairo glanced from her to the bow, a silent question. Lilith pressed her lips together in a firm line and nodded.

The bow felt strange in Lilith's hands as she took it from Cairo. She had never been a woman who used weapons, or even one who wanted to. They were not her strength, and she was fine with that. Weapons could not always protect someone. Gretchen's fate had been proof of that.

But when Lilith thought of her thirteen-year-old daughter, a girl with Cobryn's fire blazing in her eyes and an indomitable will, she realised that she wanted to do everything in her power to protect her child. Deacon would certainly not show mercy to Ayesha, and Lilith wanted to be prepared to return the favour.

Cairo handed her an arrow, fixing her grip on the bow. There was an unspoken understanding between the cousins. Cairo did not ask why Lilith suddenly wanted to learn archery, and Lilith did not ask Cairo why he had fled the meeting room with such horror in his eyes.

Lilith was a poor shot, as anticipated. She would fare even worse with knives and especially with a sword, which she lacked the strength to wield. The muscles in her arms burned in protest, but she patiently nocked one arrow after another. The burn reminded her of the way her cheek had flared with heat every time Cobryn had struck her. The burn reminded her why she was doing it.

Gretchen had known archery and swordsmanship. She would have fought in the battle during which Wendell was taken. After that, she had become something else, pushing herself down into the box that Cobryn had placed her in, as though by becoming smaller and smaller, she might cease to exist. She had fought the box at first, trying to struggle her way out, but once she realised she was stuck there, it had been like watching a bright flower wilt away.

Tears stung at the corners of Lilith's eyes, and she lowered the bow to wipe them away, causing concern to slacken Cairo's features.

"Lilith?"

"I just keep thinking about Gretchen." She choked out the words, her heart aching all over again at the thought of how fucking *unfair* it had been. "She didn't deserve that; she didn't deserve to die…"

Cairo caught her in his arms and held her close as she sobbed. She had been too preoccupied with making sure Jacen survived and Ayesha was safe after they'd fled Genera. She had never taken the opportunity to mourn her loss. Gretchen was the one solace she had in Genera, and Deacon had cruelly murdered her in case her unborn child was a son.

"It's all right." Cairo stroked her dark hair back from her face. "You're safe here. You're with us, your family."

"For how long?" Lilith's demand came out a hoarse whisper. "Deacon marches here. He will never stop. He doesn't know how to."

"He will when he's dead." Cairo's voice dropped low into a darkness that Lilith didn't recognise, and she drew back to examine her cousin. There was no sign of fear when Deacon was mentioned, just a deep loathing that burned behind his brown eyes. A shiver raced up her spine, though she could not have said why.

"I'm sorry." Lilith swiped her tears from her cheeks.

"You're allowed to break." The hint of a smile curved Cairo's lips. "We all do, from time to time."

TWENTY-ONE
THE TRAVELLING LORD
THOM DYRE

Thom had never ventured to Basium before, let alone Theron. The city perched on the edge of a glittering lake—or, more precisely, beside a lake that seeped into Theron in channels. Deacon's work, from what he had heard. During the Battle of Theron, the Primordial had flooded the city with water, costing the life of Bellona's father, Kato Lenore. Bellona had adapted the city as a response, using gondolas in the canals as a method of transport.

It was inventive, Thom thought, as he and Odessa were rowed through the canals, gliding gently across the water toward the castle looming over the city. Odessa was fanning herself down, sharp eyes flickering to every nook and crevice throughout Theron. She was an observant woman, who surveyed her surroundings at any given opportunity and took in more than she let on.

A group of people waited by the water's edge, at the foot of a staircase that led up to the castle. There were two women—one small and ginger-haired, the other fair—and a man with brown skin and dark eyes. The ginger-haired woman also had a black-haired child on her hip, who she placed on the ground when the gondola docked. Thom stepped out and helped his mother, the gondola rocking beneath them.

"Lord Dyre." The ginger-haired woman stepped forward. She must have been Bellona Lenore. She was very slight, and despite Thom knowing she was in her early twenties, for some reason she appeared younger than he'd anticipated. The child at her knee peered curiously up at him, and his stomach twisted as he recognised the little boy's violet-blue eyes. It was Zephyr Morrow, Jacen and Carissa's son.

That led Thom to the conclusion that the man must be Cristofer Santana, Bellona's husband, and the woman must be Eirian Faustus, rumoured to be Bellona's lover.

"Lady Lenore." He inclined his head, gesturing to his mother. "My mother, Odessa."

"I believe we have much to discuss." Odessa's eyes flicked between the group, resting on Zephyr. It struck Thom that the little boy was her great-grandson, and she held her arms out, surprising tenderness entering her expression. "May I?"

"Zephyr." Bellona reached down to ruffle the child's hair affectionately. "This is your great-grandmother, Odessa."

Curious, Zephyr stepped forward, and Odessa knelt down with creaking limbs to examine the toddler. A rare smile dawned on her lips. There was a lot of Carissa in the child, Thom noted. So, that was the little boy that Bellona and Sebastian fought tooth and nail over. He was more than just an innocent toddler—because of his Morrow and Darnell blood, Zephyr had claim to both Basium and Genera.

"He is a sweet child." Odessa took Thom's proffered hand to help her back up. "There is much of his mother in him."

"He has his father's temperament." Bellona examined the child as Zephyr nestled against her skirts. "Who, from what I hear, is alive."

Thom's eyes flicked around to see who was listening. Though it was no secret that Jacen Morrow was supposedly not dead, it wouldn't do to discuss such matters in the public eye. Deacon's spies could be anywhere, even there in Theron. The cloudy teal water from the canals glistened under the sun, a reminder of what Deacon was capable of.

"Best discussed in private, Lady Lenore."

When Bellona looked at the water that infiltrated the city, did she remember

153

her father's noble sacrifice? Were the canals, as beautiful as they were dangerous, a constant thorn in her side, a recollection of a time she would rather forget? He dreaded the moment when she would inevitably enquire about Carissa.

All Thom could hope was that Carissa and Jacen were successful in their endeavour and that perhaps, one day, he would welcome his nephew into Gethsemane with open arms and remind him that family could be as warm as a roaring fire in the hearth. Jacen deserved that much. Thom owed Jacen that much. Seeing Zephyr, innocent and curious with a smile that reminded Thom of a young Jacen, made him miss his sister all the more.

Annaliese, if only you could see your grandson.

Bellona had put Zephyr down for a nap when she met with Thom and Odessa in the meeting room. She was not alone—she was flanked by Cristofer and Eirian, who seemed a constant presence around the young noblewoman. After the attempt on her life, Thom could not blame her.

The scent of citrus permeated the room as the candles burned low, and Thom could finally see why the young Lady of Theron was a formidable presence. At first glance, her small stature could fool a stranger into believing she was meek and mild. There was a steel that burned in her green eyes, a determination across her freckled face that made power and control radiate off her slight form.

"So." Bellona gripped the edge of the table, leaning forward to examine the Generan newcomers. "An alliance."

"Well, yes." Odessa's voice was dry. She was seated across the other side of the table, massaging her left knee. "We need Bao."

Cristofer shook his head fervently, leaning against the mantlepiece before the fire. "Bao is impossible. We reached out to them some time ago and didn't get a positive response. They wish to remain neutral, and I feel that they will stay steadfast in that."

"What about when they see Deacon for the monster he is?" Thom pressed, arms folded over his chest as he watched Eirian. The blonde woman moved with the stealth of an assassin, silent as a crypt. "The entire continent wants this man dead. The only reason he isn't is because everyone is afraid of him."

"What of Carissa and Jacen?" Bellona folded her arms over her chest. "We know Jacen is alive, and that Carissa has fled the capital. We just haven't heard anything about either of them since. They are the ones who have the power and the ability to take Deacon down, and they're just...silent."

"Last we heard, the pair were spotted heading west." A secretive smile played about Odessa's lips. "Together."

Bellona and Eirian exchanged a baffled look, and Cristofer glanced sharply over his shoulder.

"West?" Bellona repeated, her brow furrowing. "Not south?"

"They aren't headed for Basium, Lady Lenore. Their destination is the Generan Islands."

All the colour drained from Bellona's face, illuminating her freckles. Like anyone, she had heard the tales of the Island Wars, the brutal Generan civil war that had caused Cobryn Morrow to exile the noble families and install new ones loyal to him.

"They believe they can win over the former Island lords?" Her question was asked with the quiet uncertainty of someone who hardly dared to hope.

"They want to try."

An uneasy silence settled over the room like a fog. Cristofer had turned away from the hearth, and Eirian leaned against the far wall, her arms folded over her chest as she observed everyone in the room. Her quietness was unnerving, though Thom was certain many of his mother's spies possessed a similar demeanour.

"Did you meet Carissa?" Bellona's words trembled with dread, as though she feared the answer either way.

Thom inclined his head. "I did."

"And?"

He chose his next words carefully. "She is...a strong woman."

"She shouldn't have to be," Bellona snapped, ferocity setting her green eyes ablaze. "She should be safe. She should be home in Basium, not gallivanting about Genera."

Thom bit back a retort. Bellona clearly understood the importance of what Carissa and Jacen were doing, and her fierce words were born of hurt and anger. A tear slipped down her cheek before she quickly reached up to wipe it away. The display of emotion was proof to Thom of how deeply Bellona cared for Carissa.

"She will come home." Thom did not know the Lady of Theron well enough to offer comfort, though he'd heard much about her from Carissa. The young queen had not been exaggerating when she spoke of Bellona's unwavering loyalty.

Bellona nodded fervently. "If she can survive Deacon, she can survive anything."

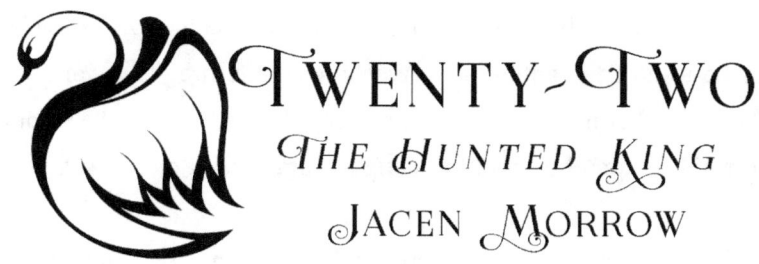

TWENTY-TWO
THE HUNTED KING
JACEN MORROW

The journey to Philemon and Severino had seemed daunting when he had been in Dalal. The idea of pleading with the former Island nobles, the families he had been responsible for exiling, filled Jacen with dread.

With Carissa by his side, it all suddenly seemed possible. His wife invigorated him, her presence a soothing balm. She had a way with words that he lacked. Knowing they shared the same goal was more than a coincidence. It felt as though, for the first time in years, the gods had smiled upon Jacen.

Jacen could not even begin to imagine the horrors that Deacon had vested upon her. He saw the darkness in her eyes when he touched her, the way she flinched at any sudden movements he made. Carissa smiled and tried to disguise the nightmares that lingered in her eyes, but Nicodemus had been hell for her. The idea that Deacon had touched her made Jacen's skin crawl, and he didn't know how she had survived it.

Gethsemane, unfortunately, remained closed to them. They had been turned away from the gates, advised that Lord Dyre and his elderly mother were indisposed. Carissa was insistent that they were not in the city—she had come to know Jacen's maternal uncle well over her months in Nicodemus and was adamant that he would never turn them away.

Jacen and Carissa were forced to travel to the coast by road, instead of the merchant ship they had planned on hiring from Lord Dyre. It was odd, thinking that they were still a married couple, when the divide between them had grown so large and so much had happened in the time they had been apart.

In some ways, it was like no time at all had passed. The way Carissa laughed at the tales he told of his antics with Ayesha over the fire. The warmth in her smile as she linked her fingers through his. Her soft breathing as she slept beside him, Jacen rigid in apprehension, knowing a single touch could wake her with a jolt.

Jacen often took longer to fall asleep than Carissa. She explained that she had barely slept when she had been on her own, but the fact she drifted off with ease showed how much she trusted him, letting her guard down around him. Jacen lay on his back and gazed up at the stars overhead. He remembered doing the same with his mother, Annaliese. Vida had squirmed impatiently beside Jacen as their mother had told them to make a wish if they ever saw a shooting star.

Tonight promised a storm. Thunder rumbled overhead, with flashes of lightning in the distance. Jacen had stretched a tarp over himself and Carissa, badly propped up with the hilt of his sword, but he doubted it would protect them if the heavens opened and the rain began to pour down.

The sound of nearby voices made Jacen tense. When it was clear they were in fact headed toward him, he gently reached down to shake Carissa awake. She lurched upwards, silenced when Jacen pressed a finger to his lips, indicating for her to listen. Their fire had been doused some hours ago, though the embers still smoked gently.

The gentle clip-clop of horseshoes on the trail and the flickering of torches made Jacen certain these were not weary travellers. The glint of their armour caught the firelight, cementing his suspicion they were soldiers. Jacen eased himself up, hand resting on the hilt of his sword. Carissa bit her lip and although he saw no change in her, he wondered if her dark magic was brimming to the surface.

"Reckon old Odessa Dyre finally joined the gods?" one of the men asked, causing laughter from his fellows. "It'd be about time. The woman's near seventy."

"No, there's something else going on in that city." A cold, clipped voice made Jacen's stomach twist as he recognised it. Nikkos Adonis, good friend of Deacon's and Lord of Belvedere. Of course Deacon had Nikkos on the hunt. "Lord Dyre has never been a friend to the King. He's shutting us out on purpose."

When Jacen swivelled to face Carissa, her face was full of dread. Jacen counted twelve men on horseback. Nikkos was certainly taking no risks. Perhaps, if Jacen and Carissa were quiet, they could avoid detection. Unfortunately, the gods were not on their side tonight, and Nikkos turned in his saddle to stare straight at them. His eyes widened like he had seen a ghost, though he recovered his senses and pointed an accusatory finger toward their faces peering out from underneath the tarp.

"It's Jacen and Carissa."

The sound of laughter died suddenly, the men uneasy as if Nikkos was attempting to swindle them. However, when they followed his shocked gaze, they could see what he was looking at. Jacen grabbed Carissa's hand in his, charging over to the horse she'd acquired and giving her a hand up into the saddle. He lurched up behind her, taking the reins and slapping them down hard.

"Go!"

The horse broke into a canter, Carissa wrapping her arms tightly around Jacen's waist to avoid being tossed off. His wife had never been much of a rider—that had always been Vida's forte. In a flight based on desperation, their odds were not good, with two people on one horse whereas their pursuers had an advantage. But that wouldn't stop him trying, not when he knew Carissa would rather die than go back to Nicodemus.

Arrows whizzed overhead, making Jacen bend down low. One of them must have struck the horse, because the creature screamed and buckled. Carissa fell hard to the ground, and Jacen only managed to grip the reins in sweaty hands for another few moments before he too was thrown. He landed on his back, pain searing up his spine.

Triumphant shouts filled the night air, and Jacen could see Nikkos's teeth bared in savage victory as he bore down upon them. He reached for his fallen sword as Nikkos jumped off his horse, only to have a heavy boot come down on his wrist. The boot twisted, making Jacen choke out a cry of pain.

"Your uncle lost his hand to that little bitch." Nikkos's eyes sparkled with glee. "You'll lose yours to me."

As Nikkos reached down to unsheathe his sword, an invisible force knocked him flying. He hit the ground and rolled, coughing as if he'd been kicked in the ribs. Jacen turned his head and sat up to marvel at the force of nature that had thrown Nikkos off him.

Carissa was on her feet, and Jacen could feel the power radiating off her. She stood tall and proud, the storm in the dark sky crackling above them, thunder rumbling ominously as Carissa advanced. A streak of lightning bore down from the sky toward her, and she reached up with both hands. To Jacen's fascinated horror, Carissa absorbed the lightning through her fingertips. In the eerie glow of the lightning, her violet-blue eyes burned with vicious triumph.

That was not a wounded woman. That was a weapon powering up, ready to be fired.

"What the fuck?" Nikkos spluttered, inspecting Carissa with a mixture of confusion and fear. "That's not possible. You're not...you're a blood mage."

"You have no idea what I am." Carissa's voice was dangerously low. Sparks danced at her fingertips as she turned on Nikkos, who scrambled away from her, tripping over his own feet in his haste to escape her wrath. "You have no idea what I can do."

Personally, Jacen was just as baffled as Nikkos. He had never completely understood blood magic, but he had never seen Carissa call lightning down from the damn sky and absorb it unscathed. Before she could unleash it, one of Nikko's soldiers hit her over the head with the pommel of his sword. She crumpled to the ground, the sparks dying from her fingers.

A smirk curved Nikkos's lips as he realised the real threat there had been incapacitated. Although Jacen was on his feet with his sword in his hand, he was outnumbered. Without Carissa, he stood no chance against Nikkos and his men.

"You lose, Jacen." Nikkos grinned. "You and Carissa will be coming with me."

"To Nicodemus?" Jacen's stomach twisted.

"To Belvedere," Nikkos confirmed. "Nice and close, so there's no chance of either of you running away in the meantime."

Jacen lifted his chin, eyes narrowed. "Are you going to execute us there?"

"We'll see what Deacon decides." Nikko's eyes glittered. "I'm going to send a letter. I'm sure he will greatly appreciate the invitation to my city, once he knows what I'm keeping there."

Twenty-Three
The Citykiller Queen
Carissa Darnell

Carissa woke to the cold darkness of a cell. Her joints ached as she sat up. Somewhere, there was a consistent dripping sound. As her eyes adjusted to the dim lighting of her cell, Carissa processed what had happened even as she tried to identify her surroundings. It wasn't Nicodemus, of that she was certain. The pungent odour of mould and mildew was thick on the stale air.

She cast around the prison for Jacen but could neither see nor hear him. The idea that they'd been separated made panic seize hold of Carissa, pulling a tight knot in her stomach and riddling her shoulders with iron-heavy tension.

She couldn't explain what had happened with the lightning. There had been instances in the past where Carissa had felt a connection with nature—when the leaves had swirled around her as she'd argued with Jacen during the tour of Basium, for one.

Carissa had read many books on blood magic, both in Basium and whatever she could get her hands on during her time in Nicodemus. The books had talked about her absorbing the power of another along with their blood...but what about when she hadn't shed any blood at all? What about when it was her own blood, coursing through her veins? She had heard it was telekinesis, but perhaps she had been wrong.

The only person who could tell her the truth had died long before she was born. Had Jameson Burnett experienced the pure power that Carissa had, unleashing the force of a storm against his enemies? Blood magic was uncommon, and as such, so was the material Carissa had access to. She could still feel the way the lightning crackled as it met her fingers. It coursed beneath her skin, hot and fast, begging to be set free.

Nikkos descended into the dark dungeons with a nasty gleam in his eyes. He had been at court several times during Deacon's reign. Carissa saw him as a feral dog on a leash, one Deacon released to do his bidding whenever necessary. He approached Carissa's cell, and she stepped back from the bars.

"You, my dear, will go back on the Obscurate. I've got enough of a supply to keep you contained."

Danger danced in Carissa's smile. "Are you certain of that?"

Nikkos's smug smile faded for only a moment, terror flaring in his eyes. He regained his composure in an instant, but it was enough. Carissa had seen his fear. Magic and lightning mingled in her blood, crackling through her body like a storm. She needed to let it out, an itch begging to be scratched.

"Where is Jacen?" Carissa demanded, her voice trembling over the words.

"I imagine they're preparing him for execution as we speak." Nikkos's tone was dismissive, but the panic that quickened Carissa's heartbeat intensified into a cold terror, a thousand shards of ice sliding beneath her skin. "Deacon has no interest in his nephew drawing breath, and I will be remembered as the man who *actually* killed Jacen Morrow."

Carissa's breath caught in her throat, a sick dizziness causing her head to spin. She would not lose Jacen, not again. She barely survived believing that he was dead, and knowing that Nikkos intended to make that real…

She stepped forward, fingers curling around the bars, cold grime coating her hands as she stared at Nikkos. Fear, she had learned over the years, was not weakness. People committed as many horrors out of fear as they did for love. Carissa had both, a lethal combination that swirled in her veins, mixing with the deep, cold rage that she always buried deep.

"I am going to rip you apart."

"You weren't so confident only a few months ago." Nikko's smile widened again. "When you were in Nicodemus, you were like a ghost. A shell of the woman you were. I thought he had broken you."

Part of her wanted to scream until her throat burned raw. Her entire body trembled. She didn't want to remember what had happened. How Deacon had never taken what she had not given. That she had let Deacon have pieces of her in exchange for more freedoms, a trickle more power in his court. Carissa shook her head vehemently, but Nikkos ignored her.

"I remember." The words were soft and ominous, and they made Carissa's skin crawl with revulsion. Bile rose in her stomach at the memories of dark rooms and the way she had kissed Deacon when she wanted to get her way. "I remember what he did to you in that castle, Carissa. But only when you wanted to. I think sometimes you even enjoyed—"

Half a decade's worth of fury and pain emanated from Carissa in a raw scream. It wasn't the sound of distress. It was a battle cry. The lightning ripped forth from her, sparking across the dungeon as she reached out a hand and in one quick *snap*, broke Nikkos's neck.

It wasn't enough. It would never be enough. Blasting the doors of her cell off its hinges, Carissa marched up the staircase. She barely acknowledged her enemy's corpse as she passed it by, lightning flashing around her.

As Carissa swept out of the castle and took in Belvedere, she realised what Jacen had been saying before. It was a war zone. Dozens of catapults. Other siege engines she recognised from the Conquest. Thick black smoke rising above the city. Nikkos was turning it into a battleground, and Carissa would be damned if she would let another fucking war take anything else from her.

If Nikkos intended to execute Jacen, he would want to make it public. He would want the world to see. With that in mind and her heart thundering in her chest, Carissa marched down the unfamiliar streets, strangely empty. Then she saw why: a wooden scaffold erected in the town square, surrounded by siege engines. Belvedere's soldiers gathered eagerly around it, and standing atop it with a noose wrapped loosely around his neck and his head bowed…

"Jacen," she whispered.

The storm crackled beneath her skin, begging to be set free. For so long, she had dulled what she was to make others comfortable, so that she would not be seen as a monster. It had almost cost her everything. Never again. The sight of her husband on those gallows, with death reaching for him yet again with its cruel talons, pushed her over the edge.

Lightning exploded out from Carissa like she was a magical bomb. She felt her surroundings as if they were connected to her, and she reached into her magic to bring it all down. The castle was torn apart stone by stone. The siege engines, the catapults, snapping like twigs from the force of her blood magic.

The scaffold buckled, and Carissa sprinted over and pulled the noose off Jacen. The crackling of the lightning around her illuminated the shock on his face. She pushed him behind her as the scaffold crumbled around them, thrusting her arms upward to hold the splintered wood back with her power. Her heart sang that her husband was safe, that he would live, but it wasn't enough.

When the lightning finally left her and wreaked all the destruction it was able, Carissa delved deeper into the power that had served her so well during the Battle of Emlen. She didn't need to understand her magic. She just needed to control it.

This is what I am, Carissa thought, *this is the only thing I am good at, what I am meant for.* Belvedere crumbled to the ground around her, a city dragged to ruins by one woman's power. She could hear the screams of the people around her, the crash of wood and bricks. She couldn't stop it. Or was it that she didn't want to? The city would become one of Deacon's most pivotal strongholds, and Carissa would not let him have anything else.

Jacen caught her arm. Carissa whirled to face him, and every dark thought in her mind, every instinct to crush and destroy, was wiped from her mind. The man she loved stared at her with bright hazel eyes full of horrified wonder. Her magic collapsed back into her as she stared at the horror she had created, the ruins she had made.

How many people had just died because of what she had done?

"I can't let him have it," Carissa choked out, tears spilling down her cheeks. "I can't let him win. Not even one small victory."

She feared that Jacen would be disgusted by what she had become. Instead, he gathered her into his arms and held her close as she sobbed, pressing her face into the warm fabric of his shirt. When Jacen held her, it felt like being home. Everything in the world was right again with his steadiness. Whatever Carissa had lost, she still had Jacen.

"I'm sorry," she cried. "I'm so sorry."

"You're all right," he promised her. "We're safe now. As long as I live, he will never hurt you again."

"No." Carissa drew back, wiping her eyes. "I proved that point myself when I took his hand. Next time we meet, I'll have the other as well."

A tight, proud smile crossed Jacen's lips before he leaned in to kiss her forehead. Over his shoulder, Carissa surveyed the smoking ruins of the city that had once been Belvedere. Through her dark magic, unleashing the lightning and telekinetically ripping the city apart, she had proved how dangerous she was. As an ally, as an enemy, as a woman, as a Maleficium.

I will rip open anything that tries to separate me from Jacen, she promised herself fiercely. It was not the time to turn herself inside out over guilt. It was the time to prove that she was a furious maelstrom of a woman who would not be used again.

TWENTY-FOUR
THE BLOODIED PRINCE
SEBASTIAN DARNELL

It was in the early hours of the morning, before the sun crested the horizon and heralded a new dawn, that Sebastian's bedroom was invaded. The door slammed open, shrieking on its hinges and making him lurch up. Such abrupt intrusions were a stark reminder of the Conquest, and how his mother had barged into his room and forced him to run. That had been the last time he had ever seen her alive, her slender frame taut with stubborn determination.

Two candles pierced the darkness, twin flames allowing Sebastian to see what was going on. Priestess Juniper stood over his bed with a satisfied smile across her lips and something dark flickering in her eyes. She was flanked by two guards that he recognised as her personal security, and both of them had their hands resting on the hilts of their swords.

"What the fuck?" Sebastian demanded, unintentionally reverting to the uncouth boy of the Emlen streets in his shock. He felt Meliora stir beside him and moved to shield her from sight.

"We will be taking control here, Your Majesty." There was a smugness to Juniper's voice that made his jaw tick.

"You need to explain better than that." There was no warmth to his words, and when he glanced at Meliora, he noted that she was alert but silent.

"Come. Let's speak on the balcony in private." Juniper cast a casual look at the guards. "Check him first. I don't want him armed. Then you may wait outside."

Sebastian was roughly hauled to his feet, and a snarl of indignation forced its way past his lips as Juniper's guards checked him for weapons. Finding nothing, they pushed him after the priestess, who sauntered over to open the doors to the balcony and step outside. Sebastian cast a look back at Meliora, whose expression was alarmed. He held up a single finger.

Juniper craned her head back and let the wind sweep her hair back, an insufferable air of triumph about her that made Sebastian want to punch her in the face. Reining in his temper, his fingers curled over the railing of the balcony.

"What is this about?"

"Did you really think no one saw you that night?" Juniper arched an eyebrow, and Sebastian's blood ran cold as he realised precisely to which night she was referring. "Oh, I was stationed in Emlen. I saw you slip outside the night that Quintin Faustus died, and when I went into his house, I found his corpse. I knew then what you had done. I've known the whole time."

"Then why serve as my advisor?" Sebastian's brow furrowed in confusion. "Why bother for a *year* with this act if you always knew?"

"Because I was biding my time." There was a vicious gleam in Juniper's eyes as she glanced at him. "Who do you think convinced General Orien that it was wise to strike out at Bellona?"

Sebastian swallowed hard. Juniper had been working to actively isolate him from potential allies. She had never believed in him. She had simply wanted to wait until the time was right before she made her move. The idea sickened him, a queasiness swirling in the pit of his stomach as realisation dawned upon him.

"*You* were the one who poisoned Meliora and murdered our child."

Juniper shrugged nonchalantly. "I wasn't about to let a sudden heir disrupt my plans. Did you really think that I wanted you as a king? How could anyone have faith in a murderer monarch? After tonight, I will hold power here, and everyone will believe you took your own life after I confronted you. It wouldn't be difficult to persuade them, considering your wife's recent miscarriage."

Sebastian's eyes flicked down to see the knife glimmering in Juniper's fingers. A smug smile danced about her lips. She wasn't even attempting to disguise her intentions now, because she didn't think there was any chance he could stop her. Unarmed and caught off-guard, perhaps she was right.

A sharp cry of rage caught Sebastian's attention, and Juniper's smile dropped as she turned to see Meliora charging toward her. She raised the knife, but the younger woman was moving too fast, arms outstretched to give Juniper one forceful shove. The speed at which Meliora had hurtled toward her was enough to send Juniper over the railing, a coarse scream resonating through the darkness followed by a sickening crack.

"Meliora." There was urgency in Sebastian's tone as the door handle shifted. Overcoming his shock at his wife's actions, he raced over to the bed. Meliora sprinted over to the bedside table. As Juniper's personal guards entered, Sebastian threw the blankets over them. They floundered in shock, but it was enough.

Meliora tossed Sebastian his dagger, and he stabbed one of the guards in the throat. The other broke free of his fabric trappings, but Sebastian was quicker, dagger plunging into his heart without a moment's hesitation. He was breathing heavily, a sheen of sweat across his forehead as he lowered the bloody dagger. Two dead men on the ground, and sheets which would forever bear the stain of the murders he'd committed.

"You...you killed Juniper." Sebastian swivelled to face Meliora. She lifted her chin and nodded, and despite the tears shimmering in her eyes, there was no regret in her expression.

"I heard what she said about our child and I just...she would have killed you."

Dropping the dagger with a clatter, Sebastian stumbled over to her and wrapped his arms around her tightly. Meliora pressed her face into his shirt, gripping onto him like her life depended on it. Tears burned in Sebastian's eyes as he recognised the gravity of what they had done. To them, it might have been self-defence, but General Orien might very well see it as cold-blooded murder.

Orien's boots clicked against the stone floor as he paced back and forth in the King's bedchamber. Meliora sat on the bed with a pillow hugged to her chest, while Sebastian felt tiredness itching at the corners of his eyes. He wished for nothing more than to go back to sleep. The bodies of Juniper's guards have been disposed of, the bloodied sheets burned and the bedclothes changed. Juniper's body had been recovered from where she had fallen beneath the balcony.

"You knew nothing of this?" Sebastian pressed, exhaustion bleeding into suspicion. If Juniper had plotted to betray him, how did he know that Orien was not a part of that plan? He felt Meliora's warm palm pressing against his shoulder.

"Of course I didn't." Orien's brow furrowed, and he raked his fingers through his thinning hair. "However, your rash reaction means there will be quite a bit of explaining to do."

"What's there to explain?" Sebastian demanded, annoyance prickling up his spine. "Juniper was a traitor to the crown. She wanted to murder—"

"You don't think anyone would question that story?" Orien threw him a sharp look, and Sebastian seethed as he stewed in his own naivety. The general was right. Monarchs committed murder with one hand and waved it away with the other all the time. He wanted to be better than that.

"Perhaps it's time I told the truth." He drew in a ragged breath, though his stomach twisted at the mere memory of what he'd done.

"Sebastian." Meliora's voice was soft, but he brushed her hand off his shoulder.

"No. Enough lies." Sebastian jerked his head up to meet Orien's quizzical expression, steeling himself for what was to come. "Jacen Morrow never killed Quintin Faustus. I know that because I did."

Meliora choked out a gasp. Orien's eyes widened and true astonishment reflected there, making Sebastian certain he was not a part of Juniper's coup attempt. For a few moments, the snap and crackle of the logs in the hearth was the only sound in the room. Orien folded his arms over his chest, the firelight casting shadows over his weary faces and throwing the lines etched across his forehead into sharp relief.

"Are you going to explain *why* you did it? I assume there is an explanation, since I know that the man saved your life when you were but twelve years old."

"Saved me but raised me like a lamb to slaughter!" Sebastian snapped, his temper fracturing like broken glass. He glowered at Orien. "Quintin didn't rescue me out of the kindness of his heart. Only a fool would believe otherwise. He wanted to decide what the future monarch of Basium would be like, and he was more than happy to dispose of any and all competition."

A nerve ticked in Orien's cheek. "I assume you refer to Carissa."

"Carissa, and her son, Zephyr." Sebastian shoved himself up off the bed, hands balling into fists as he awaited the general's judgement. "He would have murdered my sister and an innocent child in cold blood, and so I prevented that from ever happening."

"What if you chose wrong?" Orien asked, voicing a question that Sebastian had long since suppressed in his own mind. "What if Carissa returns to Basium with rage in her heart and feels you usurped a throne that is rightfully hers?"

She is welcome to it. The thoughts felt traitorous even if they were true. The people Sebastian had surrounded himself with wanted him on the throne, not his sister. When it had looked like Carissa may never return to Basium, he had accepted the throne out of a sense of duty. He would not go to war with his sister over a throne he did not even want. He would stand aside and let her have it without quarrel.

"It won't come to that."

Orien's frown deepened. "How do you know…"

"I think Carissa has bigger concerns than a petty squabble between siblings."

Sebastian's temper ebbed and flowed like the tide. "I can guess what she endured in Genera. She wants to be rid of Deacon once and for all. If she returns home, her war will not be with me."

"Very well." Orien did not appear convinced, but knew better than to push Sebastian, especially so soon after the incident with Juniper. "I will leave you both to get some rest."

The general swept from the room, leaving Sebastian alone with his wife. Meliora's expression was grim, and she touched Sebastian's cheeks, her fingers a cool balm against his warm skin.

"I don't know if you should have done that."

"The truth would have come out eventually." Sebastian sighed deeply, flopping back against the pillows. "If I bring Orien into my confidence now, it prevents any future problems occurring where he can claim I didn't trust him."

"You didn't mention the dreams," Meliora pointed out quietly.

"Nor will I." Sebastian's tone was firm. He had disclosed enough. His recurring dreams of the cave were disturbing to him, let alone a man who certainly wouldn't understand. Exhaling deeply, he acknowledged that perhaps it was time to take them seriously. "Meliora, we need to find Tycho Salus."

TWENTY-FIVE
THE PERSISTENT LADY
BELLONA LENORE

Bellona had only been on a ship once. Peregrine tried to coax her, back when they were betrothed, but she adamantly refused. It was only during the Battle of Ardelis that she had first set foot on deck. The idea of travelling across the broad ocean to the country of Bao was unsettling, but she had little choice. With several of Wendell's southern harbours resisting Generan rule, it meant they had a chance of seeking an audience with Stefan Dale upon their return.

Cristofer remained behind in Theron. That time, it was Eirian who accompanied Bellona—and, at Thom's insistence, little Zephyr. The Generan nobleman believed showing the Bao monarchs the innocent young son of Jacen and Carissa might tug at their heartstrings. The monarchs had a child of their own, perhaps fourteen or fifteen, called Miki.

Unlike Bellona, Zephyr was thrilled to be aboard a ship. He ran up and down the deck as fast as his little legs could carry him, eyes wide with wonder as they reflected the gleam of the water. Every now and then, the tumult of the waves would knock him over. It was a good thing the toddler knew how to swim — taught by Cristofer, Bellona laughing as she'd watched the pair of them in the canals that coursed through Theron's streets.

Clouds loomed over the horizon on the first night on the water, and Bellona sought refuge below deck with a churning stomach. As the waves jostled the sides of the ship, making it lurch beneath her feet, she joined Thom for dinner, eagerly listening to his stories about Nicodemus and his interactions with Carissa over salted meats and glasses of mead they gripped tightly every time the ship rocked.

"Do you really think Raiden and Perdana will listen to us?" Bellona asked over her rosemary steak. "I know Dante went to them before, and they would have nothing to do with him or with Basium's fight against Genera."

"A lot has changed since then." Thom leaned back in his seat, clasping his hands. Bellona saw some of Jacen in him—the quiet smiles, the willingness to defend everything he loved no matter the cost. "Wendell is under siege by Cirocco. Harith has turned the tables, and Deacon now bears down upon them. The continent is at war, and Bao can no longer ignore that fact."

"The ships that Deacon launched?" Bellona asked, aware that Deacon had sent his own vessels from a Wendellian harbour.

"They never made port in Mentari." Thom shook his head slowly, mischief streaking across his face and lighting up his eyes. "Blown out of the water. Dante Remington and his lot, if I am to believe rumours."

For a moment, she let herself be lulled by the swell of the sea as they crested another wave. She took a deep sip of her mead. The best way to ensure your drink didn't spill, she had gathered from the sailors, was to partake in it as hastily as possible.

"I need to know about Nicodemus." Bellona knew it was the mead that gave her such courage, though she still braced herself for the horrors her best friend had faced. "I need to know if Carissa was all right."

"No, she wasn't," Thom admitted, causing Bellona's fingers to tighten around her goblet. "But I have rarely met a woman with such a knack for survival. She is one of the smartest, bravest women I know. I'm only sorry that she didn't cut Deacon's throat instead of hacking off his hand."

Bellona smiled humourlessly, taking a sip of her mead. As much as she was viciously thrilled at Carissa's violence, she wished it had never had to happen in the first place. Carissa should be as far away from Deacon Morrow as possible at all times. Outside, she could hear someone playing the fiddle out of tune, and it tugged at her heartstrings as Jacen's easy smile flashed through her mind.

"You have done well with their son." Thom finished his meal, setting down his knife and fork with a clatter. "I have heard that you are not overly fond of children, yet Zephyr worships the ground you walk on."

In a shameful part of her being, Bellona had resented Zephyr in the first few months. He'd cried often, wanting his mother or father. Cristofer and Eirian had been better at soothing the little boy than Bellona. What sort of creature didn't melt at the cries of a baby, she had wondered. Sleep-deprived and grumpy, Bellona made a reluctant caretaker for Zephyr, but as time went on, she gradually accepted the child's presence in her life. She drummed her fingers against the table.

"I could have done better."

"Bellona." Thom's expression was sympathetic, the lines in his brow slackening and his shoulders slumping as he leaned back. "We all wanted to save Carissa. You must understand that. Deacon was paranoid about such a thing, and I never would have thought it possible until she saved herself."

"I'm not angry that no one saved Carissa." Bellona shook her head fervently. She wanted to absolve Thom of blame and the guilt she found lurking in his eyes. "I was at court with her when Deacon was in Marinel. He would have been a difficult man to escape. I'm just angry she was there to begin with."

The ship rolled over another wave, the cutlery tinkling on the table and the mead sloshing in their glasses. Bellona gripped her glass tightly, cold beneath the pads of her fingers, knuckles white. She was not worried about the young woman who was taken to Nicodemus against her will. She worried about what sort of young woman would return to Basium.

Bellona had never been to Mentari, though she had heard tales of its breathtaking beauty. The people of Bao favoured nature over man-made structure, and the palace was a fine example of their ingenuity in combining the two. Throughout the halls and corridors, plants and flowers intertwined with spiralling pillars. The throne room itself was jaw-droppingly stunning.

The glass ceiling allowed the outside weather to peer through. Ivy twined around the circular stone pillars. The thrones were situated upon a dais, a few feet in front of which the floor dipped, water separating the dais from the rest of the room. Pebbled square stepping stones created a path across to the dais, and when Bellona looked down into the water, she could see colourful fish disappearing amongst algae.

Both thrones were occupied, and Bellona steeled herself as she approached. The man with the stern features must have been Raiden, and the woman, his wife Perdana. A lanky youth of perhaps fifteen lingered behind the thrones, curious dark eyes observing everything. Their son Miki, no doubt.

"Lord and Lady Divinity." She curtsied before them, fingers twisting tightly in her dress. It was the same green as her eyes, gold thread criss-crossing across the velvet bodice. "I believe an audience was sought with you about two years ago on this same topic."

"We had our answer then. It has not changed now." Perdana's voice was sweet but firm. "I thank you for coming all this way, Lady Lenore, and you have access to our finest hospitality during your stay."

"Forgive me, Lady Divinity, but it is not the hospitality I want." Bellona straightened up, her stubborn spirit flaring. She had not come all that way to be told 'no' in the first minute of their conversation. "Things were different two years ago. Since you met with Dante Remington, Deacon Morrow now rules instead of his brother—and though he is a very different man, he too will set his sights on Bao."

"We know what Deacon is capable of." It was Raiden who spoke that time, his voice lacking any of the gentleness his wife's possessed. "He can drown cities. Concerning, yes, particularly as an island nation. Nonetheless, when

Deacon sent his ships, we destroyed them. He still needs to cross the water to get to us."

Bellona scowled. "So, you have made the first move of aggression, and expect that he will not eventually declare war?"

"What we do or do not expect is none of your concern." Raiden pushed himself up from his throne, eyes darkening. "You are young and tempestuous. Battle flows through your veins, as it did your late father's."

Steely resolve flashed through Bellona, and she spun around to face Thom. She had been dismissed in the first instance, but perhaps words were not enough. Raiden and Perdana needed something real, something tangible of the war Deacon was waging.

"Bring him in."

Thom hesitated but turned behind him and beckoned. When the door to the throne room opened, Eirian entered with Zephyr holding onto her hand. The little boy's eyes darted nervously around the room, and he hid behind Eirian, suddenly shy. Bellona refrained from smiling—that was something Carissa would have done as a child.

"I take it you know who this boy is." Bellona folded her arms, but continued on as if they did not. Even Miki had stepped out from behind the thrones, tilting his head to the side. "This is Zephyr Morrow. His parents are Jacen Morrow and Carissa Darnell. His father was presumed dead, murdered by Deacon, at which point his mother was forced to become Deacon's wife. Do you need me to tell you what happened to her, or can I leave that part to your imagination?"

Perdana arched an elegant eyebrow. "Forgive me, Lady Lenore, but what does this have to do with anything?"

"Everything." Bellona lifted her chin. Her heart thundered in her chest and at every word, she was aware she might have pushed too far, and yet she persisted. "This boy is in my care, when he should be with his parents, because of what this war has done to us. Because of what *Deacon* has done to us. If you don't want to think about what Deacon's actions might cause you, look to your son. Is this the sort of future you want for him?"

Perdana's gaze flicked to Miki, even as her son tentatively approached little Zephyr, darting easily across the stepping stones. For a moment the toddler was quiet, inspecting the older boy with inquisitive eyes. Then he beamed and held out his arms. Miki laughed and scooped Zephyr up, spinning him in a circle. The toddler shrieked in delight.

"Miki," Perdana chastised, but there was a smile playing about her lips and a softness in her dark eyes.

Bellona's gaze flicked to Thom, noting the sly smile on his face. That was the outcome he had wanted. The ice surrounding the Bethari family was beginning to thaw, and it had indeed been little Zephyr Morrow who had helped melt it. Miki set the toddler down, a flush rising in his cheeks as he inspected his parents.

"He's just so cute, Mother."

"He's a child, not a doll." Perdana rose to her feet, casting a glance over her shoulder at Raiden. There was a silent communication there, the sort of conversation that occurred between the eyes of people who knew each other well enough not to need words. It was the sort of look that Bellona might exchange with either Cristofer or Eirian.

"You should rest." Raiden's gaze locked onto Miki before shifting to their guests. "It has been a long journey, and you must be weary."

Impatience seared through Bellona like wildfire. She opened her mouth to speak, but Thom rested a hand on her arm. Biting back her irritation, Bellona realised that no good would come from speaking with a barbed tongue. Instead, she once more gathered her skirts in her hands and curtsied, dipping her head low to mask the annoyance that must surely linger on her face.

"Of course, Lord Divinity. We will speak with you tomorrow."

Dawn broke over Bao with a stunning array of pastel colours. The sky boasted various hues of pale pink and purple, reflected on the sparkling ocean beyond the port. When Bellona inhaled, the scent of jasmine permeated the room. Turning away from the bay's splendour, she took a deep breath as she tried to untangle the knots in her stomach.

Sleep had not come easily the night before, and she'd found herself tossing and turning. Though she could blame the softness of the pillow or the thinness of the blankets, the truth was concrete: everything hinged on today's meeting, and Bellona feared she did not have the temperament and charm to achieve what they'd set out to do.

Passion, she had aplenty. The fire that burned just beneath the surface of her skin served many purposes, but not when it came to negotiation and possessing a level head.

Tugging a brush through her hair and dressing in one of her plainest gowns, Bellona splashed her face with cold water and headed down to the hall, where she and Thom had been invited for breakfast with the royal family.

The aroma of poached eggs and fresh bacon made Bellona's mouth water, and she eased herself into a seat across from Perdana as Thom entered the hall. A comfortable quiet settled over the table as the sound of crunching and chiming cutlery broke what would otherwise be a silent breakfast. Bellona picked at her fish, a delicacy in Basium that seemed to be a meal staple in Bao.

If Raiden and Perdana refused, it was all for nothing. If she came back empty-handed, what good was she to Carissa? She had neither her father's experience, nor her best friend's effortless grace. All Bellona had was her rage, honed and hardened after years of suffering one loss after another by the Morrow Empire. She wanted to burn Deacon's whole world to the ground, but her fury was not a good enough reason to expect Bao's support.

What would she be, she sometimes wondered, without her anger? What motive would drive her? She could not think past it, for whenever she thought of the Morrows, she could see her father raising his hammer one last time to bring the tunnels down around them. Fresh tears welled in Bellona's eyes, and she quickly blinked them away.

"My husband and I talked well into the night about this matter." Perdana set her knife and fork down. The directness washed over Bellona like a soothing breeze, loosening the muscles that had tightened in her shoulders.

"It isn't an easy decision." Bellona poured herself some jasmine tea, studiously avoided looking at Perdana lest her desperation shine out. "I appreciate you had to consider all aspects of it."

"You lost your father to the Morrows." Raiden dabbed at his mouth with a napkin. "For you, that grief must still be fresh."

Bellona considered lying. She considered plastering a saccharine smile on her lips and offering the sort of pretty lies that would sound like truth coming from someone like Carissa. But she was tired of pushing the pain away, and as the sunlight bathed the dining hall in its golden light, she clenched her fingers around the arms of her chair and allowed herself to feel it.

The tears wouldn't be held back, and they slid down her cheeks, dripping their saltiness onto her lips. It had been over a year, but Bellona had been so focused on moving forward that she hadn't dared to look back. The grief that held her tight was a familiar embrace, but one she had always pushed away. That day, she finally sat with it and let it consume her.

"I want him to pay," Bellona admitted, and when she finally looked up at Raiden, her eyes burned with hatred. "I want Deacon to suffer for everything he's done. To my father, to Basium, to everyone I care about."

"So, is this about vengeance?" Raiden arched an eyebrow. Beside him, there was a pity in Perdana's eyes that pricked at Bellona.

"Perhaps partly, but it's more than that." The anger was setting in again, deep into her bones. "I could spin you a lovely tale of unity and friendship. I could offer you an alliance based on whatever you could dream of. But that wouldn't be *real*. What is real is the threat that Deacon poses, and the fact that no matter what happens in Basium, if he wins, you are next. What is real is that my pain is just an echo of my country's, and my loss is miniscule in comparison to the losses my people have faced."

The silence that followed made Bellona squirm in her seat. She had gone too far, as always. She had allowed her passion to overrule her decorum, in a time when Basium's fate hung in the balance, and her people desperately needed her to succeed. When she looked at Thom, though, there was hope burning bright in his eyes, making Bellona still in her seat.

"So then, this is about preventing further loss?" Perdana asked, her copper earrings tinkling as she tilted her head to the side.

Bellona smiled wryly. "I think everyone at this table knows that Deacon was the one who murdered Cobryn. If he could do that to his own brother, where do you think this ends?"

"When last we spoke with Cobryn Morrow, he talked of unity." Raiden folded his arms over his chest, but his expression was grim. "He talked of marriage between our son and his daughter, Ayesha, when they were old enough. But the discussion reminded me of another girl, barely older than Cobryn's youngest daughter now, who married into the Morrow family as her city burned."

Carissa. Hope flared in Bellona's heart as she realised that the man was talking about her best friend.

"You fear for your son," Bellona remarked.

"I fear for all children in the midst of war." It was Perdana who spoke, a steaming cup of tea halfway to her lips. "I do not want my son placed as a puppet on the throne of Bao as his world burns around him."

"Ten ships, Lady Lenore." Raiden drummed his fingers on the arm of his chair, the sunlight catching his dark hair and making it gleam like spilled oil. "So that children like Miki and Ayesha and Zephyr will grow up free of the war and oppression that has consumed so much of Razmara."

It was more than she could have dreamed of, Bellona's heart still thudding like an impending drum of war. Bao might not want battle, but at least its monarchs realised that remaining indifferent to the struggles of the rest of the continent would not bode well for them.

"Thank you, Lord Divinity." Bellona raised her head, and a genuine smile crossed her lips. "This will not be forgotten."

She had feared that her rage would burn too hot, that it would consume everything she had come to build. In the end, it had been Bellona's rage that had won them over. Her anger and her passion for her country and its people. Perhaps her fury was not misplaced after all; perhaps she was finding a place to put her grief.

That time, when the tears came, they were accompanied by a smile.

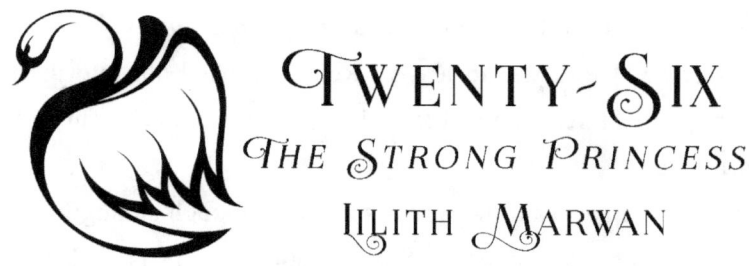

TWENTY-SIX
THE STRONG PRINCESS
LILITH MARWAN

The low peal of the warning bells sounded throughout the city. The Morrow army was on Dalal's doorstep, ready to attack. Those unable to fight fled to safety, the sound of their cries and running footsteps rising above the bells. The streets were thick with panic, people twisting themselves down alleyways and pushing their way through the crowds as they saw the bronze armour and shining steel of Harith's military.

To Lilith's concern, Ayesha could not be found as the battle horns sounded in the distance. The women and children were sent down into the tunnels to evacuate, but there was no sign of her daughter among them. Trepidation seized a hold of her stomach, a cruel and familiar twist she thought she had left behind in Genera once Cobryn had died.

Lilith waited in the training yard with a hammering heart, trusting that Ayesha would come to her. Chaos reigned supreme over Dalal, as it had many years before when Cobryn had claimed victory in Elyes. She could still remember the screams throughout the city, and the hair on her arms raised at the cacophony outside of the palace walls.

Cairo had gone to make sure that Inara was taken safely from the city, and she suspected the same could be said for Relda and Ishtar regarding Elyes.

"Mother." A slim figure strode down the steps, scimitars strapped to her hips. She was accompanied by the silent presence of Elyes Morrow. The jackal helm gleamed ominously as Ayesha Morrow tilted her head to the side and examined

Lilith. Both were garbed in armour, as though they intended to fight.

These are children, Lilith thought despairingly, *not soldiers*.

"Elyes Morrow, I told you to leave." Relda marched out into the yard, a scowl crossing her features. She had to look up at her son, neck craning back as her eyes narrowed.

"I'm fourteen." Elyes said the words simply, as though stating his age was a prerequisite for proof of manhood. "Ayesha wanted to stay as well, so we said we would fight together."

Lilith had seen the pair of them laughing and tumbling around that very same sparring yard. There was no denying that Elyes and Ayesha had become fierce fighters, but they were not soldiers. Lilith would not see Ayesha on the battlefield.

A shiver raced up her spine as she examined the jackal helm. It was a lot bigger on Ayesha than it had ever been on Cobryn, yet there was no denying it somehow suited her.

"We know you talked about Genera," Ayesha continued, nudging Elyes in the ribs. He straightened to attention beside her. "We know you want one of us on the throne there. Probably Elyes. But we aren't going in as innocent children. The Generans will want a blooded king."

Before Lilith could respond, screams ripped through the castle like a chorus of the damned. She glanced at Relda in askance, but the older woman appeared just as confused. Ishtar hurried over to them with a dagger in his hand, Cairo and Khaled accompanying him at just as frantic a pace, a limp in Khaled's step that made Lilith wonder if some injuries from the Fall of Elyes had never fully healed.

"What's going on?" Relda demanded.

"Deacon and an advance force slipped through the city unseen." Ishtar, usually so calm and practical in the face of danger, had the gleam of desperation in his eyes. "They've breached the castle. We have to get the children out of here, now."

Cairo reached Lilith and pressed a bow and quiver into her hands, and she understood immediately how dire their situation was if he was arming her, a woman who had only practised in the training yard on a handful of occasions. She was no archer. She was not a warrior in the slightest.

"Go now." Khaled drew his sword, and there was a sadness to the smile that crossed his lips that made a cold clutch of fear seize Lilith's gut. "I will give you as long as I can."

"Khaled…" It was Relda, her eyes wide with horror as she realised what Lilith already had: that the Wolf did not intend to flee. Khaled had expressed his shame over his role in the final defeat of Harith, and Lilith was not surprised that he was using the opportunity to make amends for that. Dread coiled in the pit of her stomach.

"Do not argue with me." There was a steely note to Khaled's voice, a reminder of exactly who he was to the rebellion. Before Relda could say anything more, a high-pitched whistle pierced the yard, and Khaled staggered back at the arrow embedded in his stomach. Relda screamed and reached for him, but Ishtar grabbed her and dragged her back. Elyes staggered back, eyes wide.

Lilith's head jerked up to see that Deacon and a group of his soldiers stood on one of the terraces above. So, they had infiltrated the castle. She could not see Deacon's face, but she knew that the man was toying with them. Hatred hardened her heart, and a scowl contorted her expression.

"Go." Khaled's single word was a command as the Generan soldiers descended the steps.

Where was there to go? If they took flight, Deacon would certainly chase. Khaled's sword clashed with the first of the soldiers. Lilith would not let his sacrifice be in vain, even if she feared that there was no escape. Relda sobbed and strained against Ishtar's arms. Relda, who had loved Khaled more than her own family.

Deacon moved out of the shadows, the crown that did not belong to him glimmering atop his brown hair. When Lilith looked for the hand that Carissa had cut off, her stomach twisted when she saw something shining in its place.

Deacon's missing hand had been replaced with what appeared to be sapphire. As the fingers on the gemstone hand gripped his sword, nausea rose within her as she realised it was more than just sapphire crudely attached to his arm. It moved like his own hand, as though his limb had grown back as cold, hard gemstone. As he noticed her expression of horror, a satisfied smile crossed his lips.

"Are you here to kill me, Uncle Deacon?" Ayesha asked, a scimitar in each hand, a snarl on her young face as she sank into a fighting stance . "Why don't you fight me, instead of hiding behind your magic like a coward?"

Deacon's eyes flickered with surprise before a mirthless laugh escaped from between his lips. He examined the fierce girl with a sort of twisted pride. As Khaled sank to his knees, sword blocking that of the enemy soldier's, Ayesha moved between her uncle and the rest of her family. A scream was building its way up in Lilith's throat as shock and terror immobilised her.

"You truly are Cobryn's daughter."

Taking advantage of the momentary distraction, Ayesha lunged for him. Deacon staggered back, but she still managed to land a solid stab to his side. Hissing in pain, Deacon's eyes flared with anger as he backhanded Ayesha across the face. The girl went down in a tumble of limbs, and rage coursed through Lilith's veins. No one raised a hand to her child and got away with it, not after everything she'd endured to protect Ayesha.

Lilith hefted up the bow that Cairo had handed her, nocking an arrow as Deacon advanced on Ayesha. As she struggled with the weapon, a wiry figure in a jackal helm moved in front of Ayesha, a long knife in one hand and a flail in the other.

Elyes. Lilith hadn't realised in the chaos of battle that the teenagers had swapped the helm between them. The boy lashed out with the flail, but Deacon ducked, rage glimmering deep within his hazel eyes as he used his shield to bat Elyes aside.

"That helm doesn't belong to you, little boy," Deacon hissed.

Lilith aimed the arrow at Deacon's chest, her fingers trembling. She was by no means a warrior. She never had been. But she would fight to the last if it meant saving Ayesha's life. Adrenaline surged through her veins, a steely determination to protect what she had left. Her daughter eased herself up, wiping blood from her lip and staring at her mother with shock as Lilith let the arrow fly.

Deacon stumbled back as the arrow wedged in his shoulder.

"Stay the fuck away from my daughter," Lilith snarled.

A sneer darkened Deacon's expression. Reaching into the flask at his hip, he drew water from it into the air and iced it over, sending it whizzing like an arrow right through Khaled's head.

Lilith clamped her hands over her mouth as the Wolf collapsed to the ground, instantly dead. Khaled, who had wanted a valiant death to atone for Elyes. Khaled, who had taken multiple arrows and stab wounds and continued fighting to protect the children, to protect the ones he cared about.

Ishtar had seized a hold of both Ayesha and Elyes, dragging the teenagers away from Deacon. Relda's hands were pressed over her mouth, even as her younger brother turned his malevolent attention to her.

"You traitorous bitch." Deacon's voice was cold as the ice he'd used to kill Khaled. "Cobryn should never have let you hold any power here."

He strode toward her, but Cairo pushed her aside, his frame riddled with tension, a rage building in him like nothing Lilith had ever seen. When Cairo screamed in rage and anguish, the earth around them trembled. The stone beneath their feet, the foundations of Dalal, mourned with him.

Lilith realised then the magnitude of what her cousin had been hiding. The Obscurate hadn't been for his anxiety, but to suppress his immense power...a power he clearly feared. Deacon's vicious triumph quickly morphed into panic as he realised he was dealing with someone who had magic to rival his own. He hastily drew more water from his flask, but when Deacon brought down ice, Cairo raised stone to meet it.

Lilith was filled with dread. She had seen other Anointed battle Deacon, and it had never gone well for them. But her cousin was something else. As Cairo drew plants and stone up around him, the training yard consumed by his power, Deacon took a few staggering steps backwards. He was out of his depth. Cairo might not be as practised, but he was more powerful. The idea that a mage was more powerful than Deacon—that a mage could *beat* Deacon—made Lilith swell with hope.

Deacon staggered backwards, shock flaring in his hazel eyes. It was immediately followed by a terrible sort of understanding, a wicked smile gracing his lips even as he stared down his opponent. Deacon was the sort of man who delighted in finding opponents who could match him, part of why he had become so obsessed with Carissa.

Deacon drew up an ice shield around himself, broken moments later by the stone that Cairo threw against it. Step by step, Genera's most powerful mage was being driven back.

"Retreat," Deacon barked, and Lilith's heart pulsed with vicious glee at the knowledge of how bitter that word must taste on his tongue, after he had lost Basium only a year ago. The all-powerful Morrow Empire was crumbling piece by piece.

Genera's usurper fled to the steps, all attempts to battle Cairo's magic gone. Perhaps his sapphire hand was a reminder of what pride could do to him. Lilith reached out for Ayesha, draping a weary arm around her daughter's shoulders as the Morrow army filtered out of the palace. Their surroundings had been warped and buckled by Cairo's magic, and he stared down at his hands as if he hardly dared believe what he'd done.

"The yard…" His voice cracked as he observed the damage.

"It can be rebuilt." Lilith took his hand in hers, squeezing with fierce assurance. "But you saved thousands of lives today by using your power."

Cairo snatched his hand away as though her touch burned, and Lilith stung with his rejection. Her cousin wouldn't look at her, wouldn't look at anything but Khaled's corpse. Relda approached and looked down at the man who had once led Harith's rebellion. Her lips pressed together in a thin line, and she glanced at Lilith.

"We need a new Wolf."

Lilith's brow creased. "Rebellion is open warfare at this point. Besides, you're the Fox. Aren't you in charge now?"

"I think we need someone else in charge, another Wolf." Relda spoke as though she were ruminating, but a glimmer in her eyes told Lilith she'd already made her choice. "Someone who knows Deacon, who knows Genera, and what war really costs."

Lilith's blood turned to ice as she realised what Relda's meaningful look meant, and a shiver coursed up her spine.

"We need you, Lilith. Khaled would have been honoured to have you become the Wolf."

For so many years, Lilith had stayed in the shadows, biding her time and acting cautiously. That time was over, as Deacon had proved when he had attempted to take Dalal. Lilith was no longer the woman who worked from the shadows.

Dalal was a city of grim quiet. The chimes tinkled to mourn Khaled's death. There were dark circles beneath Cairo's eyes as he sat at the meeting table with his hands clasped. Relda and Ishtar were silent, all eyes upon the powerful Anointed. It was apparent that Cairo had been hiding a lot from them, and it was time for answers.

"I need the truth," Lilith insisted from where she sat across from her cousin.

"About you. About what you can do."

"When Elyes fell…" Cairo drew in a shuddering breath, and alarm coursed through Lilith as she understood what he was trying to say. They always suspected magical involvement, but from the Morrows' side, never their own. Cairo would have been in his late teens at the time, and if he had lost control of his magic…

"The first city-killer," she breathed. The one that Jameela refused to name. After the brutal decimation of Belvedere, Jameela had confirmed suspicions that Carissa was, in fact, the third city-killer.

Cairo jerked his chin in an affirmative nod. "That's why I wanted to go on the Obscurate. I lost control. I lost us Elyes, I lost us Harith. I didn't want to be responsible for any more. So, I carried the weight of Harith's shame."

"Did your mother know?" Relda asked.

Cairo nodded again. "One of the handful who did. She agreed to protect my secret."

"You thought we would blame you," Lilith said softly, and the guilt that shone deep in her cousin's eyes was answer enough, her heart breaking for the weight of the burden he'd borne in silence. "Oh, Cairo."

"It's more important than just Harith." Ishtar leaned forward across the table, a thin gash along his cheek from loose stone caused by Cairo's destruction of the training yard. He had brought Jacen back from the brink of death, yet was incapable of healing any wounds on himself, even an insignificant scratch. "We finally have someone powerful enough to destroy Deacon Morrow."

"What about Carissa?" Lilith asked, brow furrowing.

"She has lost to him at every turn." Ishtar sucked in a deep breath. "She is powerful, but her destruction of Belvedere doesn't prove her ability to defeat the enemy. You *saw* Cairo in arcane combat with Deacon. Carissa is not strong enough to bring Deacon down."

Privately, Lilith disagreed. All the battles Carissa had faced Deacon in had been to his advantage. Besides, the girl had defeated him during the Battle of

Emlen. She had cut off his hand and fled Nicodemus. Deacon never suffered such a defeat, not even during his fight with Cairo.

"I think we should give Carissa more credit."

Ishtar's expression was sympathetic. "Lilith, I know you were in a similar situation, and for a longer time frame…"

"This isn't just about her time in Nicodemus." Lilith crossed her arms over her chest, irritation prickling under her skin at not being listened to. "You base Cairo's ability to destroy Deacon off one battle. Has Carissa not fought countless times against him?"

"Yes, but…"

She held up her hand. "No, let me finish. One victory doesn't qualify Cairo as Deacon's downfall, just as one defeat doesn't disqualify Carissa."

They wanted a saviour, and they saw that in Cairo. Yet her cousin looked upon his power with fear and shame. He had only displayed it in their darkest hour, to save his family from Deacon's wrath. If Cairo fought Deacon again, there was no telling whether his torment, riddling him from the inside out, would tear him apart. He was a wild card, something they had not counted on, but he was not their saviour.

Neither was Carissa. She had ripped a city apart for the man she loved. There was no denying her ability. Yet where Cairo fought demons, Carissa fought darkness. Lilith understood the cold rage of a woman abused, yet Carissa's deep fury had a magic behind it that Lilith could never fathom. How far would she go to avenge her family? How low could she fall to stop Deacon?

Saviours were a myth, created by those with hope and naivety flowing through their veins. Lilith had hope, but it was an angry thing, like an animal hissing as it was rattled around in a cage. She hoped for victory, not miracles.

"*We* are what can save Harith." Lilith gestured around the table, watching as Cairo slowly removed his face from his hands. "All of us. We all have shattered dreams and crushed hopes, but there is a magic stronger than anything Cairo or

Carissa wield."

"What magic?" Relda asked, curiosity sparkling within her eyes. She had found a life there, Lilith realised. Where she had simply existed in Genera, she thrived in Harith. She would not let Deacon take that away from her.

Lilith's gaze cast around the meeting room. Deacon had come expecting triumph, and he had found defeat once more. It had been not only because of Cairo, but because of their strength. Because of Khaled, who stood tall in the face of death. Because of Elyes and Ayesha, reckless teenagers full of rage who dared fight a man with power as strong as the gods.

When Lilith smiled, tears pricked at her eyes, half-grief and half-elation.

"Unity. Our magic lies in our ability to hold together, even when the world threatens to tear us apart."

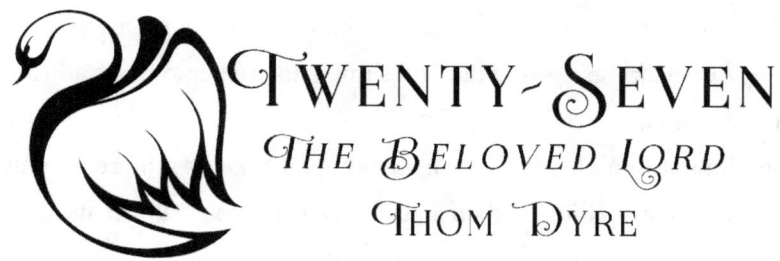

TWENTY-SEVEN
THE BELOVED LORD
THOM DYRE

Gossip in Mentari left Thom with a growing sense of dread as they prepared to set sail for Basium. The harbour was filled with the cries of gulls and the cacophony of sailors shouting to each other, overset by the ocean lapping against the wooden hulls of ships. Zephyr was, as usual, thrilled by his surroundings. Bellona must have seen the grimness about Thom's face when he approached her, because her wide smile dropped immediately.

"What is it?"

"News from Wendell." He raked a hand through his thinning hair. "Some of the Ciroccan lords have betrayed their rulers. The southern harbours were under Ciroccan control, but now…"

"They're back under the control of Deacon." Bellona bit her lip, heaving a sigh. "Fuck. Just what we need."

Cristofer had been betrayed once more. The Merciless Ones had once been mercenaries employed by Cristofer, only to take a higher offer from Deacon. Bellona's husband must be seething back in Theron, knowing he had been turned on once again.

"We need more than the southern harbours." Thom's gaze bored into hers. "We need Wendell itself."

"How do you propose we do that?" Eirian approached, arching an eyebrow. "Storm there from the harbours with our crew?"

"No; we have allies that can help us." Thom grinned. "Harith."

Bellona and Eirian exchanged an uneasy look. Harith had recently been attacked by Deacon's army—however, according to rumour, Deacon had faced an unlikely adversary in Cairo, who had shown his true colours as a Primordial. An earth elemental, no less.

Thom did not think he was a man suited to a life of adventure, of patrolling the seas and rousing allies to their cause. He had grown up in the library of Gethsemane, and the thought of adventure, of war, did not excite him as it did other men. He just wished to be left alone with his books. Unfortunately, for that to occur, evil men like Deacon needed to be put in their place.

"I heard about Deacon's hand." Eirian's tone was quiet even for her, trembling with dread.

Thom had also heard these rumours. Deacon had lost a hand to Carissa; however, when he had marched upon Dalal, he had come with a glittering sapphire hand. A hand made completely of gemstone. It was enough to unnerve anyone, particularly as the hand had functioned as an extension of his arm as certainly as if it had been his own flesh and blood. It reminded Thom of the woman he and Carissa had seen in the clinic.

"He isn't invincible," Thom reminded her gently. It may seem that way, especially to know Deacon could return with great and terrible vengeance, but he was not unscathed. Carissa had left her mark on him, just as he undoubtedly had on her.

"Any word on Carissa?" Bellona persisted. She was always eager for news of her best friend, frustrated when Thom could not provide that.

"She was last seen in Belvedere, with Jacen." Thom paused. "She destroyed the city."

The stunned silence between Bellona and Eirian was made grimmer by the morning fog that was yet to lift from the harbour. The colour drained from Bellona's face, green eyes wide with horror.

"What?" The word was barely above a whisper.

"The city was being used for military experimentation." Thom kept his tone level, hoping that relaying pure facts might help. "It's doubtful there were any civilians there. But the sort of magic that Carissa used…"

"What about it?" There was a sharp, defensive edge to Bellona's voice now. She was a woman who had supported the Queen relentlessly, and who was coming to the terrible realisation that perhaps she did not know Carissa as well as she'd thought.

"Carissa has blood magic." Thom clasped his hands, watching Zephyr peer into the murky water. "The reports from the survivors of Belvedere say this was something else. It was like she unleashed the power of a storm. The sky was alive with lightning, and it came from within her."

Bellona exchanged a troubled look with Eirian. "Then she must have spilled the blood of a mage with that power."

"Lady Lenore, there were no Primordials in Belvedere that night. Only the Queen."

Bellona shook her head vigorously, but no words followed. She was a woman of passion and fiery remarks, but her shock at what Carissa had done rendered her speechless. Thom could not blame her. He had never seen the Queen's magic, bound as she was by Obscurate during her time in Nicodemus, but it did not sound like blood magic. It was something stronger, a power none of them realised Carissa possessed.

"What about Lord Nikkos?" Eirian arched an eyebrow. "He's the one who rules Belvedere, no?"

"Nikkos is dead." Thom folded his arms over his chest, movement through the fog catching his attention as the promised ten ships slithered into the harbour. Was the fog a supernatural thing as well? "He took Carissa and Jacen into captivity, and after that…well, you know the rest."

The group lapsed into silence as the Bao ships, four sloops and six brigantines, made their way into the harbour. They were built sturdy and proud, as one would expect of vessels procured by an island nation who relied on their maritime strength.

When Thom glanced at Bellona, he saw that although the young woman stood proud, tears slipped down her cheeks.

The return journey to Basium should have been a triumph. They had formed an alliance with Bao and were granted ten ships. In every measure, it was a success. Yet after learning what had happened in Belvedere, Bellona had secluded herself in her quarters. Eirian gave excuses of seasickness, something that hadn't been an issue on their journey from Basium.

The afternoon that they spotted land on the horizon, indicating their return to the mainland, Thom slipped into the Lady of Theron's quarters while Eirian was entertaining Zephyr on deck.

Bellona sat cross-legged on her bed, and it was as though her silence and withdrawn demeanour emphasised her small stature, because she had never appeared more tiny. Her ginger hair was swept in a thin braid at the nape of her neck, and she didn't even attempt to rise at Thom's appearance.

"What do you want?" Even her voice was less demanding, instead consumed with weariness.

"To see how you are." Thom sat on the edge of the bed. "You've been out of sorts since I told you about Belvedere, and now I regret doing so."

Bellona scoffed, a derisive twist to her lips. "So, now you think keeping secrets from me would have been better?"

"What is it that troubles you about what happened?" Thom was reminded of her youth. She was not even twenty-three years old, and yet so much responsibility weighed heavy upon her shoulders. "The fact that Carissa killed people?"

"No." Bellona shook her head vehemently, a pinch appearing in her brow. "She's a survivor. She would do anything to make sure that she and Jacen were free. It's not even the fact that she destroyed a whole city, though I know it should be what shocks me most."

"Then it's her unexplained power." Thom did not phrase the words as a question, and the way Bellona pressed her lips together in a firm line made him certain he was right. "I hardly think it's something she deliberately kept from you. You are her best friend, and she trusts you with her life."

"I am not scorned by secrecy," Bellona snapped, pushing herself to her feet at last. "I am worried for her, because this is a power that none of us understand."

A thought had occurred to Thom, something he had mulled over since learning of what had happened in Belvedere. He was not as well-versed in Basiumite history as a native of the country might be, but even he'd heard of the fall of Jameson Burnett. He'd also heard other whispers, pertaining to precisely who the people involved had been.

"Carissa is Burnett's great-granddaughter, isn't she? Miriam Darnell was his daughter, the girl who defeated him at last."

Bellona's chin jerked up. "How did you know that?"

Thom smiled wryly. "My mother has an entire network dedicated to hearing such whispers, Bellona. Secrets are not safe from her."

"That doesn't make Carissa evil."

"I never said it did." Thom was quiet for a moment, feeling out the thick blanket of tension that had settled over them. "There was a fierce storm that swept over Basium the day Jameson Burnett died, did you know that?"

Bellona played with the end of her braid. "I vaguely remember the history books and the songs claiming as much."

"Maybe that storm was not a will of the gods, or even a force of nature."

The meaning of the words was not lost on Bellona, who rubbed her arms as though to fend off a sudden chill. When the young woman spoke again, her voice was cracking with the weight of her emotions.

"She is my best friend, and I am afraid for her. I know so little of what happened to her in Genera. I want to help her, but I can't until I'm with her."

"She has Jacen with her," Thom reminded her gently. "That will have to be enough for now."

"Was there anyone for you in Genera?" Bellona asked, tilting her head to the side curiously.

"No," Thom replied automatically, before realising after a moment with a twisting in his stomach that the word was a lie. Thom did not believe in romance in the traditional sense, and he was not the sort to take either women or men to his bed. But there were some platonic bonds that he had forged in fire, bonds that would last a lifetime.

"No?" Bellona pressed.

"Actually yes, I suppose." Thom breathed out the words he had never admitted to anyone else. "There's a woman there who is one of my dearest friends. She has children of her own, and she is a widow, so her future is uncertain. I know that if I were to marry her and adopt her children as my own, it would solve both our problems: give her a future, give me an heir. She did say we would make a formidable couple."

A soft smile crossed Bellona's lips. "What's her name?"

Thom swallowed the lump that itched in his throat. "Ariadne Pavlos."

"But you don't love her the way Jacen loves Carissa?" Bellona was a woman who understood that there were different kinds of love.

"I love her the way you love Carissa." Thom placed a hand on the young woman's shoulder. "I want to protect her, and I would give her my loyalty. But I do not love her in the romantic sense, no."

Bellona's breath hitched, her green eyes glimmering with tears. "You remind me of…"

"Your father?" Thom smiled ruefully. It was the only person he could think of that would move her so. He had heard tales of the late Kato Lenore, a fearsome warrior who had loved his daughter more than anything, who had given his life to save hers. "I am far from the warrior that he was."

"But you have his warmth." Bellona's smile was brittle, on the edge of breaking. It was in that moment Thom realised how much the young woman must be hurting. She had her husband and her lover, but she had inherited a city suddenly, her best friend was gone, and she was looking after a child who needed his parents.

"He would be so proud of you." Thom rested his hands on her arms, thumbs rubbing soothing circles against her freckled skin. "Look at all you've accomplished. You were the one who managed to convince Bao to aid Basium when no one else could."

Bellona's smile trembled and fell away, and she burst into tears. Thom wrapped his arms around her and held her close, a surge of emotions tumbling through him. He never wanted to be a father, but he promised himself he would be a better uncle to Jacen, and perhaps that care extended to the people his nephew valued.

"We need to redirect the ships." When Bellona drew back, her tear-streaked face bore an expression of determination. "We have our own small fleet now."

"What?" Thom followed as Bellona moved at a brisk pace, seizing her cloak and slipping out of her room onto the deck.

"We sail for Karsten." Her voice resonated across the ship, a booming command that seemed strange coming from a woman so small. When everyone exchanged looks of astonishment, Bellona smiled. "My husband's people have helped us. It's time to return the favour. Karsten is the most major southern harbour in Wendell. If we manage to claim it..."

Thom nodded slowly. They had the advantage of Bao ships, and since everyone knew Deacon was trying to send emissaries to Bao, the Wendellians might believe that the Bao were there to assist them. It was a risky strategy, but Thom admired Bellona's bold idea. They had to strike where they were least expected.

"Bellona, what about Zephyr?" Eirian strode over with the toddler on her hip.

"You'll take the smallest clipper and return to Basium, along with a tight-knit entourage." When Eirian's brow furrowed and she opened her mouth to argue, Bellona reached out to tuck a strand of blonde hair behind her ear tenderly. "I know you want to fight by my side, but keeping Zephyr safe is paramount, and there's no one I trust more."

The sailors leapt around the deck, unfurling sails, the ship steering east to Wendell instead of continuing west to Basium. Eirian pressed her lips to Bellona's in a fierce kiss before drawing back and nodding fervently. She was a woman of practicality, one who understood the role Bellona had assigned to her.

"Be careful."

"I'm coming home." Bellona's green eyes were alight with fervour. "I promise you."

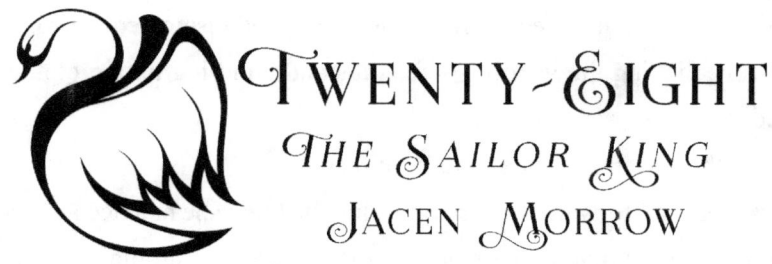

Twenty-Eight
The Sailor King
Jacen Morrow

If they could not enter Gethsemane the standard way, they would enter it by stealth. The most practical way to accomplish such a task was swimming in via one of the canals. Fortunately, both he and Carissa were up to the task. The water was cool with winter's chill as they slipped in, Carissa's teeth chattering.

Gethsemane was riddled with spies, both those of Jacen's grandmother Odessa and those of Deacon. Getting caught by the wrong person would spell trouble for both him and Carissa. Lanterns bobbed along the streets, and Jacen could recognise the Morrow colours even at a distance.

Jacen slipped out of the water, helping Carissa out. She was shivering. Obtaining new clothes would have to be their first priority. Drawing her close, he slipped into the Gethsemane night markets. As the city was renowned for its influx of merchant ships, it also had a dazzling display of wares during the night markets that ran from dusk until the early hours of the morning. Even in the absence of Thom and Odessa, the markets flourished.

Much as he tried, Jacen couldn't draw his mind from the devastation Carissa had wreaked in Belvedere. She had destroyed the entire city, as well as the weapons of war Nikkos had been manufacturing. She had been both breathtakingly beautiful and absolutely terrifying. Jacen swelled with pride at how powerful she had become…and dread at what else she might do if she got that angry again.

As Jacen stopped at a clothing stall to purchase some fresh clothes, he glanced over his shoulder to see that Carissa had paused at a book stall up the street. Whatever she had seen, there was a look of fascinated horror on her face. Quickly flicking the vendor some coins and bundling up the clothes he'd purchased, Jacen crossed over to his wife.

"I don't think we have time for a light read."

Carissa reached forward, fingers caressing the book she had been examining. It was an old black volume, the spine looking ready to crumble, but the faded silver words were legible on the bound leather.

Dark Magic: What It Is and How to Wield It

"This is a Basiumite book," Carissa murmured. "These were the sorts of volumes my grandfather banned during his reign. He didn't want Maleficiums tempted to take on more dark practices."

There was a certain yearning in her expression, and Jacen's hand dove to his pouch.

"You want it."

"I thought I understood my power," Carissa admitted, "but when I summoned down the lightning and used it to destroy Belvedere...I realised that this isn't just moving things with my mind or drawing upon the power of another mage when I spill their blood. Blood magic is something different, and I need to know what I can do."

Jacen purchased the book without a moment's hesitation. If the volume held some sort of answers for Carissa, it was worth it. It must frustrate her, the dark power in her veins that had escalated to a level neither of them comprehended. Carissa hugged the book close to her chest, breathing it in. Jacen handed her the dry clothes.

"Come on, we should change."

The pair managed to find privacy in a bathhouse off the main street, quickly stripping off their wet clothes and changing into the dry ones Jacen had purchased. Jacen gave Carissa space. He knew that she was still recovering psychologically from everything Deacon had done to her, and it was only fair to give her the room to heal.

Once they'd shed their wet clothes, the duo relinquished the safety of the bathhouse to head back out onto the streets. Fortunately, none of the Morrow soldiers could be bothered with them—there was a commotion down near the markets they were occupied with. As Jacen and Carissa slipped past, he stopped dead when he saw the source of the chaos. Praxidike Stefanos shoved one soldier away from him, raising a goblet to his lips as another roughly grabbed his arm.

"Prax," Jacen muttered, a hand on the hilt of his sword. He didn't have the heart to leave his friend, even though it could risk their exposure. He glanced at Carissa, whose violet-blue eyes were sparkling with something fierce.

"We need a ship and a crew to get to the Generan Islands," she reminded him. "Maybe Prax can help us there."

Grinning, Jacen pressed a kiss to Carissa's forehead, keeping his hand on his sword hilt as he waded through the crowd toward his friend. From what he could tell, the soldiers had a problem with Prax's drunk and disorderly behaviour.

"Gentlemen, I think you should release this man." Jacen's voice was firm. "On behalf of Lord Dyre."

One of the soldiers whirled to face him, sneering. "Who do you think you are to tell us…"

He trailed off as he realised who he was speaking to. Jacen was a man who stood out—between his tall and muscular build, his golden hair and hazel eyes, and the scar across his left eye, there could be no mistaking him.

"I'm Jacen Morrow, Lord Dyre's nephew, and you're going to release my friend right now."

Jacen followed up his words with a punch in the face that sent the man stumbling backwards. Prax's eyes were wide with disbelief and wonder. The remaining soldier released Prax and sprinted off. The secret of their presence in Gethsemane was about to be revealed, so their hasty escape was even more vital.

"Where have you been?" Prax examined his friend for a moment before pulling him into a tight embrace. "I've missed you, jackal boy."

"Come on." Carissa hurried over, glancing between the pair of them. "We need to find a ship and get out of here. I don't care how much coin it costs."

A devious glitter entered Prax's dark eyes. "Oh, don't you worry about money. I've got some friends who can help."

Jacen frowned. "You don't even know where we're going yet."

Prax barked out a laugh. "Of course I do! You're going to the Generan Islands to seek out the Farrow and Valadon families."

Jacen forgot for a moment that Prax had been there with him during the Island Wars. Of course Prax had guessed his goal, because he had seen what Jacen had done to those families. He had seen how much they despised the Morrow family.

"I came with you last time, didn't I?" Prax arched an eyebrow. "You're a fool if you think you're heading there without me."

"We could use the help," Carissa admitted, the tense set of her shoulders dropping in relief.

Jacen pinched the bridge of his nose. "Help us find a ship and a crew, get us out of Gethsemane, and you can come with us."

Bells started to toll around the city, making Jacen's stomach lurch. It was a warning, one he understood all too well. The soldiers were hunting them. Catching Carissa's hand in his, the pair ran down the narrow streets after Prax, headed for the docks where the merchant ships bobbed gently in the water.

"Linus!" Prax jumped across onto the deck of a small merchant vessel. The name *Soleless* was scrawled messily on the side of the hull in peeling gold paint. "We need to get going."

"What the fuck?" A gangly auburn-haired man descended from the crow's nest like a spider. His eyes flicked between Jacen and Carissa as they stepped from the docks onto the well-oiled deck of the ship. "Who have brought with you this time?"

"What's all the yelling about?"

A handful of other men and women, perhaps seven in total, crowded around. Their stares were polite but curious.

"Who's this?" Jacen asked, gesturing to the auburn-haired young man. Judging by the way the rest of the crew acted, he must be the captain.

"The captain of the *Soleless*." Prax walked over and slung a friendly around Linus's shoulders. They were close, then.

"I've told you not to talk shit about *Soleless*! She's sensitive." Linus pressed an affectionate kiss to Prax's cheek.

Oh. They were very close. A swell of happiness pulsed through Jacen's chest for his friend. Prax deserved some love in his life, and Jacen hoped that he'd found that in Linus.

"We need to get out of Gethsemane. We need the fleet, Linus."

A long look passed between the two, a lot that went unspoken. Linus pursed his lips, clearly displeased. Jacen didn't know what 'the fleet' entailed, but he was guessing it was more than just *Soleless*. He was confused as to why they needed more ships, though he didn't question Prax's choices. His friend had always come up with brilliant ideas under pressure.

"Lucy, go ahead and rig the *Coward*. Ronald, go get the boys from the tavern. I'm going to need the full five."

"Shit," a fair-haired man Jacen assumed to be Ronald said as he kicked down the gangplank and scurried across, disappearing into the streets.

"I need to know what we're doing here." Linus turned to face Prax, folding his arms over his chest. There was a loud splash as Lucy jumped into the canal. "Who are these two? Where are we going, why are the bells ringing, and just what sort of trouble have you gotten into now?"

"That's a lot of questions." Prax wrung his hands nervously. "We're going to the Generan Islands."

"*What?*" Something flared in Linus's eyes. Was it anger? Panic? It was gone before Jacen could decipher it.

"I'm Jacen Morrow." He stepped forward, drawing Linus's attention. "This is Carissa Darnell. We wouldn't endanger you unless we had no other choice. Prax said that he could help us."

Linus smiled humourlessly. "Prax has a knack for wanting to help whoever he can."

"What's the 'full five?'" Carissa asked, making Linus look at her.

"I've got five merchant ships. *Soleless* is my flagship. Considering the lockdown Deacon's men have on the docks, I need all my ships for an exit strategy."

"What is that strategy?" Her brow furrowed.

"You will see." Linus planted his hands on his hips as Ronald returned. "Is everyone at their stations?"

"Yes, Captain. I told them about needing the full five. They're expecting Incendiary Formation."

Linus's lips twisted bitterly. "Well, they aren't wrong."

Ronald cackled delightedly. Jacen was vaguely unsettled by the Incendiary Formation.

"Where do you need us?" Jacen asked, eager to be of assistance.

"For now, on the deck." Linus's tone was sharp, and it hadn't escaped Jacen's notice that he had been watching with suspicious eyes since he'd learned Jacen's identity. He was just as apprehensive around Linus. How was it that a man of such a young age had managed to acquire *five* merchant ships, all sailing under his command?

The gangplank was pulled up, and the *Soleless* pushed away from the docks. At the mouth of the canals, a line of Morrow vessels lay in wait—a blockade. Jacen was concerned, but Linus didn't seem too perturbed.

Jacen joined Carissa at the rail, watching as the other ships fell into formation. The ship at the front was a small vessel, not a warship—and yet, it sailed right for the blockage. He could just make out the word *Coward*. The ship that Linus had sent Lucy to prepare.

Ronald sighed. "I'm gonna miss that shitty little boat."

"What do you mean?" Alarm coursed through Jacen. "What's happening to it?"

"Keep an eye out." Ronald winked. "You're in for a show."

One of the Morrow ships fired a cannon. It appeared to be a warning shot, though Jacen pulled Carissa down and took cover nonetheless. Linus's smile broadened from where he stood at the helm, hands placed securely on the wheel.

Jacen's eyes flicked to *Coward* as a spark lit up, fire bursting along the deck. There was a splash as someone—Lucy, most likely—dove into the canal. The burning ship was headed right for the Morrow formation. If they did not break ranks, they'd light up like tinder as well. Jacen saw Linus's plan, and begrudgingly admitted how clever it was. Ronald whooped in joy, dissuaded by a stern glare from Linus.

"Ship scuttled, Captain." A dripping Lucy hauled herself back onto the deck. She was a fast swimmer, which was probably why Linus had picked her for the *Coward*.

There were shouts coming up from the Morrow armada as the ships broke formation to avoid the flaming *Coward*. The rest of Linus's fleet sailed through the gap, avoiding the burning ship and the feeble attempts to fire upon them with the cannons. The Morrow ships couldn't see through the smoke, so the cannonballs skittered across the water.

"We did it!" Carissa threw her arms around Jacen's neck, pulling him into a tight embrace. Jacen's heart did a flip at her close proximity. He could see her eyelashes, the flecks of colour in her eyes. Without hesitation, Carissa pressed her lips to his with fierce joy, and Jacen responded with enthusiasm. Perhaps it was just the heat of the moment, or perhaps she meant it, but he enjoyed the moment while it lasted.

Once the smoke and flame had cleared and they were on the open ocean on their way to the islands, Linus requested to speak to Jacen alone in his cabin. Carissa and Prax were both reluctant, but Jacen saw no reason why he shouldn't. It was quite clear Linus had an issue with him, and he wished to resolve that as quickly as possible.

"We've met before." Linus paced back and forth behind the chipped old desk in the cabin, fixing Jacen with a steely look. "Many years ago. During the Island Wars."

Shit. So, he was from Philemon or Severino, and had fought on the opposite side to Jacen. Well, that certainly explained why he didn't like him much.

"At the time, I felt sorry for you. I didn't think you had a choice. Now I'm older and I understand that there's *always* a choice."

Something about him struck Jacen as familiar. "Who are you?"

"My name is Linus." The young man's lips pressed into a firm line. "Linus Farrow."

Jacen swore softly. Linus Farrow was the name of Lord Galen Farrow's eldest grandson. The boy had been a year or two younger than Jacen during the Island Wars, and he had managed to escape into the wild forest of Philemon. He was one of the people whose approval and whose allegiance Jacen had sought to gain. He felt he'd already lost, and he hadn't even set foot on the Generan Islands.

"Then I owe you my true purpose." Jacen raked a hand through his hair. "Carissa and I have come in an attempt to unite against Deacon Morrow."

"Why should I care what king sits on the Generan throne?" Linus sneered, hurt contorting his features. "Do you know why I have these ships? Why I trade in Gethsemane, among other cities? Because that was all you and your father left us with."

Jacen gritted his teeth. "Deacon is…"

"A monster?" Linus laughed mirthlessly. "You all are. The only reason you changed was because you lost your heart to the woman who came here with you."

Annoyance seared through him. "Then what will it take?"

"To convince us to help you?" Linus arched an eyebrow. "Well, I would have nothing less than what we fought for in the first instance. Sovereignty over the Generan Islands. Besides, I'm not the only one you have to convince. Korina is even less forgiving than I am."

Jacen sucked in a breath. Korina Valadon was the oldest child and only daughter of Nestor Valadon. He had participated in the torture and murder of her younger brother. If it was Korina's mercy he had to throw himself at, he was certainly doomed.

"I took you onto this ship, even after I learned who you were, because of Prax. He is the only reason I haven't thrown you overboard. He trusts you. If you ever betray that trust, I will kill you myself. Do we have an understanding?"

Jacen accepted the hand he reached out and shook it firmly. What other choice did he have? His fate lay in the grasp of Linus and Korina. Linus might not have murdered him, but neither had he agreed to lend his support. As for Korina, Jacen feared she might be far more difficult.

TWENTY-NINE
THE SEAFARING QUEEN
CARISSA DARNELL

The revelation that Linus was head of the deposed House Farrow had been as shocking to Carissa as it was to Jacen. Everything hinged upon how their meeting went with Korina Valadon of Severino.

In the hours that had passed since their departure, and since Jacen had gone off to talk to Prax, Carissa had spent her time looking through the volume they'd purchased from the Gethsemane night markets. It was stupid to expect answers, but she needed *something*. Nothing her grandmother Miriam taught her explained how she had suddenly been able to harness lightning and wield it like a weapon.

All the book said so far was that when it came to blood magic, mages could harness the blood of themselves, or others, or the blood of the land. It made little sense to Carissa and so she tossed it aside, frustrated. What the fuck was the 'blood of the land' anyway?

The ship creaked and swayed beneath Carissa's feet, and she found herself restless, staring out the windowpane at the dark expanse of the ocean. Her breath clouded the glass. She spun around as the door opened, but it was just Jacen. He closed it behind him, breathing out a sigh.

"Sorry. We've been assigned the same cabin."

"Oh, that's fine," Carissa assured him, though her heart hammered in her chest. She kept telling herself she had nothing to fear. As she hugged her arms around herself, she found herself grateful for his company, a soothing balm in an otherwise tense environment.

"Are you sure?"

"Jacen." Carissa folded her arms over her chest. "You're so tentative with me. You treat me like I'm broken glass. You saw me in Belvedere. You know well I can look after myself."

There was tenderness in his expression as he reached out to caress her cheek. She closed her eyes and let the tips of his fingers trace her skin. How she had missed his touch, the way his lips felt against hers. His hazel eyes were bright as they bored into her, and she was overwhelmed by emotion, tears welling in her eyes. She had never thought to see Jacen alive again, and there he was, by her side as always.

"I know," Jacen admitted. "You are one of the strongest women I have ever known. I just want to help you, you know that."

Carissa pressed her lips to his, slipping her arms around his neck and closing the distance between them. Jacen responded with enthusiasm, one of his arms sliding around her waist. His hands were cool against her skin, and she relished the feeling of his chest pressed against her. As their kisses grew more passionate, Jacen backed her up against the window, the glass pane cool against her skin.

Jacen's lips were warm as they trailed down the tender skin of her neck, his hands skimming up from her waist to her chest. Carissa tilted her head back. She had almost forgotten what it was like to feel the desire pooling inside her, each of Jacen's kisses like a hot caress, stoking the fire that was building within her.

"Do you want to stop?" Jacen drew back, his voice low and breathless. "You can tell me to stop, and I…"

Carissa pressed a finger to his lips, heart racing in her chest. It wasn't Deacon, with his fingers encircling her wrists and his cold lips on her neck and his weight bearing down heavy upon her. It was Jacen, her husband, who she loved and cherished. His touch was not scalding upon her. His touch was healing, his lips soft as he kissed her with deep passion.

"I don't want to stop. I want you."

Jacen's hands roamed over the curves of her breasts, and she sucked in her breath, seizing the back of his head and tugging him down to kiss her with more ferocity. Carissa tugged his shirt over his head, her fingers tracing over the muscles of his chest. There was a pale scar at the bottom of his ribcage, and she guessed that was where Deacon had stabbed him. There were a thousand questions she wanted to ask, but there was time for them later.

Carissa tugged her skirts up, pulling Jacen close to her as he fumbled with his belt. There was no apprehension, just the giddy excitement of knowing she was with the man she loved. When he slid into her, pressing his face into her neck, Carissa gasped and let her eyes flutter shut, burying her fingers in the silken strands of his blonde hair.

When he made love to her, all the bitter venom seeped out from beneath her skin, replaced by warmth and happiness. It felt like one step closer to healing. She didn't need Jacen to fix her—she could fix herself. But the sensation of bliss with him was like a moment in paradise, and in his arms, she was safe and secure.

As dawn broke over Linus's fleet, Severino appeared on the horizon. Carissa rose from sleep earlier than her husband, heading up to the deck to take in the wild sea breeze and the scent of salt on the wind. A sense of invigoration passed over her, though she could not have said why. Perhaps Korina would not listen to Jacen, but Carissa would ensure the Valadon heir listened to her.

"Your husband is still asleep?" Linus appeared by her side, his question earning a curt nod from Carissa. He sighed, shoulders slumping. "I don't have anything against you, Carissa. I know that you have suffered a great deal at the hands of the Morrows…"

"Let me guess, we are alike." Carissa swivelled to face him, impatience coursing through her. "I know that the Island Wars meant terrible things for your family. I know you have been displaced because of them. But we are not alike,

Linus. I can see past my hatred of a name to the pure soul that's inside Jacen."

His lips tweaked into a mirthless smile. "Bold words, from the woman who loves him."

"I didn't at first." For a few moments, the only sound was the water lapping against *Soleless*'s hull. "I was determined not to. Our marriage was arranged, and I was only fourteen at the time. It wasn't until he returned from the Island Wars that I realised I wasn't married to a monster. Trust me, Linus, I *have* seen monsters."

"I don't doubt that for a moment." His voice was soft as he leaned on the railing beside her. "It's just harder for me to see past your husband's actions than it is for you. I believe he would be a better king than Deacon, but that's not saying much."

"And Korina?" Carissa persisted. "What would she think?"

Linus chuckled. "Korina is the fiercest woman I've ever met. She would like you. Jacen? Probably not so much."

Carissa remembered Jacen talking about Lord Valadon's son, how he had been tortured and killed in an effort to make his father surrender. Of course Korina wouldn't like Jacen.

The town where the Valadon family had taken refuge following the Island Wars was situated at the base of several impressive waterfalls. Carissa had to crane her neck back to see the top of them, and she was overcome by a sense of wonder. She had seen so little of Genera before that it astounded her to explore it more. Jacen was more reserved. He had been there years ago, on a far more unpleasant mission.

Jacen and Carissa let Linus lead the way, let him do the talking. He was familiar with Korina, both of them dispossessed heirs of houses that had fallen to the Morrow Empire. As they entered the dark hall, the scent of pine and fresh rain heavy on the air, Carissa's eyes were drawn to the woman sitting in the chair at the end of the hall like it was a throne. When she stood, Carissa's stomach twisted.

Korina Valadon was the tallest woman Carissa thought she had ever seen. She was physically imposing, only a few inches off Jacen's height. Her indifferent gaze raked over them, and Carissa swallowed, realising she would be far harder to convince than Linus.

"Linus." Her voice was deep and melodic. "What have you brought me today? More wealthy merchants looking for trade?"

"No, Korina." He raked a hand through his auburn hair. "I bring you Jacen Morrow and…"

Before Linus could finish his sentence, Korina was on her feet. Hefting up a spear from beside the hearth, she hurled it at Jacen with a furious strength. Carissa had a mere moment to call on the magic deep in her blood, but it surged forth, and she stopped the spear just in front of Jacen's face.

Surprise contorted Korina's face where before there had been rage. Carissa made a point of telekinetically snapping the spear in two, just to show that she could. She moved in front of Jacen and jutted her chin upwards, ignoring her husband's look of shock and admiration.

"Try something like that again, and it'll be a bone I break."

Korina's laughter rang through the hall, and she clapped her hands. "You must be Carissa Darnell, then. Maleficium. Blood Queen. I've heard what they call you. I must say, I am impressed."

"I'm not here to impress you."

"But you are." Korina folded her arms over her chest. "Linus doesn't have to tell me what you want. I know it's my allegiance. You can't have it."

"You haven't even heard what we have to say," Carissa protested.

Korina scoffed. "I don't need to. What can you promise me? Can you undo my brother's death, Jacen Morrow? My father's? Unless you can, then your words are worth nothing."

"No one can erase the past." A flicker of movement caught Carissa's eyes, and her gaze was drawn to a small child in front of the hearth, who moved forward with curiosity. He was perhaps two or three, and her heart ached as she thought of Zephyr. She wanted to go home to her son, but she had unfinished business first.

"Then you have nothing to offer me." Korina shrugged her shoulders.

"Yes, I do." Carissa took another step forward, batting away Jacen's restraining hand on her shoulder. "A future for your son."

Korina's brow furrowed. "Excuse me?"

"If we do not defeat Deacon, do you really think you will be safe here?" Carissa gestured to their surroundings. "He will stamp out any resistance he can. He knows you've survived the Island Wars, and he will see you as a future threat. If Jacen is on the Generan throne, you won't have to worry about that."

"I won't be on the Generan throne."

Jacen's words startled both Korina and Carissa. Carissa spun to face him, confusion and indignation coursing through her. Why hadn't he said that earlier? Why was she only just finding that out?

"Then who will be?"

"My sister, Ayesha." Jacen sighed heavily. "I don't want the throne, Korina. My sister might only be thirteen, but she is mature beyond her years, and her mother Lilith is one of the wisest people I know. If you can trust anyone to protect your interests, it would be them."

Korina fell silent at that, clearly contemplating as she reached down to stroke her young son's hair. Carissa could tell that they had her attention. She flicked a look at Jacen, the hint of a smile playing about her lips.

"I need assurance that the Generan Islands will remain free from Morrow influence. We wish to be self-governing."

Jacen nodded emphatically. "Done."

"I want the Pyralis family gone." Korina's eyes narrowed. "Our families will take back their rightful lands and titles. What happens to the families that have them now is up to you, but if they ever rise against us, House Morrow will back us in our claim."

"Of course."

Korina's eyes flitted to Linus, who was nodding slowly. It seemed that their words had convinced him as well.

"Very well. The Farrow and Valadon families will aid you in retaking the Generan throne."

THIRTY
THE BROKEN PRINCE
SEBASTIAN DARNELL

Sebastian had received word that Deacon Morrow was not returning to Nicodemus to lick his wounds from the Battle of Dalal—he was instead marching on Emlen. Knowing his father-in-law stood little chance against Deacon on his own, Sebastian amassed the army and marched from Marinel.

It was a perplexing move on Deacon's part. The man was normally more patient and practical, but perhaps that had been cut away along with his sword hand. Deacon had faced defeat in Dalal, and still he marched on, attempting to seize power wherever he sensed an opportunity. It was a dangerous game to play, and it reeked of desperation.

It had been difficult to say goodbye to Meliora, but he did not want her in harm's way, and there was no one he trusted more to oversee things in Marinel. Although things had settled in the capital, Sebastian had increased the guard around his wife to be on the safe side, especially after what had happened with Juniper.

Sebastian had no magical surprises up his sleeve. He did not have Cairo, with his ability to bend the earth to his will. He did not have Carissa, who had summoned lightning from the sky and unleashed it upon Belvedere. Sebastian only had the might of his army, and he prayed to the goddess that it would be enough. Last time Deacon had attacked Emlen, he had lost. That time, there was only Sebastian, and the young King was painfully aware of how few allies he had.

When he reached Emlen, scouts estimated that Deacon was just over a day's march away. Lord Ambrose had already begun preparations for Deacon's attack. He bragged to Sebastian that Emlen's walls had not been breached in many years. There were firsts for everything, Sebastian thought darkly even as he commended his father-in-law for the preparations. Jarl's expression was grim— he and Sebastian shared their dread.

On the eve of battle, Sebastian summoned Jarl, determined to speak to him alone. As he paced the hearth in his room, Jarl's eyes drawn to every movement, he whirled to face his brother-in-law.

"We cannot win this fight."

"We must try," Jarl insisted, with the insufferable pride that Sebastian thought he might have possessed in the past.

"We don't have a fucking advantage!" Sebastian threw up his arms in frustration. "Bellona is in Bao with Lord Dyre. Carissa was last seen in Gethsemane, along with Jacen. Lilith is in Dalal, and she doesn't even know who I am."

"Cirocco is…"

"Facing internal conflict now that some of the lords have turned the tide in Wendell." Sebastian shook his head fervently. "Forget Cirocco. Cristofer has a garrison force in Theron. He will not send aid."

Jarl raked his hair back. "It's worth asking…"

"It's too bloody late!" Sebastian slammed his fist into the stone above the hearth, frustration bleeding from every motion. He had nothing, and a choked sob caught in his throat as he realised he was doomed. Sebastian Darnell, the King who had lost Emlen.

The battle hadn't even begun, but he had seen the Conquest. He knew Deacon was too powerful to defeat without an Imperium or Maleficium of their own to contend with him. All the mages Sebastian had brought had rudimentary skills, nothing like Deacon's power.

"Sebastian." Jarl moved uncertainly to his side. "You have me, no matter the outcome. You know that."

"If we have to abandon the city…" Sebastian choked on the words. It hurt him to utter them. Emlen had been where he had grown up, his home following the Conquest. "I need your assurance you will heed my command."

Jarl paused, anguish burning behind his eyes. "If Emlen is lost, we *have* to fall back."

Deacon's army attacked as dawn broke over Emlen. Sebastian recognised the signs instantly: the screams of civilians fleeing, the clink of armour and the sound of soldiers calling to each other in the halls. He was out of bed in an instant, scrambling to pull on his clothes and armour. He felt ill-prepared, bile rising in his throat and tension coiling in the pit of his stomach.

"Your Majesty." The door opened and General Orien, who had accompanied Sebastian to Emlen with the experience of a seasoned commander, strode in. He walked over and helped the King with his armour before placing the black swan crown upon Sebastian's head. The young man wished for nothing more than to pull it off and cast it from the battlements.

They would not become another Theron, except with blood running through the streets instead of water. Emlen had stood for decades, and it would not fall today. Sebastian had to prove that he didn't require magic to defeat Deacon. Only…what did he have? His determination to see victory was like the last wish of a drowning man who couldn't break the surface.

"What are their numbers?"

"Close to ours, but they also have Deacon." At least Sebastian could trust Orien to be blunt about their odds. Underneath the armour, he was awfully warm, though he supposed that could be due to his trepidation.

"Have the civilians been evacuated?"

"Lady Ambrose is seeing to it as we speak."

Where would they go? If Deacon did manage to take the city, would he pursue them to slay them all out of sheer cruelty? It certainly seemed to fit with the Morrow nature. However, Sebastian also knew that Deacon was acting in desperation.

That was because of his loss at Dalal, a loss that made him both more vulnerable and more dangerous, like a wounded animal attacking out of survival instinct. It would not do to underestimate that instinct, nor to fuel the fire.

"If I fall in battle today…" Sebastian sucked in a deep breath, cold shivers coursing through him as he thought of Meliora. "I need to know that my wife will be safe."

"I cannot promise safety." Orien rested a hand on Sebastian's armoured shoulder. "But I will do whatever is in my power to protect her."

Was there such a thing as protection from a man like Deacon? Carissa had powerful magic, and even she had been reduced to a hollow shell of what she was during her time in Nicodemus.

Emlen had stood when Deacon had attacked the year before. They might have had Carissa, Jacen, and Bellona then, but Sebastian was adamant that the city would not fall simply because of their absence. Lifting his head high with a confidence that he didn't feel, he followed Orien out of the castle and onto the battlefield.

Emlen was chaos. Deacon's army had already breached the city gates, to the alarm of Lord Ambrose. Nonetheless, they fought their battle in the streets, hoping to push the Generans back outside the city walls. Sebastian knew a lost cause when he saw one, but he prayed to the goddess for some sort of advantage against Deacon.

Lord Ambrose was in the thick of the fighting. Though more a politician than a soldier, he was well-trained in the use of a sword, and he was putting that into effect. When he saw Sebastian arrive in the thick of the conflict, he raised his sword up in the sky and began to chant.

"Darnell! Darnell! Darnell!"

Sebastian couldn't help but smile, though he felt it came across as more of a grimace. Lord Ambrose hoped to boost the soldiers' morale at the sight of the King, and the chant was taken up by the other soldiers. Sebastian cast his eyes skyward. Grey clouds had gathered overhead, but thankfully no rainfall yet. They needed to push the Morrow army back before the heavens opened up.

"Push!" Jarl roared to the soldiers at the front, who had a shield wall up to prevent the Morrows gaining more ground. With a groan of effort, the soldiers heeded the command, and Jarl whirled around to the archers on the roof. "Volley!"

He was good at that, Sebastian realised. Command came naturally to Jarl, and the soldiers listened to him. Arrows rained down upon the Morrow army, earning a chorus of screams as some of the Generan soldiers were struck down. Orien nudged forward through the soldiers to grip Jarl's arm.

"Get Presta out here now. If it rains, we're doomed."

Sebastian's heart seemed to skip a beat at the mention of the most powerful Imperium they had among their ranks, an air elemental from Isadore. Jarl's eyes were wide, and he shook his head.

"Presta is our last resort."

"The Morrow army is already inside the gates!" Orien bellowed, anger contorting his features at Jarl's defiance. "Get the woman out here, now."

Jarl glanced at one of the soldiers beside him, jerking his head toward the steps. The man pushed through the throng, vanishing among the crowded mass of soldiers. Sebastian had only met Presta once or twice in passing. He glanced up to the roof when many of the soldiers began cheering, to see a blonde woman descending from the skies like the goddess herself.

"It's Presta!"

The Imperium at least had the sense to be armoured despite her magic. The moment her booted feet touched the cobblestones, Presta landing amidst the sea

221

of shocked Generan warriors, it was like watching a deadly dancer in action. She removed two knives from her belt, slashing at the soldiers closest to her, before pushing with a gust of wind to knock several of them back.

A smile dawned on Sebastian's lips. Perhaps they stood a chance after all. He was yet to sight Deacon amidst the Generans, though he knew well that the usurper would be there, hiding amongst his men. At the distraction, Jarl barked an order for the soldiers to press forward again, slowly but surely pushing Deacon's forces back toward the gate.

Through the shield wall, Sebastian observed as Presta used air currents to push the soldiers aside until she got to her target. Presta's job was simple: do not pay attention to the enemy soldiers, focus on Deacon. The brown-haired man stepped forward with a sneer, hand on the hilt of his sword.

Jarl stepped through a parting in the shield wall, and Sebastian eagerly followed, determined to see Deacon's domination first-hand. Several of the other soldiers moved through the gap, cutting through the Generans in their path.

Presta raised both hands above her head and twisted, fingers curling inward. Deacon choked, clawing at his throat as if to pry off an invisible hand. Presta's blue eyes gleamed with triumph, a savage smile crossing her lips as she drew the air from Deacon's lungs.

Something splattered on Sebastian's arm. He looked down, expecting to see blood, but instead his stomach churned in horror as he realised that it was starting to lightly patter down with rain. The goddess must be looking down at them without pity, for the rain began to fall thicker and faster.

Deacon realised the same thing, his shocked expression at Presta's attack morphing into delight at how the tables had turned. The air elemental cast her face towards the sky, lowering her hands as she saw her advantage had been lost.

"No," Sebastian choked out the single syllable before grabbing Jarl's blood-stained chainmail. "We need to pull back."

Jarl's eyes flicked up toward the sky, before over to Presta and Deacon, his expression contorting in horror. Presta stepped forward with a snarl, and Deacon laughed, saying something that Sebastian couldn't hear as he gathered water to him. As Presta had torn the air from his lungs, he forced the water down into hers. A muffled scream gurgled from her throat as she started to drown on dry land.

"No!" Sebastian charged toward them, sword slicing left and right as he disposed of any enemy soldiers who stood between him and the two Imperium. Presta was still making that horrible gurgling sound, head craned back as she fought against the water slowly consuming her. Deacon's face was alight with vicious glee as the air elemental collapsed, convulsing on the ground.

"Sebastian!" It might have been Jarl's voice, or someone else's, and it was full of panic. Sebastian ignored it, falling to his knees by Presta's side and turning her over, attempting to make her cough up the water. The glassy gleam in her unmoving eyes told him that he was too late.

"Sebastian, is it?" Deacon tilted his head to the side, examining the young King as a cat might a mouse that had foolishly stumbled into its path. "I can see it. You do look so much like your sister."

Sebastian turned on him with a snarl, rising to his feet with his sword in his hand. Presta lay by his boots. She, however, would never rise again. With the rain, they had lost their advantage, and the only magical chance they stood against Deacon.

"I'm certain you will capitulate eventually." A dark smile crossed Deacon's lips. "Your sister did."

White-hot rage flared through Sebastian at the monster speaking so casually about what he had done to Carissa. Realistically, Sebastian knew he didn't stand a chance against Deacon. He knew lashing out against him would only end in pain. But at that moment, he only felt the need to hurt the man as badly as he'd hurt Carissa.

Sebastian's sword sliced through the air toward Deacon, but of course the older man had anticipated the attack and easily blocked it with his own. He kicked Sebastian in the stomach with a booted foot, knocking the wind out of him and making him stumble backward , struggling to catch his breath.

"She should have cut off your head instead," Sebastian snarled, voice hoarse.

"Unfortunately, she missed." Deacon's hazel eyes glittered with sadistic glee. "I will be repaid tenfold for what she took from me. I'll try and ensure you're around to witness it."

Sebastian bared his teeth and aimed his sword at Deacon's heart, but his enemy easily batted aside the blow. Deacon's mocking laughter rang in his ears.

"Pathetic. Even your brother Theodore fought better than this, and in the end, I still took his head."

"Don't you talk about my family!" Sebastian roared. He was rising to the bait, just like Deacon wanted, but all the old wounds of the Conquest, the ones he had thought had healed, were painfully ripped open again.

"Sebastian." Jarl caught him by the arm, tugging him away from his enemy. "It's done. It's over. You told me that I needed to acknowledge when Emlen was lost, and it is. We aren't safe here."

"I'll kill you!" Sebastian screamed at Deacon, struggling even as Jarl hauled him away. "That's a promise!"

Deacon simply smirked, sheathing his swords as he watched the young King being forcibly removed from the battle. Tears blurred Sebastian's vision as he saw Emlen in flames, the streets overrun by Morrow soldiers. The forge where he had patiently worked on various weapons over the years was consumed by the blaze. The courtyard where he had been announced as the true Darnell heir was a mess of violence and gore.

"I'm saving your life, whether you want it or not," Jarl exclaimed, whirling Sebastian around and shaking him hard. "For my father. For my sister."

"I can't…" Sebastian choked out the words, tears blurring his vision as he was reminded of another city in flames, six years ago. "I can't do this again. I can't lose to the Morrows again."

"Look at me." Jarl's expression was fierce, eyes wild. "This isn't the end. We lost Theron once, and it's flourishing now. Please, don't sink into despair. We need you."

Sebastian nodded fervently, but he crumpled against his brother-in-law, sobbing into his shoulder as his body succumbed to the exhaustion of all he had lost.

THIRTY-ONE
THE WARRIOR LADY
BELLONA LENORE

Under the cover of darkness, Bellona's fleet slid across the black sea toward Karsten. The plan was simple: the Bao ships would go first and raise their flags, so the Wendellians believed that Bao had come to assist them. Then Bellona's personal ships would follow, launching their attack with the element of surprise.

Thom stood beside her on the deck with a steaming mug of tea in his hands. He was not a soldier, but though Bellona had insisted he accompany Eirian and Zephyr back to Theron, he wished to remain aboard for the impending battle. Besides, he knew more about Wendell than anyone else, and Bellona appreciated his insight.

"High bells." Thom took a sip of his tea as the high-pitched peal of the city bells rang out across the water. "It means they're expecting allies."

Bellona smirked. Her arms were encased by leather gauntlets, and she had her bow and quiver of arrows at the ready, though she didn't think they'd get in close enough combat for her to utilise them. If all went well, she would leave half of the Bao fleet in Karsten and take the rest back to Basium with her.

Bellona strode over to the railing and leaned against it, the cool night hair whipping her ginger hair back from her face. As she peered over at the Bao fleet, she pressed her fingers to her lips and gave a shrill whistle. Cheers erupted across the deck, and the proud fox of House Lenore rose on the wind, flag waving like a banner. Bellona craned her neck back to look at it, a ferocious smile crossing her lips.

"Low bells," Thom called, having put down his mug of tea. "They've seen the flag."

The bells were certainly deeper that time, an ominous sound that echoed through the harbour, along with the shouts of the Wendellians. Unfortunately, they were too late—the Bao ships had loaded their cannons and unleashed upon the Wendellian vessels in a glory of flame and noise, the deep booms making Bellona grip the railing that much tighter.

She trusted in the Bao ships. She trusted in their victory. With the wind swirling through her hair, she closed her eyes and prayed to the goddess Elethea to make it so. Shouts resonated across the water, and Bellona's posture tensed, rigid like a cat on the prowl as several of the ships in the harbour began to return fire.

"A hasty reaction." Thom shrugged his shoulders, unbothered. "Their ships are docked. They stand little chance. Their numbers are fewer than ours."

His words did not dissuade Bellona's concern, particularly when their ship bobbed back and forth on the water with the force of cannon fire. Striding over to rigging, she hauled herself up to get a better view of what was happening. Two of the Wendellian ships were pulling out of the harbour, while a third was sinking in the shallows, its sails on fire.

Bellona fisted a hand in the rigging as the ship rocked beneath her. She could see triumph on the horizon. The ships were of little concern, and the fortress on Karsten's shore would be easy enough to take.

"*Bellona!*" Thom's panicked shout made her look down at him, before her head jerked up again, eyes flicking to Karsten. One of the fortress cannons had shifted into position to point at their ship, and the entire crew braced themselves as a cannon splintered through the starboard hull.

Despite her strong grip on the rigging, Bellona was thrown off balance, gritting her teeth as her boot caught in the netting. Even now, they would be loading the cannon again. Reaching up and grabbing the knife from her free boot, she started to saw at the rigging, desperate to free herself.

Another of the Wendellian ships went up in flames, the screams of the sailors resonating across the water.

The fortress cannons fired again. The ship shuddered violently, and Bellona was thrown free of the rigging, plunging down into the cold ocean like a stone. For a few moments she fought the current, thrashing against the weight of the water, not knowing up from down. Then she calmed, letting her body float to the surface, gasping in a lungful of smoke-filled air.

Paddling back over to the ship, Bellona grimaced as she hauled herself up. She lost her footing and slipped, but Thom caught her arm and yanked her onto the deck. Shivering and dripping wet, she dragged herself up and clutched at the railing, too absorbed in their progress to think about how she might catch cold.

"The fortress." The words were hoarse and breathless as she cast her gaze to the thick stone and the cannons that lay in wait beyond. "We need the fortress."

The battering ram slammed home against the wooden doors of the fortress, managing to further splinter them. Bellona paced back and forth, her skin salt-kissed and her clothes only just beginning to dry. Their ships might have successfully taken the harbour, but if they didn't get the fortress, they could not declare true victory in Karsten. Bellona had not come that far only to lose, and she gritted her teeth as the soldiers pulled the battering ram back again.

Had this been how Kato had felt at the end of a relentless battle? Weariness crept over Bellona, along with a pain of grief for her deceased father. How she wished he could be there with her through this, could see how much she had achieved. Instead, she had Thom by her side. He was good company if nothing else.

The battering ram banged the doors open, and the small force that had accompanied them ashore roared their approval, surging through the broken doors with the force of a flood. Gripping the javelin that Cristofer had gifted her in one hand and her bow in the others, Bellona nudged her way past the splintered wood to follow them.

"Who is your leader?" A ferocious voice echoed through the fortress, and a brown-haired woman in her early thirties stepped forward with fury and determination burning in her eyes. She was of a similar build to Bellona, though perhaps a few inches taller. Nonetheless, she was taken aback by how much of herself she saw in the fearless woman.

"I am." Bellona moved forward, gesturing for her troops to stand down. The woman stood in front of the uncertain Wendellian soldiers with a dagger in each hand, as though she meant to single-handedly protect them. "Who are you?"

"My name is Adele Voss." The woman sneered, pointing one of her daggers at Bellona. "I am the commander of the military here. You may have defeated our ships, but you are yet to defeat me. I challenge you, girl, to single combat."

"Bellona." Thom's hand came down heavy on her shoulder even as the voices began to rise, murmuring their confusion. "You don't have to do this."

"No." She shrugged him off, handing him her bow and tightening her grip on her javelin. "But I will."

"There is no victory in a fool's death," Thom snapped.

Bellona's green eyes narrowed. "I have stayed content in Theron for long enough. This was a battle I chose to wage, and so my fate will decide its outcome."

Adele's smile was wolfish as Bellona stepped forward, inhaling deeply. Cristofer had taught her how to fight, but Eirian had taught her how to fight dirty. Combined with her speed, her skills would hopefully make her a match for Adele, whose stance indicated she was a seasoned fighter.

A bow was Bellona's weapon of choice, but circling Adele now, she only had the javelin Cristofer had gifted her and the combat training she'd developed over the past years since the Conquest. She sucked in a shaky breath.

Adele moved with the speed of a striking snake, kicking up dust in Bellona's face and making her stumble back, coughing. She barely had time to recover before the older woman was upon her, knives slashing. One of them caught Bellona's bicep, making her hiss in pain. She twirled her javelin and struck hard, but Adele nimbly dodged.

Adele was faster than her. Bellona knew that with absolute certainty, and so did Adele judging by the triumphant gleam in her eyes as she struck again. The knives would eventually slice Bellona to ribbons since she was too slow to fully block them. That time, one of them managed to nick her thigh. Taking advantage of the fresh injury, Adele swept her foot in an arc, kicking Bellona's legs from under her.

Bellona hit the ground hard, head ricocheting off the stone. Her ears rang. Adele stood over her, lips twisted in contempt and her knives at the ready as she stared down at her fallen adversary.

"You are weak. Just like your country. Just like your queen."

It was the vicious barb against Carissa that dug through Bellona's skin and roused the fire within her. A year's worth of rage flooded from her in a rush, and a roar escaped her lips as she gripped her javelin in both hands and launched it forward with all her strength. Adele stumbled back, knives clattering from her fingers, as the javelin impaled her through the torso. A shuddering gasp emerged from her lips, and she coughed up blood.

Bellona staggered to her feet, but Adele snarled, falling upon her in a maelstrom of fury. Despite the javelin impaling her, she grabbed hold of Bellona's throat, fingers tightening and making the younger woman choke. When Adele smiled, she bared crimson-stained teeth.

The world was starting to fade in and out, and Bellona could feel her head growing light, cursing a dying woman for still having such strength. Her fingers caught the javelin and she twisted hard, making Adele scream and let her go. Bellona wrenched away from her, stumbled a few steps back as the older woman fell to her knees, and then onto her side. She convulsed a few moments before falling still.

Footsteps closed in, and someone took Bellona's hand in theirs, raising her arm high. When she came to her senses, she realised that it was Thom. The Basiumite army cheered at her victory, but all Bellona could see was Adele's hateful eyes staring her down even in death.

They had won. So, why did it feel like a hollow victory?

THIRTY-TWO
THE GRIEVING PRINCESS
LILITH MARWAN

The last time Lilith visited Torvald, she was with Gretchen. The memories left a hole in her heart, a yawning ache that was difficult to fill, even if this time she was accompanied by Relda, Cairo, Elyes, and Ayesha. She shrugged her furs more tightly around her shoulders to fight the bitter cold that had set in as winter neared its end.

The welcome they received was as frosty as the weather. Torvald was still under Morrow control, and it was common knowledge that Harith had succeeded in seceding from Deacon's empire. The group were led to the great hall under heavy guard, the silence broken only by the clink of armour from the king's soldiers. King Stefan Dale rose shakily from his throne, thin frame taut with tension.

Lilith remembered Stefan well from her first venture to Torvald. If anything, he had grown thinner, the blue-and-grey woven fabrics of his clothes hanging loose on his form, dark circles under his eyes. The loss of his sister had done damage to him; Lilith hoped it would make Stefan sympathetic to their cause.

"King Stefan." Lilith curtsied deeply.

"I know why you are here." Stefan's wary eyes traced over the group, settling on Elyes and Ayesha. "You have come to convince me to join you in your quest to liberate the countries that the Morrow Empire took. To throw off my shackles."

"The idea doesn't seem to please you," Cairo noted wryly. "We will never bow to Deacon Morrow again."

Cairo had been shaken after the battle, and the revelation of his powers, but there was a new confidence in him that Lilith applauded. Steel glimmered in his dark eyes at the mention of Deacon, a sneer contorting his features.

Stefan's lips curved into the hint of a smile. "Much easier said than done."

"What about your sister?" Relda pressed. Stefan's eyes lit up with recognition upon seeing her. "I saw what my brothers were years ago. Perhaps I was not as open in rebellion as I could have been, but shaking off their oppression has been a decade's worth of work."

"Deacon murdered Gretchen." Lilith's voice quivered with barely controlled anger. "He drowned her, for no other reason than she was pregnant with Cobryn's child. Is that the man whose boots you still wish to kiss? The man who killed your beloved sister?"

Stefan paled, his mouth parting like there was something he wanted to say. Lilith supposed that Deacon hadn't told him as much. She quickly reached up to wipe away the tears that welled in her eyes. Thinking of Gretchen hurt—the fierce woman she had been, the corpse in the river that Lilith had found.

"I didn't know that," he mumbled, before raising his voice. "My stance is the same. The Ciroccan lords loyal to Deacon now have the southern harbours. I cannot fight a war within my own country."

"You're a coward," Ayesha sneered, stepping forward from her place at her mother's side. "Elyes and I fought Deacon ourselves, and we're much younger than you. I was scared, but I did the right thing."

"Ayesha," Lilith hissed in warning, though her daughter was not wrong.

"Is it you they're putting on the throne?" Stefan's voice was mildly amused, though his eyes narrowed in contempt. "You're quite the stubborn little thing."

"Or it could be me." When Lilith turned to face Elyes, he had donned the jackal helm. Stefan looked like he had seen a ghost. Physically, Elyes shared little resemblance with Cobryn, other than the set of his mouth. Nonetheless, seeing that jackal helm again had struck Stefan with the force of a blow.

"Who are you?" he asked, eyes flicking among the others as he tried to determine Elyes's heritage.

"I am Elyes Morrow. Bastard son of Ishtar Haroun and Relda Morrow."

Stefan's laugh was cutting. "They're putting a bastard child on the throne?"

Elyes yanked the helm off, eyes glittering with fury. "Better a bastard than a coward."

The words silenced Stefan's laugh, and Lilith caught the smirk growing on Relda's lips. Lilith had the feeling that as they grew up, both Elyes and Ayesha would be forces to be reckoned with. Both had the Morrow spirit, though perhaps they should be more guarded with their tongues.

"Together, we can defeat Deacon," Cairo said, his expression beseeching as he took a step forward. "Alone, you will fall, Stefan. It's not a fate I want for you or for Wendell. Gretchen deserved better."

"Don't talk about Gretchen!" Stefan snapped, pale eyes flashing with fury and grief. He physically recoiled from Cairo as though slapped. "None of you really knew her, not like I did."

"I knew her after she became Cobryn's wife." Lilith jutted her chin up, stinging at Stefan's false accusation. "A fate you condemned her to."

Stefan flinched. "Something I will regret for the rest of my life. Her death is my punishment from the gods."

"No, it was the action of a cruel man," Lilith corrected, the words acidic on her tongue.

She knew well what it was like to be cautious, to act out of self-preservation rather than true interests. The time for such a stance was gone, and Gretchen's death had been one of the catalysts. Lilith spent years afraid, tiptoeing around the Morrows for fear of incurring their wrath. Yet Stefan would not do the same, not even for his late sister.

"You think me a fool?" Stefan's brow contorted in annoyance, and he folded his arms over his narrow chest. "Were you going to tell me about the southern harbours, or did you believe I wouldn't have found out by now?"

Lilith glanced at Relda and Cairo, both who appeared as surprised as she felt. Stefan's sneer faded as he saw the genuine confusion in their expressions.

"You don't know."

"Are you going to tell us or keep us in suspense?" Relda asked smoothly, though the impatience in her hazel eyes betrayed her feigned disinterest.

"Lady Lenore has taken the southern harbours back for Cirocco. She was accompanied by a small Bao fleet."

Lilith was quick to school her features into a neutral expression. Bao had long shown they were not interested in conflict, but if Stefan's word was true and they had accompanied Bellona in taking the southern harbours, Bao had chosen their side in the conflict. Stefan sank back into his throne.

"Be thankful none of Deacon's troops are stationed here, else you would have received a far colder welcome."

"Is that a threat?" Relda bared her teeth, stepping forward. Cairo rested a hand on her arm to restrain her, but Lilith didn't miss the way Stefan recoiled, as if worried Relda would strike him.

"Deacon must be so disappointed in you." Stefan pushed himself to his feet. "His own sister, a traitor."

"My brother's disappointment is only equalled in measure by your own incompetence," Relda snapped, and Lilith couldn't quite suppress a smirk.

"I would suggest retiring for the evening." Stefan's tone would broach no argument. "You are welcome to stay the night, and one night alone. Next time I see you in my country, I will be forced to take you into custody and present you to Deacon. Pray this is the last time we cross paths."

"I pray that too." Lilith's blood surged with heated frustration at their lack of progress and Stefan's reluctance to accept Deacon's role in Gretchen's death. Perhaps he did not want retribution, but she did not need a craven King to take matters into her own hands.

Deacon had taken enough from her. It was time to start taking back.

Candlelight flickered through the halls of Torvald, caressing the walls and doors in warmth as Lilith strode down the corridor to Stefan's chambers. His guards remained behind her, close and quiet as shadows. The hands pressed to the hilts of their swords did not worry her. If they had intended to restrain her, they would have done so already. Once she received the door, she turned to glance at them, arching an eyebrow.

"If you wish to stop me from seeing King Stefan, now is your chance."

Neither of them spoke, the only sound that of the sharp wind whistling outside, rattling the panes like an angry ghost. The guards exchanged a nervous look, and a furrow creased Lilith's brow.

"You followed me here, yet you make no move to turn me away."

"The Three Fates are displeased." The bearded guard spoke softly, as if the mere mention of Wendell's gods might incite their wrath. "They say there is a ghost that lingers in these halls, my lady. It screams and it weeps and it haunts the King's sleep."

An unpleasant chill coursed up Lilith's spine. "A woman? What does she have to do with me?"

"A woman," the bearded guard confirmed, glancing at the trembling windowpane as the wind howled outside. "We thought…perhaps if you spoke to the King…it may help."

They thought the ghost was Gretchen. They thought Gretchen haunted these halls, hurt and enraged. Perhaps they believed her ghost was punishment, but why would Lilith be an atonement for that? She couldn't quite push down the uneasy churn in the pit of her stomach as she rapped her knuckles against Stefan's door, then nudged the door open and walked in without awaiting invitation.

There was an icy chill in the room, and Lilith rubbed her arms to ward off the sudden cold. Stefan stood in front of the open window, the breeze billowing his thin hair, a mug of mead clutched between his hands as he stared out into the night, its sickly-sweet scent making Lilith wrinkle her nose. When he turned to face Lilith, he blinked slowly, as if her presence was less of an intrusion and more of a curiosity.

"Why did you come to see me?"

Lilith recognised grief. It sang out to her, like the mournful notes of the sad songs Jacen would play on the fiddle. It emanated from Stefan in waves, held in the rigid line of his slim shoulders, his bloodshot eyes, the mead he was using to drown his sorrow. The ghost there was not Gretchen, no matter the guard's superstitions. It was Stefan, the shell of a man terrified to lose his country after he had already lost his sister.

"I know we exchanged harsh words earlier." Lilith picked at a loose thread at the hem of her coat's sleeve. "But I am truly sorry for your loss. More than you can imagine."

"I know what you think of me. What you all think of me." Stefan raised the mug to his lips and took a deep gulp, his gaze turning back to the star-spangled sky. When he looked out into the night, did he see defeat? Did he see the world closing in around him and only the silent, glittering stars for comfort, as Lilith once had?

She inhaled slowly. "Gretchen would have…"

"Don't tell me what my sister would have done!" Stefan snapped, wheeling to face Lilith, his sudden sharpness making her flinch at the memories of raised voices and closed fists. "I was here when Gretchen came into this world, and I watched her fight for life with a cord wrapped around her throat. My sister was strong in ways I never could be. I never thought…it never occurred to me that as I watched her enter the world, I may be alive to watch her leave it."

Gretchen had not been easy to get along with. Despite her jagged edges, she had become one of the people Lilith trusted. A warrior, even when her freedom was stripped from her and she was forced to become Cobryn's wife. A fighter until the bitter end, when she had stared up at Lilith with vacant eyes beneath the flow of the water.

Tears pricked in Lilith's eyes, a lump itching at her throat. She crossed over to Stefan, tentative as though treading across glass, and reached out to rest a gentle hand on his shoulder. He winced like her touch pained him.

"I loved her too." Lilith's voice was soft, shaking with the agony she held deep inside her, the hatred toward Deacon, and the tiny dark shard of resentment that did not know how to live in a place that no longer had Gretchen in it.

For a few moments, they stood in their grief together. Stefan closed his eyes, tears spilling down his cheeks. Lilith let hers flow freely too, allowing herself to be in this space with him. The Morrows had hollowed her out. She had replaced her emptiness first with pain, and then later with the love and tenderness for her daughter, for those she cared about that they could never rip from her.

"I heard them tell you about the ghost." Stefan's voice was hoarse, and he set his mug down on the table with a loud thunk. When he met Lilith's gaze, his eyes shone with a pain she could comprehend all too well. "I know there is no ghost. I just hoped that…even if she was with me to rain what she had suffered down upon me, it would mean part of her wasn't gone. But she is, Lilith. I must spend the rest of my life knowing that, as will you."

"Yet you will not help us." For Lilith, it was no longer just about their countries. If Stefan did not move past his loss, it would destroy him. It already ate away at him from the inside. Deacon was the one who had killed Gretchen, and the longer that Wendell stayed associated with the Morrow Empire, the further that painful shard would dig in .

"No," Stefan admitted, eyes narrowing. "If you intend to manipulate my grief for my sister, you will find I remain unmoved. This is not just about Gretchen. Thousands of my people would die, and I cannot put their lives on the line to spite Deacon."

Lilith respected his choice. In a way, she could even understand it. She had hoped for more, but she remembered what it was like to be immobilised by loss and anger and fear. Perhaps Stefan was not weak, but his strength was just different to hers. She could not pity him too deeply, for he had turned a blind eye to Gretchen's suffering far before her death.

"I wish you peace, Stefan." Lilith's smile was as bright as it was sad. She pressed a hand over her heart, the place where she held all her love and kindness. The things that the Morrows thought made her weak, but in truth had only made her stronger. "I truly do hope that one day, you can find it."

Stefan moved back to the window and cracked it open further. That time he did not look up to the sky, but down toward the darkness yawning open below the castle walls. Lilith remembered looking down in Nicodemus. She remembered clutching onto the windowsill with all her might, willing herself not to jump.

When Stefan spoke, it was a whisper in the wind. "So do I."

THIRTY-THREE
THE ACCEPTED KING
JACEN MORROW

The port of Gethsemane was open upon their return to the city, the presence of Thom and Odessa Dyre providing welcome waters rather than the risk of sinking another of Linus Farrow's prized ships. Instead of prowling the streets of the city like a criminal, Jacen and Carissa were escorted to the castle by Prax, who practically bounced on the balls of his feet as he led them into the main hall.

An elderly woman sat on the high-backed wooden chair, her neck craned forward as she was in deep conversation with a middle-aged man who stood beside her. Both lapsed into abrupt silence as Prax cleared his throat, the sound echoing through the hall. The old woman, Odessa Dyre, stared at Jacen as though she had seen a ghost, eyes round and face paling. Her lips parted as she raised herself slowly from her seat.

The man beside her, with mousy hair not quite yet grey, must have been her son. Lord Thom Dyre. Jacen glanced at Carissa, noting the wry smile on her lips. The look exchanged between her and the man was one of familiarity, only serving to further confirm Jacen's assumption.

Odessa Dyre. Thom Dyre. His grandmother and his uncle.

Jacen must have met them when he and Vida were tiny, but by all accounts, the Dyres had been on ill terms with Cobryn since the death of Annaliese. Jacen barely remembered his mother. He could recall the scent of vanilla, a soft voice singing to him at night. Cobryn rarely spoke of Annaliese, and he did not speak of her family at all.

Thom offered his arm to Odessa, and she took it, her steps cautious as she moved toward Jacen. Once she reached him, her eyes raked over him, assessing him with what seemed to be astonishment. Beside Jacen, Carissa reached for his hand and squeezed lightly. Tears welled in Odessa's eyes as she tentatively touched his cheek.

"Gods, you look so much like her."

Jacen frowned. All his life, he'd endured comparisons to Cobryn. It was only now, in the company of his late mother's family, that he understood there was an opportunity to know the woman who had brought him into the world. Odessa snatched her hand away as if burned, turning her face like Jacen's resemblance to her late daughter was a hurt instead of a comfort.

"After your mother died…" Thom spoke quietly, and Jacen wondered if he naturally had a soft voice. Everything Carissa had told him about his uncle implied the man was more a historian than a politician, someone who loved books more than people. "Cobryn and I disagreed on how to handle it. Everyone was grieving, and things were said that could not be taken back. Cobryn banished both Odessa and I from Nicodemus. Until his dying day, he declared, we were not to attend the capital."

"You and your sister…" Odessa paused on the words, mulling them over as she looked back at Jacen. She lifted her chin, and he could see the Mistress of Webs in her resolute expression. "We were your family, and it broke my heart that we were never able to see you grow as we had wished."

Family.

It was a word with which Jacen had a complicated relationship. After all, what had his family been? A father too quick to raise a fist, a father who had wanted a soldier more than a son. An uncle who wanted a crown more than a nephew. A sister who was fed their venom and believed it. Ayesha had been the only one of them who had loved Jacen unconditionally, and whom he had loved in return.

He had never been enough for them. He had never been what they had wanted, the weight of their expectations almost drowning him. It had only been when he had met Carissa that he had changed. The lonely, unloved boy had given away the key to his heart, had let her open it up. Deacon had almost stolen that life from him, but he had emerged against all odds.

Carissa and Zephyr were his family. His terror at his son's birth had choked him from the inside, a chilling fear that he would raise his son wrong leaving a bitterness beneath his tongue. A fear that he would make his own child feel as unwanted and unwelcome as Cobryn made him feel. He had vowed to do it right, and he felt the sharp sting of how much he ached to see his son once again.

Now there was the opportunity to expand that family, to have a grandmother and an uncle who might accept him for who he was. The thought flooded him with warmth, with hope. It coaxed the hint of a smile to the corners of his lips.

"I have a gift for you." Odessa clicked her fingers imperiously, and a servant rushed over with a large case and handed it to Jacen. He turned it over carefully in his hands, immediately curious. When he opened it, Carissa rested a hand on his arm, fingers tracing patterns against his skin. Inside lay a well-worn fiddle, some of the wood beginning to peel and its surface marked with several scratches. It was not a new fiddle, but a fiddle that had been deeply loved.

"It belonged to your mother." Thom said, flicking a sly smile toward Carissa. "It seems you inherited her love of music."

It had been over a year since Jacen had picked up a fiddle, and his fingers itched toward the bow. He would be rusty and out of practise, yet every instinct sang out to him to play. Setting the case on the ground, Jacen picked up the fiddle and positioned it carefully, pressing the bow to the strings. He closed his eyes and let the notes come to him, the joyful tune one he had played many times in Basium.

The music washed over him in all its raw beauty, and he did not have to open his eyes to feel the love for him in this room. It caressed him and held him close, like the first sip of a hot cocoa or a thick woollen blanket draped over his shoulders. Jacen could have sworn in that moment, his mother was watching him…and that through his music, she was smiling down at them all.

Dinner with Odessa and Thom was a light-hearted affair, and between the lively conversation and the pleasant buzz of wine, Jacen left the table brimming with joy. The room that he and Carissa had been offered overlooked the glimmering water of the port, and he had already taken the opportunity to watch the ships gliding in and out of the bay.

Carissa had politely excused herself from dinner, claiming a headache. When Jacen returned to their room, he found that she sat in the windowsill, the lights of the city illuminating a troubled expression. Frowning, he crossed over and rested a tentative hand on her shoulder. His happiness melted away like water draining through his fingers.

"Is something wrong?"

"I wanted to talk to you." Carissa eased herself off the windowsill, moving to sit on the four-poster bed. She tilted her head to the side, brow pinching. "Why didn't you tell me that you had no intention of claiming the Generan throne?"

Was that what agitated her?

"I suppose I didn't really think about it until we were talking to Linus and Korina. I realised then that I was the last thing my country needed, or wanted."

"What was it about that moment?" Carissa pressed, leaning forward and picking at the hem of her nightdress.

"Pain." Jacen muttered the word without a moment's hesitation. "The amount of pain I've caused. In Basium, in Genera. Whether I am forgiven for my crimes, my father's crimes, I will always be a reminder of it. Ayesha is different. I caused pain, but she was created and born from it."

A shadow crossed over Carissa's face, a door closing behind her eyes. Jacen's stomach twisted as he realised he had been insensitive in his insinuation of the

243

horrors that Lilith had endured. He did not know what Carissa had been through during the year she had spent in Nicodemus, though he could hazard a guess.

"You are more than pain, Jacen." Carissa swept her fingers through her dark hair. "You have atoned for your sins. If you do not want the throne, I would not blame you, but to hide behind the crimes you committed…that isn't the whole truth."

"That throne is cursed." Jacen sat down heavily beside her, his hands trembling at the thought. "Perhaps not by magic, but cursed by the blood that has been spilled to keep it. I played my part, and I want nothing more than the fall of the Morrow Empire. I do not want to be the next step in it."

Cobryn's brutal murder, Gretchen's pale corpse beneath the water…it was enough to turn Jacen's stomach. He had been raised since birth to anticipate sitting upon the Generan throne. It was only recently that he had a choice in the matter, and he chose to turn his back on his family's tainted legacy.

"When I was in Nicodemus…" Carissa's words were soft and contemplative, and acidic bile rose in Jacen's throat.

"You don't have to talk about it."

"No, but I want to." Carissa's eyes met his, defiant, challenging him to speak out against the moment she shed all the layers, took off all the masks, and showed herself bare and vulnerable. "There are things you should know, and things I need to say."

Jacen remained silent, allowing her the space to talk about the trauma she had endured. He could do nothing but listen, even if cold dread settled in his bones at the thought of what she might say.

"Deacon never forced me." Carissa's voice was deceptively even, though when Jacen looked at her, her eyes were glazed and vacant, like she had suddenly gone somewhere far away.

"The wedding night…" Jacen immediately trailed off, wondering if he had pushed too much. The biggest dilemma in Jacen and Carissa's marriage had been that it was not consummated until far later. It was something Deacon had known, and a mistake that he would never have made.

"Deacon made it a game." A bitter smile cut across Carissa's lips, even as rage shone in her violet-blue eyes. "I angered him by wearing mourning black to the wedding. I feared the worst, especially when I knew the Generan tradition of the consummation being witnessed, but…he sent the others away. He told me that there was no reason I couldn't benefit from our marriage. That if I bore him an heir, he would allow me to see Zephyr. See my son."

She reached up to wipe away angry tears, and as someone who had known Deacon for years, Jacen understood. Deacon had promised Carissa freedoms, offered her things she wanted, in exchange for gaining something in return. A sadistic, twisted game designed to elicit guilt and shame in Carissa.

"When I wanted something, I would let him visit my bed. I realise how that makes me seem, but it wasn't…I didn't want…"

"Carissa." Dread surged through Jacen, but he rubbed her arm, seeing the distress in her fingers tightening in her nightdress. "I don't judge you. I don't think anyone would. You have always been a survivor, and you did what you had to in order to survive. Deacon fucks with people's heads. It is something he has always been good at."

"The worst part is, I didn't believe he was telling the truth." Carissa's voice cracked over the words. "He wasn't going to let me see Zephyr. He wouldn't keep half of his promises, but he did keep some. A foolish shard of me hoped that maybe, one day, even if I had to work for it… He only ever dangled things over my head, just out of reach. I reached for them anyway."

Carissa buried her face in her hands and sobbed, the sound wrenching at Jacen's heart like someone had torn open his ribcage and was trying to carve it out. He wrapped his arms around her and held her close, letting her cry into the thin fabric of his shirt, feeling the moisture of her tears against his skin.

Deacon might have never tortured her physically, but the damage he had done to her psychologically left scars no one else could see. Carissa, who had struggled to trust since Jacen had known her, would find it hard to lower her barriers amongst even those she loved dearly. It broke him, but he masked his own tears by burying his face in her hair. Deeper down still lingered the violent urge to gut Deacon for what he'd done to her.

Tomorrow, they would begin the journey back to a place where they had both endured hell in their own ways. Jacen had been born in Nicodemus, grown up there, and yet it had always felt cold to him. It had never felt like home. He had found a home in Marinel with Carissa, and one day, they would return there.

Piece by piece, they would rebuild their shattered lives. They would put together the shards that Deacon had left them in, and they would be stronger for it. Then they would make sure that Deacon knew hell.

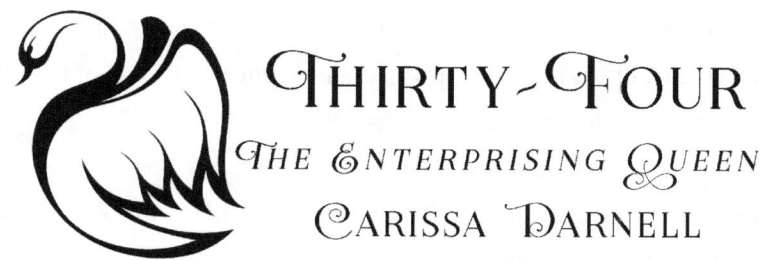

Thirty-Four

The Enterprising Queen
Carissa Darnell

The combined forces of Gethsemane and the Island heirs marched upon Nicodemus. Carissa had iron in her heart and vengeance on her mind throughout their journey, though she was comforted by the knowledge that Jacen knew the truth. It had not changed what he thought of her at all, had not diminished his love in the slightest. A weight had been lifted from Carissa's shoulders, all the mortification she had faced alone breathed out into the world.

At the city gates, they were met by a garrison force. Several filed through the gates out to meet them, while on the walls, the archers peered over the parapet. The sheen of their armour in the sunlight made Carissa wince and shield her eyes.

Her stomach clenched and roiled at the idea of more blood, more death. She did not want to kill any of these soldiers as she had during her escape. None of the soldiers raised a sword or nocked an arrow, leaving her hope that there could be a peaceful resolution instead of the siege of a city.

When Carissa dismounted her horse, she was astonished to see Ariadne amongst them.

"Carissa?" The noblewoman frowned, nudging her way through the soldiers. Carissa supposed it would make sense that Deacon would leave his mistress, a woman he thought he could trust, in command of the auxiliary forces upon his absence. Carissa faltered in her steps as she moved forward. Ariadne had helped her during her tenure as Deacon's wife, but would she still help her now?

"Ariadne."

"It's good to see you back." A tight smile crossed Ariadne's lips.

"Lady Ariadne, this is the woman who maimed our King," one of the soldiers said, stepping forward to rest a hand on her shoulder.

Ariadne scowled and shrugged him off. "And how many has Deacon maimed? Besides, you speak falsely when you claim him to be our King. The true King of Genera stands right there."

She jabbed an accusing finger at Jacen, who shifted uncomfortably at the sudden attention directed at him. The soldier who had spoken scowled, his hand resting on the hilt of his sword. Several of the others murmured amongst themselves, while three dropped to bend the knee to Jacen.

"Deacon won't be pleased about this," the soldier said darkly.

"Oh, I guarantee it." Ariadne took Carissa's hand in her own, interlinking her fingers with the younger woman's. "You are, of course, free to strike us down if you so choose. But just know that I stand with Jacen and Carissa, the *rightful* monarchs of both Genera and Basium. I have served Deacon faithfully, but we were all in thrall to a liar."

There was no magic in Ariadne's blood, but the way she defiantly tilted her chin up and the sheer willpower she displayed was a power in itself. She was a cunning woman when the situation called for it, but Carissa had never before seen such boldness in her. She admired Ariadne's conviction, even standing before a dozen soldiers who could cut her down in a moment.

Not one of them spoke up against her, not even the soldier who had initially questioned her. Smugness settled into Ariadne's smile, and with the auxiliary force unwilling to stop her, she opened the gates to Nicodemus and let Deacon's enemies through into the city beyond.

The last time Carissa had been in Nicodemus, she had fled for her life in the dead of night after cutting off Deacon's hand. It was strange how, mere months later, she could return in triumph instead of terror.

When Jacen entered the throne room, Carissa noticed how her husband's body tensed as he examined the huge throne, pewter with a snarling jackal on its back. It was the throne he had never wanted. He did not want to sit there, because he did not know what might come of it. He cast around desperately, and Carissa took his hand firmly in hers.

"You are not the King of Genera if you do not want to be."

Linus and Korina lingered by the doorway, guarded eyes on Jacen. Did they think he would change his mind and betray the promises he had made them? Carissa wondered what the pair saw when they examined the jackal throne, a reminder of what their families had lost when they had taken a stand against Cobryn.

Thom entered the throne room along with Ariadne and Myron. He had been reluctant to return to the capital, though Jacen had insisted he needed his uncle with him. Jacen raised a hand when Myron went to kneel.

"Don't. I'm not your King."

Thom's brow furrowed. "Pardon?"

"My sister Ayesha will sit on the throne."

"You're wrong about that." Myron moved forward, his footsteps quiet. "Your stepmother declared she would not let that happen. Your aunt Relda's son Elyes is the proposed candidate for the throne."

Jacen's eyes flicked to Linus and Korina, awaiting their verdict. When both nodded, his shoulders dropped like a sense of peace had come over him. He unleashed a long breath, and Carissa prayed that he might finally be able to erase the taint of his family's sins and wash his hands clean of the past.

"Until the war is over, and my cousin sits on the throne, there is only one man I trust to hold Nicodemus." Jacen turned to face Thom, determination glittering in his hazel eyes. "Uncle, I know I ask a lot of you, but I hope that you will accept."

Thom's smile was wry. "I hate this fucking city. But out of love for your late mother, anything."

Jacen's eyes lit up with joy, and he pulled his uncle into a tight embrace. Thom was the uncle he deserved, a man who wanted the best for Jacen, a man who accepted him for who he was rather than trying to mould him into something he was not. It brought tears of happiness to Carissa's eyes.

Nicodemus had been a prison for Carissa and a torment for Jacen. They had both fought demons in this place, and it would take time to undo the damage that both Cobryn and Deacon had done. Carissa did not anticipate that Deacon would forsake the capital so easily, and wondered how much more the city would have to endure before the end was over.

In private, the satisfaction of their occupation of Nicodemus became politics. Myron and Thom both had differing opinions on the two strongest candidates for the throne. Though Elyes was the suggested monarch, it was true that his bastard status would raise some concerns in the rigidly traditional Genera.

"Ayesha is the closest direct relative," Thom argued. "She is Cobryn's youngest daughter."

"Yes, but Elyes is the next *male* heir following Jacen," Myron said mildly. "Bastard or not, he does have a claim."

The conversation reminded Carissa of something that must have been discussed about her and Sebastian's claims to the throne. He was younger than her, but male. Some might argue he had the better claim, but Carissa had already been accepted as Basium's Queen.

Her heart ached at the thought of her brother, and she prayed he was all right. Deacon had taken Emlen, and the loss of the northern city was a blow not only to Sebastian, but Basium as a whole. How lonely Sebastian must be, with no allies to come to his aid. She knew that feeling all too well. She would return to Basium and reunite with her brother. No throne would come between them.

The memory of summoning lightning and unleashing it on Belvedere made Carissa's hands clench into fists. The book hadn't truly given her an explanation. In the absence of other's blood or shedding her own, she relied on 'the blood of the land.' What did it mean? Where else could she go for an explanation? Miriam had been dead for years, and her direct relation to Jameson Burnett wasn't common knowledge.

"Carissa?" Jacen placed a gentle hand on her arm, bringing her back to the conversation at the table. "Are you all right?"

She exhaled deeply and nodded. "I'm fine. I'm just...I want to see our son again."

It wasn't a lie. Zephyr had been a baby when she had been abducted from Emlen. He would be almost two years old by now, and it devastated Carissa that she had missed so many important milestones in his life. The blow was softened in knowing that Bellona was his guardian. If anyone would treat that boy with love and affection, it was her best friend.

"We will see him soon, I promise." Jacen linked his fingers through hers. If anyone understood her urge to get back to Zephyr, it was him. She had the distinct impression that Jacen's lifelong banishment from Basium would be retracted considering everything that had happened since. After all, he had *almost* died.

"What if there is another solution?" Ariadne's voice was accompanied by the click of heels as she strode into the room, her sudden presence causing Myron and Thom to lapse into silence. "Our great country is tired of tyrants and warmongers. Perhaps it's time we tried something new."

"What are you suggesting, Ariadne?" There was an exhausted edge to Myron's voice that held no patience for drawn-out conversation.

"I am suggesting that we have no king or queen at all. I think the time has come to abolish the monarchy."

"What?" Jacen's eyes were round as coins. "But...you mean to completely overturn the way Genera is governed."

"Look at what good our current structure has done." Ariadne sprawled in a chair beside Thom, draping her hands over the wooden arms, a sly smile on her lips when she realised everyone's shocked expressions were fixed upon her. "Of course, it's hardly up to me, but if it was, I would suggest a triumvirate. Three rulers, voted in for lifelong terms like they do in Cirocco, holding each other accountable."

"There so much that could go wrong there," Myron persisted. "What if the rulers simply don't like each other, and it descends into a dogfight? It could be a potential disaster, no matter your good intentions."

"The same way a monarch could order the execution of a nobleman they despised?" Ariadne arched an eyebrow.

"I agree with her." It was Jacen who spoke this time, causing all heads to turn to him. "The people are tired of Morrow Kings. Elyes and Ayesha might be different, but they're still children. Right now, we need change. I propose that we have people stand for an election, and that way, they can be voted into power."

"There's only one problem with this." Carissa twisted her fingers in the folds of her dress, finally bringing herself to voice the uneasiness that settled deep within the pit of her stomach. "We've taken the capital, but Deacon is out there with his army. He's far from dead and gone, and yet you're talking like he is."

"We need to plan, Carissa." Ariadne poured herself a glass of water. "We're aware of the threat Deacon poses, but…"

"So, what is the plan for him?" Carissa demanded, leaning forward and resting her elbows on the table in a way her mother would have reprimanded her for during her childhood. "Are we letting him rot in a cell for the rest of his life? Plying him with Obscurate so he's never a threat? Beheading him in front of a crowd so everyone can see justice done?"

The silence and looks exchanged across the mahogany table were answer enough. They had no idea what to do with Deacon once they took him on. A death in battle would have been glorious to the man, a fitting end to a life of violence and conquest. Just as Cobryn had been denied such an end, so too would Carissa deprive Deacon of it.

"Well, then. I request that, should it be possible, Deacon Morrow will be delivered into my hands if he is apprehended, so that I may invoke justice."

Myron frowned deeply. "Your Majesty, if this is about revenge..."

"Of course it's about revenge," Carissa snapped, swelling with indignation at his pacifying tone. There was no point in tying a pretty bow around her choice and calling it an execution. It would be brutal, and it would be ugly, just as the events that had ripped her family from her had been.

"How do you plan to go about this?" Thom asked, his tone less condescending than Myron's, but no less grating on Carissa's frayed nerves.

"I am going to kill him, Lord Dyre. I should have thought that much was obvious."

"Together." Jacen's voice caused silence to fall over the table once again, but even though they all looked at him, his eyes were on Carissa. Her irritation faded away, replaced by a steely conviction that with her husband by her side, nothing was impossible. Though she wanted blood for what had been done to her family, her country, her...she was not the only one Deacon had wronged.

"Together," she agreed.

THIRTY-FIVE
THE COMMANDING LADY
BELLONA LENORE

With a Bao fleet at her back, Bellona thought she could have taken any news in her stride. However, when she returned to Cristofer telling her that Emlen had fallen, it felt like she had been slapped in the face. Deacon had a foothold in Basium now, and Sebastian and his army had retreated to Marinel.

Privately, Bellona chastised herself for her stubbornness. If she had been more friendly toward Sebastian, if she had lent her forces in support, would that still have happened? She supposed his advisors had always painted her as a rival instead of a friend.

There was no point in deliberating about what could have happened. Instead, she needed to focus on the cold, hard facts: Deacon was gaining ground. He might have lost Dalal, but Emlen was a significant victory.

Bellona's fingers shook as she placed the jackal marker on Emlen, surveying the map of Razmara. She swore it would be the last city that Deacon got a hold of. She had reached out to Sebastian in Marinel, asking how she could be of assistance. The time had come to let old rivalries die. There was only one enemy, and he was amassing an army in the heart of their country.

"Tell me the latest." Her green eyes flicked across to watch Cristofer, standing in front of the hearth.

"Jacen and Carissa were spotted leaving the Generan Islands with a fleet of four."

Bellona frowned. What in the name of the goddess were they doing? Though she was thrilled that her best friend had been reunited with Jacen, she didn't understand Carissa's movements. Why wasn't she coming home? So much was happening in Basium, and yet Carissa remained in Genera.

"For what purpose?"

"Unknown, but it likely involves the Generan throne." Cristofer raked his fingers through his dark hair. "If they can obtain it while Deacon is in Emlen, he has nowhere to run if he decides to fall back."

So, they were cutting Deacon off at all corners. It was a wise choice when Bellona thought about it. Deacon had been allowed to flee back to Nicodemus before—and look where that had gotten them.

"Lilith?"

"Last seen in Wendell."

Harith had celebrated freedom from Deacon's iron fist when they had defeated him in battle. A sound victory, especially since they had been part of the Morrow Empire for over a decade. Wendell was the only country still fully under Deacon's control, and that needed to change if the tide of war was to turn in their favour.

They were too spread out. The only way they could defeat Deacon was together. Sebastian had done admirably in even attempting to hold Emlen against Deacon, but he was doomed from the start. There was no one in his ranks powerful enough to pose a real threat to the Imperium.

"Bellona." Eirian touched her arm. "We need Lady Benedict."

Bellona recalled the Lady of Fortua, who had been unintentionally outed as a Maleficium during Jacen and Carissa's tour of Basium. As a shadow mage, the woman had the potential to be a strong ally. She rubbed at her temples, embarrassed that she had needed the reminder from Eirian to even consider Lady Benedict.

"Going to Fortua is ill-advised," Cristofer said.

Eirian folded her arms. "So, we summon Lady Benedict here."

Lady Benedict had remained in Fortua since the death of her husband to raise their two children. It pleased Bellona to see more women finding power across Basium, where once men had tried to silence them. Lord Benedict had sworn allegiance to Deacon, and he had paid for it with his life.

"Perhaps we should summon them all," Bellona murmured.

Eirian and Cristofer exchanged a look, the kind they always did when Bellona made a suggestion they thought outlandish.

"Calling in all the major houses?" Cristofer arched an eyebrow. "Don't you think that's something Sebastian should be doing? It's something the monarch would do, not..."

Bellona held up a hand, and he lapsed into silence. "Sebastian is currently busy, engaged in what's happening in Emlen. I am not acting to usurp the King's authority, nor am I acting on his behalf. I am acting in the best interest of Basium, to help Sebastian, to help all of us. We have the Bao fleet, and the southern Wendell harbours. We can do this, but we need to do it together."

It was a bold choice, and some of the other nobles might be affronted by Bellona's request for aid. However, it was a card she needed to play. She had not gotten as far as she had by meekly sitting in Theron waiting for Deacon's next move. She would not see her city suffer again. She closed her eyes and still saw the darkness of the tunnels, heard her own ragged scream as Kato sealed it off, giving his life to save hers.

"I love you. Both of you. I need to know that you are with me on this."

Eirian crossed over to Bellona and pressed a tender kiss to her lips, wrapping her arms around her. Bellona held her close as Cristofer joined them, an arm around each of them. In that space, with the two people she valued most, Bellona felt the warmth of their love as though it was a welcoming hearth.

"I've called upon the King and Queen of Cirocco." Cristofer was smiling as he drew back. "They have agreed to send in our troops. It's time."

The whole of Razmara was going to war, a continent erupting in turmoil because of one family's greed. Bellona could only hope that they escaped these next battles with as few scars as possible, because she didn't know how much more she could stand to lose.

THIRTY-SIX
THE VENGEFUL KING
JACEN MORROW

The journey back to Basium would take them to Theron. With Deacon holding Emlen, it made the most sense to go to Bellona. Where would Deacon strike next? It was hard to tell if he would set his sights on Marinel, Theron, or another of Basium's major cities. He probably had not yet learned there was nowhere for him to retreat, and once he did, he would hit even harder.

Each day they travelled, Jacen and Carissa's relationship blossomed. The barriers between them were slowly coming down. With their common goal of returning to Zephyr, they were stronger than ever. Deacon had wanted to break them, to tear them apart with such savagery that they would return damaged and unable to fit back together. Instead, they had risen above what he had done to them. They had come together fractured and helped make each other whole.

Jacen and Carissa had been on the run for so long they had forgotten what it was like to stop and take a breath. While Thom, Myron, and Ariadne remained in Nicodemus, Jacen relished the opportunity to spend time with his wife. They both knew it was the calm before the storm, battle about to bloody the horizon, but they cherished it.

"Have you thought about how we're going to kill Deacon?" Jacen asked as Carissa warmed her hands over the campfire. When she spoke of it in Genera, he had seen the danger flaring in her violet-blue eyes. He had seen the woman who had destroyed Belvedere, though he could not hold it against her for wanting to kill the man who'd caused her so much pain.

"Part of me wants it to be just and fair, without emotion."

The logs in the fire crackled, Korina's booming laugh resonating through the camp. Her adamance on joining them in the war to come had astounded Jacen. He had thought, once they'd taken control of Nicodemus, she would return to the Generan Islands. There was a conversation coming about the throne since Ayesha would no longer be sitting on it as Jacen had promised.

"The other part of you?" Jacen pressed, banishing thoughts of the Generan throne as he took in the rage that simmered deep within Carissa.

"The other part wants it to be vicious." Carissa's voice trembled. "To repay almost a decade's worth of bloodshed and cruelty. But if I return to Basium and prove I am the violent Blood Queen some call me…"

"Carissa." Jacen leaned forward and rested a hand on her shoulder. "Fuck what people think. Basium suffered under the Morrows too. Anyone with sense would understand."

In the past, before his uncle had attempted to kill him, perhaps Jacen would have approached the matter with apprehension. He had been so intent on getting the people of Basium to like him, but those who judged him for his Morrow heritage would hate him regardless of his benevolence. The time for being who he thought other people wanted him to be was over. He embraced who he was, and Carissa was so close to doing the same.

"You're right." Carissa's voice was soft, barely audible over the crackle of the fire, but she raised it. "I will give Deacon the end he deserves. We decide what punishment fits his immeasurable crimes. Fuck what people think."

Jacen grinned and pressed a kiss to the top of her head. Carissa was accepting of physical affection, though sudden touches had a tendency to startle her. Perhaps, in a way, Deacon had killed both of them, and they were reborn from the ashes of the boy and girl who had stepped so tentatively around the opinions of others.

"There's some people I need to talk to." Jacen eased himself to his feet, seeing that Korina had extricated herself from her tight-knit group to pour herself a drink. His heart hammered in his chest as he braced himself for how she would take the news. She arched an eyebrow at his appearance.

"Quite the victory in Nicodemus. We didn't even need to fight."

"There's something you should know." Jacen clenched his hands into tight fists. "Ayesha won't be ruling Genera, but neither will I."

"Then who will be?" Linus approached with a drink in hand, a terse expression on his face. "This was not our bargain, Morrow."

"We're disbanding the monarchy." Jacen's rushed words were met with incredulous silence, as Korina looked to Linus for his reaction. "A triumvirate will rule in place of a king or queen. After everything the Morrows have done to Genera…we thought the change should be more than just which Morrow sits on the throne."

There was a moment where he thought one of them might punch him. Probably Korina. Instead, she burst out laughing. Linus's mouth was slack with shock, and Jacen examined Korina with a mix of astonishment and apprehension. The laughter was genuine, as were the tears of mirth she wiped from her eyes.

"Is…is this somehow funny?"

"I admit, I thought you were like the others." Korina's grin spread across her whole face. "All empty promises and hollow words. But you, Jacen Morrow… it's like finding a diamond in pig shit."

"Flattering," Jacen muttered, but his cheeks burned in embarrassment at the unexpected compliment.

"You aren't like the others." Linus's voice was softer, more reflective. "You just proved it. Your father would never have been able to see past his own greed to what was good for Genera…your uncle, either. You're something else."

Korina and Linus's praise made unexpected tears well in his eyes. Jacen had only ever wanted to be a better man than Cobryn. His father would have snarled at him to wipe his eyes, swearing that crying was a weakness, but Jacen shed the tears openly in front of his unexpected allies.

The credit for the idea went to Ariadne Pavlos, yet he would not shrug off his own role in how things had panned out. If Jacen could confront the sins of his past, then he deserved to acknowledge the good choices he was making in the present. His country came before any throne, and he was relieved that finally, people were beginning to see that he had as much love in his heart as Cobryn had hate.

Thunder rumbled over the camp in the early hours of the morning, low and ominous. When Jacen turned over in his sleep, it was to an empty space where Carissa had been. Kicking the blankets off, he rolled out of bed and padded from the tent to find her standing outside, her gaze fixed on the sky. Lightning flashed through the darkness, illuminating the gathering clouds. She turned to glance over her shoulder at him, black hair unruly in the breeze.

"Can't sleep either?" A rueful smile played about her lips.

Jacen shook his head in response. The time would come when he and Carissa would talk about the demons that plagued them, the ghosts that visited them in their nightmares. But for both of them, the trauma of their experiences was far too fresh, and giving voice to them would be like digging a knife into an open wound. They needed to heal first, and Jacen gave Carissa a space of love and respect in which to do so.

"Does it remind you of Belvedere?" Jacen asked, moving beside her and watching her crane her neck up to look at the sky.

"It reminds me there's a lot about my magic I still don't understand and can't control." Carissa looked at him with unshed tears in her eyes. "I don't want to hurt people I care about because of that. Even in the volume I read, there wasn't much of an answer. I thought I knew the limits of my blood magic, but...this is something else. Something dangerous."

"You didn't know the limits of your blood magic at first," Jacen reminded her, brushing his hand against hers. "Maybe this is something you need to give time to understand. Your magic saved us. It did damage, but without it, I don't want to think about where we might be."

The hint of a smile graced Carissa's lips and she threaded her fingers through his, giving his hand a squeeze. Perhaps Jacen should have been afraid of the power that flowed through her veins, how destructive it could be. But he loved her, and he trusted her, and that was enough for him to believe in her magic.

"You didn't want the Generan throne." Carissa exhaled deeply. "What if I want the Basiumite throne?"

"That's different." The Generan throne was tainted by a bloody legacy, one that kept Jacen awake at night. The Basiumite throne didn't fill him with the same dread. If Carissa chose to rule Basium, he would do so by her side.

"I don't want to fight Sebastian." Carissa swept her hair out of her face. "The last thing Basium needs is a civil war. I know it's been years since I really knew who he was, but...I don't think Sebastian wants the throne. I think he rules out of a sense of duty and responsibility rather than ambition."

Jacen hoped that Carissa's assumption was not misplaced. He had seen firsthand the devastation that a civil war could bring, and he did not wish Genera's fate upon Basium. The wind swept Carissa's dark hair across her face, and she closed her eyes, a peaceful expression crossing her face even as lightning streaked across the midnight sky once again.

The wild chaos of the storm suited her...perhaps a little too much.

THIRTY-SEVEN
THE DREAMER PRINCE
SEBASTIAN DARNELL

The waning candlelight flickered over the set of volumes Sebastian had set on the grass in front of him, his eyes itching with weariness as he searched for a mention of General Tycho. All records of him vanished after the defeat of Jameson Burnett, and even as Sebastian hungrily pored over those brief mentions, there was no note of Tycho's role in the Maleficium's downfall, just that he had been one of the handful of survivors.

In truth, Sebastian had far bigger concerns. They were on the run after Deacon's victory in Emlen, and he didn't know that returning to the capital was safe. It had been at General Luce's suggestion that they head for Theron, after word reached them of Lady Lenore gathering forces there. Sebastian had sensed another betrayal but was pleasantly surprised to learn Bellona intended to help, not harm.

"You're still looking at those."

"Fuck!" Sebastian jumped, almost knocking over the candle as he looked up to see Meliora approaching with her arms folded over her chest. His heart hammered against his ribcage, and he took a steadying breath. "You should be sleeping, Mel."

"So should you," she responded nonchalantly, sitting down beside him. "But you're not even focusing on Emlen. Instead, it's this nightmare, the cave, the idea that maybe Tycho Salus has something to do with it all."

Guilt surged through Sebastian at her words. Meliora had lost her father during the battle of Emlen, an uncertain Jarl taking over leadership with his mother's guidance. His wife had shed tears for her father, but Meliora was as pragmatic as ever. There was no accusation in her voice, only the truth.

"I wish I could stop thinking about it." Sebastian's voice was hoarse. "But every time I have a dream, it's the same. Juniper was a treasonous bitch, but maybe she was right about this. It's an omen, and I need Tycho to find out what it means."

"So, you think those dusty old books will help you?" A mischievous smile spread across Meliora's lips. "Don't you know the best way to find out gossip is through free-flowing wine?"

"People are drinking out of sorrow, not celebration," Sebastian reminded her, raking his fingers through his black hair. He slammed the volume shut with more force than was necessary, frustration flowing through him. He had lost Emlen. He didn't have any leads on his dreams, if they were even anything more than a fiction his mind had concocted.

"You need sleep." Meliora's tone was firm this time, and Sebastian pinched the bridge of his nose. She was right, which happened more often than not. He flopped back on the blankets he'd spread across the grass, staring up at the stars spangled across the sky overhead.

"It's a nice night. I might sleep out here."

"All right." Meliora seemed to know a lost cause when she saw one, because she shook her head in disapproval but headed back to their tent without another word.

Sebastian closed his eyes, letting the cool breeze caress his skin. There was a slight chill to the air, but it was peaceful nonetheless. Sleep came more easily than it had in weeks, the ambient sounds of the night lulling Sebastian into restful slumber.

It wasn't the cave.

It was a field of green grass, sprawling as far as the eye could see. The sun beat down golden over a flock of sheep and cattle, happily grazing as a black-and-white dog padded around to check on them all. The sky was a clear azure blue, and when he closed his eyes, he could feel a warm sense of lethargy sweeping over him. Here there was no war, no battles to fight...just tranquillity.

When Sebastian turned, he could see a cottage nearby, smoke billowing from the chimney. Outside, a grey-haired man was tending to what appeared to be a vegetable garden. Sebastian moved closer, feeling like a puppet on strings as his feet moved him toward the man even though he should have been more guarded. The man cursed as he stepped on a small tomato, squelching it under his boot.

"Excuse me." The man looked up at Sebastian's words. He was old, more than seventy, with wrinkles across his forehead and a face leathered from too much time in the sun. "Who are you?"

"What are you doing here?" The lines across his forehead deepened as he frowned. "You aren't meant to be here."

Sebastian held up his hands. "I don't mean any trouble. I'm just trying to understand where I am."

There was a richness to the garden, the pops of colour of vegetables growing in the soil and the scent of freshly tilled earth on the wind. The old man's suspicious gaze relaxed, and he jammed his shovel into the dirt, leaning against the handle. He reached up to wipe the glistening sweat from his brow.

"My name is Tycho Salus."

Sebastian stepped forward, a twig snapping under his boot. That was the retired general who had been with his grandparents in that cave when Jameson Burnett had died. He was the last person who knew the truth. The lines between dream and reality blurred, until Sebastian wasn't sure if his subconscious was conjuring up Tycho because of his own desperation. Was he losing his mind, or finding it?

"The cave..." The words were barely above a whisper, but Tycho flinched at

them as though Sebastian had screamed them.

"I swore an oath never to speak about what happened that day. Elethea rest the souls of the others who were there…"

"Miriam and Patrick."

Tycho's eyes widened. "Yes. I won't ask how you know that, since I may not like the answer. Nonetheless, though they are gone, I am a man of my word. I am never talking about what transpired there."

Sebastian had come so far, reaching out for something only to have his fingertips brushing against an immovable force. He pushed forward, frustration and excitement mingling within him as he came so close to solving the mystery of the cave.

"Can you at least tell me where the cave is? Even drawing it on a map or something…"

He trailed off as Tycho shook his head, squeezing his eyes shut. "No. But…I can show you."

THIRTY-EIGHT
THE RECONCILED LADY
BELLONA LENORE

Dusk settled over Theron like a violet cloak when the Morrow jackal was sighted on the horizon. Fear thundered through Bellona's heart; she was about to issue the call to arms when it was accompanied by the gold and cream colours of House Darnell glimmering in the dying rays of the sun.

Not Deacon. Jacen and Carissa.

After Zephyr had finished making a mess of his dinner, smashed potato all over his face and clothes, Bellona cleaned him up and took him down to the canals. It would not only be the first time that she had seen her best friend in over a year, but also the first time Carissa had seen Zephyr since he was a baby. He was closer to his second birthday than his first now, a little boy instead of a squalling infant.

Carissa and Jacen's boat inched closer to the edge of the canal, and Bellona gave Zephyr's hand a small squeeze. A cry tore from Carissa's mouth as her eyes locked onto her son, and she tripped on the hem of her dress in her haste to disembark the boat. It rocked violently back and forth as Jacen stepped off too, helping Carissa to her feet.

How could two people that Bellona knew so well be so different and yet so similar to when she'd last seen them? There was a grimness in Jacen's expression, dark circles under Carissa's eyes. They were older, gaunter. She supposed she must be too. Taking a deep breath, she leaned down and gently nudged Zephyr forward.

"Do you remember me, Zephyr?" Carissa knelt down on the cobblestones in front of her son, her eyes glimmering with unshed tears. When the little boy shook his head, shyly clinging to Bellona's skirts, she choked out a sob. "I'm your mother."

Carissa wiped tears from her cheeks as she gestured to Jacen, who stood staring at his son with fierce love in his eyes.

"This is Papa."

Carissa held out her arms and Bellona noticed how they trembled. She feared rejection from the small child, feared that her son would turn away from a woman he did not recognise. Zephyr's eyes, so like Carissa's, darted between his parents, before he threw himself into Carissa's embrace. She laughed and cried as she held him close, fingers threading through his hair.

"Thank you." They were the first words Jacen had spoken to Bellona since he had been exiled from Basium. She noted the scar on his left cheek. "You took care of our son when neither of us could. I can never repay you for that."

Jacen, who had consistently responded to Bellona's distrust and contempt with patience. Jacen, who had risked his life to fight on their side and been punished for it. Jacen, who loved Carissa and Zephyr with all his heart. After all these years, after all he had done to prove himself worthy of Carissa, she considered him a friend, and a dear one at that. His words warmed her like an open hearth, and she wrapped her arms around him and embraced him tightly.

Jacen staggered back slightly before he tentatively put his arms around her to return the hug. Perhaps it was as unexpected to him as it was to her. She glanced at Carissa, who had risen to her feet and scooped up Zephyr. The child played quietly with his mother's dark hair, much like he had as a baby.

"I think there's a lot we need to discuss." Bellona disentangled herself from Jacen, examining her best friend. "I'll let you both settle in, spend some time with Zephyr. After dinner, we should have a meeting."

Bellona was not a woman easily consumed by dread. She had survived the flooding of Theron, travelled to Bao, and launched an attack on the southern harbours of Wendell. Yet her stomach twisted at the idea of hearing the ordeal that Carissa had been through, not to mention Jacen's own near-death experience. They had all been through so much, and she could only wonder at how much damage their trauma had caused them.

Carissa sat by the hearth, the leaping flames illuminating her face as she stared into their depths. Jacen stood with his arms folded, leaning against the mantlepiece. Bellona sank into a chair, drumming her fingers against her thigh as she watched the melancholy that settled in between the cracks of their joy.

"You cut off Deacon's hand." Bellona had never been much good at small talk, so she launched right into where she wanted to be in the conversation.

The hint of a smile curved Carissa's lips, something vicious gleaming in her violet-blue eyes.

"I should have slit his throat instead."

Her words were full of venomous hatred, and there was an unspoken understanding between the three of them, a knowledge of precisely what Carissa had endured in Nicodemus. She would not push Carissa to speak of such an atrocity. Yet the Queen continued of her own accord, her breath hitching.

"I was never forced into anything, Bell. Deacon manipulated me, toyed with my mind. The insinuations that my compliance would gain me things I wanted…I went along with it. Firstly because I desperately wanted to believe, and secondly because I wanted some tiny shred of control."

Bellona mulled over her words in horrified silence, for somehow, that was worse. Deacon had thrown Carissa into a gilded cage and dangled a key over her, and watched how hard she would try to obtain it. Carissa had survived the Conquest and its aftermath with grace, and Deacon would have known that she was a woman not averse to shedding her pride like a second skin. Carissa had made sacrifices Bellona never could have, and she had never thought her best friend was stronger.

"Ariadne Pavlos." Carissa looked to Jacen, whose brow furrowed at the name Bellona didn't recognise. "A widowed noblewoman. Along with Thom Dyre and Myron, she was one of the few friends I had there. When Deacon… when he grew bored of me, he took her as his mistress."

Jacen stepped up behind her chair and tentatively placed a hand on her shoulder. Carissa reached up to rest her fingers over his, a dark shadow passing over her face. She did not need to imagine what hell was like. She had been there.

"What about you, Jacen?" Bellona asked, wanting to give her friend a reprieve from the darkness of her year in Nicodemus. "We heard you had died. Deacon killed you. How did you survive?"

"Pure luck, I suppose." Jacen smiled tightly. "Lilith found Ishtar, the Harithian ambassador, before he escaped the camp. They took me from the river where Deacon had left me, and Ishtar healed me. Brought me back from the brink of death. I suspect Deacon's men had a decoy body burned so he never knew the truth."

Deacon. It was always Deacon. Once it had been Cobryn that Bellona despised, the man accountable for what had happened to Basium, and to her mother. But where Cobryn's power had waned, Deacon's rose in its stead. He had delivered cruelty and pain. Bellona was too exhausted by war to want to repay it, and neither was it her place. She just wanted Deacon where he belonged, buried in the ground.

Thirty-Nine
The Recovering Princess
Lilith Marwan

The only time Lilith had been to Basium, she had been under Cobryn's thumb. Returning free from his oppression was like a whisper of fresh air against her skin, with the forces of Harith at her back. Rumours of Deacon's activity in the north, of current unrest in Nicodemus, made Lilith certain that it was the right thing to do. Bellona Lenore had always been one of Carissa's fiercest allies, and Relda believed an alliance was likely.

Deacon would not return to Dalal, not after the humiliating defeat he had suffered there. It was content in that knowledge that Lilith had felt safe leaving Elyes and Ayesha in Samara's capable hands while the rest of them prepared for battle. She had been hesitant, concerned that her non-warrior status would make her ill-suited for the task. However, she did not intend to fight, but to lead. Her aunt had done so many times, and like Lilith, she lacked swordsmanship and archery capabilities.

A cool wind whistled through the camp as Lilith raised her hands to warm them over one of the numerous fires burning bright through the darkness. Relda joined her with an exaggerated huff, sinking down and staring into the flames. Lilith wondered if she had any doubts about going up against her brother.

"Gretchen would have been here with us." Relda's voice was soft and contemplative, and Lilith's head jerked up at the use of her fellow wife's name, like a squeaking door hinge that hadn't been used in some time.

Lilith had never known Gretchen when she had been a warrior, only when she had been Cobryn's resentful third wife. Lilith's outstretched fingers curled into fists. The memory of Gretchen's body drifting in the water was a half-healed wound, and sometimes it still pained her.

"What we do to Deacon will be in her name," Lilith vowed darkly.

Her daughter would never sit on a Generan throne, and it lifted a weight from Lilith's shoulders. Ayesha deserved more than a target out of her head, courtesy of being a Morrow Queen. She would grow up free from the might of her father's legacy, and it was a gift no one but Jacen had been able to bestow upon her.

Lilith had failed Gretchen and the poor baby that had died with her. She had not failed Jacen and Ayesha.

Closing her eyes, she tilted her head back and let the thick smoke of the fire wash over her face and fill her nostrils. Tears welled behind her closed eyelids, born of a heart wrenching sadness and an ecstatic happiness combined. She could not undo the damage her husband and his brother had done, but she could move forward, creating the sort of world where Gretchen and her child could have lived in peace.

Lilith appraised Theron with a critical eye and could see where Deacon had left his mark. The streets were flooded with water from the lake by the city, but it was in the people's resilience that she found her admiration. The waterways were scattered with gondolas, many fitted with brightly-coloured umbrellas to shield them from the sun's rays.

"This is certainly an interesting way to travel." Relda trailed her fingers over the surface of the water, the sun casting glimmers of green and blue across the silvery expanse. "They've adapted well."

Lilith remained silent. The slow trickle of water and the gentle lull of it against the side of the gondola reminded her of finding Gretchen, skin pale and eyes wide, the life long since having left her after Deacon's cruelty ripped her from this world.

"Did you always know what your brothers were like?" Lilith's voice was soft over the lapping water.

Relda glanced at her with a wry twist to her lips. "Is it terrible that I did, but because it didn't impact me, I didn't care much?"

Lilith mulled over her words and how the harsh truth of them dug beneath her skin. Relda's honesty was like smothering a soothing balm over a slap to the face. A brief sting, a brief comfort. She supposed it was better than the gilded lies that poured from Deacon's mouth, or the blatant hostility from Cobryn's. One of those mouths had been forever silenced, and the second soon to follow.

"So, when was it that you did care?" The words were delivered with more bitterness than Lilith intended, especially since in a way, she could understand Relda. The woman was born into wealth and privilege, unburdened by marriage. She never saw the consequences of Cobryn and Deacon's actions.

"When I was stationed in Harith"—quiet chagrin gentled Relda's words—"I saw the devastation that followed Cobryn's bloodthirst. I didn't expect to meet Ishtar, or have a child with him, but I regret none of it."

The gondola bobbed to a halt, and Relda wasted no time vaulting unceremoniously out onto the stone pavement. She reached out a hand to Lilith and after a moment's hesitation, Lilith took it. She remembered the tale of how Relda had spiked her would-be husband's drink with broken glass to avoid marrying him.

"I can't change what I did in the past." Relda helped Lilith out onto the steady stone. "I have worked for years to atone for my brothers' actions. Much like my nephew, Jacen, some people will always hold me accountable for their crimes."

Lilith's thoughts of her stepson were often a mixture of pride and sorrow. The young man had endured so much over the course of his lifetime. Lilith was not even a decade older than him, but she felt a maternal protectiveness toward him all the same. Not a moment went by where she regretted saving Jacen's life.

When she had found him, broken and bleeding, she'd known she would never find peace if she left him to die. It had been the gods smiling down upon her, perhaps, that Ishtar had not yet left the camp. Together in the darkness, they had dragged Jacen out of danger and healed his wounds to the best of Ishtar's ability before fleeing to Harith.

"My forgiveness doesn't change anything, but…" Lilith inhaled deeply, casting her eyes over the glittering canals. "For what it's worth, I forgive any role you had in what your brothers did."

Relief crossed Relda's face, and Lilith thought maybe her forgiveness was worth more than she'd previously imagined. When she had first met Relda, her initial impression had been of Vida. Now she could see Jacen in that relief, in the desperate desire to be proved as something other than just a Morrow.

"Your forgiveness is more than I could ask for." Relda linked her arm through Lilith's, eyeing the imposing castle of Theron with dread. "I am not looking forward to braving this particular meeting with Queen Carissa tomorrow."

"Relda! Lilith!"

Cairo's voice echoed over the water, his steps hurried as he approached them. Relda arched an eyebrow, while Lilith's stomach twisted as she waited for bad news. It seemed the only sort of news she heard these days.

"What is it?"

"Sebastian Darnell's army." Cairo swept his errant hair back from his face. "They've just arrived and are setting up camp as we speak."

Gratitude flooded through Lilith, her shoulders slumping as the tension left her body. So, the boy had come to fight beside his sister after all. For once, she could actually believe that they might hold out against Deacon. She had never met Sebastian, and was curious why he had left the security of Emlen.

"No doubt he will also come to meet with Carissa tomorrow." Relda sighed dramatically. "This has been quite a day. I think now that I've experienced a gondola, I'll head back to my tent and sleep until dawn."

Tomorrow. Lilith's gaze was drawn to the castle, the red fox on a green background fluttering on the flags. They were all in Theron for the same purpose. They all had the same goal in mind: end Deacon Morrow. Perhaps they all had different reasons, but Lilith's was clear. She wanted a future for her daughter beyond violence and bloodshed. No matter what happened to Lilith, Ayesha deserved that.

FORTY
THE DESPERATE QUEEN
CARISSA DARNELL

Carissa had never seen more boats in the canals of Theron, bobbing along the water with their torches lighting up the darkness. The night was full of dozens of such lights, visible from her balcony in the castle before she turned away and strode back inside.

The remainder of Sebastian's army traipsed into Theron with a weariness hanging over them like a dark cloud. They were accompanied by refugees from Emlen, those who had managed to escape Deacon's wrath. Bellona hadn't known that Sebastian and his entourage would take shelter in Theron until they had arrived, but she had accepted him with begrudging grace that would have made Kato proud. The people were sheltered, clothed, and fed.

With Cyprian Ambrose dead, it had fallen to Jarl to take his place, and anxiety twisted knots in Carissa's stomach as she entered the hall to meet with the young lord. Jarl had always been one of Sebastian's most ardent supporters, and she doubted he was pleased with having to flee to Theron. Instead of anger burning in his eyes, there was a deep sorrow etched across his face. His dislike of her was eclipsed by his grief.

Sebastian and Meliora were not, as Carissa had anticipated, the centre of the congregation. Defeat weighed heavy upon her younger brother's shoulders, and his fingers were clasped with his wife's as he stood back, as though not wanting to draw attention to himself. It was not the demeanour of a king, but of a young man broken.

Jarl glanced at the pair, a furrow in his brow, before he turned to Carissa. He fell to one knee before her, eliciting a gasp from Meliora. Cold shivers raced upon Carissa's spine as Jarl bowed his head. Across the room, General Orien Luce, recently arrived from the capital, clenched his jaw.

"Your Majesty."

Carissa's eyes flicked to Sebastian. One of his most vocal followers had just acknowledged her as the Queen. There was no bitterness or jealousy in Sebastian's violet-blue eyes, simply resignation. He offered her a curt nod, and she understood that while he had sat upon the throne while she had been in Genera, it was not something he wanted.

"Jarl, how could you?" It was Meliora who spoke, hurt flashing across her face as she extricated her hand from Sebastian's and stepped forward. "Sebastian is our monarch. Carissa is..."

"We both know the crown is never what he wanted," Jarl snapped, lurching to his feet and whirling around to glare at his younger sister. "Carissa might be the Blood Queen, but she is the greatest hope we have. I know what Sebastian wants, Meliora. Do you?"

The question made Meliora lapse into silence, brow furrowed. Carissa was mildly surprised and concerned that her brother did not speak up for himself. It was as though the loss of Emlen had cost Sebastian his voice. Swallowing hard, Carissa reached out a hand to her brother. She expected him to bat it away, but instead he took it, stepping forward and kissing the back of it.

"I have lost our family." Sebastian drew in a ragged breath, eyes meeting hers for the first time since he'd arrived. "I have lost a father-in-law, a child..."

His voice choked up, and Carissa's heart ached at the unexpected loss, a cold stone dropping in the pit of her stomach. She hadn't known that Meliora was expecting, but how would she? Deacon had not exactly kept her updated on the news in Basium.

"Sebastian, I'm so sorry."

"I wore the crown because there was no one else." Tears glistened in Sebastian's eyes as he shook his head fervently. "But I don't want it. I am not suited to it. I was not made for politics or court intrigue. I miss the forge, and the life I had before everyone knew who I was."

Carissa had grown up in a pit of snakes, and Sebastian had grown up in the heat of the forge. Their lives had been forever changed since the Conquest. There was no going back to the people they had been before that. In another world, Sebastian might have one day worn the crown, but in this one, he had no desire for it. Carissa clasped his hand in hers and squeezed tightly.

"You have done an admirable job, Sebastian. I can think of no one else I would rather leave in charge in my absence."

She spoke as though she had left for a holiday, instead of facing the truth of what had happened in Genera. Yet in that darkness there were pinpoints of light, blinking like stars in the night sky. She had caused instability in Deacon's rule. She had made unlikely friends, who supported her through her ordeal. Perhaps, in some way, the changes being made in Genera were as much to do with her as they were the Generans.

Sebastian scoffed. "I can think of plenty of people who would have done better than me."

Carissa couldn't help but smile, and an answering grin was echoed on Sebastian's face. For the first time, she could see the young boy who had teased her and stolen apple tarts from her plate during dessert. They had changed, but perhaps in some ways, the ghosts of who they'd once been would remain with them.

The arrival of the Harithian army was cause for much cheer in Theron. Carissa's curiosity burned hotter than most since she had heard tales of Prince Cairo Amir's power. When Deacon had attempted to seize the city, Cairo made the earth tremble beneath them, like the whole world had shuddered at his might.

He was like her, with power pulsing through his veins, a power he might not yet be able to control. In order to understand herself, Carissa hoped that she could understand Cairo. Impatience itched at her, prickling beneath her skin, though she waited until the army settled in before she invited Cairo for tea in her rooms. The scent of cinnamon and cloves lingered over them as Carissa let the warm liquid slide down her throat, examining Cairo across the table.

"I heard about what you did in Dalal."

Cairo smiled tightly, setting his porcelain cup down. "I believe everyone has by now. Cairo Amir, the Anointed."

There was a bitterness in the words that the tea didn't quite wash away as Carissa took another sip. She understood what it was to fear power, as she had spent years being afraid of her own.

"My power is like yours. Volatile, difficult to control. Like trying to cup water in your hands and watching it trickle through your fingers."

Cairo's dark eyes flicked up to meet hers. "Water doesn't destroy the way we do."

Carissa thought of Deacon's power, how he had tried to drown Theron, how he had taken down Isadore with a sweep of his hand. She had only ever seen water cause destruction. It had not been something gentle for her, but a violent reminder of what her enemy was capable of.

"Yes, it does," she said quietly.

"I know what you want, Carissa." Cairo leaned back in his chair, smoothing a hand over his brow. A bone-deep weariness settled in his expression. "You want me to help you defeat Deacon. You want me to reach into that magic again."

"It's no longer about what I want." Carissa set her cup down with a clatter. A storm built beneath her skin, not one born of her magic that time, but a desperation to protect her people. It churned and raged, unwilling to be silenced. "If you and I do not stand together against him, we will fall. Our countries will fall, as they once did. We've both experienced enough loss."

"As you heard of my exploits, so I have heard of yours." Cairo smiled humourlessly, dark eyes shining with accusation. "Quite the feat you accomplished in Belvedere."

Cold dread slithered down Carissa's back at the memory of the destruction she had caused. Was it worse that she did not regret it? She wore the mantle of Blood Queen like a battle scar.

"I cannot do this on my own." The words were soft, a desperate plea barely audible above the trill of birdsong outside the window. "I know you are afraid. I'm fucking terrified. But if you and I do not stand together, what sort of legacy do we leave behind for our children? What do you think happens to your daughter and my son?"

Cairo considered that in silence, staring down into the brown depths of his tea. He and Carissa lived in the shadow of their families' defeats, left to pick up the pieces of what had once been proud nations. They were both powerful but damaged, shattered by the brutality of House Morrow's greed.

Carissa could not fix what had happened to her family. She could not go back in time and undo those horrors. She once held their demise clumsily in her hands like something she could put back together, the way her mother Imogen had patiently fixed Sebastian's broken toys. There was no going back, and that trauma would always be a part of her, a sharp shard lingering and waiting to cut her.

Carissa had a family of her own now. A husband, a son, a brother. She could not heal the wounds that Cobryn and Deacon had inflicted upon her, but the people she loved were a soothing balm. They would never make the scars go away, and yet, they would make moving forward easier. A lighter heart, an easier smile. That was all she had ever wanted.

"I just…" Cairo's voice was barely above a whisper, shaking with a mix of anger and agony that Carissa felt in her own heartbeat. "I want this to be over. I want a future for my country, not more of the same. Lilith deserves better. Ayesha deserves better. They have suffered for years, and I turned my head because it was easier not to look."

"We have all suffered." Carissa reached across to rest a hand over his. "It does end, Cairo. It ends with us."

Carissa enjoyed walks with Zephyr through Theron, marvelling in his wide-eyed fascination with his surroundings. It grieved her that she hadn't been around to hear the first word he had uttered, to witness his first steps. It burned beneath her skin like a half-healed wound, all the things she had missed in her son's life. Zephyr had gained confidence, toddling through the cobblestone streets with his tiny hand curled tightly in Carissa's.

The last time she'd seen Lilith Marwan, Carissa had been pregnant and grieving her grandmother's death. Though she'd heard of the woman's flight to Harith, she certainly hadn't expected Lilith to lead the Harithian army to Theron. She was accompanied by a woman in her late thirties whose resemblance to Vida made Carissa's breath catch in her throat.

"You look like you've seen a ghost." The woman's voice was deep and throaty, a stark contrast to Vida's. There was no bow, no formal greeting, simply a wide grin that spread across a face lightly freckled by the sun. Her eyes flicked to Zephyr, who hid shyly behind his mother's skirts.

"Your Majesty." Lilith curtsied deeply, the picture of grace even in riding pants and an oversized shirt. It was a far cry from the jewel-toned velvet dresses she had worn in Basium, but there was a glimmer in her dark eyes that she'd never possessed as a woman trapped in matrimony. "Forgive Relda her lack of manners."

"Relda Morrow?" The name was familiar, and Carissa recalled that she was the middle sibling of the older Morrow generation, Cobryn and Deacon's sister who had been in Harith since the country had been conquered.

"The very same." Relda's grin didn't fade. She had been described as a bold woman, and Carissa saw that description was apt. She had a bastard son by a Harithian nobleman, from what little Carissa could remember of discussions of Relda. "This must be your son, Zephyr. He has your colouring, but I can see my nephew in the shape of his face."

Carissa smiled tightly, reaching down to stroke Zephyr's dark hair. Her son's shyness with strangers was reminiscent of her as a young girl. From what she'd heard, Jacen had been an outgoing child, prone to laughter and mischief with Vida, approaching strangers without fear.

"There is someone who wants to speak with you." Lilith glanced over her shoulder as a stunning woman with braids piled atop her head approached. Something about her made Carissa prickle with unease, a metallic tang coating her tongue. "This is Jameela. She is an Anointed, and she sees the future."

Like Miriam. Carissa still yearned for her grandmother years after her execution, as she yearned for her parents, grandfather, and older brothers. If Jameela was determined to speak with her upon arrival, then she had seen something in Carissa's future, and Carissa was not certain she would like it.

"Your Majesty." Jameela dipped a shallow curtsy, arching an eyebrow. "May we walk?"

"Of course."

Carissa liked strolling along the edge of the waterway, though it filled her with unease. She and Bellona had agreed that their final battle against Deacon could not be in Theron, lest the water be used against them. They both remembered the darkness closing in around them as the tunnels were sealed, Bellona's desperate scream for her father.

When Zephyr tired, his small steps faltering with weariness, Carissa picked him and propped him against her hip. His warm weight was a comforting balm to her, his little fingers toying with her dark hair.

"I doubt you've heard the prophecy of the city-killers." Jameela's voice rose over the gentle lull of water lapping against stone. "Three cities will be in the age of the Morrow Empire. The mages who are responsible are two men and one woman ."

Cold dread washed over Carissa as she thought of Belvedere. "I was one of them. I was the woman."

"Yes, the third city-killer." Jameela didn't sound perturbed. "The two men came before you."

"Deacon," Carissa whispered, her mind drawn to the colossal waves that drowned Isadore.

"He was the second."

Carissa stopped, her dress swirling around her ankles, Zephyr clutched tight to her. "Then who was the first?"

Jameela cast a look out over the water, shielding her eyes from the afternoon sun.

"Until recently, it was a secret I was content to take to my grave. But it is a secret no longer. Cairo Amir was the first city-killer, the destroyer of Elyes. He revealed his power a second time when Deacon's army marched on Dalal. He is the most powerful mage this continent has ever seen."

"Cairo destroyed Elyes?" Something clicked into place. All the things Cairo had left unsaid during their conversation. The shame and the pain that glimmered in his dark eyes. The way he feared his power enough to take Obscurate, the familiar sickly sweet scent making Carissa's stomach churn with revulsion when she had first inhaled it.

"Not deliberately. Cairo's power, like most, is tied to his emotions, and the city's destruction was a misguided attempt to stop the Generan oppressor."

Carissa considered her words in stunned silence. She understood that all too well, recalling the damage she had wreaked during her grandmother's execution. Cairo had just done it on a far larger, more devastating scale. She clenched her jaw and lifted her chin, examining Jameela imperiously.

"Is that why you wished to speak to me? To remind me what I am? To tell me that all I can do is destroy?"

"No." Jameela swept her braids back. "I have seen what you must do to defeat Deacon Morrow, but you will not like it."

Carissa's skin crawled, but she persevered. "Tell me anyway."

"You have to confront your past, and the sins of your family's past."

Irritation prickled at her. "What does that even mean?"

"You know where your magic came from." Jameela's tone was grim and understanding dawned on Carissa. Her dark legacy as Jameson Burnett's great-granddaughter was no longer a secret. "You may not know where to look, but there's another who does."

"I am tired of enigmas, Jameela." Carissa reached up with her free hand to rub her temple. Queen, mother, wife...all these roles were giving her a headache. She was expected to don one mantle after another, play her parts perfectly.

Jameela examined her curiously, as though expecting to see something in her expression that she did not find.

"Your Majesty, another Darnell with magic in their blood lives."

Carissa's brow pinched. Did she mean Zephyr? The boy was a child, not even two years old. Jameela saw Carissa's gaze drawn down to her son and shook her head.

"Your brother. Sebastian."

Forty-One
The Blood Prince
Sebastian Darnell

The idea that magic coursed through his blood was ridiculous to Sebastian. Yet, how could he deny it? He had countless nightmares about the cave where Burnett had died. He had seen Tycho Salus in his dreams. When Carissa came to him with questions, it chilled him to the bone to realise he had the answers, like pieces of a puzzle slotting together. As the city slept, Carissa and Sebastian departed under the cloak of darkness.

He told Meliora where they were going, of course. There was nothing he didn't share with his wife. She had nodded with grim satisfaction, like she had known that was where his journey would take him all along. Sebastian would find Tycho, in his place of sunshine and peace, and bring death and war to his door once more. It made his stomach turn.

From Theron, it took half a day on horseback riding north to reach the quiet country that Tycho called home.

When Sebastian rapped on the door, the weathered face that answered was the old man from his dreams. He swallowed hard. Tycho took in their garments, the riding clothes that Carissa pushed to wear to avoid being recognised, but it was when his eyes travelled up to their faces that he paused, fingers splayed against the wood of the doorframe.

"When I went into retirement, your father hadn't even been born yet." Tycho shook his head slowly. "But I would recognise you two anywhere. Carissa and Sebastian Darnell, at my doorstep."

"It's a pleasure to meet you, General Tycho." Carissa was all pretty words and a polite smile, but Tycho's scowl deepened.

"Don't call me that. It's just Tycho. I don't know what you two are looking for, but you are not going to find it here."

He made to close the door, but Sebastian wedged his boot in to stop him.

"We've travelled a long way, Tycho. All we want is answers."

Tycho's eyes lit up with fear. "I swore I would never speak about what happened that day."

"The people you gave that oath to are dead now." Carissa planted her hands on her hips. Even in riding leathers, she looked every inch the Queen. "I cannot force you to talk to us, but please know, we would not have come to disturb you if we had any other choice."

Tycho's expression was one of exasperation, before he blew out a long breath and yanked the door open wide, muttering under his breath. Carissa exchanged a look with Sebastian. Whatever she had been expecting from the former general, it hadn't been a bad-tempered old man.

Tycho's house was modestly furnished. Sebastian's eyes cast around the wooden flooring, the brick walls. It was sparse, with little decoration. Tycho struck him as a practical man, and that was reflected in the way he had set up his home. There was no sign that anyone aside from Tycho resided there, leaving Sebastian to guess the man had been alone, for the most part, since his retirement. Was that a lonely existence, or a peaceful one?

"Your choices of tea are peppermint, lemon myrtle, or black with a dash of milk." Tycho's words were brusque as he bustled about the kitchen, silverware clanging and the kettle whistling as he put it on to boil.

"Oh, um, lemon myrtle, please." Carissa perched herself on a chair, clasping her hands in her lap. Sebastian didn't know her as well as he used to, but he could tell by her rigid demeanour that she was on edge.

"I'll have the same," Sebastian added quickly, hoping that if they weren't too difficult, Tycho would be more inclined to be open with them. He sat down as well, the sharp citrus aroma of the tea filling the space as Tycho crossed over with a pot of boiling water filled with herbal tea leaves.

"Now, I want to make this a quick visit." Tycho reclined in a chair with a huff as Carissa poured each of them tea. "This is about what happened with Burnett, isn't it?"

"Yes." Sebastian raked his fingers through his hair, unkempt and windswept. "I've been having…nightmares. About a dark cave beneath a waterfall. I don't know for sure, but I remember that Burnett was killed in a cave. It was his lair, or something."

"You have magic?" Curiosity sparked in Tycho's eyes as they flicked to Carissa. "I knew the girl did, but you…"

"It's a recent discovery." Sebastian's smile was more of a grimace. "I have visions of the past, just as my grandmother Miriam did of the future. That's all there is to it. Magic is rare in the men of our family's line, so it makes sense mine is not strong."

"What is it you can do?" Tycho sipped his tea as he kept his gaze on Carissa. "Blood magic?"

"Yes, and…" Carissa chewed at her lip. "Recently, I found out that I possess something else. Storm magic."

Tycho lurched back in his chair as though she had physically struck him. The table jolted, hot tea splashing across its surface as he regarded Carissa with a horrified expression. Her own look turned to bewilderment.

"I can't do this," Tycho muttered, gripping the back of the chair so tightly his knuckles shone white.

"What is that supposed to mean?" Sebastian demanded, realising that something in Carissa's words had triggered such a strong reaction in the old man. "You were fine with us until she said that. Storm magic."

"Because, boy," Tycho snapped, eyes flaring with anger, "that was the sort of magic that killed Jameson Burnett and every single other person in that cave, save for myself and your grandparents."

Carissa shook her head vehemently as she dabbed at the spilt tea with a cloth.

"But...that's not possible. Our grandmother had the ability to heal wounds and see the future."

Tycho's laugh was mirthless, and he ran a hand down his weathered cheek.

"If only that was all Miriam had."

A tense silence settled over them like a heavy cloak. Sebastian had not seen his grandmother since the Conquest, but he certainly remembered her magic. It wasn't anything like Tycho was saying. Surely they would have known if Miriam had storm magic, as Carissa had discovered she did. Yet...all the stories said a wild storm had raged through Basium the day that Burnett fell. An omen from the goddess Elethea, or something else?

"Then tell us." Carissa gestured to the chair he had leapt from. "Tell us what really happened that day."

Tycho exhaled deeply, sitting down and taking a sip of the lemon myrtle tea. The quiet stretched on for a few moments, and Sebastian wondered if he would speak at all. When he did, his tone was soft and grim.

"You know, of course, that Burnett was a blood mage. When he took the blood of others, he was able to conjure their power, as you can, Carissa. He went about this unchallenged, for there were few mages who possessed the sort of power to stop him. One of these was an Imperium, Elinor. She was a close friend of Miriam's, with the power to manipulate metal. She went up against Burnett, and she failed.

"Elinor was captured by Burnett, because he saw potential in her magic and wanted it for himself. There was a cave where he conducted these...experiments. He tortured, maimed, and killed these mages to grow his own magic. The only person who knew where it was located was his daughter, Miriam. She had remained neutral in the conflict, but once Burnett took Elinor, she came before young King Patrick and struck a deal: she would lead him to Burnett and help destroy him if it meant saving Elinor."

A queasiness swirled in the pit of Sebastian's stomach. He had never heard of Elinor, and that could not bode well for where the tale was going. His fingers curled tightly in the hem of his shirt. Miriam and Patrick had not often spoken about their past, or how they had met. He wondered if his father Frederick had known the truth.

Tycho took another sip of his tea, his hands trembling around the mug.

"I was, as you would be aware, the General of the King's armies at this point. Along with two dozen other soldiers, I accompanied Patrick and Miriam to the cave where Burnett had his stronghold. We were too late to save Elinor. By the time we arrived, Burnett already had her blood staining his hands."

Sebastian snuck a glance at Carissa. His sister had paled at the reminder of how much damage blood magic, *her* magic, could do.

"Miriam was…she was enraged. She confronted her father with a desire for retribution. The soldiers could not move against Burnett, for they were all in armour. All aside from myself and Patrick, who were in riding leathers, for we had stripped ourselves of it the moment we realised he had spilled Elinor's blood."

A shadow crossed over Tycho's face, and Sebastian realised they had not yet heard the worst of it. Burnett's experiments, Elinor's death…they were nothing compared to what was coming, and he braced himself for it, drawing up all the walls and barriers that had once separated Sebastian the prince from the blacksmith boy he'd wanted to be so desperately.

"I have heard that mages can sometimes unlock more than one ability if they possess it. If it is in their blood, in moments of extreme emotion, a second power can be discovered. In some, very rarely, even a third. That is what Miriam did that day, and I truly believe that she did not know she could control the power of the storm, that she did not realise what she would do…"

"No," Carissa gasped, her violet-blue eyes shining with trepidation.

"Miriam called down lightning, and everyone in that cave, everyone save herself and Patrick and I, was electrocuted instantly. Including Burnett."

Carissa pressed a hand over her mouth. Icy shock coursed through Sebastian. There was so much he did not know about his grandmother, about their bloody legacy, and that had to be the most shocking of all.

Burnett had never killed all of those soldiers.

Miriam had.

"The three of us, the sole survivors, agreed never to speak of what happened in that cave. Burnett was dead, and that was enough. We buried him and the soldiers in that darkness. Patrick was enraptured by Miriam, and they married not long after. But I...I could never forget the sins of the past. I was too close to it in Marinel, so I sought out early retirement because I wanted to forget what had happened."

"Tycho, I..." Carissa stumbled over her words. "I'm so sorry. I didn't want to dig up something so painful."

"Unfortunately, there's something else I need to ask of you." Sebastian steeled himself, drawing in a heavy breath. "We need to know where the cave is."

He expected a barrage of angry retorts, assurance that Tycho would sooner die than go back to that place. Instead, when he looked at the old man, he saw tears leaking down his wrinkled face. It was as though he had known that day would come: the day where he must return to the darkest part of his past.

"I will take you there." Tycho's voice came out hoarse, making Carissa's head snap up. "But I would rather plunge a knife through my own heart than go into that cave again. You hear me? I'll bring you there, but if you enter, it's on your own."

Forty-Two

The Storm Queen
Carissa Darnell

The roar of the waterfall drowned out every other sound, overwhelming Carissa's senses. She stared up at the tranquil trees swaying in the light breeze, the sunlight dappling through the leaves. How deceptive that the place appeared so calm when so much death had happened there. She dreaded what lay in wait behind the curtain of clear water, the darkness that she and Sebastian had to confront.

Why was *that* what it took to defeat Deacon? Frustration coursed through Carissa. She had left her husband and son behind. She had left everyone else to plan the next move, all while she and Sebastian went chasing ghosts. If Jameela was wrong, Carissa didn't know what she would do. She had to have faith that it wasn't for nothing.

Beside her, Sebastian's eyes were round as coins, and if that didn't prove he recognised the place from his nightmares, she wasn't sure what would. She reached across and gripped his hand in hers, giving it a reassuring squeeze. They had once been rivals, but they were still siblings, the last of the Darnells. They were in it together, for better or worse.

"This is the place." Tycho pointed a shaking finger toward the waterfall. He did not seem like a man easily spooked, but Carissa could not blame him for his fear, after the atrocities that had occurred in the cave. "If you head up those rocks, that's how you get behind the waterfall. That's where the cave is."

"Thank you, Tycho." Carissa glanced at him with genuine gratitude. "We couldn't have done this without you. We won't trouble you any further."

She was glad for choosing to wear her riding gear as she stepped over the rocks, slimy from exposure to the elements. With each step, she made sure her footing was secure. Her boots were sturdy, crunching over loose pebbles as every footfall drew her toward darkness. Her stomach twisted when she reached the edge of the waterfall, peering behind it into the yawning chasm that was the cave.

"This is it." Sebastian's voice was quiet, trembling with trepidation as he stepped up behind her to peer into the cave. "This is exactly where my nightmares take me."

Carissa raised her arms to balance herself as she took a big step from the rock into the cave, almost losing her balance and teetering on the heel of her boot. Sebastian's hands firmly gripped her shoulders from behind, easing her forward. She turned and offered a hand, pulling him up and into darkness.

Deep in the cave, there was a wide circle of light. Carissa's eyes flicked up to take in the trees overhead, shadowing what was a jagged circle in the ceiling of the cave. Was that where Miriam had called down the storm, or had it always been there? Biting down on her lip, Carissa moved through the cave, uncertain what she was meant to find.

The scent of moisture and mould clogged her nostrils, her boots squelching over mud. Metal glimmered ominously in the dimness, catching her gaze. As her sight adjusted to the gloom, her stomach lurched when she realised they were a series of swords, planted blade-first in the dirt. Sebastian caught her arm, and she whirled to face him, noting the apprehension in his eyes.

"They're graves. For the fallen soldiers."

He was right. Though unmarked, it was clear that the dirt had been moved here, a long time ago, the soil uneven. Something cracked under Carissa's boot, and she gasped and flinched backward when the pearly gleam of bone appeared beneath her foot. She reached back blindly, her hand nudging Sebastian's until his fingers curled through hers.

"This is as far as I came in my nightmares." Sebastian's voice was a whisper, the dull roar of the waterfall a low hum as they ventured further into the cave. His magic had gotten them that far, and she feared it was up to her for what was to come. A cold sweat broke out across her body as she saw something glimmering in the pale light. She knelt, knees trembling, and unearthed a skull.

"Is this…"

"Jameson Burnett." Sebastian choked out the words. "Yes."

The evil within the cave was palpable to Carissa, like a cloying odour that filled her nostrils and wouldn't let her breathe. It reached for her with greedy fingers, caressing her trembling form and threatening to consume her. She reminded herself that it was just a place. A place full of death, but a place that could not hurt her.

Comprehension dawned on Carissa, a light in the darkness. It was not a welcome revelation, making her choke in a breath.

"I know why we're here. I know what we have to do."

She turned the skull over in her fingers, nausea rolling in the pit of her stomach. Once, to save her country from ruin, she had consumed blood to boost her power. What would happen, she wondered, if she was to consume bone? Her books had spoken in passing of the Bone Rite, but remained either silent or enigmatic about what it did. Could it be such an unspeakable horror that even the scholars dare not breathe a word of it?

The skull snapped like a twig between the pressure of her hands, and Carissa raised its powdery remains to her lips with shaking fingers, tears welling in her eyes as she forced it into her mouth.

The scent of smoke was thick in the air, distant screams pricking at her ears. The flames licked at Carissa's feet, and when she stumbled back, she looked over a city in flames. Marinel, the night of the Conquest. Everywhere she looked, fire edged her vision, hemming her in and making her breath rattle in her chest as

293

smoke filtered into her lungs.

"Why am I seeing this?" Carissa demanded of no one at all. "Why would Burnett's skull show me this?"

"You don't think that he could see the future, as his daughter did?" Theodore Darnell stepped out of the fire, cocking his head to the side. He had always most closely resembled Miriam, with his brown hair and laughing brown eyes. In another life, Theodore would have become Basium's King. He stared Carissa down with a hollowness he had never possessed in life.

She shook her head fervently. "You're dead."

His smile was strained. "But I'm alive within you, Carissa. We all are. Burnett's malice and magic will eat away at you if you don't fight back against it."

"I don't understand." Carissa fell to her knees before him, tilting her head up to stare beseechingly up at him. "How is this meant to help me defeat Deacon? Why is coming back to this place, reliving these memories, necessary?"

Theodore reached out a hand to sweep Carissa's hair back from her face. Her oldest brother had always seemed so grown-up and mature when she had been fourteen, but she was almost the same age he had been when he'd died, and it felt painfully young and inexperienced.

"Because you never accepted it. Some part of you still clings to what happened that night, and to our grandmother's execution. You need to let go of the girl you were and become the woman you were born to be."

"Avenge us." Peregrine moved from the flames to stand beside Theodore, ash smeared across his freckled face. She was older than her middle brother had been when he had died. Sebastian was almost older, too.

"I don't know how." Carissa's words came out as a plea, cracking with despair. "I have tried to be what they wanted, and then I tried being myself. I've been in Genera for a year. How can they ever think I'm the rightful Queen? How can I bring down Deacon when I've failed so many times?"

"Wake up, Carissa!" Peregrine snapped, clicking his fingers in her face, a gesture so reminiscent of his impatience with her when he'd be alive that she almost laughed. "Jarl Ambrose was one of Sebastian's most loyal, and he swore to *you*. Everyone recognises your power, your potential. Everyone but you."

"My darling girl." Imogen joined her children, moving gracefully through the smoke to help Carissa to her feet and take her face in her hands. "Look how much you've grown. You are a mother yourself now, and you know how important the bond of family is. You and your little brother will do wonders. You just need to have faith in yourself, and in each other."

Patrick and Frederick emerged from the smoke side by side, and Carissa turned her accusing gaze upon her grandfather.

"There was so much you never told me."

"You were a child, dear girl." Patrick shook his head slowly, his eyes brimming with sorrow. "You grew up far too fast."

"Embrace your magic." Frederick placed his hands on Carissa's shoulders, staring deeply into her eyes as Imogen drew back. "You are so close. You accepted what you were in Genera; why not in Basium?"

"Because I'm afraid of what my magic will do," Carissa whispered.

The smoke blurred their faces, obscuring them from her vision. When she blinked again, they faded away. A cry tore from her lips, tears streaming down her cheeks as she reached out for the family that she had lost. Their violent deaths had been the end of the Conquest, but they had merely been the beginning of Carissa's path of vengeance. She fell to her knees and sobbed, her heart aching for those who had been ripped from her, leaving behind holes she could never fill.

"Carissa?"

There was no fire, no smoke. She was back in the eerie darkness of the cave, Sebastian leaning over her with concern etched across his pale face. Little Sebastian, who had been twelve when he had been orphaned. Above them, where the sun had shone through the leaves of the trees, clouds gathered and thunder rumbled ominously.

"Stay back." Carissa held her hands up as she eased herself to her feet. She could feel the magic thrumming in her veins, the pit of her power yawning open. The last person she wanted to hurt was her brother. "I can't control my storm magic."

"Yes, you can." Sebastian took a bold step forward instead. "I'm not scared of you, Carissa. Maybe I was once, but you are my sister. Call down the storm."

"No." Carissa shook her head vehemently. She had done so when she had nothing to lose, back in Genera when she was dozens of cracks barely held together. She was almost whole again, and she feared her volatile magic would break her.

"I believe in you." Sebastian's voice trembled, eyes glassing over with tears. "I know I have doubted you in the past, and I'm sorry. I'm so sorry. I'm here for you now, I promise. You just need to let it go."

Perhaps, after all these years, it had never been Jacen's assurance she had needed. Perhaps it was meant to be Sebastian, the brother she had lost and found again. She took a deep breath and relinquished control, battering down the wall that had housed her grief and her pain for so long.

A raw scream erupted from Carissa as she reached her hands up toward the sky, something terrifying and enthralling tingling within her. An ancient magic surged through her veins, and she was not going to control it any longer. She was going to set it free.

Was that what it had felt like for Miriam, when she had accepted the power of the storm? Lightning crackled overhead and speared down to her waiting fingertips. It lit the darkness, purple-white sparks illuminating the broad grin on Sebastian's face. Even as the lightning streaked down and flared around them, he never once stepped back. He never once looked away. He had once looked at his sister with horror, but instead, he looked at her with hope.

Carissa inhaled and exhaled, drawing the crackling currents deep within her bones. She didn't fight them, but instead she welcomed them. The wild magic was a part of her, just like the blood magic she had feared.

She did not control the storm. She *was* the storm.

Carissa was tired of losing places and people she cared about. As Cairo had once unleashed hell upon the Morrows in Elyes, so too would she rain down her magic on the man who had tormented her for years.

Next time, they would not lose any cities. Next time, she would do it right. With the storm in her bones and lightning crackling at her fingertips, a savage smile graced Carissa's lips, and she saw it answered in the glee shining in Sebastian's eyes.

"Let's go kill some monsters."

Forty-Three
The Beloved King
Jacen Morrow

The quiet that lingered over Theron was a welcome boon. Tomorrow, there would be the chaos of clanging metal and the cacophony of people shouting as they moved out to Fortua. The streets had been a hubbub of movement and sound, the Ciroccan troops that had arrived earlier in the afternoon being settled into the campsite beyond the city walls. King Alessandro and Queen Bianca had kept their promise of aid at last.

Tonight, there was the chirp of crickets and Zephyr making incoherent noises as he toddled around the bedroom, curiously inspecting everything and grabbing at blankets and pillows with small hands.

Jacen couldn't help but crack a smile as he watched his son. His colouring was almost all Carissa, but some of his mannerisms were so reminiscent of Jacen. Zephyr eventually tired of exploration and settled on the floor with a wooden toy, turning it over clumsily in his fingers. Jacen had doubted himself as a father, but he had taken each step tentatively, acknowledging that Zephyr didn't really know him.

Carissa's furtive mission made Jacen uneasy, though he would never have said so, as he also understood its importance. Sebastian's role in it was more of a question, though it went unasked. Jacen trusted his wife. She knew what she was doing.

A tap on the door made Jacen ease himself to his feet, Zephyr's curious eyes following him across the room. He turned the handle, mildly surprised to see

Bellona as he opened the door. She smiled ruefully, sweeping her errant ginger hair back from her face.

"Can I come in?"

"Of course." Jacen pushed the door open wider, and Zephyr's eyes lit up at the sight of his former guardian. It made Jacen's heart ache, wishing that one day, his son would look at him with such wonder.

"Bell!"

"Zephyr." Bellona smiled fondly as he rushed over to her, and she scooped him up and rested him on her hip. For a woman who was not overly enthusiastic about children, she had done an incredible job of raising Zephyr in Jacen and Carissa's absence.

"I hope he loves me that much someday."

A year or two ago, it would have been too vulnerable to confess to Bellona, but he considered her one of his closest friends. Her green eyes flashed with surprise as she raised a hand to ruffle Zephyr's dark hair.

"He just hasn't seen you and Carissa since he was a baby. Give him time, and he'll become accustomed to you as he did to me."

"Do you really think this will work?" Jacen asked quietly, his mind drifting to his wife and the dire mission she and Sebastian had set out on.

"Yes." Bellona responded without a beat of hesitation, eyes burning with a determined fire. "She is strong, and she knows it. She just fears it, too. I hope that, whatever they find there, it will be enough for her to overcome that fear and to defeat Deacon."

Jacen had not seen Deacon since his uncle had attempted to kill him. He wanted to rend open Deacon's chest and pull out his still-beating heart with his bare hands for what the man had done to Carissa, to all of them. Though he wanted vengeance, he also believed the ultimate decision should be Carissa's.

"She can do it." Jacen fully believed that much with all his heart. His doubt stemmed from Carissa's drive, not her ability. "With us by her side, hopefully she *will* do it."

"When you first returned to Basium, I didn't like you at all." Bellona swept a strand of dark hair back from Zephyr's face.

Jacen feigned shock. "Really? I wouldn't have guessed."

Bellona rolled her eyes. "Hilarious. I was protective of Carissa. I saw how much she suffered after what happened to her family, and I assumed you'd be the cause of more suffering. I was wrong about you, and I realised that pretty early on; I just didn't want to admit it. So, I kept you under suspicion, and that wasn't fair."

Jacen remained silent, giving Bellona the space to speak what was on her mind without interrupting her train of thought. The scent of musk and cloves lingered over the room, along with the last remnants of lavender that reminded him of Carissa.

"Now I see that you are a good man, and you are deserving of love. You deserve Carissa, you deserve Zephyr. You don't deserve what has happened to you, and I am sorry that it did."

Her words stunned Jacen, for he didn't think he could recall people saying he deserved good things, that he deserved love. Jacen's life had been a series of duties, and then resentment for the acts he had committed in the midst of those duties. It had not occurred to him that others, aside from Carissa, might believe he was worthy of something more.

"I'm grateful." Jacen smiled, reaching out with hesitant hands to take Zephyr from Bellona. The child examined him quietly. "For you, and your friendship with Carissa. You've been there for her through so much, and you've never once wavered. I admire that about you."

Bellona's eyes welled with tears, and she threw her arms around Jacen. He hugged her back, surprised at the embrace and the force of it. Zephyr giggled and reached out to pat Bellona's ginger hair. For a moment, there was peace. He could believe, with his son in his arms and a woman who'd become a close and unlikely friend to him, that there was a future for him in Basium—something he could never picture in Genera.

This was his home, and he would fight for it to the bitter end.

 Forty-Four
The Powerful Prince
Sebastian Darnell

Brilliant dawn stretched across the sky in various violet and pink hues as Sebastian stood at the edge of camp, away from the grind of steel against stone and the chatter of the people. The torches blinked and burned like fireflies, the heady scent of campfire smoke thick on the gentle morning breeze.

Sebastian enjoyed travelling. In the cities, he sought refuge in the quiet places, like the heat of the forge. Places where he could concentrate. Traversing the countryside, it was easier. The hustle around the camp was subdued by the calls of the wildlife, owls hooting their indignation from the tree and foxes snarling somewhere in the depths of the woods. Unfortunately in the past few days, tranquillity meant time for Sebastian to reflect on the cave.

The memories of the cave imprinted themselves in Sebastian's mind, an echo of the power he had not truly begun to understand. Part of him had hoped the cave was a wild hunch, and yet…he had been right. About Tycho, about all of it. Carissa was not the only grandchild of Miriam Darnell to inherit some of her magic, which both enthralled and troubled Sebastian. What was he meant to do now, knowing he was an Imperium?

A gentle hand rested on Sebastian's shoulder, the light touch causing him to jolt out of his reverie. Meliora glided to his side, linking her fingers through his. She carried herself with such grace that sometimes he forgot, with a churn of guilt in the pit of his stomach, how much she had endured these past months as well. The loss of their baby weighed heavily on her, exacerbating dark shadows under her eyes.

"You still haven't told me what happened."

Mild accusation tainted her tone, the hurt of a girl used to being held deep in her husband's trust. It wasn't a matter of trust this time. It was Sebastian coming to terms with everything that had happened.

"We found the past, and maybe the future."

A smile quirked the corners of Meliora's lips. "Well, that's infuriatingly vague."

"Sorry." Sebastian shook his head to rid it of the darkness of the cave, turning to give her his full attention. "The truth is…I don't really know what happened. I thought I was one thing, but it turns out maybe I'm something else."

"You mean, you're concerned because you're an Imperium?" A furrow etched itself in Meliora's smooth brow.

In the inky black, Sebastian had finally seen Carissa for what she truly was. She had lit up the darkness with the might of a storm, lightning sparking around her and thunder roaring its approval. They had been taught the legends of how the Darnell family were descended from the goddess, but it was Miriam's power that had been bestowed upon Carissa.

Carissa was a queen. A wife. A mother. A sister.

Now, he believed that she was as close to a god walking upon Razmaran soil as ever existed. Now, his fear of her power had been replaced by something more dangerous still: hope. Hope that Carissa could help win the war.

"I'll never be as powerful as my sister." Sebastian exhaled a deep breath, watching as it fogged the chilly air and feeling the light burn of the cold in his lungs as he inhaled once more. "I don't want to be. But maybe I understand her more because of it. Our combined magic has led us here. Maybe the goddess has smiled down on our family once again."

Their family had endured loss, death, humiliation. Sebastian had approached the throne with a sense of duty— it was something he felt obligated to rather than because it was something he wanted . Carissa, though…she was a natural. Perhaps not as outspoken or as confident as monarchs before her, but a thoughtful and compassionate leader. When everything was over, Carissa should be on the Basiumite throne with no questions asked.

Across the years since he had emerged from the tunnels beneath Marinel, bloodstained and sobbing, Sebastian never questioned whether there was magic flowing through his veins. It had always been the women in his family born with such power. Understated though it was, magic lived in him. Magic that connected him to Carissa, magic that brought them to Tycho and the cave.

They would avenge their family. They could never undo the damage that had been done, the pain that they had experienced to come so far, but they could make sure their future burned as bright as the midsummer sun.

Sebastian turned back to the camp, but Meliora's hand tightened around his. "Wait."

When Sebastian spun back, he followed her line of sight into the blanket of morning fog. There was movement on the horizon. Panic seized Sebastian with cruel talons. They hadn't expected the Generan forces until they reached Fortua—which was precisely what Deacon was counting on.

All of the waiting for the final battle, and it had arrived early. Far too early.

FORTY-FIVE
THE DOOMED LADY
BELLONA LENORE

The camp was a cacophony of panic, feet flying across the soil as Deacon Morrow's army approached. Anger and vengeance, slumbering so long in Bellona's chest, uncoiled. She could taste the sourness of them on her lips. The man who had so callously ripped her father from this world, who had piled one atrocity onto another, would be upon them in less than an hour.

He had the element of surprise, but there was one particular element that he had not given himself enough of: water. There was sure to be moisture in the morning air, but would that be enough to let Deacon tip the scales of the battle?

Bellona strode over to Cristofer with a sword strapped to each hip, ginger hair braided in a tight crown back from her face. In her armour, she felt twelve feet tall. She wanted to crush Deacon beneath her heel and grind him to dust. Shielding her eyes from the rising sun, Cristofer barked orders to the Ciroccan troops staggering to assemble with minimal notice. He raked a hand through his dark hair, apprehension bleeding into his eyes.

"We barely have enough time to get the troops together." Cristofer shook his head slowly, kicking at the dirt. "Fuck. This is going to be a disaster."

"Not this time." Bellona rested a gloved hand on his shoulder, squeezing lightly. "We have Cirocco. We have Harith. The ships of Bao are no good to us this far inland, but if they flee to the water, we will catch them."

Tents brought crumbling down to the earth were replaced by rising flags, the gold and cream of House Darnell glimmering proud in the sunlight. Seeing them inflated Bellona with euphoria. They had been defeated time and again, but today was different. With her father's final words a refrain in her mind, she spun to glance over her shoulder as the chatter of the soldiers crescendoed into a roar.

Carissa and Sebastian. The Darnell siblings, together and unbreakable. Carissa with the golden swan crown adorning her raven hair, and Sebastian with his grandfather's swan-pommelled sword at his hip. Fractured and embittered, they had faced only loss. Now, whatever had happened in that cave tied a ribbon of unity between them and held them close.

"Bellona." The soldiers, flocking toward them less in haste and more in curiosity, lapsed into silence as the Queen approached the Lady of Theron. Dressed all in black, Carissa was a striking sight to behold. She threw her arms around her best friend and held her close. Bellona could feel Carissa's heartbeat racing.

"Your Majesty."

"You are my sister." Carissa clung to Bellona tightly, her voice cracking as the words warmed Bellona's heart and soothed the ache for the father she had lost. "In every way that matters, you are my *sister*. I just needed to say that before…"

"Carissa, we are going to survive this." Bellona extricated herself from her friend's fierce embrace and stared hard into her tearful violet-blue eyes.

Carissa smiled softly, taking Bellona's face in her hands and pressing a kiss to her forehead. She moved away, leaving Bellona perplexed with concern creeping up close behind. There was no time to mull on it, with the shouts of the Generans resounding across the field. Spinning to face the loathsome smirk of the man who had torn their lives apart, Bellona led the charge into battle.

Her breaths came hard and fast, the stampeding feet of the Ciroccan soldiers reminding her that she was not alone. She gripped the hilts of her blades and drew them free the moment she collided with the first soldier in black-and-silver armour. The sharp bite of metal tore through skin and bone, and the man went down with a gurgled scream.

Bellona's blood pulsed through her veins with an itch of impatience, and she cast around for the one man whose death could end it once and for all. She found him through a flash of sunlight, the taste of ash on her tongue as she saw he had replaced the hand Carissa had taken with one that sparkled deep blue in the clearness of day.

A sapphire hand, one that flexed and moved and hit like anything made of flesh. Bile rose in her throat, but she fought it back down.

Deacon wheeled around and must have seen the horrified look on her face, because a delighted gleam caught in his hazel eyes, a smug smile tugging at the corners of his lips as he approached her. Bellona gripped her swords tight, eyes narrowing on the man who had flooded her city.

"Don't you remember what happened the last time you tried to fight me?" His disdain rose above the din of battle, the clash of swords and cries of the fallen. "Don't you remember what happened to your father?"

"You don't have the right to besmirch his name, you vile fuck," Bellona snarled, slim frame tensing at the memory of the tunnels. Kato, raising his warhammer to bring down the stone around them. Kato, whose last act had been protecting Bellona and the people of his city.

Patience was never Bellona's strong suit, and she did not intend to stand there and trade verbal barbs with Deacon. She intended to cut out his heart and raise it, dripping scarlet gore, to cement their victory. Lunging at him with a sharp cry, she feinted right before spinning left, landing a slice across his mailed arm that made him hiss.

Bellona had trained for months with Cristofer and Eirian. She had pushed her body to the limit, freckled skin covered in a sheen of sweat along with old bruises and scars, all for a chance to defeat this man. Deacon might not have full access to his magic here, but he was just as deadly with a blade, and she would not be foolish enough to underestimate him.

307

Where Bellona was all speed and ferocity, Deacon was strength and precision. He had one sword for her two, but he deflected each strike she tried to rain down upon him. She gritted her teeth and persevered, despite the muscles in her arms screaming at her.

"Didn't you ever wonder what happened to your beloved queen in Genera?" Deacon arched an eyebrow, cruelty contorting his face into vicious glee. "Didn't you ever think that perhaps she is a monster just like I am?"

Bellona staggered backwards with the force of the blow that belted against both her swords, unpleasant surprise coursing through her at Deacon's words. She had worried about her best friend, and Deacon bringing up that dark time for Carissa reopened a wound that Bellona thought had healed: the death of her mother.

Deacon tilted his sapphire hand, an unholy mixture of magic and science. It dazzled in the sun and Bellona winced at its brightness, lifting one arm to shield her eyes from the brilliant light. In that split second of hesitation, the sapphire hand dropped down and forward, and a terrible agony tore through Bellona like her entire body had split with the force of a thousand daggers.

Not a thousand daggers. Just one sword, Deacon's sword up to the hilt embedded in her stomach. Horror and shock mingled with the pain, and when Bellona choked, blood spattered from between her lips. Deacon's eyes shone with a cold madness, and in one harsh tug, he ripped the sword from her.

Bellona's scream was riddled with torment as it echoed across the battlefield. She collapsed to her knees, keeping her head bowed, and waited for the killing blow as both of her shaking hands tried to staunch the blood that flowed from her in a crimson fountain .

"You think I would grant you the mercy of a quick death?" Deacon's sadistic taunt was soft as a caress.

Tears spilled down Bellona's cheeks as she closed her eyes. Kato had always told her a gut wound was one of the worst. It could take days to die, a long death spent in torturous agony. Every part of her body was screaming in a pain beyond anything she'd ever known, and she resisted the urge to beg with blood-stained lips for the end.

Another scream ripped across the battlefield, one born of a dark and terrible fury. Thunder rumbled across the sky, and when Bellona managed to lift her head, it was to grey clouds and a woman in black striding across the field as if it belonged to her alone. Bellona could taste her power, electrifying and sugar-sweet.

As Bellona's strength faded and she collapsed onto her side, the life ebbing from her, Carissa raised her hands high to the sky, and the might of the impending storm bent to her will.

FORTY-SIX

THE FORLORN PRINCESS
LILITH MARWAN

"I can't do it."

On the edge of the battlefield, wind whistling through her hair, Lilith gripped Cairo's hand tightly in her own. Impatience seared through her at his reluctance, though she supposed she should be more understanding. Cairo had used his powers against Deacon, but before that, he had used them to destroy a city.

Lilith was not a warrior. She would not engage in the conflict erupting around them, but her task was vital: help Cairo let go of his fear, or they risked losing the war they so desperately needed to win. She was a woman of honeyed words and soft touches, the gentle nudge in the right direction. Today, she was not feeling so gentle.

"Pull yourself together." The words were sharp as a knife as she seized hold of Cairo's shoulders and shook. He was a grown man, by the gods. His trauma was as valid as her own, but at the moment they needed to put aside their pasts, or they could never embrace their vision of the future.

"What if I fail again?" Cairo's eyes searched Lilith's face, as though he would find answers there.

"You didn't fail in Dalal. You will not fail now."

Lilith spun to face the battlefield with apprehension twisting her stomach. A glimpse of ginger hair on the ground. Lightning crackled in the clouds above them as Carissa walked into the chaos like she was born to it.

They had lost Elyes because Cairo had succumbed to his rage. The worst of him had been brought out in those moments, and a city had died because of it. They could not risk the same happening now.

"You can't fail." A steely resolve cinched Lilith's words as she faced Cairo, her jaw setting in determination. "You see those people out there? They need you. Queen Carissa needs you, or else we risk a repeat of the past."

Cairo nodded, pushing a hard breath out through his nostrils. Something savage burned in his dark eyes, and it made a proud smile curve Lilith's lips. Her cousin was ready, and she hoped he would hold nothing back.

Lilith's eyes once more caught a streak of ginger hair amongst silver steel and grey armour. Bellona lay on the ground, hands over the crimson stain blossoming out from her stomach. She was pale as snow. Panic bloomed like a dangerous flower with thorns, and Lilith drew the knife from her belt and marched toward the battlefield.

"Lilith!" Cairo's shout was riddled with alarm, but she ignored him. Bellona had to survive, or else she feared the destruction Carissa was capable of. She had already destroyed a city, like Cairo, like Deacon. What more would she do if her best friend died at the hands of her enemy?

Lilith was not a warrior, but she had killed before, and she would do so again.

Two familiar figures, a blonde woman and a dark-haired man, cut through the chaos to where Bellona was curled up, forgotten by Deacon in light of the appearance of his true adversary. Relda and Ishtar reached Bellona's side first, the spymaster placing his healing hands on her while Relda stood by with her crossbow, ready to aim at anyone who would interrupt.

"Lilith?" Her brow furrowed in confusion as her sister-in-law arrived at the scene. Lilith fell to her knees so fast that the grass and dirt scraped at her skin. Bellona was alive, but hanging by a thread. If Ishtar had worked his healing magic upon Jacen, surely he could heal the Lady of Theron.

"We need to get her off the battlefield." Lilith's breaths came in ragged gasps, unused to exertion. "It's not safe for her here."

"Traitorous bitch!" The venomous words made both women turn, a Morrow soldier charging toward Relda with hatred in his eyes. She gritted her teeth and refitted the crossbow, but he was upon her before she could fire, backhanding her with a mailed fist. Relda went reeling, the crossbow falling from her hands.

Lilith glanced desperately to where Ishtar had his hands placed over her terrible wound through Bellona's stomach. They needed to buy him time, the most precious asset they could give him to complete his work. As Relda kicked dirt up into the soldier's face, Lilith reached down and picked up the abandoned crossbow.

The earth trembled beneath them, and Lilith staggered for balance. Across the battlefield, Cairo walked through the pandemonium like a god amongst mortals. Wherever he went, the earth turned and shook, shifting to obey his will. What must it be like, to have the kind of power to turn the tide of battle? The Harithian soldiers cried his name like a prayer.

Lilith spun back to Relda and fired the bolt straight through the Morrow soldier's chest. When he fell, she realised he was not alone—another soldier in black and silver had nocked an arrow, and it was aimed at Relda's head. Before she could cry out to warn her, someone grabbed Relda and pulled her aside, just as the archer released the arrow.

At first, Lilith thought it had been a narrow miss, until she heard Relda's horrified scream.

Ishtar stumbled backward, the arrow lodged through his throat. Relda took her lover's sword and, in one mighty swing, cut off the archer's head. The damage was already done, though. For all of Ishtar's healing power, Lilith remembered with a twist of shock that he only had the ability to heal others, not himself.

When Ishtar collapsed, Relda was at his side in an instant, but it was too late. Ishtar choked once and then lay still. Relda bent her head over his body and sobbed, the woman who brushed off her emotions broken by her lover's death.

Her anguished wail resonated across the battlefield.

Lilith glanced at Bellona. The young woman was alive, and the wound appeared less critical, but she was still pale, and her breath rattled out through her lips. It was unclear if Ishtar had progressed enough to save her. Tears welled in Lilith's eyes for her fallen friend, a man who had died protecting people he cared about.

"Relda." The word was hoarse, but it caught Relda's attention, making her jerk her head up. "We need to get Lady Lenore off the battlefield if she's going to survive. The wound is still deep, we need to…"

"All right." Pain glimmered in Relda's eyes. She paused, tears spilling onto Ishtar's peaceful face as she leaned down to kiss the top of his head. Lilith could not imagine the pain she felt over the loss of the man she loved, the father of her child, a pain that Relda admirably suppressed in the face of battle. Relda moved over to Bellona, and together, she and Lilith eased the young woman to her feet, eliciting a hiss of pain from her.

"I'm going to survive this." Bellona's voice was a determined rasp. "I won't have Ishtar's last act be in vain."

Lilith marvelled at her tenacity, but would it be enough? Her freckles were bright against her skin as stars in the night sky, and there was blood all over. Ishtar might have brought her back from the brink, but Bellona's fate still hung in the balance.

FORTY-SEVEN
THE VICTORIOUS QUEEN
CARISSA DARNELL

The earth churned and shook beneath Carissa's boots. Above her, the sky darkened with the promise of rain, thunder growling its disapproval and lightning lashing across the battlefield as she marched over to Deacon Morrow with murder in her heart. She would not lose anyone else, not today. Deacon reached the cruel hand of death toward Bellona, and Carissa was batting it away.

"How predictable." An indolent smile curved Deacon's lips, vicious glee dancing in his hazel eyes. "They always need you to protect them, don't they? It's a shame that my nephew survived my blade, but he won't today. Neither will Lady Lenore."

"Go on, spit some more venom." Carissa folded her arms over her chest. Once, perhaps, Deacon's words would have sent chills of terror up her spine. Now, she just found him tiresome. "Do you remember when I first met you, during the Conquest? You threw my brother's head at my feet. That night, I knew I was destined to one day take yours."

Deacon laughed. "You see the true threat on this battlefield? It isn't you."

Carissa glanced over at Prince Cairo, watched as the soil turned itself over at a curl of his fingers. She'd never imagined the Harithian prince wielded such power, but Deacon was right. He was stronger than either of them. Regardless, a mocking smile graced Carissa's lips.

"You're right. It isn't me. But the true threat wants you dead."

Cairo's furious dark gaze locked upon them, and he strode over with rocks rising into the air in his wake. They soared toward Deacon, making him stagger backwards as dirt and dust began to rain down upon him. A snarl twisted his lips, hazel eyes alight with savagery as he raised a hand and drew down moisture from the air, a quick twist of his fingers shaping it into something tangible. A thin stream of water materialised before him, a whip made of water.

"So, it was you," Deacon sneered at Cairo, a mocking edge sharpening the cruelty in his voice. "You who brought your own city to dust."

Cairo's response was not in words, but action. He raised his arms into the sky, fingers splayed, and the earth trembled and groaned beneath Deacon's feet. A decade's worth of rage, of hiding a dangerous truth that burdened his soul, poured forth from Cairo. Carissa knew that anger well and could feel its searing heat burn within her too. The ground itself moved to the tilt of Cairo's fingers, tendrils of grass pulling together to rope around Deacon's feet.

Deacon stumbled again, moving to steady himself. When his head shot up, there was murder in his eyes. Batting aside another hurtling rock with his water whip, Deacon immediately iced the whip over and drew it back to his side as one might a spear.

Cold panic surged through Carissa. "Cairo!"

Cairo's eyes widened as the ice spear whizzed toward him. Though he stepped back, he was too late to avoid it piercing him through the shoulder. An agonised cry tore from his lips and he crumbled like the walls of the city he'd destroyed, knees buckling from beneath him as a scarlet stain spread from where the ice spear was still embedded in him.

Carissa sprinted over to him, uncertain fingers prodding around the melting ice and making Cairo clamp down on his teeth. The wound, to her judgement, would not be fatal. However, it was dire, and it would prevent Cairo from further engaging in combat. She had lost her most important ally in the battle of their lives, and the sting of impending defeat made tears burn in her eyes.

"Carissa." Cairo's voice was a rasp. "You know what to do."

When he looked up from his wound, there was hope sparkling in his eyes. Hope, the very thing she found most dangerous of all. It could be an intoxicating thing, but it could also lead them to their doom. Hope would make them, or it would break them.

Cairo reached with shaking fingers to streak his blood across her palm, and understanding dawned over her, like a bright sun rising over a pale morning.

Cairo's earth magic sang to her, luring her in like a siren's song. It was powerful and intoxicating, sweet as a lick of honey, causing her to suck in a deep breath as she pushed herself back to her feet. She swung to face Deacon, who stalked over to them with a wild grin, and spread her arms wide as if to embrace the magic she had gained.

The ground shuddered beneath them, stones and plants rising to Carissa's outstretched hands as if to answer an unspoken call. Without hesitation, she flung her hands forward, pelting him with dirt and dust and rocks. Deacon raised his arms over his face to protect himself from harm, but the sharp hiss her actions elicited brought a thrill of triumph.

"You little bitch," he snapped, crossing over and seizing her by the throat before she could enact more vengeance with the lethal magic that thrummed in her veins. The flesh of his fingers grew cold against her skin, and he lifted so that her toes barely skimmed the ground. Carissa choked, attempting to pry him off as her vision spun. She could see the glimmer of his sapphire hand, his sadistic smile.

The cold bit against her neck, and then into it, ice piercing her skin. The metallic tang of blood clogged her nostrils, the sting crescendoing into sharp pain and dragging a strangled scream from between her lips.

Terror and fury coursed through Carissa in an unstoppable tide, firing her into movement. She reached out and gripped a hold of Deacon's hair, pulling hard, so hard that she tore out a fistful of it. With a strained shout, Deacon released her. Carissa's feet touched the ground, and as blood dribbled down her neck from a dozen icy wounds, she seized a firm hold of Cairo's power once again and backhanded Deacon across the face with an airborne rock.

Deacon's smile dropped, and she saw panic spark in his eyes. Triumph swelled within her. Something dark was calling for his blood, there and then, and she was more than happy to oblige that particular temptation.

He had been afraid of her when he had brought her to Genera. It was why he had drugged her with Obscurate. He was afraid of her again now, even if his fleeting moment of fear was replaced by a defiant sneer.

"Where is your power, Deacon?" Carissa taunted, head cocking to the side. "Where is your water, your magic?"

Deacon threw his arms up to the sky, calling up the rain that had gathered within the dark clouds. As the rain poured from the heavens like a waterfall, Carissa raised her hands in turn, creating a telekinetic bubble around them so that none of the droplets came anywhere Deacon. The strain burned through her like fire, teeth bared in a grimace.

"I won't let you have it."

"You have never been as strong as me," Deacon snapped, rage contorting his features. "You will bend until you break, as you always have."

Carissa felt the tug of his magic, straining to push through the bubble she had created. The weight of her own magic ground her down, but she was not giving up. She didn't have anyone to help her take Deacon down. It all rested on her.

In her desperate hour, Miriam had called down the lightning upon her father and killed all of Patrick's soldiers. Could Carissa wield that kind of power without damaging anyone except Deacon? Certainly, she had to try. Armour did not fare well against lightning, but there was something else that could also devastate.

When Sebastian had been a child, he'd kept a small school of fish in a little pond out in the gardens. He fed them every day, except for the morning after a vicious storm when he ran inside crying. All of the fish in the pond were dead. Their mother had comforted him and explained that when lightning hit a small area of water like that, anything dwelling in it died instantly.

The fish had not survived the lightning. Deacon, master of water magic, would not either.

Inhaling deeply, Carissa's telekinetic bubble allowed for a small breach, right above Deacon. Surprise and confusion furrowed his brows as the rain came down solely upon him, eyes resting on Carissa. At what should have been a moment of victory, the water making its way to its caller, she brought down the storm.

Deacon screamed as the lightning bounced off the water, tearing at him with its violet tendrils of sheer power. Carissa held on for as long as she could, her breath catching as the lightning crackled and seared anything in its path. As Deacon dropped to the ground, she let it go, the rain tumbling down over the battlefield as she released her hold on the storm.

Carissa drew her knife with blood-slick fingers and marched over to her enemy. She nudged Deacon with a tentative boot, and he coughed. She kicked him onto his back and her stomach churned, bitterness coating her tongue as she inspected his ruined face.

It looked as though a hundred blades had carved into Deacon's face, a thousand shards of glass into his body. Unfortunately, he still breathed. The storm had not killed him, but it had torn him up and spat him back out. Carissa's fingers tightened on the hilt of the blade, and she knelt down beside him, letting him see the way the steel shone.

"You don't deserve a quick and merciful death." Her voice trembled with the weight of years of his cruelty bearing down upon her, the memories of the family that he and Cobryn had ripped from her. "So, know I don't give it to you for your sake. I give it to you for *mine*."

"Carissa!" Jacen jogged over to her, scarlet-stained sword in his hand. His face was covered in blood and dirt, jaw clenching as he stared down at the mutilated man who had once been his powerful uncle. His eyes landed on his wife, knife in hand, poised for the kill. She tilted her chin up.

"I'm ending it here and now."

"No." The word was sharp and firm, cutting beneath Carissa's skin so she could feel the sting from it, the same way the wounds on her neck throbbed and protested.

"*No?*"

"This is what he wants." Jacen stared hard down at Deacon, loathing burning in his eyes as he inspected the man who had almost taken his life. "A glorious death, a death in battle. He might be different from my father in many ways, but in that, they are similar. Don't give him this one last triumph."

"Then what do you suggest?" Carissa spat, indignation pumping through her blood as she pushed herself to her feet. "We cannot leave him alive, he's far too dangerous for that."

"An execution." Jacen strode over to his wife, sheathing his sword and placing his hands on her shoulders. "On your terms. Quick and quiet. He will die alone, without any of his supporters to mourn him."

Tears slid down Carissa's cheeks, a choked sob forcing its way from her mouth. She.wanted vengeance, without caring how much it would rip from her. Jacen pressed a kiss to her forehead, and she hated that he was right. Her victory would be hollow, tasting lemon-sour instead of sugar-sweet, but it would be *justice*.

Not vengeance for her family's deaths, but justice for them.

"On your terms," Jacen repeated quietly, thumbs brushing away the hot tears that tracked down his wife's face, gently tilting her head to examine the cuts where Deacon's ice had sliced into her neck.

Carissa tugged away and stared contemptuously down at her fallen foe. He was breathing, but he had not said a word. She didn't know if he couldn't speak or chose not to. He watched her with angry hazel eyes, and his fury coaxed a vicious smile to adorn her face.

"My love for him is stronger than my hatred for you. That's where my power comes from, Deacon. The darkness might bring out the worst in me, but Jacen is the light that brings out the best."

The gardens of Marinel began to blossom with life, spring heralded by blooming flowers and an abundance of green leaves. Winter's chill no longer bit at Carissa after dusk. As she waited in the gardens a week after they had won the Battle of Basium, she took in a deep breath and allowed herself to bask in the heavy scent of rose and the accompanying sharpness of pine.

The evening sky was dappled with lilac purple and pale orange hues, leaves whispering in the soft breeze and dancing through Carissa's black hair as she wrapped her arms tightly around herself, wondering whether she made the right choice. There were a thousand ways she could have imagined Deacon's demise. Jacen had been correct to say it was her decision.

In the bitterness of a private execution, of her enemy's demise a whisper rather than a scream, Carissa found sweetness in the irony of it.

The fountain tinkled as water spilled down from the ornate swans into its basin. She had splashed through the fountain with her siblings, with Vida and Bellona. Her best friend was still recovering from the grievous wounds that Deacon had dealt her, and Carissa visited her daily. Bellona's skin had some of its colour back, and she could even laugh without grimacing. Carissa's own wounds had nearly healed, though she would bear scars on her neck from them.

The guards led Deacon out into the sunset, Sebastian sweeping out behind them with his hands clasped behind his back. He had insisted upon being present, and Carissa could not deny him without feeling the heat of his wrath for the rest of their lives. Jacen stepped closer to his wife, resting his hand on the small of her back.

The cuts all over Deacon's face and body were hideous and gave Carissa no small degree of satisfaction. Her lips curved into a smirk, inhaling the sickly-sweet smell of Obscurate as the guards pushed Deacon forward. How had she once feared this man? He was a shadow of the powerful Imperium he had once been. Once, he had taken everything from Carissa. Now, she returned the favour.

"How does it feel without even the barest spark of your magic?" Carissa relished the words, took vindictive delight in the way Deacon's jaw tightened. "You are nothing, Deacon Morrow."

"I will always be something." There was cold defiance in his words. "I will always be there in your nightmares. I took your country from you, and more."

Carissa sneered, her hand cracking across Deacon's face. Blood from his split lip dripped onto her palm.

"Bold of you to assume I would think of you at all."

"Yet the idea still angers you enough that you would strike me." The smugness in Deacon's tone was unbearable, even if it was misplaced.

"Oh, no." Carissa's smile held all of winter's coldness that spring had staved off. "The Obscurate pumping through you means that you have no way of controlling your power. But I can still use your magic if I spill your blood."

The complacent mask dropped from Deacon's face, replaced by horror. Jacen moved behind his uncle, grabbing Deacon's shoulders and propelling him forward. Once he stood in front of the fountain, he pushed the once-powerful Imperium to his knees. Carissa planted her hands on her hips as she felt the tug of Deacon's magic and watched her nemesis stare down into the water with pure dread.

Carissa tilted her face up to bask in the sun's dying light.

Imogen, slaughtered protecting Sebastian. Patrick, brought down by five arrows. Theodore, beheaded by Deacon. Frederick and Peregrine, murdered in these gardens. Miriam, unfairly executed.

She thought of her family and the fond memories she had of them, and the future with them that had been stolen by the Morrows' cruelty. When she glanced at Sebastian, his quick nod was all the incentive she needed.

321

Carissa raised her palm, spattered with Deacon's blood, and the water from the fountain swirled up to reach out and drag him beneath it. Deacon fought it, pushing back against the element that had once served him so faithfully. There was no hint of mercy in Carissa's mind as she held him under, his writhing becoming weak spasms as the water seeped into his lungs to replace the air.

Jacen's arms were folded over his chest, his eyes hard as he examined his drowning uncle. A dark smile crossed Sebastian's lips, and Carissa wondered if he too was remembering what the dying man had done to their family.

Carissa did not know how much time had passed before Deacon finally went still. It could have been seconds or minutes or hours. She relinquished her hold on his magic, the last time she would ever use it. Her body trembled violently as she stared down at the dead man beneath the water, and her frame wracked with sudden sobs.

She did not cry because she mourned him. She cried because after years, a weight had fallen from her shoulders, a knot untied itself from deep within her stomach. She had not felt freedom that clearly since she had been fourteen years old. With Deacon dead, Carissa finally had peace.

Sebastian strode over to her and pulled her into his arms. Silent tears coursed down his own cheeks as he held her close. The Darnell siblings had been divided by rivalry, reunited by a duty to protect their country. In that moment, they were closer than they had ever been, a bond forged through despair and solace, vengeance and justice.

They were finally, truly free.

Forty-Eight
The Redeemed King
Jacen Morrow

It was ironic that discussion of the Generan triumvirate should take place in Marinel, yet Jacen was determined to prove swiftly that he was a man of his word. The weight of the Generan crown had loomed over him like a dark cloud promising a downpour since he could remember, but it had been shifted from his shoulders. He would never have to sit upon that cursed throne. Elation swelled within him as he glanced over his steepled fingers around the table at the others who had joined him.

Relda was as silent and solemn as he had ever seen her, hands clasped in her lap and eyes red-rimmed. Did part of her mourn the loss of her younger brother? Jacen wanted to think Deacon's death did not perturb her, but had Vida's not troubled him though he had known she was a traitor? Combined with the grief of losing Ishtar, it was clear his aunt had a lot on her mind.

Also amongst the party were Lilith, Cairo, and Carissa. The latter two were present as a witness to negotiations rather than active participants, but Jacen found his wife's quiet presence a soothing balm to his frayed nerves. He wanted to be better than his father and uncle. He wanted to be a good man, and he believed that turning his back on the throne he hated with such passion was a good place to begin.

"Who will this triumvirate consist of?" Lilith leaned forward, dark eyes glimmering with concern. Though not Generan, as the mother of Cobryn's youngest child, she had an undeniable place at this table. "Though I agree they should be voted in, the fact is that Genera without leadership currently is too unstable. We should have three members now and vote in a year or so when things have settled."

"She's right," Cairo added hoarsely, shifting with a grimace in his chair, fingers picking at the bandages around his shoulder. Lilith shot him a warning look. He was there as a witness, not to take part in the negotiations.

"I won't be part of it." Jacen raised his hands in the air and leaned back in his chair. "I belong in Basium with Carissa. Genera will always be my birthplace, but it has not been my home for some time. Besides, no good would come of the man who would have been king worming his way into power another way."

"You." Relda's quiet syllable made them all look to her, and Jacen noted her gaze was fixed upon Lilith. "I have rarely seen a more compassionate woman than you, Lilith. You may not believe it, but you commanded much respect in your years as Cobryn's wife."

"No." Lilith shook her head fervently. "I promised to keep my daughter away from the Generan throne. If, once she is of age, she wishes to be in the running for the triumvirate, that is her right as a Morrow. Until that day comes, she and I will return to Dalal."

"We need people that the Generans trust." Jacen's fingers brushed through his unkempt blonde hair. "People like…"

"Ariadne Pavlos." Carissa's voice was soft as silk. The wicked cuts on her neck were still deep crimson against her pale skin, though they were superficial wounds.

Jacen's eyebrows flew upward at the mention of Deacon's mistress. He did not know the woman well, but Carissa vouched for her, calling her a woman of great intelligence and kindness.

Relda nodded, a slow smile tweaking at the corners of her lips. "An ambitious woman. I like it."

"Perhaps this is a discussion best had in Nicodemus with all candidates present." Lilith suggested, toying with the ends of her dark hair. "We cannot be certain this is what Lady Pavlos wants, and it should be an open discussion."

"Agreed." Cairo sprang to his feet, all too eager to leave the table, the movement causing him to pause and grit his teeth momentarily. "Besides, we have celebrating to do, don't we? Let's take a moment to enjoy our victory. We've earned it."

The iron weight of responsibility had chained Jacen down for so long that celebration seemed like frivolity. Cairo was right, though. They had all suffered enough of the Morrow Empire, and it was a new day. He pushed his wandering mind away from potential candidates, thinking instead of his wife and son.

Carissa deserved a night without a care in the world. A night spent with her family. Deacon's execution may have seemed satisfying, but Jacen knew well how death could linger.

The night sky flared with a thousand colours as another set of fireworks snapped overhead, lighting Carissa's face as she stood beside Jacen on the balcony. Her arms were wrapped firmly around Zephyr, who was attempting to clamber onto the ledge to get a better view of the festivities. With an arm around his wife's shoulders and his son squirming impatiently, there was nowhere else Jacen would rather be.

"I think we should put him to bed." Carissa hoisted Zephyr onto her hip and slipped through the curtain back into their room. Nudging the door open with her foot, she moved into the corridor with Jacen at her heels. Their son would be two years old soon, and Jacen marvelled at the fact that he was more child than baby now.

"No," Zephyr grumbled as his mother wrangled him into bed. Again, it showed just how much he had grown that he was in a bed rather than a cot. Jacen leaned in the doorway, arms folded over his chest as Carissa stroked Zephyr's hair and sang an off-key lullaby he didn't recognise. Perhaps Imogen had once sung it to her when she was a child.

Zephyr's stubbornness faded like water trickling through fingers, and his eyes fluttered closed. After a few minutes, his deep breathing assured Jacen that he was sound asleep. Carissa eased herself gently off the bed so as not to wake him and crossed over to her husband. Jacen pushed himself off the doorframe to loop an arm around her waist.

"We made a beautiful boy, didn't we?"

"Certainly did." Carissa leaned her head against his shoulder.

"The rest will be just as amazing."

Carissa smacked him in the chest, though she flashed a wicked grin. "Don't get ahead of yourself, Morrow."

The sweet melody of the music outside was a tempting prospect. Spending time with his wife though was infinitely more appealing. As they trudged back into their bedroom, Carissa closed the door and leaned against it, biting back an unusually shy smile.

"I have something for you." Pushing off the door, she crossed the room and picked up a familiar case, making Jacen's breath catch in his throat.

"Is that…?"

Carissa handed it to him, smile broadening as he set it down on the bed to open it. Jacen's well-worn fiddle was nestled safely in the velvet. Without hesitation, he snatched the fiddle and bow, his fingers readjusting to what it was like to hold the instrument. It had been over a year since he'd touched the fiddle.

As he started to play a joyful tune, his initial uncertainty morphed quickly into giddy confidence in his own ability and the happiness it exuded. Music was magic in itself, and Carissa's delighted smile as he played was everything he could have wanted, warming him as surely as a fire in the hearth. When he was with her, he shed his doubts like an old skin, leaving behind only the certainty that he loved her and was loved in return.

Carissa's laughter was infectious, a broad grin spreading across Jacen's lips as she caught her skirts and twirled to the beat of the music. Her steps fumbled and she swore as she almost tripped on Soot, who had made his way out from under the bed to see what was going on. Jacen swiftly set the fiddle down to catch her clumsily by the waist and steady her. When she stared up at him, it was like falling into blissful oblivion.

Carissa reached up and took his face in her hands, kissing him deeply. Jacen returned the kiss with eager fervour, arms looping tighter around her waist. All the pain of the past melted away when she kissed him, her fingers threading through his hair drawing him into that moment, where there was only love and lust and longing.

Jacen had spent his life being defined by other people. His father, his enemies. He brimmed with clarity: *he* was the only one who could define who and what he was. He was a loving husband, a doting father, and a king who had defended Basium to death's door and beyond.

He forgave himself. For the sins of the past, the mistakes and terrible choices he had made , he forgave himself.

Forty-Nine

The Blacksmith Prince
Sebastian Darnell

Effortless grace was not Sebastian's style. He was convinced that, for Basium to fully accept he intended to relinquish his claim to the throne, he had to do so publicly. Unfortunately, that meant presenting himself in front of hundreds of prying eyes to bend the knee to his sister and make a statement. Fussing irritably over his cream-and-gold tunic, Sebastian ruminated on how much he hated speeches and how much he hated public attention. That, he supposed, was why Carissa was far better suited to ruling than him.

"Stop fussing, you look perfect." Meliora gave his tunic a sharp tug, making Sebastian yelp and swat at her arm. She rolled her eyes. "Look, you can go and make yourself a sword in the forge afterwards, how about that?"

"I was thinking of something for my nephew." Zephyr was a child with Carissa's temperament and Jacen's indignation when he didn't get his way. A brat, but a brat that Sebastian had grown fond of since meeting him. "Perhaps a knife to start with."

"That can wait until he's older," Meliora admonished, dusting off Sebastian's shoulders.

A rap at the door made them both pause, and all words flew from Sebastian's mouth as the last person he had expected to see stepped into the room. Tycho Salus clasped his hands behind his back and examined Sebastian with mild disdain.

"You look ridiculous."

"Excuse me?" Meliora prickled, eyes narrowing at the man she didn't recognise. Sebastian touched her hand with gentle assurance. They had known each other long enough for Meliora to heave a sigh. "I'll leave you both to talk, then."

An amused smile played about Tycho's lips as he watched Meliora march from the room.

"Your wife, I expect? Spirited thing."

"I...I never expected to see you again." Sebastian's brow furrowed, a cool chill racing up his spine. "After the cave..."

Tycho waved a dismissive hand. "Public life isn't for me, but even I attend social functions once in a while."

"Not for a long time." Sebastian couldn't help the suspicion gnawing at him. "What changed?"

Tycho was quiet for a long moment, the aged lines of his face shifting into sorrow as his eyes pierced Sebastian.

"After what happened in the cave, I hid myself away. Even following the Conquest and the deaths of the people I cared for, I remained in solitude. Perhaps I have more sins that need atoning for than I thought."

Sebastian shook his head. "There is no sin in..."

"Shut up and listen." The sharpness in Tycho's voice silenced Sebastian. "You and Carissa were so young. Twelve and fourteen. You were still children. It was not hard seeing you at my property because you were Patrick and Miriam's grandchildren. It was hard because I saw the last two of that bloodline and was reminded that I turned my back."

Sebastian was not yet nineteen, but if he had learned anything, it was that there was never any turning your back. The only way to move was forward, even for a man as old as Tycho. He reached out a hand and was warmly surprised when Tycho clasped it.

"You could stay, you know. Here in the capital. I'm planning on rescinding my claim to the throne, and my sister…"

"Will announce that you are the General of her armies."

Sebastian's nose wrinkled in confusion. *"What?"*

"I am old, boy, not deaf. I hear whispers. Your sister does not trust Orien Luce, and I cannot blame her. She wants to give you a proper position, one that you might enjoy more thoroughly than ruling."

Sebastian was stunned into silence. It was exactly the sort of position that would interest him. He was of military mind, not political. It would not take away from his days in the forge, a dream that he intended to follow since he was no longer shackled to the throne. Carissa understood him.

"So no, I will not stay in the capital." Tycho sniffed contemptuously. "I can imagine nothing worse. However, should you or your sister ever wish to visit… well, sending notice would be nice, but know that you are welcome."

Warmth flooded through Sebastian, though he did not imagine Tycho was exactly the sort to appreciate a hug. Instead, he squeezed the older man's hand tightly, and caught a glimpse of a rare smile on Tycho's lips. After years of having rivals and enemies, perhaps Sebastian was actually making friends.

Sebastian bit back a snicker as he knelt at his sister's feet. It was important that the pair of them remain serious, but with a heavy velvet cloak around his shoulders and the black swan crown adorning his hair, it felt like one of the plays they'd put on for their family as children. Reaching up with steady fingers, he removed the crown from his head and placed it at Carissa's feet. More accurately, at the hem of her ridiculously long lavender silk dress.

"I, Sebastian Darnell, hereby renounce my claim to the throne of Basium." The words were so formal they sounded like they came from someone else, though they flooded him with relief. "I have no intention of being King. I would remain as my sister's heir, should anything befall her son."

"Thank you, Sebastian." Carissa extended her hands to him, and he caught them in his own and rose to his feet. "I accept this. I would also like to offer you the title of General of the Basiumite armies. Hopefully there will be peace in Basium for many days to come, but should war ever arise, I would be in need of you."

"I graciously accept this title, Your Majesty." Sebastian bowed deeply from the waist. When he looked up, Carissa was biting back the smile on her lips. As the crowd around them applauded, the tension left Sebastian's shoulders and he sighed deeply. The people dispersed in excited chatter, while Carissa approached Sebastian with a spring in her step.

"Does the General want a drink?" Carissa teased, throwing an arm around her brother's shoulders and reaching up to ruffle his hair as she'd done when they were children. Formality eased into familiarity. Jacen crossed over to them, Zephyr clasping tightly at his hand as he toddled along beside him.

"Congratulations, Sebastian."

"I'll have you know that I only stayed for this particular honour." Sebastian shook his head, allowing Carissa and Jacen to lead him from the throne room into the banquet hall. "Meliora and I plan on returning to Emlen in the next few days."

"Of course." There was a troubled pinch in Carissa's brow, making Sebastian examine her with impatience.

"Are you going to say what's on your mind, or do I have to guess?"

"I just..." Carissa bit down on her lip, before turning to Jacen. "Do you think you could get us some sparkling wine?"

Jacen's inquisitive hazel gaze darted between them, but he nodded, leading Zephyr over to the dining table. Carissa seized hold of Sebastian's sleeve and led him over to the corner, clearly not intending to have the conversation in the middle of the banquet hall.

"I have everything back." Carissa's voice was soft, tears shining in her violet-blue eyes as she stared him down. "My home, my family...you. I'm so scared that now, right when things are going well…"

"Rissa." It was a nickname he hadn't called her since he'd been a small child who couldn't quite get a handle on her name. "We will always be siblings, Darnells. But Marinel…it's not home. Not anymore."

Carissa nodded fervently, a weak smile pulling at her lips as she reached up to wipe away her tears. They had been through so much together these past few months, and he understood her reluctance for him to leave. Sebastian would always be bound to Carissa, both in blood and experience. He was the only other person who had been there in the cave, something he'd not soon forget.

"I'll miss you." She tilted her chin up, a defiant gleam entering her eyes. "You'd better come visit."

Sebastian snorted. "Well, you know where Emlen is. You can come visit too."

"Sparkling wine?" Jacen reappeared with three glasses of bubbling drinks, frowning down at his son when Zephyr offered a mischievous 'yes please.' "No, not you."

Carissa and Sebastian both accepted their glasses. If Jacen questioned why his wife had been crying, he had the good grace not to mention it. A smile shone on Carissa's face, bright as the dawn as she raised her glass.

"To the future."

"To the future," Jacen and Sebastian echoed, clinking their glasses with hers.

The clear chime echoed across the room. Sebastian glanced over his shoulder to see Meliora and Jarl helping themselves to some cheese and crackers, and he raised his glass in a salute as he caught their attention. Meliora raised her cheese in return, causing Jarl to bark out a laugh.

They had all lost so much. Jarl and Meliora had lost a sister and a father to the Morrows' cruelty, but Sebastian would no longer make the mistake of blaming Jacen for his family's crimes. Jacen was just as much a victim as the rest of them, and Sebastian found that he actually rather liked him.

Soon, Sebastian and the Ambroses would return to Emlen and start to rebuild. That was what he had been destined for. Not a throne and a crown, but the sweat on his brow and the hard work of his hands. Brick by brick, they would restore Emlen.

Sebastian was reborn from flame and ash, just as his family had once thought he died in. He was not the boy consumed by hatred and vengeance, but a man filled with love and a hope for a better tomorrow.

FIFTY
THE SEABOUND LADY
BELLONA LENORE

Bellona's brush with death, much like Jacen's, had consequences. Her half-healed wound caused pain whenever she stretched or laughed, and her impatience prickled at the fact that it would be several weeks before she could even think about getting back in the training yard. Cristofer slyly reminded her that there were other activities it prohibited, earning a sullen punch to the arm from his wife.

In truth, Bellona was fortunate to be alive, and relieved to be out of bed. The fresh morning breeze caressed her face and teased her hair as she strode out into the gardens, knowing that Carissa would be there. The Queen had spent a lot of time there, especially since Sebastian's departure. Though it pained Bellona to part from Carissa, she would be the next to leave Marinel.

"Bell." Carissa smiled from her perch on the fountain's ledge, fingers skimming over the water's surface. She patted the spot beside her, and Bellona sat with more difficulty than she was happy with. "I wanted to wait until you were feeling better before we spoke about Deacon."

"I know that he was defeated and executed." Bellona shrugged her slim shoulders. "That's enough for me."

An itch at the back of her mind told her that it wasn't. The Morrows had been their enemies for so long that Bellona craved validation. Deacon had almost killed her. If it had not been for Ishtar's intervention, and the ultimate sacrifice of his own life, Bellona would likely be among the dead they had burned.

"I killed him." Carissa gripped Bellona's hand in hers, their fingers interlocking. "I drowned him in this fountain, with his own power. It felt like justice. I wanted to look back and regret it…but I don't."

"Why would you?" Bellona frowned. "The man has caused you nothing but pain for years. I'm glad he's dead, and I'm glad you were the one to do it. Feeling satisfied by it makes you human, not a monster."

"How do you always know what to say?" Carissa shook her head slowly, tilting her head back so that her glossy black hair caught the sunlight. "I was scared that there was something dark in me. Now…well, there's darkness in everyone. I'm not afraid of what I am or what I can do anymore. I control the magic, not the other way around."

"Where you and Sebastian went…" Bellona trailed off into silence, letting Carissa decide if she wanted to continue down that line of conversation.

"We found the cave where Jameson Burnett died." Carissa chewed thoughtfully at her lip. "I had a sort of…revelation. People are always going to have opinions on me, and I can't change all of those. It's up to me to decide what sort of person I want to be. What sort of queen I want to be."

Pride swelled within Bellona, warm as the spring sun. Carissa had grown so much from the uncertain young queen she had been immediately following the Conquest. Bellona could not think of a better person to rule Basium, even if she was perhaps slightly biased in that opinion.

"We've been through a lot together." Bellona's eyes stung with unshed tears as she thought of Kato. Somehow, it started to hurt less as time went on. The wound of his death was closing up. "We are sisters, even if I never married your brother. You are my best friend, and I love you. I've been by your side for so much, but…it's time that I left."

"You're returning to Theron?" Carissa swept her hair back. "I suppose it was only a matter of time."

"Not exactly." Bellona shook her head, a smile spreading across her lips.

"Cristofer, Eirian, and I are going to visit Bao. After their help with the southern harbours in Wendell, we figured we owed them thanks in person. Besides, I've not really spent much time in Bao."

It had been Peregrine Darnell who loved the ocean more than the land, more than he ever could have loved Bellona. It was his memory she hoped to honour by braving the sea again, something she had complained constantly about when he was alive. If only he could see her now, developing the sea legs he'd teased she didn't have.

"Maybe one day I'll visit Bao, too." Carissa sighed wistfully. "There are so many places I want to go. So many things I want to do."

"Now you can do them all." Bellona was overcome with a swell of affection for her best friend. "Goddess, they would be so proud of you, Carissa. Your whole family. If they saw how far you had come…"

"I know." Carissa's voice trembled, her smile fierce as her eyes glistened. "Sebastian and I both. It's been years since we lost them, but I never want to forget that loss. I want to make sure I continue to honour their sacrifice."

Bellona thought of Kato's own sacrifice, the way he had nobly laid down his life to protect her and his people. Sometimes, sacrifice ended in death, but other times it didn't have to. They had all made enough sacrifices over the past few years. It was the time for love and healing, and Bellona could hardly wait for it all to begin.

The sun set over the harbour as the last of the trunks were loaded onto the ship. Bellona stood at the docks with her hands clasped, closing her eyes and inhaling the fresh salt that stung at her skin. Part of her ached for home, but part of her was exhilarated about the new adventure. The demise of Deacon Morrow had led to opportunities, ones that she grasped eagerly with both hands.

"Bell!" The shout and thundering of footsteps along the wooden dock made her turn away from the ocean. Zephyr charged toward her, and she grinned, kneeling down as he threw himself into her arms. He smelled like his mother, lavender clinging to his hair and clothes. Her stomach wound twinged in protest, but she ignored it. When Bellona straightened, she saw Carissa and Jacen approaching at a more leisurely pace.

"He's going to miss you," Jacen remarked as Zephyr buried his face in Bellona's shoulder.

"Well, he needs to start behaving like a prince." Bellona smirked as she set the toddler down. "We can't have him barrelling about the place, almost knocking people off their feet, can we?"

"Gets it from his mother," Jacen deadpanned, a statement that fooled absolutely no one.

"Oh, is he coming with us?" Cristofer swaggered down the gangplank and onto the docks with an arched eyebrow, Eirian trailing behind him in her customary quiet fashion.

"Yes!" Zephyr insisted.

"Maybe when you're older," Carissa said, reaching out to take her son's hand and patiently ignoring his pout.

Bellona had never been fond of children, but Zephyr was her ward for a year. She would miss the little boy as dearly as she would miss his parents. They had been divided for a year, scattered across Razmara, but they were together as a family, and Bellona had never seen so much love as she did between Zephyr and his parents.

"Who knows?" Bellona tilted her head to the side as she smiled at him. "Your uncle Peregrine loved the ocean. Maybe you will too."

"We need to head out soon before the tide rises." Dante Remington jumped down from the rigging and strode across the deck, his impatience prompting Eirian to scowl over her shoulder at him.

"We're saying our goodbyes, Captain Remington."

"It won't be the same in Marinel without you." Carissa put on a brave smile, but Bellona could see the way that her chin trembled. "We've spent so much time together that it…it just feels strange."

"Marinel needs change anyway." Bellona pressed a kiss to her best friend's cheek, before kneeling down with a suppressed grimace to kiss the top of Zephyr's head. "You're going to be instigating that change."

"What will I do without you?" Tears streamed down Carissa's cheeks as Jacen put a comforting arm around her shoulders. "You've been my rock for so many years, and I just…"

"Don't act like I'm not coming back." Bellona couldn't help but laugh, though she could feel a lump itching in her throat. "I'll be back in a few weeks at most. Back in Theron, where you're always welcome. I suppose you can even bring Jacen too."

Carissa choked out a laugh before flinging her arms around Bellona's neck. The two held on tightly, each having always been the anchor for the other. Bellona could not imagine her life without Carissa. It was goodbye for now, but not forever. They each had their own responsibilities, and Bellona was certain that she would see Carissa again soon.

Bellona extricated herself from the Queen's iron grasp, taking Eirian's proffered hand and stepping up onto the deck. The setting sun made Bellona's ginger hair look as bright as a burning fire. She reached up to wipe her eyes, raising her hand to wave as Carissa and Jacen strode back down the docks.

"Look at the pair of you, getting so sappy," Cristofer teased, pressing a kiss to Bellona's temple as she gripped the railing.

"We've been so entwined in each other's lives that it just feels strange." Bellona took a deep breath, wondering why moving forward was as terrifying as looking back. They were entering a golden era, and her elation was wrapped up in terror at the thought of relinquishing her grief and accepting her own healing. Sorrow and salvation, all at once.

"She will always be there for you." Eirian touched Bellona's hand with gentle fingers. "And you for her. Distance and time won't change that."

The sun sank below the horizon, and Bellona cast her gaze skyward as she pushed aside her apprehension of the open water. The sky was lit with pale yellow and vibrant orange hues. The cries of the gulls and the lap of the waves against the hull were a strange comfort. She closed her eyes and offered a quick prayer to the goddess Elethea.

Mother and Father, wherever you are, I want you to know that I'm at peace now.

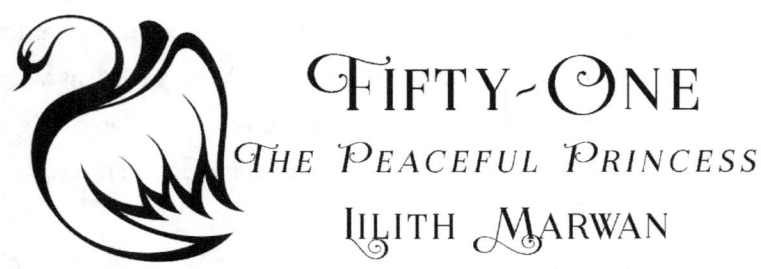FIFTY-ONE
THE PEACEFUL PRINCESS
LILITH MARWAN

The Harithian sun beamed down warm on Lilith's skin as she skirted through the markets, basket full of assorted fruits and candied sweets, her sandals padding against the stone streets. The lively tune of a banjo thrummed through the bustling afternoon, coaxing a smile to Lilith's lips.

Across the lane, Ayesha was admiring some gaudy Generan jewellery, holding it up to the oval mirror in the shop and asking Elyes for his opinion. Elyes's bored expression spoke volumes in itself, though every now and then the hint of a smile presented itself on his face before he seemed to catch himself.

"Despite the fact she'll never sit on the Generan throne, she still wants to dress herself up like a princess." Cairo appeared at Lilith's elbow, shaking his head as he examined the pair of cousins. For once, he didn't reek of Obscurate. Since the Battle of Basium, he seemed to have reconsidered his stance on suppressing his magic.

"Let her preen." Lilith nudged him with her basket. "She's spent her whole life in Genera, but here in Harith…she shines like the sun."

"They are absolutely intending mischief." Relda strode over, weighing a peach in her hand before taking a deep bite. Once she had shed her tears over Ishtar's death, Relda bounced back to her bold self. She said that Ishtar would want her to celebrate life, and their son's life, instead of wasting her time on mourning. Indeed, she was a strange woman, Lilith thought.

"I hear you're the new Generan ambassador." Cairo flashed Relda a grin.

"So, you'll be going between Harith and Genera?" Lilith asked, linking her arm through Relda's and ignoring how peach juice splashed upon her skin. At the shop across from them, Ayesha beamed as she paid for a ruby necklace and bossed Elyes into doing it up around her neck.

"I want to make sure the new triumvirate settles in well." A wicked smile graced Relda's lips. "Gently bully them into doing the right thing, you know. We don't need any more Cobryns or Deacons."

"Oh, did they decide already?" Lilith's eyebrows flew up in astonishment. She had thought it would take time, though she supposed it made sense that a fractured country like Genera wanted to get the cogs of progress churning as quickly as possible. "Who's on the triumvirate?"

"I expect I'll find out once I return." Relda gave a nonchalant shrug.

Ayesha rushed past in a whirl of laughter and colour, leaving only the scent of jasmine perfume behind her. Elyes followed his cousin at a more measured pace, taking her hands and spinning her around as she danced to the beat of the banjo. Lilith's proud smile was unrestrained as she examined how radiant and full of life her daughter had become.

The memories of her dark days in Genera wouldn't simply go away. They still came in nightmares, but with less intensity and frequency as the weeks passed. The horrors of the past were washing away, replaced with memories full of love and laughter, like the one Lilith currently experienced.

Cobryn was gone. The jackal helm he had once used to inspire fear among the countries he'd conquered was no more than an ornament kept in Ayesha's room, though one she and Elyes had a tendency of wearing on occasion in the training yard. Neither Lilith nor Ayesha needed to live in fear anymore.

If Ayesha decided she wanted to live in Genera when she was older, that was her choice. She was half-Generan and had every right to prefer the country in which she was born. In that moment, though, there was happiness and unity. Elyes and Ayesha, children of both Generan and Harithian blood, dancing through the streets without a care in the world and with laughter bubbling from their lips.

Home. Lilith was at home for the first time in so many years, and not even the sugared candies of the street markets could compare to that sweetness. She had spent enough time in the darkness, and now, she was ready to step into the sunlight.

FIFTY-TWO
THE HAPPY LORD
THOM DYRE

Nicodemus teemed with activity in anticipation of the first official meeting of the Triumvirate. The scent of fresh bread from the bakeries wafted down the streets, mixing with the honeyed taste of mead that was rich on Thom's tongue as he strode into the meeting room. Although not a member of the Triumvirate, he had been invited as a valued lord who had a good deal of ideas to contribute.

As he entered the meeting room, he scowled at the sight of a familiar former pirate treating the mahogany table like it was his personal footrest.

"Will you get your boots off the table? You're a member of the Triumvirate, act like it."

Linus Farrow rolled his eyes and removed his gold-studded boots, letting his feet clatter dramatically to the floor. Beside him, Prax was shaking his head and offered Thom an apologetic smile on his lover's behalf.

"Linus is still adjusting."

"Linus is fine," the man in question retorted. "Am I early, or are the other two late?"

"I would say late." Thom sat down across from the pair, casting a look to the open door. "Perhaps deliberately so."

It was a surprise when Linus had stepped up to volunteer himself as a member of the Triumvirate. Korina Valadon had also been offered the opportunity, but her response of 'fuck no' and retreating back to tend to the Generan Islands had been a strong answer. Linus wasn't after the lordship of his ancestral home, since it had been taken from him when he'd still been a boy. Korina, he said, could manage Severino and Philemon well enough on her own.

"Forgive an old woman her tardiness, would you?" Odessa Dyre, the Mistress of Webs, ambled into the meeting room and sank herself into the closest seat with a relieved sigh.

Thom was not astonished at his mother joining the Triumvirate. Odessa had complained about the travel to Nicodemus and that she would miss Gethsemane, but also expressed regret that she had not intervened more directly in Generan matters in the past. She came with a country-wide network of spies, meaning the Triumvirate would always remain well-informed of what was happening around Genera.

"Sorry I'm late." Ariadne Pavlos sauntered into the meeting room with a smirk that assured everyone present she wasn't apologetic in the slightest. Her hair fell about her shoulders in perfect curls, leaving Thom with no guesses as to what she'd been doing before the meeting. Her emerald velvet dress complemented her pale skin perfectly.

"Now that all of the Triumvirate is here, can we get down to business?" Thom arched an eyebrow, and Ariadne responded by tipping him a wink. "Firstly, I would like to welcome you all to this first meeting…"

"We don't need the spiel." Linus waved an impatient hand. "Look, this country is a mess and has been for some time. We as the Triumvirate need to do whatever is in our power to fix it."

"Well, we can start with the Generan Islands." Ariadne leaned back in her chair, drumming her fingers against the table. "Though I believe Korina is making some headway there."

"The experimentation of melding flesh and gem has to stop." Linus's brow furrowed. "Generan soldiers aren't test subjects. I saw many of them return from Basium with gem limbs , and it's quite horrifying."

So many problems, Thom ruminated. Genera was a broken country, torn apart by Cobryn and Deacon's greed. It would take some time to heal the fractures, and a lot of patience. Thom would continue to run the pirate trade in Gethsemane, since all three of the Triumvirate were aware of its existence and the profits that it could turn over.

"There is also unrest about this new form of government." Odessa sipped her glass of water. "Many people, especially those closer to my age, are uneasy about stripping down the monarchy. The Triumvirate is a good idea, but it will take time to build trust. People don't always like change."

"What about a festival?" Thom suggested, prompting all eyes to turn on him. "I know Genera is in some debt after the wars, but I could host it in Gethsemane and pay for it all. Something to renew the people's spirits."

"We could definitely gain some revenue through local businesses contributing as well," Ariadne added, tapping her chin thoughtfully. "Plus, I do love a good party."

"We should invite the rulers of the other countries too." Linus slung an arm around Prax's shoulders. "To show that we welcome peace and unity."

"Definitely," Thom said, already looking forward to the chance to see his nephew and Carissa again.

When he looked around the table, he saw a group of people determined to make Genera a better place. It made his heart soar, and he wondered what Annaliese would have to say if she was still alive. His sister had always loved and cared for others more than herself. There, in that room, was Genera's future. A future that didn't rely on conquest and violence to sustain itself. A future that was as beautiful as the stars that spangled across the midnight sky.

Genera was evolving and changing in ways that the Morrow brothers had never been able to envision. Thom was thrilled to be a part of that future, laying down the framework for his country's growth. Once, he had been ashamed to be Generan, to be part of the Morrow regime. Now, his elation could make him take flight.

It was a brave new world, and Thom could hardly wait to see how radiantly it would glow.

EPILOGUE
CARISSA DARNELL

"Zeph, wait!"

Aurora Morrow toddled through the garden on unsteady feet, stumbling over herself in an effort to keep up with her older brother. Carissa observed the pair from her perch on the fountain's edge, one hand drifting lazily through the water. Zephyr slowed not to match his sister's pace, but to observe the series of graves that stood among the roses. Carefully, he plucked some to place over the graves. When he yelped and drew back, Carissa sighed and eased herself to her feet.

"I've told you to be careful, Zephyr. Those have thorns."

Zephyr met his mother's gaze with a typical five-year-old's defiance, raising his pricked finger to suck on it. Carissa knelt in front of him and gently took his hand.

"Let me see."

It had been ten years to the day since the Conquest, and Carissa had chosen to have a celebration. Not to mark what had happened on that day, but to drink to all they had accomplished since. She had long since stopped letting herself be defined by the pain of the past, which was why she had put the graves of her family in the garden where she came so often.

The dead rotted and fed new life. From the bones of their family, Carissa and Sebastian had blossomed.

"Mama." Determined not to let her brother occupy Carissa's attention, Aurora presented her mother with a daisy, which Carissa took with a smile. She pressed a kiss to her daughter's forehead. Barely two years old and a tiny blonde whirlwind, there was a lot of Jacen in Aurora, especially as she was adamant that she should play the fiddle too.

"Thank you, darling." Carissa scooped Aurora up and pushed up off the grass. Jacen strode into the garden, blonde hair shining like gold in the warm sunlight. Seeing his wife and children, a grin spread across his features. Abandoning his rose-picking attempt, Zephyr sprinted over to his father.

"Sebastian and Meliora should be here today." Jacen picked up Zephyr and spun him around, making the boy shriek in delight. "Bellona and her entourage tomorrow or the next day."

Marinel had been a whirlwind of preparation all week. Carissa had commissioned more gold-and-cream decorations, and swan ornaments, than she had in her entire decade as Queen. The mead merchants had benefited greatly, as had many of the city's bakeries. She was not one for frivolous expenses; however, the occasion was something important, both to Basium and her personally.

"I'm surprised that Meliora came at all." Carissa swept Aurora's blonde hair back from her face. "Isn't she seven months pregnant now?"

"Eight," Jacen corrected.

Carissa wouldn't be surprised if the baby, Sebastian and Meliora's first child, was born in Marinel during the celebrations. An exciting time for the expecting parents, who had been praying for a child for the past few years. It would be something more for them to honour, another commemoration of life in a place that had once known only death.

The weight of her memories bore down upon her, and Carissa's breath caught in her throat.

"Do you mind taking the children inside for a bit?" Carissa pressed a kiss to Jacen's cheek, setting Aurora down on her feet. "I want a few moments alone. Just before all the partying gets started."

"Will you play the fiddle for us, Father?" Zephyr asked.

"Yes!" Aurora clapped her hands.

Their combined enthusiasm made Jacen's smile brighten, his love for the children reaching out like the rays of the sun to caress everything around him.

"Of course." He spared Carissa one last look before leading Zephyr and Aurora inside, the pair of them chattering excitedly. Their enthusiasm was infectious, and Carissa found herself smiling as well, despite the thoughts that clouded her mind. Once she could no longer hear them, Carissa knelt in the grass in front of the graves, examining each of the names carved into the headstones.

Patrick Darnell.

Frederick Darnell.

Imogen Darnell.

Theodore Darnell.

Peregrine Darnell.

Miriam Darnell.

Carissa cast a look around the gardens that were so dear to her. The gardens where her family had been slaughtered; the fountain where she had drowned Deacon. Yet despite the atrocities that had occurred there, for each memory of darkness and death, there were a hundred of love and laughter.

All those years ago, she had been right when she had told Deacon that her love for Jacen was more powerful than her hatred for him and Cobryn. What was the bitter taste of loathing when compared to the honey-sweetness of love? She cherished her husband and her children, each of them a bright and brilliant spark in a life she now adored.

"I love you all." Carissa's words were soft, spoken only for the departed she did not know would hear her. "I miss you every single day, and I wish you were here to see how much I've accomplished, to watch my children grow."

Carissa would never have them back. She had accepted that almost as soon as she had lost them. But in the midst of the sharp sting of their deaths, there were memories she cherished.

Frederick's laughter as they ran rampant through the halls. Imogen fitting butterfly pins into Carissa's hair. Theodore drunkenly serenading his siblings and the servants. Peregrine tossing Sebastian over the side over the ship he gave them a tour of.

A cool breeze swept over the garden, the leaves rustling and Carissa's hair brushing against her face. A smile crossed her lips as she closed her eyes, tears slipping down her cheeks as she listened to the wind.

The dead weren't gone and forgotten. They lived on in her. They always would.

Pronunciation Guide

People

Bellona Lenore—BELL-OWN-AH LE-NORR

Carissa Darnell—CAR-ISS-AH DARN-ELLE

Cobryn Morrow—CO-BRIN MO-RO

Cyprian Ambrose—SIGH-PREE-IN AMB-ROSE

Deacon Morrow—DEE-KIN MO-RO

Kato Lenore—KAY-TO LE-NORR

Jacen Morrow—JAY-SIN MO-RO

Jarl Ambrose—YAH-L AMB-ROSE

Lilith Marwan—LILL-ITH MAH-WEN

Meliora Ambrose—MELL-EE-OR-AH AMB-ROSE

Miriam Darnell—MIH-REE-AM DARN-ELLE

Quintin Faustus—KWIN-TIN FOUR-STUS

Sebastian Darnell—SEB-AS-CHUN DARN-ELLE

Tiago Benedict—TEE-AH-GO BEN-EH-DICT

Vida Morrow—VEE-DAH MO-RO

Places

Ardelis—AH-DELL-ISS

Basium—BASS-EE-UM

Bao—BOW

Cirocco—SI-ROCK-OH

Fortua—FOUR-CHEW-AH

Genera—JEN-EAR-AH

Harith—HA-RI-TH

Isadore—ISS-AH-DOOR

Marinel—MA-RIN-ELLE

Nicodemus—NICK-OH-DEE-MUS

Seneca—SIN-ICK-AH

Theron—THE-RON

Wendell—WEN-DALL

OTHER

Imperium—IM-PEER-EE-UM

Maleficium—MAL-IF-UH-SEE-UM

Primordial—PRIME-OR-DEE-ALL

ACKNOWLEDGEMENTS

I wish I'd known, in complaining about the second book, just how much more of a trial this one would be. This book kicked my ass from the beginning, and there were points when I questioned whether I'd ever get it finished. It was a longer process than I wanted, but I am truly happy with how things have wrapped up for my beloved characters. It's been over 5 years since I started writing Blood of Queens in 2018, a journey I never imagined would bring me to where I am today.

Of course, there are always people who have been supportive the whole way through, and whole helped me to get things where they are now.

To my CP and proofreader, Camilla. Thank you for being a set of eyes on this when I was stressed that no one wanted to read it, and for all the help in making this book the best that it could possibly be.

To Cass, for this map that I've used throughout this series, and being a voice of reason and support whenever I'm doubting myself and the world I've created.

To my copy editor, Cassidy. Thank you for all your hard work on this book, and for the kind words that I still hold close to heart on how this series has ended.

To my cover designer and formatter, Celin, for producing yet another amazing cover that gets compliments wherever I go.

To my beta readers Lina, Ilona & Margie for your feedback and commentary, especially on parts of the book where I feared that I was going in the wrong direction.

To my readers. I appreciate you so much, and I truly hope that the end of this trilogy was as satisfying to you as it was to me. Thank you for being on this adventure with me for the past few years.

ABOUT THE AUTHOR

Maddie is an author from Sydney, Australia. She has been reading and writing from a very young age, and is particularly invested in complex characters, healthy relationships, and well-written female protagonists. She's the oldest of three siblings and the owner of two very cute bunnies called Kenobi and Kylo. She has a Bachelor of Arts in Journalism, though she works in administration.

www.ingramcontent.com/pod-product-compliance
Lightning Source LLC
Chambersburg PA
CBHW061938130726
47909CB00013B/2035